FORBIDDEN LOVE

"You're the most beautiful woman I've ever seen," Rayne said to the innocent Indian beauty.

Falling Water had to tilt back her head to look into his eyes. The passion he saw reflected in her gaze and the alluring scent of her silken flesh were almost more than he could withstand.

She took several steps backward in surprise and fear. "You have sweet words," she said, "but I have heard sweet words before."

She moved to pass him and suddenly found herself bound agianst his hard-muscled chest, his two iron arms holding her securely. She could feel the length of his powerful body pressed to hers. Before she could protest, his mouth swept down and captured hers in an ecstasy-filled kiss that nearly defeated her. Something within her seemed to shatter, filling her with brilliant touches of flame. His mouth hungered for her response, and she was helpless as he drew it from her with the intensity of his searching lips.

"If there's a way to be found, I will find it," he said. "I want you as I have never wanted a woman before. One day, you will be my woman. One day," he repeated softly, "I will make you mine . . ."

Sylvie F. Sommerfield

Savage Kiss

ZEBRA BOOKS
KENSINGTON PUBLISHING CORP.

ZEBRA BOOKS

are published by

Kensington Publishing Corp.
475 Park Avenue South
New York, NY 10016

First printing: October 1985

Printed in the United States of America

To Betty Archibald, for her support; and to Phyllis Gipson, for the charitable donation of her time and energy.

Prologue

Cade Holliday, half-white, half-Cheyenne, had been raised in the village of his blood brother, White Eagle, where he remained until he was seventeen. His white father, a doctor, then took him to Washington to train him in medicine. Both men were aware that the freedom enjoyed by the Indian people they loved would soon be no more than a memory.

Cade returned to the Cheyenne as a doctor and married a woman from his tribe who had loved him from his childhood days. She was the beautiful Snow Blossom, sister of his blood brother. But a white woman, Lauren Brent, also believed herself in love with Cade and followed him to the Cheyenne village.

The conflict that arose between them disappeared when greater dangers presented themselves, first in the form of the dreaded disease, smallpox, and then in a brutal attack on their village. A bloody massacre directed by Major John Chevington drew many tribes together, and in the turmoil Lauren sought a new love and a new direction for her life. She married Running Wolf, becoming medicine woman of the Cheyenne village and a respected leader among her adopted people. At the death of the great Chief Tekata, White Eagle became ruler of the tribe. Soon after, he happened upon two white people traveling alone, one of whom was the golden-haired Rebecca. She immediately captured his heart, and although there was much against them, their love carried them through, and they married.

Major John Chevington, mortal enemy of the Indians, discovered the presence of a white woman in the Cheyenne village. He attacked the village and took as captives the wives of both White Eagle and Cade Holliday.

In retaliation, they destroyed the fort. White Eagle rescued Rebecca, but Snow Blossom had been given to a trapper, Josiah Tucker. Cade followed their trail, only to be led back to his own village.

Again, the tribe faced the threat of Major Chevington and his troops, but at the last minute they were saved from extinction. Though Cade knew his people were in jeopardy, he worked diligently with them so that together they might build a future for their children. This is a story of those children. It is the sequel to *Savage Rapture*, and it follows the children of these brave people into conflicts and passions of their own.

Chapter 1

Washington . . . 1848

It was a comfortably cool night with a light, whispering breeze that rustled the trees standing along the darkened street. A brief rainfall had wet the cobbled surface and sent little rivulets running through the gutters.

Few lights shone from the houses that lined the street. One particular house was completely darkened except for the pale glow of yellow light that emanated from a single downstairs window.

Within the room a low fire burned, and two men sat facing each other before it. They were sipping brandy, and, for the moment, both were silent, each thinking over the words that had recently been exchanged.

Martin Preston was a man just a little over forty. A tall man, his figure was still as slim and erect as it had been when he was twenty. His dark hair showed no sign of gray, and his eyes were even darker. His face was all sharp angles and planes, reminding one of a seriously intent predator. He had the sleek grace and cultured look of a man who had indulged himself in the finest of everything. His exquisitely groomed clothes were obviously expensive. A tie tack and cuff links of glittering diamonds adorned a white lace, ruffled shirt of delicate material. Even the cigar gripped between his square white teeth was the best that money could buy.

He sat facing Major John Chevington, who sat as he stood—ramrod straight. He, too, still retained the same slim, muscular build of his youth, perhaps because he spent many hours at physical endeavors. He was over fifty, but even the most astute eye would never have guessed his age. His face was leathery tan, and his hair a flowing white mane with mustache to match. His eyes were an amber color and glowed with a fanatic's fire, the kind of flame that would, without a touch of conscience, set ablaze and destroy anything that stood between him and what he wanted.

Some time passed before the silence was broken.

"Hundreds of thousands of acres of land. Good land, choice land. A valley very beautiful and rich . . . rich," Martin said. "John, how reliable is this information?"

John Chevington smiled and gazed at Martin Preston. "Most reliable, Martin. There is gold there. I let that valley slip through my fingers once; now the land is being held in trust for this Indian tribe by Lauren Brent and her father."

"Alexander Brent is hardly a man to be toyed with, and his daughter is a fool to have chosen marriage to an Indian rather than the life I could have given her here. Together, we could have driven those Indians from the valley and made it ours," Martin replied bitterly.

"It is still not a lost battle," John said. "Alexander Brent is not a well man. If anything should happen to

10

him, the land would go to his daughter."

"Damn her! She would never give it up."

"We don't need her to give it up," John said softly. "We will take it from her."

"Take it from her," Martin replied slowly, "and take her from it. I have much to repay her for."

"We must tread carefully and not make the same mistakes twice. I underestimated both Cade Holliday and his blood brother once, but I will never do it again. When next I move against them, I will see to it that it is with so much force that none of the tribe will survive it."

"Then you think what I suggested might be of some help?"

"Yes, I do. Tell me again about your son and these two friends of his."

"I don't know what Thomas sees in these two ruffians, but he admires them. He listens to their stories of trapping in the wild and is overwhelmed with them. Can you imagine a man—raised as well as he has been—interested in such a life? I cannot, yet all he talks about is wanting to go with them."

"They are leaving Washington soon?"

"Yes. The one man only came here to settle an estate of some relative. It seems he prefers the wild life. Thomas says he is most anxious to leave Washington."

"Tell me more about them."

"Well the two seem to have been together for a long time. Their trapping has been quite profitable for both. I suppose it's because they seem to get on well with the savages. I imagine they are quite savage themselves."

"Rayne Freeman, Mackenzie Weaver . . . it seems I've heard those names before," John Chevington said thoughtfully. "Somewhere . . ."

"You have." Martin laughed. "At least you have heard the name Freeman. It seems the young man has always been a bit independent and wayward; rather wicked with the women, also. I believe his father was quite upset over some incident and told him to rearrange his life or he would toss him out on his ear without a cent."

"They were a wealthy family?"

"Reasonably so."

"Why should he have given up all that to trap furs in the wild?"

"Rumor has it there was a woman involved, but no one knows the truth of the story."

"What are your plans?"

"I have finally let my son convince me to allow him to make this trip with them."

"What good will that do us?"

"You, at the same time, will be put in command at Fort Ramsey, which, I might add, is the closest to the Indians."

"Then?"

"Then you will build up your command and prepare them. I will see to it that as time goes by men will be sent to add to your command. When my son and his two friends are attacked by . . ."—he smiled—"Indians, it will be a tragedy. Of course, my son will be the only survivor. He will bring home word of the bloody murder of two innocent men of rather prestigious families. It will incense some very important people. You will probably receive orders to find the killers. In the process, you might find a battle you cannot avoid. Then"—he shrugged—"you might be forced to eliminate the entire village . . . except, of course, for its white inhabitants."

"No," John Chevington said softly as his mind vividly

brought forth a picture of Rebecca. He had not been able to force her from his thoughts from the first day he had gazed into her blue eyes. He would take her from her Indian husband as his final act of revenge against White Eagle. "Not the white inhabitants. There are much better uses for them."

"When my son sees savages kill his two friends without mercy, he too will be filled with the desire for revenge. It will be the most useful tool we have—his righteous indignation."

"It is a good plan, most excellent. Of course, you are prepared to buy up the land immediately?"

"Of course, but first there is the little problem of Alexander Brent."

John Chevington and Martin Preston remained silent for a moment, then their eyes met in complete understanding. One way or another the obstacle of Alexander Brent would be eliminated. The faint sound of a malicious chuckle echoed in the room.

Several streets away, two others lay together, talking of very nearly the same subject, yet discussing it from a completely different point of view.

Grant Jamison had been for many years a friend to the Indians who lived in that distant valley. He had helped Cade Holliday in his transition from the Indian world to the white one, had long ago seen the difficulties that lay in Cade's path. Grant had chosen to stay in Washington to help as much as he could. He had married Martha Sanders, and together they had used their combined wealth and influence with that of Alexander Brent to protect their distant friends.

He had awakened in the wee hours of the morning, disturbed by consistent and most irritating dreams. He lay very still, not wanting to awaken Martha, but she stirred despite his effort.

"Grant?" she whispered softly.

"I'm sorry, my dear. Did I wake you?"

"The same dreams again, Grant?"

Grant laughed. "I'm sure the Indians would tell me there is much to be learned from my dreams, but if there's a message in them, I swear I can't see it. All I see is senseless fighting, and I can't even see the outcome of it. It's frustrating."

"You spoke with Alexander today?"

"Yes, I did. Alex related a few things. It seems Martin Preston is trying to buy up more land—as close to the valley as he can get."

"But he can't touch them, can't do them any harm?"

"Not as long as Lauren and Alex own the land. If something is going on, I wish to God I knew what it was. I have a feeling Martin and his crowd are up to no good."

"Maybe you had best try to sleep, Grant. Tomorrow you and Alex can try to find a way to learn what they are doing."

Grant chuckled and turned on his side to draw a warm and willing Martha into his arms. He heard the soft sound of Martha's laugh.

"Now that I'm completely awake, my love," he said, "I can't seem to get my mind off better things than sleep."

"Your friends?" she inquired with a soft chuckle.

"You are not even close," he whispered as he sought her lips with his own.

Grant and Martha had found in each other a deep, rich

love, which had steadily grown in the eighteen years of their marriage. They had surrendered the burning flame of their youthful ardor to nurture a diamond-bright core that had sustained them and would continue to sustain them through an eventful marriage.

They reached for each other with the sure knowledge that their need was mutual. Martha was a woman of deep passions, and she had found an answering intensity in Grant.

Slowly, he caressed her still-slim form, his hands expertly arousing her until he could feel her body vibrating beneath his touch. Their mouths blended in a kiss that lifted them both with the depth of its searching.

Her hands drew him even closer, and with sensitive fingers she caressed his hard muscles, enjoying the feel of them rippling under his skin. She had found sensual joy in Grant from the first time they had shared each other; now she helped to deepen that joy by responding to his questing touch with all the desire she possessed.

Spiraling passions ignited and raged to a crescendo. It heightened Grant's pleasure even more when he heard Martha's softly murmured words of desire.

He pressed himself deep within her, driving rhythmically with sure, hard strokes that sent her every sense into rapturous oblivion. She lifted herself to meet him, needing more, demanding more, and receiving more until they lay gasping and clinging to each other in silent satisfaction.

Grant kissed her gently and held her close, giving thanks, as he had on so many other occasions, that she was his.

* * *

In another section of Washington, three men sat at a table sharing drinks and conversation, although the conversation was rather difficult amidst the laughter and noise of the tavern. None of the three were adverse to the lingering smiles of the pretty girls about the room, and none of the three were entirely sober.

Two of the men were several years older than the third, who was bent toward them now, leaning on the table with a look of near pleading in his eyes.

"C'mon, Rayne," he said, "I won't be any trouble to you. You know I can take care of myself, and I can bring all the supplies I need. Let me go with you just this one time."

He was a handsome young man of about twenty. His hair was thick and dark and had an obstinate curl to it. His face was thin, dominated by wide, darkly intelligent eyes. His body, though slim, was sleekly muscled, for he enjoyed strenuous activity.

The man who sat next to him watched the exchange of words with a touch of amusement about his sparkling blue eyes and his wide mouth. He was the product of a Scottish bondservant and an English planter. Tall and broad shouldered, he was handsome in a rugged, rough-hewn way. He possessed a deep sense of sparkling humor and a will of iron that was matched only by his honest sense of commitment. He chose friends carefully, then never lost them, for he gave totally to those he cared for. He chuckled softly now.

"The laddie seems to be intent on trying his wings. Why don't ye let him come along, Rayne, and let him have a real taste of what he's been dreamin' about"—he waved his hand airily—"the wide and beautiful frontier."

"Don't encourage him, Mack," the third man replied.

16

"It's not quite that simple, and you know it. It's dangerous. You have any idea what his father could do if we went and got him killed?"

"I've already talked it over with my father, and he's agreed to let me go if you'll accept me. He said he knew your reputation and that if he had to let me go, it would be best I go with someone who knew what he was doing."

"Your father said that?" The reply came rather suspiciously.

"I wouldn't lie to you, Rayne, and you know it," the young man asserted belligerently.

Rayne Freeman sat back in his chair and took another drink from a nearly empty bottle. Rayne was the kind of man another man would look at twice in envy and a woman would look at as many times as she possibly could. At thirty-two, he had the self-possessed look of someone who had experienced both good and bad in his life. He stood four inches over Mack's six feet. His shoulders were awesome in their breadth, and any observant gaze would have found that the heavily muscled chest and arms were not padded material but belonged to the man. His skin was tanned a deep golden color that brought his startling green eyes to prominence. They were eyes that could smile with warmth or turn cold and hard enough to shake the confidence of the strongest man. His hair was thick and the hue of rich, dark wine. It framed his chiseled features, the eyes set wide, the nose straight and rather Roman. His mouth was firm and wide, and his smile appeared broad and white against the tan of his skin.

"I know you wouldn't, boy," Rayne said softly.

"I'm not a boy, Rayne: I'm twenty. I'm a man."

Rayne would have argued the point with him, but he

liked Thomas and regretted the insult to his masculinity. "Sorry," he replied, and before Thomas could answer, he questioned him again. "You said your father agreed to your going with us. That came as a surprise, didn't it?"

"I sort of convinced him"—Thomas grinned—"but I didn't lie, Rayne. He did say it was all right with him if I went. Is . . . Is it all right with you and Mack? I won't be any trouble, Rayne. I'll do anything you tell me to do."

Rayne remained silent, but he was thinking of the strange change in plans. Some inner sense told him something was wrong, but he couldn't put his finger on what or why.

"Rayne?"

"All right, Thomas, you go. But you're new at this, so I expect you to be quiet and learn, and if you want to stay alive, you listen to both Mack and me. Neither of us," he said softly, "is going to tolerate stupidity."

Thomas's eyes brightened in ecstatic delight.

"Don't be too happy about this," Rayne added. "You might be sorry you ever wanted to come along."

"I won't be," Thomas said quickly. "I won't be."

"We're leaving before dawn tomorrow," Rayne informed him. "I think you'd best get your things ready." Thomas nodded and rose hastily. "We'll meet you in front of our hotel in the morning."

"Yes sir! I'll be there."

"Before dawn."

"Before dawn." Thomas nodded. "Thanks, Rayne, Mack. You won't regret it, either of you. You won't regret it."

Thomas was still chattering as he backed away, then he turned and left quickly. Mack laughed heartily as they watched Thomas's rapid disappearance.

18

"The boy is anxious," Mack said. "Too bad he doesn't know what he's gettin' into." Again he chuckled. "You won't regret it, Rayne?"

"I think"—Rayne grinned—"that I'm beginning to regret it already. It's hard enough without taking a green boy along. I wonder—"

"Wonder what, laddie?"

"I wonder why Thomas's father agreed after all this time of swearing his precious boy wouldn't leave this city where his influence is so powerful. Doesn't it seem strange to you that suddenly he's letting his little boy slip away from him?"

"You aren't particularly fond of the boy's father?"

"No, not very. Thomas is a good boy, but his father is trying to shape him, heart and soul. He won't let the boy grow unless he grows the way he wants him."

"If the boy is going to be his own man, Rayne, he has to walk away on his own. He's got to cut the ties himself. Nobody can do it for him."

"That's the only reason I agreed, Mack. I think that's what he's trying to do now."

"Then what's botherin' you?"

"The real reason his father agreed. It's too easy. Something just doesn't feel right."

"What are you going to do about it? You told the boy he could go."

"He can go, all right, but we'll keep looking back over our shoulders just in case. I don't know how true they are, but I've heard some stories."

"What kinds of stories?"

"About some mix-up between the Prestons and the Brents. Happened some time ago. Seems it concerned this man who was, from what I hear, half-white, half-

Indian. Anyway, his father was Dr. Michael Holliday."

Mack whistled lightly in surprise, as Rayne continued to tell him the bits and pieces of the story he had heard.

Mack added, "I heard Holliday got killed out in the Indian's territory."

"He did. I suppose there's more to the story, but I've never been among his son's people. Maybe we'll cross their territory this time. Anyway, I've got a strange feeling that Thomas's trip with us, his father's agreement, and the people in the Cheyenne village are somehow connected. I just don't know where we fit in. And I can't help wondering if the information Senator Miles asked us to gather secretly figures into the picture as well."

"And you're just going to take him along, knowing there might be more to it?" Mack smiled. "Why don't you just tell the boy to forget it?"

"I'm curious"—Rayne laughed—"and how will I answer all the questions I have if I don't play along?"

"And you like the idea of maybe besting Thomas's father and proving to him that you are able to outsmart him."

Rayne chuckled, lifting the bottle for the last drink, then he stood up. "Come on, old grandmother, let's get some sleep. We have to be on our way by daylight."

Mack laughed in response, and both men made their ways unsteadily to the door. Outside, they hired a carriage to take them back to their hotel.

Both Rayne and Mack slept soundly, and as promised, they were standing in front of their hotel before the first rays of the morning sun touched the sky, watching the Preston carriage deliver an extremely excited Thomas.

Both Rayne and Mack gazed incredulously at the huge

amount of luggage being deposited with him.

"Boy!" Mack exclaimed in amazement. "What in hell are you planning to do with all of that?"

"Why, take it with me," Thomas replied. At this answer, both Rayne and Mack began to laugh.

Thomas looked at them, first in surprise, then with wounded dignity. His face flushed with the beginnings of anger. It was with considerable effort that Rayne controlled his amusement.

"Thomas, send all that back home with your carriage. Not only will you not be able to use it, but you also won't find an animal alive that will be able to carry it for you. All you need to bring for now is money. We'll buy what we need at the end of the stage line. We'll buy our horses and pack horses there. You won't need any of what I suspect might be in those cases."

Not really knowing what to bring, Thomas had packed most of his worldly possessions. He grinned sheepishly when he realized that neither Rayne nor Mack meant to insult him, then ordered the carriage to return to his home with all his luggage still on board.

"I . . . I wasn't sure . . ." he began.

"No, I don't suppose you were," Rayne said, "and I'm stupid for not explaining to you last night. We'll go by train as far as we can, then by stage as far as it goes. At the end of the line we'll buy our equipment at one time." He grinned at Thomas. "I forgot to ask how you handle a horse. We'll be on horseback so long, you'll think you're part of the animal."

"I've had riding lessons since I was six. I think I can manage a horse pretty well."

"Well then"—Rayne smiled as he clapped Thomas heartily on the shoulder—"suppose we get this show on

21

the road."

The three left Washington by train. A little over a week and a half later, they exchanged their railroad car for a stagecoach, and, after another two weeks of hard travel, they arrived at the end of the stagecoach line. In the last hotel they would see for a long time, a very tired and dirty threesome took hot baths, ate heartily, and went directly to their beds.

The next morning they rose early to purchase supplies at the store down the street from their hotel. It was the only store in the small town. Before noon, three riders leading pack horses left the small town and headed into uncharted territory.

Chapter 2

The valley had been kissed by the magic touch of Spring. It was alive with beauty. The pines stood tall and green on the mountainsides, and brilliant wildflowers bloomed in gay profusion everywhere.

The sun was high and the day was very warm, but all these things remained temporarily unnoticed by the three riders racing across the valley floor. The three ponies flew side by side, their riders bending low over their stretched necks.

Laughter was caught on the wind and tossed behind them as each tried to urge his pony ahead of the others' before their imaginary finish line brought an end to the race. Slowly, one rider pulled ahead. Though the lead was short, it was enough to induce a wild cry of triumph as rider and horse crossed the finish line first.

Their horses were drawn to a halt, and the riders slid gracefully to the ground with quick, lithe movements of youth well accustomed to such performances.

The winner of the race was a young man. He was slim, yet sleekly muscled. An extremely handsome man, his square-jawed face displayed high cheekbones that be-spoke his race. His eyes were ebony and filled with laughter, laughter that was also quick to come from his wide, smiling mouth.

"Too bad, Little Sister," he chuckled. "You and Falling Water must try harder."

The girl to whom he spoke was a feminine image of him, for, in fact, she was his twin. They both wore the same well-tanned buckskin. His hair was caught on each side of his face with a band of brown rawhide, and a red band of beaded leather circled his head. He was naked to the waist, and his buckskin pants hugged his lean hips and legs.

Her smile, wide and white, reflected the pleasure she had shared with the brother she loved so dearly, the brother who had shared the moment of birth with her. From that day forward, they had been inseparable. Night Sky was the first born of White Eagle, chief of the tribe, and his beloved wife Rebecca Wade. Lone Star was the girl child who had shared that moment of birth.

She was slender, yet her body was softly rounded. Her features were a soft reflection of his, the ebony eyes filled with laughter and a touch of mystery that had already caught the interest of many of the young braves of the tribe. Her dark hair hung in two braids to her hips, and the same red-beaded band circled her head.

The third person in the riding party was a woman the same age as the others. That she was Indian was quite obvious, yet there was something different about her, something that made her stand out from the two with whom she rode.

Falling Water was tall for a woman and startlingly

beautiful. Her skin was several shades lighter than that of her two companions, and her thick, dark hair was the color of deep mahogany. It was held by a band around her head and flowed about her slim shoulders. Her wide mouth smiled easily, showing square white teeth, and her eyes were wide and deep amber in color, with gold flecks dancing within. High cheekbones suggested her Indian blood, yet the white blood that surged within her was just as apparent. Pride in both races sparkled in her clear eyes and erect posture.

"I shall win next time, Brother." Lone Star laughed. "I nearly beat you this time."

"Not really." He grinned arrogantly and insisted, "I only let you remain close to ease your loss. You owe me a new shirt, Sister, and it should be done well. I will wear it at the next gathering to show the other braves how well you work. Who knows"—he shrugged—"you might catch a husband yet."

Lone Star's smile wavered, and she averted her head so her brother would not see the quick start of tears in her eyes. "I do not look for a husband yet," she said softly.

"You are nearing eighteen summers, Lone Star. There are many who say you are too choosy and will never accept a husband. You do not want to be an old one with no tepee of your own, do you?"

He was teasing her and had no idea how close to her heart he had struck. He loved her completely and never would have deliberately hurt her. Therefore he was taken by surprise when she turned on him. She had never before been truly angry with him in their eighteen years.

"I am the daughter of White Eagle, as you are the son! I have the right to choose carefully, just as you do." She

25

lifted her chin proudly, adding, "The daughter of White Eagle will choose her own husband when she is ready, and not before. I will make your shirt, Brother, but do not try to choose a mate for me. You would do better to look for a woman for yourself."

Night Sky stared at her in stunned amazement as she turned from him and gracefully leapt upon her pony's back. Without another word, she spun the horse about and rode back toward the village.

Night Sky shifted his astounded gaze to Falling Water, who almost laughed aloud at his shock. She knew he had absolutely no idea of what he had said to bring on his sister's anger.

"What did I say? What has made her so angry?" he asked in concern.

"Oh, Night Sky, how little you seem to understand women."

"I was only teasing her. She . . . she didn't take me seriously?"

"You were teasing her about a very sensitive subject."

"I don't understand."

"As well as you know your sister, do you not see that her heart already belongs to someone? It has from the time she was a little girl."

"Who?"

"That is not for me to say. If she chooses to keep it a secret, then it is her secret to keep."

"Falling Water, I am her brother. I would not hurt her again with foolish words. Tell me so I do not stumble over my own tongue."

"You will not speak of it?"

"Of course not!"

"To anyone—especially Lone Star? She would be very angry with me."

"I will say nothing, Falling Water. Who is he that she cannot let him know? I do not believe there is a brave in our village who would not give any bride price if she would but smile at him."

"Only one, and he does not see her as anything other than a child he remembers."

Night Sky chuckled. "Even a brother can see when a sister is no longer a child."

"I wish Little Eagle were as observant," she replied.

Night Sky's earlier surprise was nothing compared to the shock he received from hearing this name. Little Eagle was several years older than he and his sister and was the son of their half-white medicine man and doctor, Sun Knife.

"Little Eagle?" He appeared shocked. "But he's . . ."

"I know." She laughed. "He's older than she by six or seven years, a warrior who has already suffered the *okipa* rite and has given blood at the sun pole. He is brave; he is the son of the most important man in our village. Still, she loves him and has loved him from the time she was a child. It breaks her heart that he never looks at her as a woman."

"But she is the chief's daughter! She could have him if she desired it so. All she need do is ask . . ."

"Night Sky! I do not believe what you say. You know your own pride as the chief's son. Do you think hers is any less? She would go to no man on her knees. She would beg no man to take her as wife—not even the man she loves more than her own life."

Night Sky remained silent as these words touched him.

For a moment he felt pity for his sister, but he soon realized pity was the last thing Lone Star would ever want—from him or any other.

"I must go back to the village," Falling Water was saying. Her words brought his wandering attention back to her. "My mother has much to do, and she will expect me to help."

"I will ride on for a while," Night Sky replied.

Falling Water mounted and Night Sky stood watching her ride away. Falling Water had been his and his sister's companion since they were all small children. They had established a camaraderie based on many things, among them the facts that the three had been born at almost the same time and their parents had always been very close. But more important, their bond remained strong because the three of them were a mixture of Indian and white. The blood of both races flowed through the veins of each, making them somehow different from all the children with whom they had grown up.

The only white people Night Sky had ever seen were his mother, Falling Water's mother, and the trapper, Josiah Tucker, who lived among them. Cade Holliday, or Sun Knife, the man who was the tribe's medicine man, had the strange light eyes, light eyes he had given to his son, Little Eagle. Those orbs still had a profound effect on Night Sky when Little Eagle looked at him. Eyes the color of a cloudless sky were beyond Night Sky's understanding, but he had heard the stories of Sun Knife's father and had seen the almost magical skill Sun Knife had in healing.

Night Sky thought of his own father, White Eagle, and pride moved warmly through him. He felt the truth of

Falling Water's words and understood Lone Star's pride. Still he wondered what his sister would do if Little Eagle persisted in thinking of her as a child.

He shook his head and remounted. The day was beautiful, and he was young and filled with restless energy. He would leave such problems behind and enjoy the day. The gods would care for all that needed caring for. He rode into the hills seeking meat for the evening meal.

Lone Star rode toward the village, remembering the sting of her brother's innocent banter. She knew he had not meant to hurt her, and she regretted her anger, yet she still could feel the choking pain his words had brought.

"Little Eagle . . ." She spoke his name aloud. She had cared for him, she realized, from the first moment she had known him. He had been fifteen and she was only eight, and to her he had seemed so tall, so very handsome, with his sky blue eyes and quick, white smile. As they both grew, the breadth of his shoulders and his blue eyes filled her world more and more until it seemed she dreamed only of him. Sometimes it angered her that she could not control this need that seemed to possess her whenever he was near. She continually promised herself she would leash her emotions, but to no avail.

She had confided her dreams only to Falling Water, for they were as sisters, and she felt certain her friend would not betray her. Only with Falling Water had she cried her tears of frustration, for she would never do so before anyone else.

After today's episode, she vowed that she would push Little Eagle from her mind and accept one of the many braves who sought her hand in marriage. Yet she knew such a promise would be difficult, if not impossible, to keep, for no matter how many good qualities her suitors possessed, she found herself comparing them to Little Eagle, and she always found them wanting.

Suddenly, as if she had conjured him up with her thoughts, she saw Little Eagle riding toward her. Even at this distance, she knew him, recognizing the way he sat his horse as if he and the animal were one, admiring the breadth of his shoulders as the sun glistened on his bronzed skin. She knew him as a woman in love knows the man of her choice not just with her eyes, but with her senses, with the rapid pounding of her heart.

His body seemed to be alert to everything about him, and she sensed the moment he spotted her. With a movement so slight that only a trained eye would see it, he turned his horse in her direction and rode rapidly toward her.

Her breath seemed to catch in the center of her breast and refuse to be expelled. She could feel herself tremble, and inwardly raged at the emotions she tried in vain to control.

He stopped close beside her and smiled as he would at any friend he met in the valley. "Good morning, Lone Star."

"Good morning," she murmured.

"I am looking for Night Sky. Have you seen him?"

"Yes, we were riding together. He is not far from here. I believe he goes to hunt. Falling Water is still with him."

Before Little Eagle could speak again, the sound of an

approaching horse drew their attention. Soon Falling Water rode up to them.

While his attention was drawn to Falling Water, Lone Star took the opportunity to gaze at him more fully. Until now she had refused to look into the miracle of his blue eyes, fearing what he would see in her own eyes would betray her. She wanted him to see her, but she wanted it to be with his heart and not just his eyes.

The sun glistened on his skin, and she was breathlessly aware of the latent strength that seemed to ripple beneath it. She fondly regarded his chiseled square-jawed face and noted how masterfully the long, slim fingers of his large hands held the reins of his horse. He seemed to be in complete control not only of the animal beneath him, but of all that surrounded him. She watched his quick grin as Falling Water stopped beside them.

She envied Falling Water's easy smile. Why could she not look at him, smile at him with ease as Falling Water did? Why did she feel this trembling within her that took words and smiles away and left her silent and wanting?

"Good morning, Little Eagle." Falling Water laughed, then asked, "You are hunting or just enjoying the day?"

He chuckled in response. "I'm looking for Night Sky. I would hunt, and I thought he might like to join me. Our tepee is in need of meat."

"Night Sky has ridden toward the clear water valley," Falling Water answered. "Maybe he goes to hunt also."

"Good. My thanks, Falling Water." He expertly touched his horse, and it leapt to his command. In a moment, he was riding away.

Falling Water gazed at Lone Star in sympathy as she watched her friend's eyes follow Little Eagle until he was gone from their sight. Lone Star needed no words from anyone. Abruptly, she turned her horse in silence, and the two friends made their way back to the village.

Little Eagle rode with the ease and self-assurance of a man in control of everything around him. As he gazed at his surroundings, he was struck by the majestic splendor of his world. Contentment filled him completely. He thought of his world and the people who inhabited it. His father, Sun Knife, had enriched his life with every dream his mind had held from the first day they had seen each other. He remembered well the mother who had cared for him in his beginning years, before he had known who his father was. He was grateful to her for her surrender of him and still often prayed to the gods for her well being, for she had vanished from his life when his father had entered it. He thought also of his foster mother, Snow Blossom, who had been to him all a mother could be.

A younger sister completed his family. She was Spring, born when he was eight or nine. He had nearly smothered her with brotherly love in his gratitude for the way she had seemed to complete the circle of happiness in his family.

Now he had all he wanted. The valley was his world, and he was happy with it. He could hunt and fish and, as the son of the medicine man, he was treated with deference by all. His pride very closely bordered on arrogance. He was sure this life would have no end. Always he would be master of his existence. One day he would choose a wife from among all the young girls who fluttered about him. He would have sons and gift them with the beauty of the valley and the life of pleasure he enjoyed so fully.

A wife? he reflected. Who would he choose of all the pretty girls he knew? He envisioned each separately and examined each one's qualities coolly and abstractly, without emotion or desire. He gave no thought to Lone Star, nor did he suspect her yearnings or her determination.

Once he found Night Sky, he abandoned all thought of women and marriage. Together they enjoyed the bright spring day, unaware that other forces were already determining their futures.

The village lay sprawled in the valley. As was always the custom, tepees had been erected near the river that wound across the valley floor, for water was of utmost importance. The tepees formed a semicircle, with all entrances facing the rising sun.

Amidst the bustling activity, small children frolicked while older children involved themselves in more serious play, which would help them develop their roles in life. Here and there women worked at assorted chores, some kneeling over pegged buffalo hides, some building fires or grinding corn. It was a serene and well-ordered village.

Standing out from the lavishly decorated dwellings along the river was a huge tepee, situated near the center of the village. It was a massive abode, and also unique in that it was without decoration, for the others were brightly painted with scenes depicting the accomplishments of their owners.

It was the sight of this tepee that greeted Falling Water

and Lone Star as they crested the hill and rode into the village. In fact, the large, unpainted tepee was the one toward which they rode. They dismounted in front of it, but, before they could enter, the flap was pushed aside.

Sun Knife, healer of the tribe, stepped out into the sunlight. He was the model from which Little Eagle was formed. His crystal blue eyes confirmed their kinship. He carried his years well, for he was still slim and muscular, and his hair was still a gleaming raven black. A smile of greeting came quickly as he welcomed the daughters of his friends.

"Good morning. You have been riding early?" he asked.

"We have been racing Night Sky," Falling Water explained. "But, as usual, we lost. Lone Star owes him a new shirt for our efforts."

"I must make it," Lone Star replied. "Falling Water has already acquired the beads and the deer hide."

"I'm sure it will be beautiful, Lone Star. Your work is always so," he remarked kindly.

She smiled her pleasure at a compliment from one so important in the tribe as Sun Knife. "My mother—" Falling Water questioned, "is she with you; does she need my help?"

"No. Our work here is finished for a while. She has gone to her tepee."

"I shall go to see if she needs me. If she does not, Lone Star, would you like to go to the river and swim?"

"Yes, I shall wait at my tepee should you decide to go."

Falling Water strode purposefully across the open area between the tepees. She walked with a graceful step that bespoke her ease in the place she lived. As she came to her tepee, she stopped, then, pushing the flap aside, she bent slightly and entered.

She was not surprised to find her mother, Lauren, present, but she had not expected to find her father, Running Wolf. Normally, her father would be hunting or trapping the animals from which they would make winter clothing.

She smiled as a sense of warm pleasure filled her. It was obvious they had been holding each other and whispering about something. It always gave her a feeling of delight when she saw them together, for their deep love for each other enhanced her life as well.

Running Wolf, her tall, strong, handsome, and always laughing father whom she loved deeply, had always shown her kindness and gentleness. He had given her pride in all that she was.

Her eyes touched her mother. How beautiful she still was. Though her deep auburn hair hung in two thick braids and her skin had tanned to a deep gold, her sea green eyes vividly proclaimed her white blood.

"Mother, do you have need of me now?"

"No, there's nothing pressing. Do you have plans?"

"I thought if you didn't need me I would go to the river with Lone Star and swim."

"Go child; there's time for work later," Lauren replied with a laugh.

With a quick smile, Falling Water turned and left. Running Wolf chuckled as he slid his arm about Lauren's waist and drew her close to him. Leisurely and very thoroughly, he kissed her.

"I look in our daughter's eyes and I see the beauty of her mother," he said softly.

"You see with blind eyes, my husband. She is a beauty.

I am an old woman.''

"Old woman!" he scoffed as he drew her closer. "You are still the girl I was wise enough to capture before she could fly away. You are still Summer Rain, and I love you. I always will.''

He drew her down to the blankets with him, and they shared once again the love they had nurtured over the years.

Chapter 3

Falling Water rode alone, for Lone Star had been unable to accompany her. Most times she preferred privacy, loving the freedom of her world and never feeling lonely when surrounded by its beauty. And she rode with the ease of one who had been taught to ride before learning to walk.

She left the village at a slow trot, but that was not enough for her exuberant spirit. She bent low over her horse's back, urging him into a run. Soon they were flying. As her dark hair billowed out behind her to catch the rays of the morning sun, it seemed a flame-touched mass. Her slim, supple body swayed with the horse's rhythmic movement, and she gloried in the feel of the wind against her face and the throbbing, muscular power of the horse beneath her.

The river toward which she rode was quite some distance from the village. There were closer places to swim, but she preferred this one for the seclusion it offered. She slowed her horse when she felt him begin to labor and walked him to let him cool. After a while, they came to the banks of the river.

Though the river was not too wide, it seemed to move with a swift current, and she realized she would not be able to match her strength to it. Slowly, she rode along the river bank to a familiar spot where the river nestled into deep, quiet pools overhung with shady trees. It was here she would enjoy the cool, quiet waters.

First, she tended her mount. Horses were the Indians' most prized possessions, and they never neglected or abused them. Falling Water brushed the animal, then led him to drink. When he was finished, she took him to a nearby grassy spot and hobbled him so he would not drift too far. Then she walked back to the cool, inviting water.

She turned her eyes upward to the blue, cloudless sky. Something within her lifted and soared like the lone eagle that drifted above her. She felt she belonged to this place, was a part of it. And she was filled with both a sense of joyous pleasure and expectancy, as if some great event in her life were about to occur.

With deft fingers she untied her dress, slipped it from her, and cast it on the bank. Her moccasins followed. Finally she stood naked, savoring the freedom of it. Her slim body was a masterpiece of beauty, displaying long, slender legs, a flat, taut stomach, a slender, curved waist, and high, proud, rose-tipped breasts. Her bronze skin, kissed by the sun, completed the compelling picture.

She waded into the shallow water until she was waist deep, then, with expert movements, she dove beneath the surface without making a splash.

Like a graceful otter, she swam downward until she could no longer fight the need for air. Kicking upward, she shot to the surface with an exuberant laugh.

Leisurely, she floated on her back and watched the branches of the trees as they swayed over her. Then she turned, and, with surprising strength, she swam toward the shore until she could again stand in the shallows. The water swirled about her slim legs as she stood to squeeze the water from the lengths of her dark hair.

An instant later, she froze and remained motionless while her eyes studied the surrounding area. Accustomed to the forest noises, she was always alert for any alien sound. Now she was like a wild animal, poised for flight, waiting only to be sure from which direction her danger was coming. Enemy tribes often cut into Cheyenne territory to steal horses and women, for the women were well known for their beauty.

It came again, the sound that had first caught her attention. A low, almost unbearable moan. She listened intently and let her eyes follow the sound.

Around the protective outcropping of land was a rocky shore, beyond which tall grass grew thickly. It seemed the sound was coming from the grassy area, and though she knew an enemy could easily hide in the tall grass, some instinct told her to search out the cause of the sound.

She moved slowly through the water, prepared to leap into the river instantly should an enemy appear.

As she drew closer, the sound repeated itself, and now she was certain it was a groan of pain. Then she saw a man's form lying half in the grass and half on the rocky ground.

She bent low and moved toward it, alert for any other sounds about her. When she finally reached him, she could not tell just how badly hurt he might be. He was a very large man, and she had difficulty turning him over.

Blood soaked the front of his shirt, so much of it that she would not tell at first where the wound was. She finally discovered it was high on the left side of his chest, near the shoulder.

He groaned again as her hands searched for more wounds. She noted a superficial one on his left leg, and saw that blood was clotted over a wound on his temple.

Satisfied that he would live if he received care, she knelt on her knees beside him for a moment to consider her options. Should she leave him and go for help? she wondered, then grew concerned that a wild animal would find him defenseless in the meantime.

Before she could determine what to do, his eyes fluttered open. Their look was vague, disoriented, then suddenly communicated disbelief. A shaky hand reached to touch her, his fingers making contact with her shoulder and tracing a path down her still-wet arm.

"My God," he rasped. She smiled, knowing he thought she was something he was imagining. "Mack," he groaned. "Thomas . . . Mack."

He was calling for others. The names were strange to her, and she surmised that he must have had companions with him. Slowly, she rose to her feet and began to look about. A few moments later, deeper in the high grass, she found another man, completely unconscious. A further search uncovered no sign of the third man she had heard him call for, and she returned to his side to find him also unconscious.

She made her decision, then went to her horse and got a blanket, food, and her water sack. Then she dressed quickly and went to the first man. As gently as possible, she washed his wounds, padded them with soft moss and a leather strip, then formed a pillow of the soft grass and

40

covered him with her blanket. Then she turned to the second man.

The wound in his side was still seeping warm blood, so she knew the attack had not occurred too long ago.

It took all her strength to drag the second man close enough to the first so that a fire between them would warm them both. She built the fire carefully, hoping it would keep animals away until she could return with help. She took a last look at the first man. Her eyes told her that she had not seen one so handsome ever before. It was strange that her flesh still tingled from his touch, and she was surprised by her desire to see him look at her, know her, say her name. She shook off the thought, turned and mounted her horse, and rode rapidly toward the village.

They had traveled slowly. It was early spring, the time Rayne most enjoyed in the wild territory. He, like Mack, delighted in Thomas's pleasure. As he watched Thomas, Rayne remembered the first times he had seen and fallen in love with the wild, untamed country. No matter how often he had tried to make his parents happy by returning to civilization and the responsibilities of the family fortune, in the end he had to be honest with himself and them. This place called for him in a voice no one else could hear. It was the only place in the world he felt he truly belonged—the only place he was happy.

"Rayne?"

"What?" Rayne responded, his reverie interrupted.

"We goin' to make the river before we camp?" Mack questioned.

"We should. It's not far from here. We'll make it a

short night. Come morning, we'll feel more like riding again."

"I could use a little walking now," Thomas laughed in youthful pleasure.

Rayne chuckled as he replied, "Getting a sore rump, boy?"

"To put it mildly," Thomas confessed. "I've got blisters on my blisters."

"Well, we'll camp by the river. In the morning you can soak your behind in the river. We'll stay a few days, then push on. I'm not sure, but I think there's an Indian village somewhere near here."

"Rayne?" Thomas ventured. "I don't want to get nosy, but are you lookin' for a particular village?"

Rayne was silent for a moment. Then he replied, "What gives you that idea?"

"I don't know. You just . . . seem to be lookin' for something."

"You're imagining things, kid. I'm lookin' for a comfortable place to light, that's all."

Thomas was silent, and both Rayne and Mack wondered if he doubted what Rayne had said.

They reached the swiftly flowing river and made an early evening camp. Thomas and Mack fished for the night's supper, since all three needed a change from a diet of roasted rabbit and other game.

After supper, they swam for a while, then lay talking until the moon was high. Finally they slept, unaware that hidden eyes watched their every move.

Dawn had barely streaked the sky when the three rose and began to pack their horses. They were preparing to mount when the first shrill cry of the attackers shattered the morning air. Rayne and Mack were not so much shocked by the unexpected attack as they were surprised when they saw the painted Indians.

Taken completely unaware, neither Rayne nor Mack had time to reach for a gun. Rayne heard Mack cry out and spun about to see him fall. Then a sharp, burning pain in Rayne's head was matched by one in his chest, and darkness enveloped him.

A war club quickly knocked Thomas senseless, and none of the three knew that the attackers quickly dismounted.

"Run off their horses," the leader ordered. "Then get the boy and bring him along. Leave the other two. They'll die soon enough."

Thomas was tossed across a horse, and within moments they were gone, leaving Rayne and Mack lying quietly in the tall, waving grass.

The first thing Rayne could remember was pain—red, hot pain that seemed to crush his chest and pound ceaselessly in his head. He felt himself being moved and struggled to regain his consciousness. Grimly, he tried to force his eyes open, and, when he succeeded, the shock of what he saw paralyzed him.

She bent above him—the most beautiful woman he had ever seen. She was glistening with silver drops of water and she was . . . completely naked. Her beauty was so absolute that he could not believe she was real, and he reached out to touch this golden vision.

He could feel the damp, cool skin beneath his fingers, like smooth velvet. It was beyond his comprehension that he could conjure up such an amazing beauty in his mind.

"My God," he muttered in disbelief. Then once again the pain overwhelmed him. He felt the blackness overtaking him and called out for Mack and Thomas. Were they dead? Was he dead and this glorious woman some part of heaven? He hoped it was so as the dark cloud of unconsciousness took all thought away.

After a time, pain again gripped him and shook him into foggy awareness. Hands seemed to be lifting him. He tried to pull himself from the black oblivion but could not quite do so. Voices came to him, then movement, pain, and again darkness.

Much later, he opened heavy-lidded eyes and peered into semidarkness. He looked up to see pale sunlight filtering down through the open flap of the tepee. He was lying on something soft and furry. Desperately, he tried to sort out what had happened and where he might be. He wondered if he had been captured by either Crow or Ute, for they were the most warlike Indians in the region. Then his mind drifted to what he had thought was a dream—to the slim beauty who had bent over him in her naked splendor. Had she been real? Could such a delicate beauty have been Crow?

With painful effort, he turned his head to see Mack lying on a buffalo hide across the low-burning fire from him. Mack's eyes were closed, but he was breathing evenly, which indicated to Rayne that he was all right.

"Mack," he rasped. Mack's eyes slowly opened, and he turned his head to look at Rayne. "You all right, Mack?"

"I'm not sure. Everything I own hurts. What the hell happened?"

"We were stupid, that's what happened. We lowered our guard and got caught with our pants down. We knew

44

we were being followed. We should have been more careful."

"Where's the kid?"

"I don't know. Christ, I hope they didn't kill the boy."

"Rayne?"

"Yeah?"

"They wasn't Indians."

"I know. I wonder . . ."

"Sure is a good sign that what Senator Miles thinks is true."

"We've got to find out what's going on. I'm just wondering whose village we're in."

"Could be Grey Elk, maybe . . . or White Eagle. They're both close about here."

"Could be. Mack?"

"What?"

"Did you see anything . . . different, after we were attacked?"

"Different? You mean because they were whites painted and dressed to look like Indians?"

"No," Rayne said hesitantly. "I mean after the attack was over."

"Hell, Rayne, I was out like the dead."

"You mean you never felt anyone move us—never saw anyone?"

"No. What are you getting at, Rayne?"

"I . . . I must have been imagining things," Rayne muttered. "God, what a dream that was. With something like that, I could spend the rest of my life asleep."

"Tell me about it." Mack grinned. "I could use a little relief from this pain."

Rayne told him of the vision he had seen. He described

the woman so accurately that Mack could almost see her.

"Boy, I have to say when you use your imagination, you sure know how to use it. Why don't you conjure up one for me while you're about it."

Rayne laughed, but he couldn't believe he could still see her in his mind's eye, could still feel the fine texture of her damp, soft skin. His senses were still alive with the memory of her. "I wish I could move," Rayne said. "I'd like to know the situation we're in, where we are, and where Thomas is. If he had been wounded, he'd be here with us. I'm just praying he's alive and well."

"I wonder how long we've been here."

"It's midday," Rayne explained. "But we don't have any idea if there've been days in between."

"Well, somebody has patched us up pretty good."

Rayne examined himself for the first time and realized he was bandaged—bandaged in the white man's way. This was totally unexpected. "How the—"

Before he could finish speaking, the flap was pushed aside and a man bent to enter. Both men were unprepared for what they saw. When he stood erect, he was almost as tall as Rayne, broad shouldered, and very handsome. What drew their attention was the startling blue of his eyes. In his bronzed face the color was shocking. He smiled and surprised them again by using English, the English of one well educated.

"Good afternoon. I'm glad to see you are awake." He could not resist laughing at their obvious shock. "I'm Sun Knife, the man of medicine here, but I'm also Cade Holliday, son of Dr. Michael Holliday. You might have heard of him."

"Heard of him?" Rayne chuckled. "He's practically a

46

legend. I've often wondered if the stories were true."

Sun Knife grinned. "When you're feeling better, you can tell me what you've heard; then I'll tell you just how much of it is true and how much is legend."

He knelt beside Rayne as he spoke and began to check the bandages. Then he moved to Mack and did the same. Satisfied, he sat back on his heels and studied them. "How do you feel?"

"Like a freshly weaned kitten," Rayne replied. "How long have we been here like this?"

"A little over a week."

"Damn," Rayne muttered. "I didn't realize it had been that long. Can you tell me how our other friend is?"

"Other friend?"

"The young man who was with us."

"We searched the area very carefully. There was no one else. Believe me, we would have found him if he had been there."

"I don't understand. What could have happened to him? He was with us when the Indians attacked."

"Indians!" Sun Knife said with a frown. "You believe some of my people attacked you and left you for dead? We would not leave even a wounded animal to suffer so."

Mack remained silent and watched both men carefully. He knew Rayne was aware that the attackers had not been Indians, and he wondered what Rayne was doing.

"What do you suggest happened?" Rayne said softly.

Sun Knife's eyes met Rayne's and held them as he spoke firmly and with conviction. "I have not questioned the ones who found you, nor have I questioned our chief, my blood brother, White Eagle. But even without their answers, I would swear on my life that none of our people attacked you. We live in peace here and would like to keep it so."

"Maybe," Rayne said softly. "We can talk to these people together and go to the spot where we were attacked and examine it. It might tell us a story. Besides, I have to know just what happened to the boy who was with us."

"It would be wise to do so"—again Sun Knife smiled—"but don't judge my people too quickly or by such a deed. You will be with us for a while. You will see and understand."

"Yes," Rayne replied. "That is what I would like to do—see . . . and understand."

Sun Knife rose and walked to the tepee door. He turned and looked back at both men. "You may try to get up and eat. I will have food brought to you. The wounds are healing nicely. You might be stiff and feel some pain, but both of you are well enough to begin moving. I shall return before dark to make sure all is well. In the meantime, eat and drink; it's what your bodies need now."

"I'm not too sure I can move"—Mack chuckled—"but I sure as hell could eat. My stomach thinks my throat's been cut."

The resulting laughter eased the tension. "I shall see that someone brings you food soon." He turned and left the tepee. For a moment Rayne and Mack stared at each other in silence.

"You know it wasn't Indians, Rayne. I could tell with just one look. Why was you pushin' him?"

"I just wanted to watch his eyes."

"What do you think?"

"He was telling the truth. He has no idea what happened out there."

48

"Now what?"

"Now we have to play our cards close to our chests until we find out for sure if anyone else in this village does. In the meantime, we have to start a search for Thomas. If he had been killed, they would have found him; if he had been wounded and wandered away, he would have left a trail. One way or the other, we have to know."

"Until we're well enough to ride, we'd better concentrate on gettin' up and eating."

"You're right," Rayne replied. With a few moans and groans, he forced himself to a sitting position. Then he watched Mack struggle to do the same. As they sat facing each other across the fire, they laughed simultaneously at each other's helplessness.

With grim determination, Rayne stood. His body was weak, but he was surprised that there was less pain than he had thought there would be. Resolutely, Mack followed his example. With a few mild curses, he too stood erect.

"God," Mack complained, "I feel like hell."

"I don't think even food is going to make me feel like doing much right now," Rayne remarked with a chuckle.

There was a rustle of movement outside the door, then the flap was again pushed aside. Mack merely saw a pretty girl stepping inside with a bowl of food in each hand. But Rayne was stunned to realize his mystical vision was in fact a very live and very beautiful woman.

Her eyes flew to his and widened. She had seen him helpless and unconscious, and she had been aware of him then, but not as much as she was now. He seemed to fill the room with his height and powerful build. Suddenly she became aware of his gaze, which seemed to pierce her flesh and seek the very center of her being. Her breath caught and her heart began to pound. She tore her eyes from him as she smiled hesitantly, trying to regain control of herself. It was not proper, she felt, for a woman to be so ragingly aware of a man who was nothing more than a stranger.

"Sun Knife says you are to eat. I have brought you warm soup. Later I will bring meat."

Gently, she set down the bowls and, without meeting his eyes again, she swiftly left the tepee. Once outside, she stood very still, fiercely determined to regain command of herself. She had been courted by most of the men in her village, as well as men from those nearby, and no man had ever affected her so. But he was different from any man she had ever known—so tall, so wildly handsome. She imagined again the gentle touch of his fingers on her skin, the way his eyes seemed to search the very depths of her. It made her wayward body tremble.

She stormed at her thoughts angrily, and, just as fiercely, they fought back. They would not let her forget a thing about him; nor would they let her forget the touch of his hand.

"I am no child," she muttered. "He is probably a husband, the father of many children. I will put him from my mind."

Determinedly, she walked toward her teepe, but thoughts of Rayne persistently followed.

Chapter 4

Rayne could only gaze helplessly at her, overcome by the reality of his dream. As he watched her disappear, all the thoughts in his mind were reflected on his features, and Mack did not miss them.

"So," Mack said softly, "you weren't imagining things?"

"No," Rayne replied. "She is quite beyong anything I have ever imagined. I wonder who she is, and I wonder—"

"If she's married and the mother of five or six kids." Mack chuckled. "Maybe she's got a big buck for a husband, and he'll wear your hair if you lay a hand on her."

"I sure hope not," Rayne breathed softly. "I wouldn't want any trouble, but I'm sure not going to be here much longer before I get those questions answered." He turned to face Mack, and Mack's smile faded. He realized that for the first time a woman had reached inside Rayne Freeman and touched a place he had never before let a woman touch.

51

"Rayne, we have to remember just why we're here. We can't stir up any trouble. At least keep this easy until we get some answers."

"I don't intend to drag her behind a bush and rape her, for God's sake. I just want to . . . to—"

"To be with her, to find out if your dream woman is real or just another empty shell."

"Mack . . ."

"I'm just telling you to be careful, Rayne. I know what kind of man you are. Maybe it will be hard, but you'll do what you have to do. I . . . I don't want you to have any problems you can't handle."

Rayne smiled. "I know, Mack. Trust me. I won't do anything stupid."

Mack smiled, and slowly Rayne walked to the entrance, bent, and left, the door flap closing behind him with a soft rustling sound. Mack stared after him. "I don't want you hurt, either, my friend," he said softly as he gazed at the closed door flap. Then he sighed deeply and returned to his fur-covered couch and lay down.

As Rayne stepped outside into the bright midday sun, he was soothed by its warmth, though he still felt a twinge in his shoulder and his body resisted the movement after so much time spent in bed. He gazed at the village that surrounded him. It was a large village, and slowly he began walking through it. Curious eyes followed him, but no one attempted to stop him from moving about.

Then he approached what appeared to be the largest tepee he had ever seen. He stood before it, marveling at its immense size. After a few moments, Sun Knife stepped out, followed by a slim woman. The medicine man smiled as he stopped, and the woman came up beside him.

"I told you to move around, but I didn't say you had to walk all over the village."

"I'm feeling fine," Rayne assured him with a smile.

"This is my wife, Snow Blossom."

"I'm Rayne Freeman, and I'm grateful to your people for taking me in when I was in trouble."

"You are welcome in our village, Mr. Freeman." Snow Blossom smiled. "And we are grateful to the gods that we found you in time."

It was obvious to Rayne she was a woman of strength and character. Still beautiful and gracefully slim despite her years, she looked at Rayne with shrewd eyes that missed nothing.

Before Rayne could answer, another woman emerged from the large dwelling. His face registered surprise as he realized she was white.

"This is Lauren Brent, wife of Running Wolf."

"I have heard of you," Rayne said honestly. "There are many rumors circulating in Washington."

"Oh?" Lauren smiled. "Then maybe we should talk, so that what you have heard can be proven either false or true. If you have come from Washington, you may have been told stories that are not only exaggerated, but unflattering as well."

"We set out from Washington nearly a month ago, and if you can tell me the real story of Michael Holliday, it will be enough to make the whole trip worthwhile. I've heard a lot of different reports and would love nothing better than to know the truth."

"Come along then." Lauren smiled. "You can eat the evening meal in my tepee. By the time I tell you the whole story, Running Wolf will be insisting on his supper."

Rayne smiled and fell into step beside her as she

53

walked toward a tepee that sat some distance away. As they walked, Rayne could not help but ask himself why a beautiful and wealthy white woman with a prestigious name would come to this remote area to live. She must have read his thoughts well for she laughed softly.

"Because it is beautiful and peaceful, and when you meet my husband and my daughter, Falling Water, you will truly understand why."

Rayne laughed. "Was I that obvious?"

"It is a reaction I have seen before. But it does not bother me. I have the best of everything here. When I compare the world I've known, I can feel this place call to me. I'm certain I belong here."

Rayne was silent for a moment, then he replied in a quiet voice, "Yes, I know what you mean."

"You have felt it too?"

"Yes, I guess that's why I keep coming back."

"You have returned to Washington often?"

"Only for short periods. I feel much better out here."

"You have not been to our village before."

"I have been near, but not here."

"You will stay with us long?"

"For a while."

They reached her tepee, and she stopped and turned to face him. Smiling warmly, she said, "I hope you find pleasure in your stay with us and return often."

"Thank you," he replied, surprised at the sense of belonging her words gave him. She bent and entered the tepee, and he followed. It was then he received his second shock of the day.

She knelt beside a low-burning fire, and her eyes widened with surprise at seeing him. It was the last place she had expected him to be. She had come to the privacy

54

of her family dwelling to try to gather together her thoughts and emotions, but now her mother had brought the agent of her confusion to her only sanctuary. She could not seem to pull her eyes away from him, and she desperately fought the sensation that he was reaching across the space between them and touching her.

Mentally, he had done just that. He had dived into the depths of her eyes and allowed renewed feelings to flood him, memories of her slim, golden body, its soft, round, pink-tipped breasts, and the delicate curve of her waist. He could almost feel the smooth texture of her skin on his fingertips, and the desire to touch her again overwhelmed him.

"Falling Water, this is our guest, Rayne Freeman. Mr. Freeman, my daughter is the one who found you and carefully nursed you while you were so ill."

"I know," Rayne said softly, and Falling Water could feel her cheeks become pink. Her eyes fled from his, and she found herself unable to speak. It was a startling experience, for she had never before been without laughter or words. She became angry with herself for her childish behavior.

"I am grateful to you for finding and caring for us, Falling Water. I should like to give you some gift to show a little of our appreciation."

Rayne knew quite well that it was customary for the Indians to give and accept gifts. Usually the gifts were exorbitant, costing the givers much in order to show sufficient appreciation to the recipients. He also knew Falling Water would not be able to refuse a gift offered in gratitude. Above all, he was delighted to have found her in her parents' tepee, for it meant she was as yet unmarried.

"It . . . it is not necessary to give me a gift," she said quietly. "I found you by accident and the others brought you home. It is Sun Knife who should be given a gift, for he is the healer who made you well."

"But," Rayne argued resolutely, "if you had not found me, I would have died out there. I owe you my life." He laughed. "It may not mean much to some, but I place great value on it. I shall decide soon what the best gift would be, and I would be greatly disappointed if you did not choose to accept it."

Falling Water saw that her mother's curious eyes were upon her, and she knew her mother's wisdom. There was no way she could refuse his gift. She bent her head so her eyes would not meet his, replying, "I will accept, for I am grateful that the spirits led me to you and you did not die."

"Come," Lauren said, "sit by the fire and I will tell you our story."

Rayne moved to sit as close to Falling Water as he could. He felt her awareness of him but knew it could not possibly match the sensations engulfing him. He would have liked nothing better than to have her rest her head against his shoulder while he put his arm about her slim waist.

Falling Water knew she could no longer bear the unfamiliar feelings this stranger caused within her. Abruptly, she rose to her feet.

"I will leave you to talk," she whispered. "I have much to do." With these words, she rapidly left the tepee, and Lauren's eyes contained both surprise and understanding as they followed her retreating figure. Rayne listened to Lauren's story of the white doctor with only half his mind. The other half followed Falling Water and was

56

tangled helplessly in thoughts of her.

He was not surprised by the story, for, piece by piece, he had heard most of it before. He asked few questions, but the ones he asked were answered swiftly and honestly.

Lauren had been keeping an eye on food that had been cooking at the edge of the fire. It hung from a tripod, and the scent of it had begun to entice Rayne. Lauren noticed this also.

"You will eat the evening meal with us?"

"I would be pleased." He grinned. "It smells too good to pass up. Your . . . your daughter will return to eat with us?"

"Perhaps." Lauren smiled. "Perhaps not. Often she goes her way and does not eat her meals here."

"Oh," Rayne replied, and Lauren could have laughed at his obvious disappointment.

Rayne stood up. "I will go back to see about my friend, then return to eat."

"Bring your friend with you," Lauren invited. "I'm sure he must be hungry for some meat after all he has been eating."

"We'll eat all the food you can supply," he warned with a chuckle.

"My husband is a good provider," she replied, humor sparkling in her eyes. "You are always welcome at our fire."

"I look forward to meeting him." Rayne left the tepee and stopped outside. His eyes scanned the area, but he soon realized he would find no sign of Falling Water.

He was annoyed, and his annoyance rapidly became frustration. As the days moved along, it seemed obvious she was deliberately avoiding him. He would catch a glimpse of her now and then, but she would seem to fade from sight whenever he approached her. Before too long, grim determination began to replace frustration. Mack watched the transition in silence. He was well aware that Rayne had been more than successful with women in the past, and it amused him that this was one time Rayne was not finding the going too easy.

It was just before dawn when Rayne rose from his bed. Mack stirred, only half awake. "Where you goin'?" he mumbled.

"Go back to sleep, Mack. I'm just goin' out back."

Mack was already asleep again even before Rayne left the tepee. He walked softly, not wanting to disturb anyone, especially the dogs that slept between and in front of some of the tepees.

He made his way from the village to a spot he had watched carefully for some time, near the stream that ran by the village. A secluded and quiet area, it was the place Falling Water came to get water for her mother. She came each day at dawn.

In the preceding days, he had waited and observed her daily routine. He was certain this was a place she would not see him until it was too late to disappear.

At the moment he was slightly angry with himself. Why should he go to such trouble to meet one woman, when there were so many other pretty maidens in the village? Of course, he knew the answer even before the question was fully formed in his mind. He could not keep his thoughts from her any more than he could keep his senses from conjuring her up so vividly that he could almost taste and feel her presence.

He found a place and waited motionless and silently for what seemed to him like hours. Well accustomed to the wild, he had developed a sense of hearing that rivaled any Indian's. Falling Water walked softly from habit, yet he heard her footsteps. His heart skipped a beat, and again he was amazed at himself. He was feeling new, alien emotions, and he was not sure he liked their effect. Standing with his back braced against a tree, he watched her walk by. He had remembered her beauty well.

He remained quiet for a while longer, enjoying the way the sun touched the gold of her skin and shimmered in her dark hair. The sway of her slim hips drew his attention, and he sought again the memory of her wet, slim body.

She bent to fill a water skin. When it was full, she hung it on a tree branch, removed her moccasins, and proceeded to wade into the cool water. He took advantage of that moment to speak her name softly. "Falling Water."

She spun about and gazed at him in surprise.

"I'm sorry," he said. "I didn't mean to frighten you." He regretted those words immediately when he saw the spark of anger in her eyes and the defiant tilt of her chin.

"The man does not breathe of whom I am afraid—" she said arrogantly, "much less a white man."

He knew quite well she preferred his anger, for this she could fight, and he had no intention of falling into her trap. "Then come out of the water and talk to me . . . unless, of course . . ." He grinned and shrugged, pointing out without words that he would consider her afraid if she did not. Anger pinkened her cheeks as she walked slowly from the water.

She stood beside him, defiant and so beautiful it left

him with a hollow feeling in the pit of his stomach, and only self-control kept him from pulling her into his arms. He didn't want her anger and resistance, and he searched for words to alter her feelings. "Falling Water, I come only to thank you for saving my life and the life of my friend."

"So you lie in wait for me?"

"It was necessary. I could not seem to get to talk to you alone."

"It . . . it is unnecessary to thank me," she replied, but her eyes fell from his, and he sensed her uncertainty return. She knew she had nothing to fight, yet she felt a strange kind of fear—a fear she could not name.

"Oh," he said mildly with a half smile, "you think my life is of so little value that I should not be grateful for its safety?"

"I didn't . . . I didn't mean that!" She was startled. Trained well in Indian customs, she found it difficult to be rude to a guest her mother had welcomed to their tepee. "I only meant—"

"You meant," he supplied gently, "that you did not want to talk to me alone. Why, Falling Water? I owe you much. I did not mean to upset you, only to tell you how grateful I am." He chuckled. "Worthless as it may be, it's the only life I have, and I value it. So . . . please," he added softly, "let me talk to you for a while."

She looked up at him, and he could see a responding smile tug at the corners of her soft lips.

He lost himself in the amber pools of her eyes where golden flakes danced and sparkled, and he was touched with the sudden but sure knowledge that she was a rare, beautiful creature with whom he could happily spend the rest of his days.

"I accept your thanks." She smiled. "You are most welcome. I am grateful to the gods for allowing me to find you before you died."

"It was a strange place for you to be. Why were you alone?"

"Are you so sure I was alone?" She laughed, but the laughter faded at his reply.

"I remember a moment . . . a single, beautiful moment when an angel bent over me—quite the most beautiful angel I have ever seen."

Again her cheeks grew pink, but her eyes held his in an unspoken attempt to deny what she knew he had seen. "What is an . . . angel?"

"A messenger from the gods—the most beautiful of all creatures."

"I am not an angel," she protested, but she was pleased with the novel compliment.

"But surely you believe, as all your people do, in the existence of Fate?" He stepped closer as he spoke, raising his hand to softly touch her cheek. "Whether it was Fate, the will of the gods, or an angel that rescued me, you are still the most beautiful woman I have ever seen." His eyes were warm and gentle, his touch a light caress that sent ripples of warmth through her.

Mesmerized by the intensity of his gaze, she found herself enjoying the feeling of oneness that seemed to envelop and hold her. He was tall, so tall that she had to tip her face up to look into his eyes.

Her nearness and her sweet, vulnerable lips inviting his were more than he could withstand. He bent his head and gently touched her warm lips with his own.

Something within her seemed to shatter and fill her with brilliant touches of flame. He could feel her tremble

61

as he drew her into his arms to savor her sweet taste.

She moved from his arms, gazing up into his face with a look of combined surprise and fear. Did he think because she was alone and . . . naked when she found him that she was the kind of woman who would give herself to any man?

The Cheyenne women were known as much for their chastity as for their beauty. Did he believe that she would surrender herself so easily, and to one who might be gone tomorrow?

She took several steps backward and fought the fact that she felt a sudden sense of loss and emptiness when she did. "You have sweet words," she said. "But I have heard sweet words before. I give you your life. You owe me nothing. Now leave me alone, for I am not one who gives herself to any man who reaches for her. If you are used to those women, as I'm sure you are, then find another. But do not think to take my pride in addition to what I've given you."

"I did not mean to insult you, Falling Water," Rayne replied. "Is it an insult to tell you that you are kind and beautiful and generous? Is it an insult to say that what I feel for you is much more than just desire for a woman? There have been many I've desired, but never has there been one like you."

"Again sweet words."

"No."

"What do you want of me?"

"To talk with you, be with you, understand you as I want you to understand me. Time to let you know what I feel is true. Then I will seek your trust."

"You ask too much."

"Are you afraid?" he challenged.

"Of course I am not afraid." She smiled. "My father would hang your scalp on his lodge pole if you harmed me."

"Then why is it too much?"

"Because it would be frowned upon if I allowed this. Many would talk, and my parents would be shamed and angry. It is not done."

"Then tell me what I must do."

A smile again touched her face, and a glow of mischief lit her eyes. Now it was her turn to challenge him. "If your words are true and if you really want to know our customs, then"—she chuckled—"there are many ways for you to learn them."

"But you could tell me now and make it easier."

"Those who seek Falling Water have never found it easy. Why should it be so for you? Strong warriors have failed. Are you as good as they?"

He accepted the challenge with a smile on his lips and a glint in his eye that should have warned her of the battle to come.

Thinking she had already won, she moved to pass him and suddenly found herself bound against a hard, muscular chest, his two iron arms holding her securely. She could feel the length of his powerful body pressed to hers. Before she could protest, his mouth swept down and captured hers in a passion-filled kiss that nearly defeated her. Her senses swirled as if in a white-hot cauldron, until she was weak and dizzy from the force of his embrace. His mouth hungered for the feel of her response, and she was helpless as he drew it from her with the intensity of his searching lips.

When he released her, she felt as if she had been caught in a violent storm. Her knees trembled and almost

63

refused to hold her erect.

In firm, yet gentle words, he assured her, "If there's a way to be found, I will find it. I will tell you now that I will, and that I want you as I have never wanted a woman before. You are proud and you are strong, and I admire that strength, but I will not let it or anything else get in my way. My heart speaks to you, Falling Water, and I can hear your heart answer, even if you refuse to hear it. One day, you will be my woman."

Defiance was in her eyes, but now it was accompanied by awareness. "We will see," she said, then she turned and walked away. He watched her go, knowing he would have a battle on his hands, yet he smiled. The reward would be all the better when he won . . . if he won.

"One day," he repeated softly, "I will make you mine."

Chapter 5

His words echoed in her mind as she walked away. They were joined by anger, anger at the weakness of her wayward body that still shook with the warmth his touch had brought.

She denied the existence of any emotion except resentment at his confident words. His admission still grated that women had always been easy conquests for him, and she assumed he must think her an ignorant savage, ready to fall beneath his attach.

She was grateful to her mother and Rebecca for successfully teaching her to read and write the language of the white man. She did not enjoy the confinement of being a student, but still she preferred to be what she felt she was—the daughter of Running Wolf, a Cheyenne maiden content with the security and freedom of her life.

She forced her thoughts to move from Rayne to the warriors who had also sought her, strong, capable warriors willing to share the kind of life she already enjoyed. Rayne was different. Was the difference between them too wide to cross? *Yes!* her mind declared angrily, though her body subtly insisted, *No!*

I want you. His words lingered in her heart. Wanting was far removed from love, she thought. It was the lust of one animal for another. He had not done or said anything that would have been considered proper among those of her tribe, but instead had calmly told her he wanted her, as if she were a trifle he could bargain for. Her cheeks flushed in shame as she thought of the way she had reacted to his touch. Silently she vowed it would not happen again, ignoring the small voice that challenged her, "If it did, what would you really do?" Could she truly resist the strange magic his kiss had awakened in her?

She trembled violently as her bravado deserted her. She returned to her tepee, glad to find it empty. As she lay on the fur-covered mat, for the first time in her life she felt touched by something she did not understand and feared she could not control.

After some time she sat up. A new light of determination lit her eyes. She berated herself for being a fool, telling herself she did not have to succumb to his charm. He was a white man. One day he would ride away and she would never see him again. No, she would not be a fool, she vowed. She would not be left gazing at the empty horizon and weeping for a man who would never look back over his shoulder.

Rayne had watched her walk away. God, but she was wild and lovely, untamed as the elements about her, he had thought. Yet he also remembered that one unguarded moment of surrender, that one moment of vulnerability that had lifted his hopes along with his desire.

If Falling Water summoned the determination to resist

him, he would just have to breech her defenses. He would prove to her that his honor was as deep and demanding as hers. He would show her he was a man with qualities to surpass those of the braves in her village.

The next few days were warm, bright, and beautiful. But Rayne was heedless of nature's beauty as he continued his vigil for another beauty who expertly eluded him.

He went again to the river in the early morning, but Falling Water did not come, and he knew she would not return to the spot again. He would have to be more careful. He was still in no physical condition to risk angering any male in the tribe, especially one with the strength and power of Running Wolf.

He was here for another reason, and he knew he would soon have to seek the answers the senator wanted. But he was also a tenacious and very patient man when it came to something he wanted for himself. He rationalized that following a dream could not be a waste of time when he felt himself drawn after it so relentlessly.

Rayne wisely let a few days pass. He regained his own strength while absorbing the color and the culture about him. In the past he had trapped in this wild and uncharted wilderness and loved it with a fierce passion even he could not fully understand. He knew he belonged here, and he wondered if he could convince a slender, dark-eyed girl that he did.

Mack watched Rayne and instinctively sensed what had occurred. He smiled often to himself, thinking it was about time Rayne learned that all women would not fall at his feet. Falling Water had a pride that matched Rayne's, and Mack wondered just how this contest would end.

The next confrontation was startling to both combatants. Falling Water had studiously avoided Rayne. Yet, though her days had been carefully planned, her nights had been free for dreaming, and she had not enjoyed her dreams. They had made her much more cautious in the daytime.

The day was nearly over. A pale, half-shadowed dusk had fallen, and low fires lit each tepee. Few people were moving about, most of them warriors checking their horses or returning home from the hunt. It was a contented and peaceful time.

Falling Water stepped outside her parents' tepee, breathing deeply of the cool evening air. She closed her eyes for a moment to savor the scents of the wind-rustled trees and blooming wild flowers. She was filled with the urge to ride with the wind and could not restrain her need.

She walked across the open area to where the horses were kept. Quickly she bridled one and drew it away from the rest. In one fluid motion she leapt upon its back and let it drift from the camp toward the flat valley floor, unaware that very pleased eyes had followed her every move. It took Rayne only a few moments to saddle his horse and quietly follow her.

She raced across the valley floor with a graceful abandon that filled Rayne with admiration. She was a woman of chameleonlike changes that fascinated him. He had seen her still and quiet, had tasted her cold resistance, and now he sensed again the flame that ignited her spirit.

He followed at a distance, knowing she would rest her horse soon before she rode back to the village.

She slowed and allowed her mount to lead her to a

trickling stream, a small tributary to the river where she had found him. Stopping beside it, she let her horse drink.

After dismounting, she knelt and watched ripples as they settled into calm water again. Seeing her face reflected in shadows, she studied it seriously. He had told her she was beautiful. She could feel the warmth of remembrance touch her skin with its heat. She placed her damp, cool hand upon her brow to ease this unwelcome feeling. Again, helpless anger filled her. Would she ever be able to wipe away the touch of his hands or the taste of his hungry mouth?

Lost in her reverie, she did not hear his approach at first. Suddenly she rose and spun about as sounds of hoofbeats finally reached her consciousness. Her heart pounded furiously and she mentally tried to calm herself as she recognized the figure astride the horse.

He stopped beside her and slid lightly to the ground. For a few moments they stood in silence, regarding each other as might two foes preparing for a life or death battle.

"I saw you ride from the village," he said. "I followed you."

"Why?" she demanded.

"To talk with you."

"There is nothing for us to say."

"There is much to be said," he countered. "Only you have been running from me. Why are you afraid?"

She was half in shadow from the setting sun behind her, and he did not see the spark of fury that leapt to her eyes. She laughed softly.

"I am not afraid of you," she insisted.

"I didn't say you were afraid of me," he replied with

69

aggravating coolness. "I think you are more afraid of yourself."

"You are an arrogant one!"

"No, not arrogant. Maybe 'honest' is the word."

"Why do you linger here in our village? You are well; your wounds are healed. Why do you not go away?"

"I like it here."

"For a time," she responded. "When you are tired of it, you will go."

"Is that what you really think, Falling Water? That I am just someone passing by?"

"Most white ones are like you. They come sometimes. They linger for a while, then they go and are not seen again."

He chuckled softly. "It is extremely difficult for you to trust me, isn't it?"

"Is that what you want from me?" she questioned with sarcasm in her tone. He stepped closer, and though she was aware of him with every sense she had, she refused to back away.

"To begin with, yes," he replied.

A tingle of warning moved through her, and she yielded her pride and moved back a step.

"We do not begin here," she snapped. "There is no beginning." She lifted her head proudly. "I am Falling Water, daughter of Running Wolf. I can choose any warrior in my tribe. I do not come to a white man because he calls to me and says 'I want you.' Do not say those words to me! What you want is to take me like a worthless one and have the freedom to leave when you choose. I say leave now! I do not want you!"

His anger blazed for a moment, and he reached out suddenly to grab her arm, jerking her toward him.

70

Startled and completely unprepared, she began to fight seconds too late.

She was strong, but he was stronger. He held her in a grip she could not break. She regained her control and ceased to fight, yet she glared up at him, fury darkening her eyes.

"I think," he said softly, "that you are lying to both of us."

Only grim determination kept her wild emotions under control. His nearness stormed her senses, and she could feel the strength and warmth of him begin to draw her under their spell.

It was a silent duel. He held her stiff, resisting body close to him, enjoying the feel of her soft, pliant curves. Yet he knew the battle had only begun. He was in a dilemma his unbridled temper had caused. If he held her and did what he wanted to do, he would only convince her that what she assumed about him was true. If he let her go, she would never give him a moment to explain that he had not meant for this situation to occur.

"Falling Water, just listen to me for a moment," he said.

He was too near, she realized. The vital magnetism about him was slowly enveloping her. She had to get away. Purposefully, she relaxed in his arms. Completely deceived, he loosened his hold. It was all she needed. She struck him—hard. Her hand left a print on his cheek and snapped his head back. In total surprise he released her; but his shock lasted only a moment.

She spun about and headed for her horse, though not quite quickly enough. He caught her, turning her about into his arms. Binding her helplessly to him, he bent his head and caught her mouth with his, stifling her cry of anger. He ravaged her mouth while she fought him. When he finally released her, they stood panting, both momentarily blinded by a combination of anger and desire.

At that moment he wanted to do many things. He wanted to throw her to the ground and take her; yet he wanted to hold her and love her gently. He had to try to explain. He reached for her, but this time he stopped, his eyes focusing on the heavy blade she held in her hand, its point inches from his chest. He knew too well that his own temper had destroyed all he had set out to do.

"Falling Water . . ." he began.

She was afraid of what she saw in his eyes, afraid that he had the power to reach her. She could feel the tingle that still remained as a memory of his touch, and knew she had to get away from him, had to bring her reeling senses under control.

"Put the knife away," he said gently. "I won't touch you again. I just want you to listen to me for a few minutes. It's all I ask. I swear, I won't touch you again." They stood in silence, the knife between them.

Could she believe him? she wondered inwardly.

Would she believe? he mentally asked.

She backed away a few steps, her eyes wary. As she slid the knife back into the sheath at her waist, he breathed a silent sigh of relief.

"I never meant for this to happen, Falling Water. It was my anger that made me foolish for a moment. I ask you to forget this."

Why did she feel truth in his words when she did not want to, she raged at herself.

"Leave our village," she said softly. "There is nothing that holds you here."

72

He sighed raggedly. "I'm sorry. I won't do that. You are wrong. I cannot leave here now. Not until you see the truth."

"I have seen the truth."

"No, you refuse to see."

"My father has spoken many times of the deceptions of the white man—how he tried before I was born to steal our valley. I do not want to hear your . . . truth. I do not believe it is mine. And I do not choose to listen."

She spun about and was on her horse's back in one graceful movement. Without another word she rode back toward the village.

Defeat was not a thing that sat well with Rayne. He had heard her words, but he felt the silent undercurrent of other, unspoken ones. He mounted and rode back toward the village. His hand touched the cheek that still flamed from the sting of her not-too-gentle touch.

For the next few days he moved among her people, listening and asking questions. He heard the story of the threat to her village that had occurred years before. Many explained to him why it was difficult for those of the village to trust the white man. But he could gather no information for Senator Miles as to why tribes that had previously been at war were suddenly gathering in peace. He realized this mission would be more difficult than he had originally expected.

Now he listened for two purposes—to discover the reason for the gathering of the tribes and to find a way to get Falling Water to believe that he had no intention of betraying either her or her village.

Somewhere in the back of his mind lingered the thought that there was a reason for the unrest in this wild frontier, separate and apart from the gathering of the tribes. There was something else happening, and he had to find out what it was. He laughed to himself, knowing he wanted to find out more for Falling Water than for his friend Senator Miles.

Several nights later, there was a celebration. A hunting party had returned with a good supply of meat. This was an occasion the Indians would mark with revelry and the sounding of the drums.

The night was bright with the glow of fires and the sounds of laughter. The drums thundered the invitation to all to join in the festivities. In the air was the scent of cooking food and the murmur of contented chatter.

Men gathered in small groups, their participation in such an activity one of the enormous pleasures of their lives. Hosts of young people were caught up in the fun of the games and the dancing. Rayne watched the dancers, noting that although the participants did not touch each other, they used the dances as a means of conveying affection. He kept one eye on the surrounding activities but continually searched the crowd for any sign of Falling Water.

When he found her it startled him, only because he could hardly believe what his eyes saw. She was dressed in soft, white beaded buckskin. Her dark hair hung free about her, held by a band of white beaded leather around her forehead. She was a vision of loveliness that took his breath away.

She stood with a group of young women. For a few moments he was content just to watch her, admiring the toss of her head as she laughed at something someone had said. The fire glow touched her skin, turning it amber gold, and shimmered in the dark flame of her hair.

Rayne had learned enough of their customs to know that no warrior would walk to a group of women and ask one of them to talk with him. Therefore he waited patiently for the moment she would be alone.

In less than half an hour he found it. She left the group and started for her own tepee, perhaps to get something she had forgotten. She walked between the tepees, and finally he saw her enter her own. Deliberately, he moved toward it.

He was still several steps away when the tepee flap was pushed aside and she stepped out. He saw surprise on her face, but only for the instant before it closed to him.

"Hello, Falling Water." He smiled, trying to ease her suspicion. "It is a grand celebration. I thought you might help me."

"Help you?"

"I don't really understand a lot of your ceremonies and celebrations. The dances are interesting, but I'm confused. I thought we might talk for a while and you could explain."

He could see an unspoken refusal rising in her eyes. "I don't mean here and alone." He laughed. "We could join the others. It looks like a lot of fun. I don't mean to dishonor your customs," he added, referring to the fact that they were alone, away from the others.

She nodded, and he fell in beside her as they slowly walked back toward the fire and the joyous festivities.

Her tension lessened as the hours went by, for Rayne displayed an avid interest in all that was happening about him. He asked her questions and listened intently to her answers, putting every word into the care of his very good memory.

Slowly the celebration drew to a close. The fires died down, and people began to drift back to their tepees. Falling Water found herself walking through the dark village with Rayne beside her.

The moon was high enough above the horizon to shed some light, but still they were barely able to see each other. For a while they walked in silence.

"I enjoyed this night very much," Rayne said. "Do you have such celebrations often?"

Falling Water giggled. "White Eagle enjoys celebrations. He has them as often as he has reasons."

"And I'll bet he finds reasons very easily." Again she laughed, and he found himself enjoying the sound of it. He stopped in a darkened area, and she turned in surprise to look at him.

"Falling Water," he said. "Ride with me tomorrow. Show me your valley."

Again a faint tingle of warning coursed through her. Was he here for a reason they did not know? Did he plan to use her as a means to that end? She wanted to refuse but knew he would again accuse her of fearing him. Her pride would not accept that. Perhaps, if she rode with him just once, he would somehow reveal the real reason he had been near their village.

As she sought logical reasons for accepting his offer, she pushed to the back of her mind the warm emotional response swirling within her. She nodded her head in agreement.

He was surprised when she agreed. He had been prepared to try to convince her that what had happened before would not happen again. He vowed he would move cautiously from now on.

They continued their walk. He left her at her tepee,

then strode away, well aware that her eyes followed him. A frown furrowed her brow as she watched him leave. Question after question filled her mind, but no answers followed. She would have to attempt to find those answers tomorrow.

She went inside her tepee, but sleep did not come easily for her that night. When it did, it came with strange, disoriented dreams that left her questions still unanswered.

He marveled at the way she rode, as if she were part of the huge stallion beneath her. She had complete control of the animal.

Each time he was with her, he discovered a new facet of her beauty. The sun kissed her golden skin, and he found it difficult to keep his eyes from her.

The valley was her world; she knew every inch of it and took great pride in showing it to him. He absorbed everything he saw, wondering what might be here that could cause the turmoil he sensed was brewing.

By midday they stopped to eat and drink. After tethering their horses, they sat beneath a huge tree to share the food she had brought.

For a time they were silent. Rayne turned to her, able to watch her unobserved for a few moments as she gazed out over the valley she loved.

Suddenly, she sensed his stare and moved to look at him. Their eyes met.

She had tempted herself, and she knew it. Her pride-filled mind refused to let her run from him now. It commanded her to cease this wordless warfare, but her wayward body refused to cooperate.

In the very depths of her, something stirred to warm, vibrant life. It tingled through her body, leaving her suddenly weak and breathless.

He bent slowly toward her, not touching her with anything but his seeking, longing gaze.

Very gently his lips brushed hers, and within them twin battles raged. He tried to resist the overwhelming desire to pull her into his arms and claim her. She tried to resist the desire to rest against the hard expanse of his chest and feel the strength of him surround her.

A sense of unknown danger moved through her. She still suspected that there was more to Rayne than he had told her. She couldn't allow his deception! She couldn't let this strange fascination draw her deeper into his spell.

She pulled away, but he reached an arm to encircle her waist and draw her resisting body closer to him.

Her closed fists pressed against his chest, and their eyes held each other's.

"No," she murmured raggedly as his mouth came closer to hers. A strange, warm lassitude held her mesmerized as their lips met. She felt herself weakening. Her senses began to reel, and she fought desperately to regain control.

With a cry of anguish, she twisted in his arms, thrusting him away with all the force she could muster.

Her body shrieked out for her to assuage the wild need that blossomed within her. Grimly she fought the desire to return to the strong arms and passionate kisses that left her with this unquenched yearning.

"Let me go!" she ordered. She had meant the words to be angry, but they came out in an almost moaning sound of despair. She had to gain control! she told herself. She had to!

78

"Is this how you ask for trust, white one?" she snarled, bringing all her anger into play. She needed such anger desperately to fight the demand of her body to return to him. Until she knew what dangers lurked behind those magnetic eyes and that fiery touch, she could not surrender to what her aching body cried out to experience.

He released her and she rose swiftly to her feet. Her need to get away from him was so strong she could taste it. She was unable to think clearly when he touched her.

"Falling Water," Rayne began hesitantly as he gazed at her rigid back. He rose and walked close to her, taking her shoulders in his hands. "Falling Water, I do ask for trust. I ask for trust and so much more from you." His voice was soft and persuasive as he drew her back to rest against him. "You felt what I did, I know. I could hear your heart beat. Don't leave. Let me show you what we were meant to share."

With a soft cry she tore herself from his arms and ran to her horse. In seconds she was riding away.

Rayne's eyes followed her. He had failed to reach her this time, but he was far from defeated. He realized he would have to discover why she seemed so afraid.

He rode slowly back to the village, deep in thought.

Chapter 6

Rayne returned to the tepee he shared with Mack. He found his friend there, who had just awakened and was beginning to dress. It had taken Mack no time at all to adjust to the slow and easy life the Indians lived.

Rayne sat on the fur-covered couch opposite Mack. "Mack, I need a little friendly help." He grinned sheepishly as Mack gazed at him with a puzzled expression.

"Help? With what?"

"Well . . . it means a little prying into your past. I don't want to stir up any bad memories or cause you any hurt, but you are the only one I know who has the answers."

"What do you want to know?"

"Mack, you . . . you lived with another group of Cheyenne a long time back, didn't you?"

"Yes . . . a few years before I met you. Why?"

"I heard that you married once."

Mack looked at Rayne, who held his gaze in silence, and he was still for a long time as old, unwelcome memories flooded his mind. "Yes," he replied softly. "Yes, I was . . . once." Rayne could see pain flickering in his eyes.

"Mack," Rayne said in a quiet voice. "I want her. I want her to belong to me. I don't want to offend her or her family, and I don't know the customs."

For the first time since Rayne had come in, Mack smiled. "What happened, she chew you up and spit you out?"

"Something like that." Rayne chuckled. He proceeded to tell Mack what had happened, omitting certain parts he intended to savor privately.

"You sure pulled a dumb trick. You don't remember just how proud these people are? They hold their women and kids higher than their own lives. Her pa's Running Wolf, and her ma's the closest thing to their gods they can make her. She's their medicine woman. They ain't people to play with. He'll have you buried and your hair hangin' on his lodge pole if you touch that girl."

"I made a mistake, Mack. I'll admit that. But I'm not backing away. I need you to tell me just how to go about convincing her I've got good intentions."

"Do you?" Mack asked seriously.

Again, Rayne was silent for a moment; then he allowed Mack to pass the barrier of his eyes and see within. "Yes, Mack . . . I do. Maybe I didn't believe that myself at first, but . . . well . . . she's the kind of woman a man doesn't play with."

"If my advice is worth a nickel, then I'll tell you. You've played a lot . . . maybe too much. But if you have plans for this one, let me tell you this—you dishonor Running Wolf and his family and I'll stand by and watch them skin you. You were right about one thing—I lived

81

with them; I know them; and I respect them."

"I know that, Mack. It's why I want to know their customs. I want to do this their way."

"Why?"

"Because," he added softly, "I think it's the best way, and maybe the only way . . . and . . . I want her."

Mack's eyes held his, and Rayne had the feeling his very soul was being read like an open book. Rayne was again surprised at himself when he found he was holding his breath, waiting for Mack's verdict. He expelled it in relief as Mack smiled.

"This isn't going to be easy. You're outside of their tribe, so, first, they have to trust you."

"You didn't seem to find that so hard. You married into the tribe."

"Yeah"—Mack chuckled—"but I've got a real trustworthy face. You look like the devil lives behind those eyes. You're a handsome buck, and parents don't exactly trust that kind so easy. Besides, you're white; that's another thing against you."

"Sun Knife's father was white."

"It was a long time before they accepted him, and only after he had become blood brother to Long Arrow."

"What about Falling Water's mother, Lauren Brent, and White Eagle's wife, Rebecca?"

"They're women, and Rebecca became Long Arrow's blood daughter before she married White Eagle."

"This sounds harder by the minute," Rayne complained.

"That ain't nothing. After—and if—they accept you as a part of the tribe, then you have to talk to her parents and offer a bride price."

"Bride price! What the hell is that? Sounds like I have

to buy her!"

"My friend, you don't have enough worldly possessions to *buy* the daughter of Running Wolf."

"Then what's a bride price?"

"You got to prove to her parents you're rich enough, man enough, and strong enough to take care of their daughter. The bride price is given to the parents of the one you wish to marry to prove you'll be a good provider. It tells them a lot, like how high you value their daughter and just how badly you want her. It also tells them your attitude toward marriage."

"All right, Mack," Rayne said. "Let's say I find a way to achieve all these things?"

"Then, my friend," Mark laughed, "you got to convince the girl she wants you as badly as you want her."

"Lord, they don't make getting married so easy around here, do they?" Rayne remarked thoughtfully.

"No," Mack said quietly. "But they sure try to make marriages happy and permanent." Mack watched with amusement as Rayne's eyes began to sparkle with the light of challenge. He knew Rayne well, perhaps better than Rayne knew himself. What Rayne wanted and set out to get he usually got. Mack wondered if this was going to be a successful quest. Deep inside, he had a feeling it just might be. But he was also eager to watch his friend's progress. He thought it might prove to be a constructive lesson for Rayne as well.

"All right, Mack. What do you suggest I do first?"

"Make a couple of friends. Get close. Help them any way you can. Then ask their help in collecting the bride price."

"What is it?"

"Buffalo robes, horses, furs, anything necessary."

"How many?"

"In the case of Falling Water, I think it will be a lot. You have to talk to her pa about that. Make him an offer. But you better start high; they get insulted real easy, and he ain't a man to insult."

"Mack, what about her?"

"Well"—Mack grinned—"a more resourceful man can find a way to meet her . . . by accident, of course. If she's agreeable, she won't say so; she'll just let it happen. If she's not, you won't find her alone anywhere."

"Any other impossible things I should know?"

Now Mack really laughed. "Yep. After all this, you have to court her." Rayne chuckled helplessly. "Give her some gifts; be with her every chance you get. Tell her how you feel."

"I think," Rayne replied with a short laugh, "that she already has an idea how I feel."

"The rest," Mack added, "is up to you and her."

Rayne rose. "Thanks, Mack. I owe you."

"Don't be too sure."

"I'll manage."

"Rayne?"

"What?"

"What are you going to do when we've found out what we've been sent to find out, when it's time for us to report back? You just going to leave?"

"You think I'd do that to her, Mack?"

"I'd sure like to think you wouldn't."

Rayne smiled and left the tepee without answering, leaving Mack to wonder about his thoughts.

* * *

Running Wolf was an astute and quick-witted man. He knew very well what was happening and was not pleased with the idea that a white man cast his eyes on his beloved Falling Water. Lauren was amused by the entire situation, because, from what she had read in her daughter's eyes, she knew Falling Water was as attracted to Rayne as he was to her. She wondered just how long it would take before Rayne made a visit to their tepee to speak with Running Wolf.

Both Little Eagle and Night Sky were pleased when Rayne decided to spend more time with them. He was a good hunter and very adept at capturing wild horses. Each time they hunted, Rayne acquired another buffalo hide. In the search for horses, he almost always came home with two or three.

He was a good comrade, and, in the three weeks following his talk with Mack, Rayne worked hard on developing solid friendships with the sons of the chief and the medicine man. As their friendships grew, he just as patiently acquired what the Indians considered wealth. And while he was doing so, he was also carefully stalking Falling Water.

She found him near whenever he could manage an encounter, and her awareness of him continued to grow, even as she fought to control it.

Their eyes would meet across the evening fire on the occasions when he came to her tepee. And he took every opportunity to let her see exactly what he felt.

Falling Water awoke one morning very early, which was her habit. Her parents still slept, and she allowed herself the luxury of lying still and letting her mind wander freely. Her thoughts immediately strayed to Rayne.

She smiled to herself, for she now often dreamed of him. She could bring him to her mind easily, and with such thoughts came strange sensations that began somewhere in the center of her being and expanded until they filled her. She could still feel the branding touch of his lips on hers and the strength in his lean, muscular frame as he had bound her to him.

She rose quietly so she would not disturb anyone. She liked to ride early in the morning and often left and returned before the day began for others. Silently, she stepped outside and then stoped in shock. A look of pleasure crossed her face, and she looked about quickly to see if Rayne were near. He did not seem to be in sight, but before her tepee stood the most beautiful horse she had ever seen. No one had to tell her it was a gift from Rayne, for she and all those in her tribe had seen and admired it among his horses.

She moved to its side and gently brushed her hand down the dark, silky neck. Rayne knew well her ability to ride any horse, so he had gifted her with the largest, speediest one he could find. It was completely black and shone with a gloss that bespoke Rayne's careful keeping.

He was a magnificent creature, and Falling Water was well aware of the many long, hard hours Rayne had spent in capturing and breaking the animal. To make it more valuable, the horse carried a bright blanket and saddle. She wondered who had crafted the saddle for him and what it had cost in trade.

She quickly mounted, feeling the hard, muscular power beneath her. With agile hands, she guided the horse from the village toward the surrounding trees.

Within their shadows, she would move slowly until she reached the flat plains beyond. There she would test the strength and power of her new possession.

She had just reached the trees when his voice touched her. "I knew he was meant for you the first time I saw him."

She reined to a stop and remained motionless. She sensed him more than saw him until he moved his horse toward hers and stopped beside her. She could feel him mentally reach to touch her, although she knew he did not move.

"Falling Water," he said gently, "I would ride with you."

She could have said no—even felt that she should have—yet she could not lie to herself. She wanted him to ride beside her. She did not need to answer. He felt her acceptance and smiled.

They moved together through the deep shadows of the trees to the plains beyond. Once on the valley floor, she urged the black horse ahead. She would test his speed and strength against Rayne's mount.

They raced across the flat plain. Falling Water was thrilled with the grace and power of the horse beneath her. She did not want to push him too far, so she began to slow him. Rayne had kept a steady pace with her, and, when they finally came to a stop, they were side by side. It surprised them both when the realization came to them that they were very near the same spot where she had found him.

When their eyes met, neither had words to put to the vibrant emotion that seemed to hold them. Rayne reached out a hand and very gently caressed her long, silken hair. "You remember as clearly as I," he said softly. "It is a moment I have held within me for a long time. I love you, Falling Water, and I have said those words to no other woman before you. I have not felt for any woman this desire I feel for you. Look at me and tell me you do not share what I feel. Speak the truth. Tell me to leave you and I will."

She knew it was wrong. She knew she should be angry and tell him to leave her, but within his eyes she saw warmth and the reflection of the need she had battled for so long. But to speak the truth meant to tell him she felt as he. She said nothing.

Rayne reached out and grasped the reins of her horse, drawing it behind his. He rode down to the tree-shaded riverbank. There he dismounted, tied both horses, then moved close to her horse's side. Wordlessly, he reached up for her. Falling Water placed her hands on his shoulders. Gently and slowly, he lifted her down to stand beside him.

They were inches from each other, and his eyes held hers while his hands rested gently on her slim waist. "Tell me," he whispered. "Tell me what I see in your eyes is a lie."

His nearness played havoc with her senses. With all her heart, she wanted his strong body pressed to hers, to feel his powerful arms hold her, to experience the vibrant warmth of his lips on hers.

She wanted it with every ounce of her being, except for one lone, rational thought. She still had the suspicion he was being less than honest. She still had the vague sense that he was here for another reason. And she still retained the fear that he would one day be gone.

She needed to eliminate the doubt that lingered in her

heart. She wanted answers but did not know the questions.

"For two to share their lives, there must be honesty between them. They should hold no secrets in their hearts," she replied hopefully. She needed only his assurance that he spoke the truth.

"Secrets?" he questioned with a puzzled frown on his face. "I will tell you what my life has held. I am ashamed of very few things in my life, but I will tell you those things also."

Her heart leapt with happiness. It had all been her imagination. He would give her the words she needed to hear. All of the strange suspicions she had harbored would be washed away.

"Come and sit beside me," he invited.

They moved to the grassy bank of the river and sat together. Silently he made note of the fact that she kept some distance between them. There was still an invisible yet immovable barrier between them.

"Well, let me see." He grinned. "I suppose I should begin at the beginning. I was born in Washington."

"Washington?"

"A city a long, long way from here." She remained silent, listening.

"I was raised with a lot of love in a reasonably well-to-do family. My parents still live there, and I have one brother. I'm sure Greg has been more of what my parents wanted us to be than I, but"—he shrugged—"I was cursed with wanderlust."

"Wanderlust?" she queried. "What is that?"

"I couldn't seem to stay in one place too long . . . at least until now." He did not get the encouraging response he had hoped for. He continued. "I've been tracking out here for some years with Mack, drifting from home to here to home, never satisfied . . . always looking . . ." He let his voice drift to a moment of silence as he looked back for the first time in a long time.

"Anyway"—he sighed—"I just couldn't stay put." He went on to tell her about all the details of his life he felt were important, conveniently leaving out his reason for being sent here. He didn't want his real reason revealed yet. He felt she might repeat it to the other women who would carry the word to White Eagle and the other leaders. He was completely unaware that some sense had already warned her of his omission. Her heart beat painfully as she studied his face. His eyes refused to hold hers for a few brief moments, but it was enough time for her to ascertain that he was indeed hiding something, lying to her.

She had to force back the tears that burned her eyes.

He was surprised when she abruptly rose to her feet and turned from him. He rose quickly to stand behind her.

"Falling Water?" he questioned.

"I must go back now," she answered. "I will return your gift to you. The horse is beautiful, but I cannot accept it."

He gripped her arm, and, though she resisted, he turned her to look at him.

"Why?"

"I do not choose to keep it," she replied defiantly. It took all her effort to hold back her words. She wanted to strike out at him somehow, to make him feel what she was feeling. "A woman does not accept gifts from a man she does not choose to know."

His gaze was so intense that she felt her pulse grow unsteady. It was as if he could penetrate both her mind and her heart.

Very slowly he drew her to him. She wanted to resist, but she was getting lost in the depths of his eyes.

"You spoke of truth," he said softly. "Then why do you deny it?"

She couldn't reply; he was too near. The strength of him and his overpowering magnetism had a spellbinding effect.

He pulled her closer, one arm holding her slim form against him. Her body trembled beneath his heated gaze. He was taut with desire, and there was no doubt of it in her mind as she felt the length of his body pressed against her.

She felt her heart begin to beat rapidly, and every sense she had was aware of him. She knew he would touch her, kiss her, and, if he did, would she be able to resist any longer what her disobedient body cried out for? An excitement broiled through her like the heat of a prairie fire.

His mouth lowered slowly to claim hers, and she moaned softly, her lips yielding to his demanding kiss. Flames, once ignited, grew in intensity as his open mouth plundered hers.

Her mind slipped from all but the need that was building within her. She molded herself to him, and his hands crept down her slim waist to her buttocks to pull her against him. His mouth demanded a response, and her resistance began to melt as the embers of her desire were fanned to life.

He raised his head, and his eyes burned deeply into hers, seeking his answer. His bold, unspoken question was answered in the molten glow of her half-closed, passion-filled eyes. She was lost.

Her heart, pressed against him, matched his in quickening rhythm. She slipped her arms up around his neck, and again his mouth sought hers, open and warm, teasing and playing with her lips until the fire grew to a heat neither could contain.

Slowly Rayne drew her down beside him on the soft grass. The breadth of his shoulders filled her world as he bent above her to again sear her senses with a gentle, questing kiss. Despite the attempts of her logical mind to bring herself under control, she could no longer fight his passion.

Gentle fingers sought the ties of her dress, loosening them to let his hands discover soft skin that burned beneath his touch.

In moments they lay naked together, pressed to each other and lost in the wonder of discovery. The hot, sweet torment possessed them both. Arms clung, legs entwined, tongues fought the eternal battle and both won. His hands glided over the smoothness of her skin, turning her to fire. Hers followed his example by discovering the hard, sinewy muscle that rippled under the bronzed skin.

With an urgency that neither could control, they sought the deepest pleasure. Swept away by searing passion, the dam to ecstasy burst, and they gasped at the blissful sensations engulfing them as he thrust to the depths of her with strokes that drove her to frantic rapture.

She clung to him, arching to meet him with an exultant cry. Her body sang in joyous, heated pleasure as they rose higher and higher among the stars until a brilliant fulfillment dazzled their senses and left them clinging to each other in the rose-colored afterglow of sensual delight.

She lay still, her head resting on his shoulder, her eyes closed. His hands gently caressed her skin in a soothing motion. Slowly, ever so slowly, her mind began to regain control. She had been defeated by her body and the driving need he had so skillfully built within.

Tears touched her eyes as she realized that nothing had changed. She still had her doubts about why he was here, as well as her fears that one day he would leave her. She would still have to fight the battle and knew that, if she did not find some way to resist, he would always have the power to reach within her at will and ignite the flame of desire.

Rayne rose on one elbow and looked down at her. A slow smile touched the corners of his mouth. He reached out to gently caress her hair, then rested his hand softly against her cheek. Slowly he bent forward to brush her lips with a soft kiss.

"I love you, Falling Water," he whispered. "There is no lie to that. It is the purest truth I know. I love you."

She could not reply. Fear tangled the words that were in her heart. Her tears glistened, and one slid slowly down her cheek.

"Do you weep for joy?" he questioned anxiously. "Or do you weep for pain? Can you not say, 'I love you, Rayne?' I have felt your body speak to me. Can you deny what we shared?"

"I do not know," she said softly. It made her heart ache when she saw the flicker of hurt in his eyes. "I know

I have never felt such joy, such wonder. But . . . is it enough to build our world on? Should there not be something else?"

She wanted him to say the words, to open himself in trust. She prayed for it, but it was not to be.

"Falling Water, I will go to your father. I want you for my wife. You will see in time that we can have a good life together."

"I must have time to think," she replied.

"It will be some time before you father agrees, I know. In that time I will convince you that you are part of me and I am part of you. I will wipe away what doubts you have. I will drive them from your mind, never to return."

Hope warred with doubt. Would he come to her one day with all the truth on his lips? Only then would she agree to join with him. Until that day, she vowed, she would not allow such intimacy again. She knew the power he wielded over her senses. She could no longer let him control her as he had done so easily with just a touch. She would wait and see, but she would not be caught in this ecstatic trap again, where she had no will of her own.

"We must go back before I am missed," she said.

Reluctantly, he rose from her side and reached down a hand to help her. She put her hand in his, looking up and stealing the few instants to admire the strength of his lean, hard-muscled body. His skin was bronzed and glowed with good health and the vibrant tautness of controlled strength. She savored the look of him and the heat of his gaze as he drew her up into the circle of his arms.

"I will take you back now," he whispered softly against her hair. "But one day you will be mine, and I will never let you go . . . never."

94

She looked up at him, and he took the moment to kiss her leisurely and thoroughly. She moved from him, knowing if his branding lips held hers a moment longer she would again be lost.

They dressed and rode back to the village in silence. Her mind wept with the thought that no matter how her body cried out for him, her mind still held the same doubts and fears.

It was the custom, if Running Wolf chose to follow it, for the father to accept the husband for the daughter. She trembled with the thought of the outcome, for she wanted both his love and the truth and she knew she could have only one.

Chapter 7

With deliberate effort, Mack stifled all the funny remarks he wanted to make, for the threatening glint in Rayne's eyes bespoke his lack of humor. He sat quietly, contemplating a very tense and nervous Rayne.

This was the man who had traveled this country and trapped with him for several years, he thought, a man who, he knew, was afraid of nothing; yet he could not seem to sit still, and the steady hand he had always had now trembled slightly with restrained tension.

For the fifth time in the past hour, Rayne rose from his couch and paced the floor. It was still the hour for the evening meal, too early for Rayne to go, yet he had not eaten a bite and didn't appear as if he were going to.

He had bathed and dressed carefully in fringed buckskin that clung to his muscular frame like a second skin. Mack could easily see how he had captured the heart of Falling Water. He was startlingly handsome and exuded a magnetic aura of power and strength. Running Wolf would find it difficult to find fault. More than familiar with Indian ways of judging a man, Mack knew

Running Wolf would not see anything less than a strong and virile man. He also knew Running Wolf, and he suspected Rayne would have some moments of difficulty under his watchful and very clever dark eyes.

"Light and eat," Mack said. "You got plenty of time. You don't want to go over there until he's done eating, or he might not be in the best of humor. Besides, it will give Falling Water and her mother some time to soften him up."

"I'm not hungry. This is ridiculous!" Rayne stormed. "She should just be able to marry me if she wants to. Why should I have to do all this?"

"I'll tell you one thing, Rayne. These people have their way, and if you don't follow it, you don't stand a snowball's chance in hell of getting her to marry you."

"She would say no, even if she wants to?"

"Their pride means a lot to them. If she went against her father's will, it would bring shame on him. She wouldn't even think of doing that to a man like Running Wolf. She loves him and respects him too much. You can go through with it, can't you?"

Mack added the last question with a gleam in his eye that was not lost on Rayne, who chuckled in response. "I can do what needs to be done. If I have to face the whole Cheyenne nation, I'll do it. Her father can't be that hard to deal with."

"He'll hate to let her go; probably give you the battle of his life."

"Well, he'll know he's been in a fight."

"Want me to come along and pick up the pieces? I could nurse you back to health in time."

Rayne smiled, then sat down opposite Mack again. This time there was a faint touch of worry on his face.

"Mack, all joking aside, what if he says no. Can I convince her anyhow?"

"Maybe, but I wouldn't. Rayne, we're white. If we step on their toes, we'll liable to stir up a hornet's nest. We were sent to get information, not start a war. You just keep away from her if he says no. Don't lay a hand on her."

"Mack . . . it's too late for that advice," Rayne replied. Mack's face registered sincere alarm.

"You aren't stupid enough to have . . . Rayne . . . ?"

"It wasn't planned. Neither of us intended for anything to happen. It just happened."

"And you couldn't have stopped it?"

"Maybe . . . but I didn't want to. Mack, I'm going to have her if I have to steal her and take her back East with us."

"She'd die there. Boy, I hope Running Wolf listens to you. If he don't, there will be hell to pay."

Again, Rayne rose, a grim look on his face. "He'll listen. If I have to promise him my life, I'll make him listen."

"You still don't know what can happen, do you? He finds out you two been together, he'll get you out of this camp, send you away, but it will go worse for her. She's the one who'll pay the price. That was a fool thing to do, Rayne."

"He won't find out."

"Good luck. That man has got eyes like a hawk, and he's a lot wiser than you think. He'll probably look through you like an open window."

Rayne moved to the door. "Thanks for the good wishes. I'm as stubborn as he is. One way or another she's going to be with me."

"I hope it goes well, Rayne," Mack offered honestly. Any doubts he still held he kept within his own mind.

"Thanks," Rayne replied. A moment later he was gone.

Falling Water had been sent from her parents' tepee, ostensibly to carry fresh water from the stream. The water bags had been empty only because Lauren had made a special point not to fill them. Falling Water was well aware that her parents wanted to talk alone.

Running Wolf had eaten very lightly, and Lauren knew he had his daughter's future on his mind. She also knew that Running Wolf felt there was not a man alive to whom he would willingly give his beloved daughter.

Lauren had watched Rayne, and she had listened not only to his voice, but to the voices of others. She knew he was respected among the warriors. Having lived so long among the Cheyenne, she knew this was an accomplishment. She had also watched her daughter, and she knew what Falling Water felt for Rayne was a deep and solid love.

Lauren sat down beside Running Wolf. To Rayne, Running Wolf looked like a fierce stranger, but Lauren knew his surprising gentleness and the man of good humor that lived beneath his deceiving exterior.

"You have not eaten well."

"I have much on my mind," he replied.

"Our daughter?" Lauren answered gently. Running Wolf's eyes turned to her, to Lauren, his beloved wife, the white woman who had come into his life and had made it beautiful.

He remembered well the first time he had seen her at Sun Knife's wedding. She had taken his heart then and had held it through the years. Even now, there were still times he could not quite believe she had chosen to stay with him.

Then there was Falling Water, the beautiful expression of their love. She had been the light in his world from the day of her birth. He had seen how the handsome white trapper had looked at his daughter, and fear quickly touched him. This man, this white man, threatened something deep within him that even he did not understand. His world had begun to shake, and he was, for the first time in his life, unsure . . . and maybe a little afraid.

"Do you know every thought in my head?" he asked with a quick smile.

"Of course." She laughed softly. "I have not lived with you all these years without learning to understand you."

"You know the white trapper looks at our daughter?"

"Yes," she replied.

"She is too young to think of him," Running Wolf said angrily.

"She is as old as I was when we married," Lauren gently reminded him. "Of course, you were not a grumpy old bear then."

"He is white, Summer Rain."

"As I am."

"But he may go from us at any time. He could leave her hurt and alone. I would not have it so."

"At one time, you thought I might leave, too, but I chose to stay. I chose out of love for you. Can he not do the same?"

Lauren reached to touch him. "One day you said to me, 'Stay Summer Rain, and let me show you my world.' You let me see a world of love and happiness. Don't deny that to Falling Water. I know what you feel, but Falling Water is much like you, and if he learns, as I did, of the love that exists here, he will not go."

Lauren knew Running Wolf was looking for any reason to deny Rayne, but she knew also of the gentle, loving heart beating beneath his formidable exterior. "Running Wolf, let him talk to you. Let him come as a man and ask for what he wants." Again, Running Wolf's eyes held hers. "I ask only that you remember," she said softly, "remember our young days and the love we shared. Remember, and let them have their young years as we had ours."

"Why is it"—he grinned—"that you still—after all these years—have a way of turning my stubbornness to water and my anger to hot air?"

She chuckled as he drew her against him and kissed her firmly. "I remember well," he said gently, "the place of ours where the water falls like thunder, the place you first came to me."

"Then you will listen when he speaks?"

"I will listen," he agreed reluctantly. "But," he added swiftly, "I did not say I would agree; I only said I will listen."

"That," she replied, "is all I ask."

Rayne walked slowly from his tepee toward Running Wolf's. In his mind, he was forming words, and, when he realized what he was doing, he was surprised at his nervousness. Women had always come easily to Rayne, and he was completely unprepared for these courtship rituals. But if he wondered why he was facing such challenges, he had only to bring Falling Water to his mind's eye. He thought of her, sweet and warm in his arms, giving him all of her love and faith. It was enough to hurry his feet.

As was the custom with the Indians, Rayne announced himself from outside the tepee. He was immediately invited in and made welcome. Seated opposite Running Wolf with the glow of the fire between them, Rayne was offered food and drink. He ate and drank a little, aware of the hard, dark eyes that seemed to be dissecting him.

Lauren moved to the back of the tepee and began quilling a new shirt for Running Wolf. This added nothing to Rayne's comfort for he was acutely aware of her presence. It still seemed to him that he was trying to buy Falling Water, and he wasn't too sure how to begin this strange conversation. To make matters worse, Falling Water took that moment to return with the water. If he had been uncomfortable before, her appearance made it worse. How did a man make an offer for a wife? If he offered too much, they would think him foolish; and if he didn't offer enough, the whole family would be insulted.

Falling Water hung the water bags and joined her mother at the back of the tepee. Her dark eyes met Rayne's for one brief moment.

He had no idea that the wise eyes of Running Wolf had seen in his gaze all he needed to see. There was no doubt in Running Wolf's mind that Rayne indeed felt for his daughter the same emotion that had stirred him at the moment he had first seen Lauren.

With utter control, Running Wolf allowed no trace of this understanding to be read on his face. The brief sparkle of humor in his dark eyes was lost to Rayne, who only saw the stern, cold set of his features. Rayne inhaled deeply and began.

"I have come to speak to Running Wolf about something of great importance."

"Speak," Running Wolf replied shortly. It was obvious to Rayne that Falling Water's father had no intention of helping him.

"I wish to ask Running Wolf for something."

Generosity was taught to all in the tribe. Sharing and giving were qualities they learned early. It was also their custom to give gifts easily. Yet Running Wolf was not interested in giving what he knew Rayne wanted.

"You are our guest," Running Wolf reminded gently. "If there is something you need, you must ask."

Rayne took a deep breath. "I would ask for your daughter, Falling Water, to be my wife. I value her highly and believe she would be a good wife. I would do my best to be a good husband and would provide well for her. To show my good faith, I offer Running Wolf and his wife gifts.

"I know how much Falling Water means to you. To help ease her departure from your tepee, and to show my esteem for Falling Water, I would give Running Wolf the fifteen horses I now have, and twenty more as I acquire them. I would also give ten buffalo hides and"—he unwrapped the bundle he had carried with him, pulling out an object that widened Running Wolf's eyes and drew amazed gasps from both women—"I would give Running Wolf this to help him hunt for his village." It was a new and very shiny rifle.

Very few Cheyenne Indians possessed a rifle and to own one such as this would make Running Wolf a very envied warrior. Yet, despite his desire for it, he knew he would be giving his daughter in return. He would speak to

Falling Water first, before he made a decision, for there was nothing valuable enough to exchange for her happiness. The thought of her being discontented would take away all the pleasure of owning the rifle.

Still, Running Wolf could not resist taking the rifle in his hands, to hold it and examine it closely. He took it gently and touched it with sensitive, caressing fingers. He examined it closely and knew it was of excellent quality. He wanted it more than he had wanted many other things.

Quietly, he returned the rifle to Rayne. His desire for the rifle was still second to his daughter's happiness. "I have watched you in our village," Running Wolf said. "You have been a welcome guest, and the warriors respect you. I will think on this. Soon our chief returns and there will be a celebration. Then I will tell you of my decision."

Rayne knew there could be no argument. Once the head of a family spoke, it was usually final, for, otherwise, his fragile pride might be damaged in the eyes of his family. He nodded, then asked, "Your chief has been away long?"

Running Wolf responded, "For many weeks. He has gone to speak to other chiefs." Running Wolf grinned. "They speak of the white man."

This was Rayne's original reason for being here—to find out what was drawing the tribes together and why they had stopped warring among themselves—and Rayne knew that it must have taken a strong man with strong reasons to bring them together peacefully. He was more than curious about Chief White Eagle and his white wife, Rebecca.

Rayne smiled in return. "In the white chief's village,

104

we speak of the Indians too. Maybe we should join and speak together."

Running Wolf's eyes closed against him and Rayne could read nothing on his immobile face. But Lauren could, and she was struck once again by the knowledge that she and the people she loved so dearly had to live in fear of the white man and all the problems and troubles he seemed to bring with him.

"Perhaps," Running Wolf said softly. "Perhaps you should speak to our chief and listen to his words."

"I would like nothing better," Rayne replied. "When he returns, after the celebration."

Again Running Wolf's eyes sparkled with mischief. "We will smoke and speak of many things." Rayne nodded. He returned the rifle to its cover and rose to leave.

What he wanted and needed most was to reach out to Falling Water. He wanted to hold her, to feel her close to him, and to let her know that he would never give her up.

It would have been a breach of courtesy to speak to her at such a time, but, as he turned to leave, he was grimly determined that it would not be too long before he did so.

Slowly, he walked back to his tepee. Mack watched him in silence as he moved to his couch and lay down, his hands behind his neck. Unsure of the reception Rayne had had in Running Wolf's tepee, Mack remained silent until Rayne offered to speak.

"That man won't budge an inch," Rayne grieved.

"Did he say no?"

"No, he said he'd think about it."

"That's a lot of budging for a man like him. What did you offer?"

"Just about all I own and then some." Rayne laughed.

"I'll have to work like hell to get the rest of those ponies and buffalo robes. I offered him a rifle, too."

"I'll bet his tongue was hanging out."

"It was, but he still gave it back to me. He said when White Eagle returns they'll have a celebration. He'll give me an answer then."

"I'd sure as hell like to know where White Eagle and the warriors he took with him have been."

"Having some kind of big conference with some of the other chiefs. Running Wolf says they're talking about the white man."

"You think White Eagle's behind this gathering of the tribes?"

"I wouldn't be surprised."

"I wonder what brought all this on. From what I hear, White Eagle is a pretty strong leader. You think he can get all the Cheyenne tribes and the others to join forces?"

"That's what we're here to find out. Senator Miles would like the names of the men who are stirring up all the trouble. If I've put the pieces together right from what I've already heard, I can be fairly certain this tribe has already had a run-in with some whites."

Rayne went on to tell Mack the story Lauren had told him. Of course, she had omitted some parts, but Rayne was an astute man, and his imagination had supplied the parts she had artfully left out. "From what I can make out," Rayne added, "Lauren—or Summer Rain, as Running Wolf calls her—and her father, Alexander Brent, are owners of this valley. Our white law says no Indians can own land. Can you imagine—the people that have roamed this land for thousands of years before we came are being told it's no longer theirs?"

"Rayne, what if someone got the obstacles of Brent

and his daughter out of the way?"

"Then the land would revert to the government . . . or slip into the hands of whoever it is that wants it. These people would be forced to move . . . or to fight."

"And?"

"They'd fight," Rayne said softly. "They'd fight and die here before they'd give it up."

"Kind of makes you curious about who's behind all this."

"I want to talk to Sun Knife, and I want to talk to White Eagle. Maybe I can put some more pieces together, and we'll have something to report."

"Well, I guess all we can do for the moment is wait, keep our eyes and ears open, and ask questions. When White Eagle gets back, we can get some answers."

"Yes." Rayne grinned. "But in the meantime, I'm going to concentrate on doing some courting and gathering some ponies. I'm going to convince Running Wolf that I'm the best man in this village to be Falling Water's husband, and I'm going to try to keep her convinced I'm the best man for her to marry . . . just as soon as you tell me what I can and can't do so I won't get into any trouble."

Mack chuckled. "Since when have you ever been worried about rules?"

"Since I opened my eyes and saw her," Rayne answered. "She's some woman, Mack, and I don't want to lose her because I've done something stupid. I want peace here, because after I report to the senator, I intend to come back and make this a permanent home."

"No more wandering?" Mack said in surprise.

"Not if I can help it."

"Well, I'll be damned." Mack laughed. "I never

thought I'd see the day."

"I guess I didn't either, but"—Rayne chuckled—"here it is, and I'm not going to let it slip away. So, come on Mack, fill me in on those rules so I don't step on any toes."

"Well, in the first place, you'd better practice a little abstinence. You get that girl with child before the wedding and you're liable to find your hair swinging from her papa's war lance."

To this Rayne made no answer, for in his heart he wondered if he could control himself if she came to him without doubts or fears of some unknown thing. He felt there was no way in the world he could resist the touch of her, the taste of her, the wonder of possessing her.

Mack continued to talk, and some of it registered, but Rayne's mind and body drifted to a sweeter, more fulfilling moment. . . .

The appetite Rayne had lost earlier magically seemed to reappear, and he ate the meal that had previously been brought to him. They sat and talked for a while, of the village and its inhabitants and of the peace both of them seemed to have found here. After a while, Mack slept, but Rayne lay watching the dying fire and thinking of Falling Water.

Falling Water also lay awake in the dark silence of her tepee. Her parents slept, but the same state seemed impossible for her. Why was it that when she tried to close her eyes she only found visions of warm eyes and sensitive touches? she wondered. Why was her body so defiant, so warm and then so cold?

She tossed on a mat that felt first empty and then filled with poignant memories that would not allow her to rest in their company.

She fought a battle that left her weak, and she was losing it. She brushed her hair away from her moist forehead, then lifted its weight from the back of her neck. Nothing eased the heat that burned in the depths of her. No matter how she tried to reason it away, she wanted Rayne. She wanted the touch of his hard body next to hers; she wanted to feel again the vibrant fulfillment only his touch could give.

She rose from her mat and stepped outside, hoping the cool air would comfort her.

She would ride! she decided suddenly. It had always helped her in the past. She found her horse, but, before she could mount, she turned to look once at the village, her eyes drawn to the tepee in which Rayne slept. Desire and hunger filled her, and all her being called to him.

An exhilarated sleeplessness possessed Rayne, and he couldn't seem to lie still any longer. It was as if something called to him. He rose from his bed and walked to the tepee entrance. Pushing aside the hide flap, he stepped outside.

The night was bright. A full yellow moon dominated a black velvet sky filled with millions of brilliant stars. If he had wanted Falling Water before, he wanted her now even more so that they could share this beauty. And then he instinctively knew, as his heart began a rapid beating, just what had called to him.

She stood at the edge of the forest, the reins of her horse held in one hand, her eyes intently gazing toward him. He could actually feel her, as if she had reached a hand to touch him.

He smiled, knowing they shared some deep, vibrant thing that would always make words unnecessary. With no hesitation, he walked to his horse, saddled it, and mounted. He rode toward her and saw the bright gleam of her smile as he approached.

He stopped by her side and looked down into her dark eyes. "You called to me," he stated softly.

"Yes," came the reply.

"I could feel you call." He reached down to touch her cheek gently. "Come with me?"

She did not reply; instead she gracefully mounted her horse. Together they turned, and the dark shadows of the forest silently swallowed them.

Chapter 8

The river glistened in the moonlight, and a gentle breeze whispered softly through the trees. Rayne and Falling Water stood together, his arm about her waist, sharing the beauty of the evening for a quiet moment. Slowly he drew her close to him and brushed a kiss against the silkiness of her hair.

"Rayne," Falling Water breathed softly. "Why is this happening? What hold do you have on me that I cannot sleep, that I cannot feel alive until you are near? This is wrong. I should not be here."

He caught her face between his hands, and his intent gaze studied her. He smiled as he bent to take her moist, willing mouth with his. Slowly, with infinite gentleness, he parted her lips and savored the taste of her sweet giving. Any words Mack might have told him fled from his mind. The heated desire that filled his blood would not allow him to think of anything else but the warmth of her in his arms.

"Falling Water, you are here for the same reason I am—because we are meant to be together. I love you. It's hard to be without you even for a moment. Being with you only makes me want you more."

"I want to be with you," she said quietly.

"Did your father say anything to you after I left?"

"He and my mother spoke quietly. I could not hear all they said . . . but . . . I do not think he was angry with you. In fact, I could hear them laughing a little."

"Well, I hope his laughter means something good, because I don't give up easily. I told you that one day you would be my woman, and if I had to fight Lucifer himself, I'd do it to get you."

"You speak strangely, Rayne. Angels . . . then this . . . Lucifer. What is a Lucifer?"

He laughed a deep, warm laugh and pulled her to him. "The one who's responsible for any temptation, kind of like what I'm thinking now."

She liked the sound of his laughter and the feel of it as he pressed her against him.

"I've told you," he said, "about you, my angel, and I've told you about me, your Lucifer. Now let me show you a little of the heaven that you own and I would like to share."

He drew her down beside him in the soft grass. Holding her nestled close in the sanctuary of one hard-muscled arm, he slowly untied the laces of her tunic and slipped his hand inside to caress the warm, soft skin beneath. He was pleased with the soft sound of pleasure she uttered as he found the curve of her throat with his lips and journeyed leisurely down to the pulsing beat of her heart. He circled one hardened nipple and then the other with his mouth, lightly flicking his tongue and sucking gently.

It seemed to her that exquisitely torturous flames seemed to follow each touch. He continued to attack her

112

senses with his lips while his hand slowly pushed the tunic away from her. Skillful fingers now sought more sensitive flesh, burning a path of wondrous delight to the throbbing, moist place that opened to his search, pulsing with the need that filled her and drove her to complete abandon.

Falling Water's hands moved from his thick hair to the hard muscles of his shoulders and back, clinging and drawing him closer to taste more fully this still new and heady emotion.

His fingers deepened their gentle caress until she stirred and moaned softly at the ecstasy his touch inspired within her. It seemed to her a magical torture when his mouth invaded hers, and his hands explored and stimulated until she was almost mad with yearning. Desire throbbed throughout her body like drums of war, and she was unable to withstand the need to join with him.

Rayne wanted to maintain this white-hot fever they shared as long as possible. He wanted her to reach the highest peaks and fly with him. Gently he rose, then swiftly discarded his clothes. Kneeling beside her, he took her hand and drew her to a sitting position.

In the light of the moon, he saw her passion-filled eyes and moist, parted lips and knew she craved fulfillment as much as he. Tenderly, he took her hands and drew them to his chest. "Touch me, Falling Water," he said softly. "Know me as I want to know you. Tell me as I tell you of the magic we share."

At first her touch was shy, and he simply held her as slowly she began to explore. Her slim fingers brushed lightly down his broad chest with its matt of dark hair, then to his waist and down to caress his hard, muscled hips. Hesitantly, they continued their journey until his hard, throbbing manhood was captured between her hands.

He groaned softly as his hands, with a will of their own, created havoc by continuing their intimate search of her slim, trembling body. Their lips touched, tasted, and savored, and each kiss became deeper and more demanding until his open, hungry mouth closed over hers in a kiss that drained what little reality was left to her.

She was breathless and no longer able to restrain the wild need that filled her. She moved tightly against him, her hands urging him, her voice calling to him.

He eased her to the ground and knelt to push her legs apart. Sheer, ecstatic rapture filled her as he bent his head to taste the depths of her need. It burned to the very soul of her, and she cried out, writhing beneath the iron-hard hands that held her.

Then, when she could bear it no more, when she felt her heart would cease to beat, he was within her, filling her, moving with sure, hard strokes and feeling her body respond with the same urgency.

Slim legs wrapped about him, soft hands caressed, and her sobbing voice filled his mind and heart as they moved together into the flames of ecstasy.

They lay together, their bodies entwined, unable to speak or move. Slowly, rasping breaths returned to normal; slowly, trembling bodies stilled; and very slowly, hearts began beating more steadily.

He rose on one elbow and looked again into her eyes. There he saw all he would ever need to sustain him in his life. He lifted one hand and gently touched her cheek. The warmth of tears was there, and he bent his head to taste the tears as he had tasted the love that had created them.

"God, I love you, Falling Water," he said softly. "You are as much a part of me as my heart, as my body. You are the sweetest thing in my life. I want you always to be part of everything I do. I want to love you, to share my life with you. I want to give you children. I want to be a part of you."

"I never believed there could be such a thing as we have just shared."

"Falling Water, if your father . . . if he refuses us . . ."

"I do not know his heart," she replied slowly. "I only know mine."

He was completely captivated by her words. She was willing to give up all for him! He vowed silently he would do everything in his power to make that sacrifice unnecessary.

Neither of them wanted to leave the warmth of each other's arms. They lay together and spoke quietly of the future they would one day share. Soon their words dissolved into a vibrant renewal of their promises to each other.

It was in the small hours of the morning that both reluctantly returned to camp. Rayne slipped into the tepee he shared with Mack. It was silent and dark, and he made his way to his bed to dream of the beauty he and Falling Water had experienced and the day when she would belong to him forever.

Rayne had no idea that Mack had been awake for hours, knowing without a doubt where Rayne was and praying the lovers would not be discovered. He also hoped Rayne would be wise enough not to jeopardize their mission. Many lives might depend on what they did here, maybe even that of the woman he loved.

It was two days later when a young rider approached the village. He brought the news that White Eagle would arrive before the day was over.

Both Rayne and Mack were amazed at the reaction that swept through the village. Every man, woman, and child seemed filled with excitement.

"They sure must love their chief," Mack said.

"It seems that way," Rayne replied. "I can't wait to meet him. His activities are part of the reason we came out here. I hope Senator Miles was right, Mack. I sure hope we can help keep the peace out here."

"Well, today's the day we try to find out. Let's talk and listen . . . and pray."

"Mack, I'd sure like to know exactly what happened to Thomas. If the boy had been killed, he would have been found with us. If he had been wounded, all those scouts we sent out would have found him. I have a strange feeling his disappearance has something to do with this village."

"I can't seem to shake that feeling either. I'd just like to know why this valley seems so important to someone. I've got the sense we're not seeing something that's right under our noses."

"Maybe we can find some idea from White Eagle when he gets here."

"Let's stay close to camp," Mack suggested. "I want to be here when he gets here. Sometimes you can watch a man when he doesn't know it, and you can find out what kind of a man you have to face."

116

Rayne agreed with this and the two of them did just that, remaining close to their tepee as they waited and watched.

It was mid-afternoon when dust on the horizon told of the large group of riders approaching the village. Rayne and Mack stood by their tepee and silently observed the procession. Both were fascinated, first by the magnificent man who was White Eagle, chief of the Cheyenne, and second by the still very beautiful white woman who rode beside him—Rebecca, wife of the handsome chief.

They rode side by side, in itself unusual, for it was customary for a woman to ride behind the man. It exemplified both the power of White Eagle and the love this village seemed to have for Rebecca.

Rayne was unaware of the look of shock that suddenly transformed Mack's face, and just as unaware that Mack's eyes were no longer on the chief and his wife. He was staring instead at the slim, dark girl that rode behind them.

As the returning leader rode by them, Rayne and Mack were certain that nothing had passed the astute gaze of the granite-faced Chief White Eagle. They realized that he had probably already been told of the presence of white visitors in his village.

Most of the warriors and other travelers dispersed in order to be welcomed in their own tepees. White Eagle dismounted in front of his tepee and went to Rebecca's side to help her. His strong arms lifted her with ease to stand beside him.

White Eagle motioned to a dark-eyed child who played nearby, and the child approached him with wide-eyed admiration, pleased that the chief in his village, the mighty warrior, White Eagle, would single him out. "Go to Sun Knife's tepee," White Eagle said with a smile to ease the strength of his voice. "Tell him White Eagle would speak with him."

The child ran as fast as he could, and both White Eagle and Rebecca laughed as they watched him. The child ran to Sun Knife's tepee and called to those within. In a moment Snow Blossom appeared.

"Our chief would speak with Sun Knife," the child exclaimed proudly. Snow Blossom smothered her smile and spoke to him as if to a grown warrior.

"He is not here now. He is with Long Arrow. Go to his tepee and bring word." Almost before she could finish speaking, the child was moving away.

Inside Long Arrow's tepee, three were in conversation. Long Arrow, his wife, Water Flower, and her son, Sun Knife. As blood brother to Sun Knife's father, Long Arrow had raised Sun Knife from boyhood.

The years had touched both Long Arrow and Water Flower, but it had also given them a gentleness, and love had given them a serenity that was obvious to all who knew them.

Long Arrow was recovering from a recurrent illness that had this time left him weakened, and a worried Sun Knife berated him for rising from his bed. To all his words, Long Arrow only smiled, and soon Sun Knife had to laugh, for, as always, he knew his stepfather would do exactly what he wanted to do whenever he chose to do it.

"You are a stubborn one," Sun Knife claimed. "At least, will you take the medicine I have given you?"

"It tastes evil," Long Arrow replied with a chuckle.

"Evil or no, you need it. Must I force it down you?" Sun Knife asked with a sparkle of humor in his eyes that was matched in Long Arrow's.

"My son has become a man of violence."

"Only when faced with an immovable object such as your stubbornness. Father, for my sake, take the medicine. Who will I argue with when you become ill?"

"I suspect," Long Arrow retorted, "with everyone."

All three laughed at this, but before Sun Knife could reply, the child's voice called to him. Water Flower went to the tepee entrance and brought a now completely overwhelmed boy inside. "He would speak to you, my son," Water Flower said.

"Are you sick?" Sun Knife questioned.

"No, Sun Knife, I am well. White Eagle is home. He has sent me to tell you he would speak with you."

There was a quick flash of pleasure in Sun Knife's eyes as he rose to his feet. "Good. I'm anxious to find out just what the other chiefs had to say."

"Return quickly, my son," Water Flower said with a smile, "or your father will be driven mad with curiosity."

Again, the three laughed. Sun Knife left the tepee and crossed the village to the dwelling of his blood brother, White Eagle.

He called out to him, and the invitation came quickly for him to enter. Once he was inside, the two men greeted each other warmly, for many memories and much love existed between them.

"I am glad you are back, White Eagle," Sun Knife said. "I am anxious to hear all that has happened."

"I will tell you, but first we must speak of another thing. I am told there are strange white visitors in our village."

"Yes."

"They have been here long?"

"Since the day after you left—almost six weeks."

"How did they come here . . . why did they come?"

"I will tell you what I know. I brought them here." Sun Knife went on to explain how Falling Water had found them wounded and had come for help. "I had them brought here and cared for their wounds. I thought it best they stay until you returned. You can question them and decide why they might be here. They say they are fur trappers and want to stay with us this winter to trap beaver."

"They say—but you don't sound as if you believe them."

"It isn't that I don't believe them. I and many others have secretly tested them. They are good fur trappers. Both are excellent riders and horse traders."

"But?"

"But when I talk with them I get the feeling they are that and more, and it is the more that worries me."

"What is it about them that arouses your suspicions, brother?"

"For one thing, they are very well educated, and fur trappers are not usually so. Then, they have eyes that seem to be trying to record all they see and hear, as if . . . as if they must report everything to someone else."

"Sun Knife," Rebecca said softly, fear tinging her voice, "you don't think it will be like before? You don't think they will make any danger for us?"

"I don't know, Rebecca. I just think it would be a good idea to keep a close eye on them. By the way, there's another situation to consider."

"What?"

"The white trapper named Rayne Freeman has asked Running Wolf if he can marry his daughter. He has offered the bride price and has given Falling Water many gifts. It seems he knows our ways well."

"What does Running Wolf say of this?"

"Nothing yet. He has told Rayne he will think about it. Tomorrow night the celebration for your return will be held. It is then that Running Wolf will decide. I think he would like to speak to you first. I think Running Wolf is well aware himself that these men are more than they say they are."

"I will speak to Running Wolf. Perhaps he has ideas we can add to ours."

Sun Knife nodded. "White Eagle, what news do you have?"

"They are building a new fort, five days' ride from here," White Eagle replied grimly. "They are calling it Fort Ramsey."

"Damn," Sun Knife said softly.

"Josiah has gone there to see if he can find the reasons for their coming here again. I thought that when I burned the fort it would keep them away for a while."

"When will Josiah be back?"

"In a few days."

"Good. In the meantime, we will let these visitors stay without letting them know we are suspicious of anything. When Josiah comes back, maybe we will have more answers. Then we can begin asking them some more questions."

They agreed on this and began to talk of other things.

Mack had quietly suggested to Rayne that they move about the village separately to see what they could find out. Rayne agreed to this, not realizing Mack had other reasons in mind.

Mack drifted toward a group of young warriors who had just arrived with their chief. They welcomed him into their group and continued to talk while Mack listened.

One by one, they drifted away until Mack was left alone with one, a young brave who was filled with good humor and quite willing to talk. It was only then that Mack asked the questions that had been burning in his mind.

He pointed out the slim, dark girl who worked in front of a nearby tepee. She knelt before the dwelling preparing food.

"Who is she?" he questioned.

"She is Little Dove," the young man replied.

"Is she married?"

"No."

"That is her parents' tepee?"

"No."

Mack looked at him in surprise, for he well knew what kind of woman had a tepee of her own, and this girl did not look like such a woman. At Mack's surprised look, the young warrior laughed.

"It is a good thing I am not Running Wolf. If I were, you might have a battle on your hands. That is Little Dove, Running Wolf's young sister."

"Then that is the tepee of Running Wolf's parents?"

"Their mother died when Little Dove was born. She lives with her father and an old aunt."

"I see. Does she look at any of the braves with favor?"

"I and many others wish she did. Any of us would be happy to take her as wife. Little Dove is a very quiet, good-natured girl and would make a good wife, but her heart refuses to hear any of us."

Mack's face registered no emotion at these words, and he continued the conversation, speaking of many other things, yet his eyes moved again and again to the girl. He left the young brave after a while and walked slowly toward her.

No one knew the customs as well as Mack, and he had no intention of stopping to talk to her, yet he could not resist pausing for a moment to look at her closely.

Little Dove looked up from her work at the tall man who stared at her with such a startled expression.

It was only a brief encounter, and Mack quickly continued on. But now Little Dove's eyes followed his broad-shouldered frame. The strange sensation touched her that he had wanted to speak to her, to tell her something that would change her life. The feeling passed as fast as it had come. Little Dove continued with her work, but the gaze of the white visitor lingered in her mind.

After a while, she paused and sat back on her heels allowing her mind the freedom to drift again to the white visitor. He had been handsome—her quick glance had told her that immediately—but she had seen many handsome faces in her village. There was something about him that was different. What was it? she asked herself, picturing him clearly in her mind. It was his eyes, she decided, and the way he had looked at her, as if . . . as if he had been hurt and was asking for her help.

She laughed softly, chiding herself for such foolish ideas. Her father and her brother, Running Wolf, had often teasingly accused her of being a dreamer, and now she was creating strange ideas in her mind about a man she did not even know.

123

She rose and entered her tepee, carrying the food she had been preparing for her father's meal, determined to put the tall white man from her mind. Little Dove was completely happy with her life at the moment and had no intention of seeking anything that might change it.

From some distance away, Mack watched her enter her tepee. Even after the door flap closed behind her, he stood immobile. It was as if he were no longer seeing her but looking instead at some distant vision only he could conceive.

And though no other person was aware of it, Mack was spellbound. It was as if the dark wing of something forgotten had fluttered near, and he felt the breeze of it stir his thoughts, his memory, and his heart.

Chapter 9

The celebration began almost immediately after White Eagle's return. Buffalo was plentiful, and, for the feast, was supplemented by antelope, deer, and elk. It was a time for relaxation, for escaping tedious daily chores, an opportunity for gossiping or participating in games of chance and skill. While the women prepared the food, men displayed their skills, wagering skins, dogs, food, and clothing.

Not surprisingly, there were disputes that occasionally turned into fights. Again, White Eagle's authority was evidence, for he knew well that the survival of the village depended on unity within. With a strong hand, he enforced the tradition of internal discipline.

Excitement was evident in every tepee as all prepared for the dancing that would follow the feast. Rayne, too, prepared, and it was before he realized that his friend was inordinately quiet. Mack was seated on his couch, silently contemplating the low-burning fire.

"Mack?" he said quietly, and, when no response came, he repeated the name. "Mack?"

Mack was startled into an awareness that Rayne was talking to him. "What?"

"What's the matter?"

"Matter . . . with me? Nothing. Why?"

"You've been sitting there staring at the fire for the past half hour. Aren't you coming to the rest of the celebration? It will be our first chance to meet White Eagle."

"Sure . . . sure, I'm coming."

"What is it, Mack? What's wrong?"

Mack stood up and smiled. "Nothing is wrong. I'm looking forward to meeting White Eagle too. Maybe we can find out a few things. The sooner we get some answers, the sooner we'll be goin' back to report."

"You're anxious to leave, Mack?"

"No, just trying to get a job done."

"Mack, when we first came you never asked me just how long I intended to stay."

"I just took it for granted we'd leave before the snows came."

"No, we're staying through the winter . . . until spring."

Mack's face became strangely still, as if he were holding his thoughts in firm control.

"Mack, if there's something on your mind, if there's something you want to say . . ."

"No, Rayne." Mack laughed. "I'm fine. C'mon, let's get going. This should prove to be an interesting evening."

Mack brushed past Rayne and moved to the door. Slowly Rayne followed, aware that Mack was holding something inside. It was the first time in the few years they had been together that Mack had been secretive, and it shook Rayne. He followed Mack outside where they stood for a few moments, absorbing the scene about them.

The village was a beehive of activity. A huge fire had been built in the center, and the villagers had begun to gather around it. Many were seated in a wide circle, well away from the fire, leaving room for those who would dance in the area between. Several places were empty, and their strategic positions suggested to Rayne that they were places of honor for the chief, White Eagle, and his family.

Neither Long Arrow, Sun Knife, or Running Wolf had yet appeared. Rayne's eyes searched the faces until he found Falling Water, busy with a group of laughing, single women. She had not seen him yet, and he leisurely enjoyed watching her slim, graceful movements.

Throbbing drums softly began to echo through the village, sending out the message that all were called to celebrate the homecoming of their beloved chief. All who were not present at the moment soon began to arrive.

Rayne and Mack found a place near a group of young men. Soon they were being served food and drink and found themselves caught up in the festivities.

No matter how exciting it was, there still seemed an aura of expectancy surrounding the gathering. Then suddenly the drums ceased, and all eyes were drawn to White Eagle's tepee as he stepped out.

Rayne and Mack gazed at the man whose strength and wisdom ruled this village. They were both more than a little impressed by him. Rayne was a large and powerfully built man, but White Eagle was larger. Rayne found himself hoping he would never have to face him in hand-to-hand combat.

White Eagle stood four inches over six feet. He had a face that could have been chiseled from granite, his jaw firm and square, his features sharply cut planes and angles.

Only the obsidian eyes bespoke the man beneath the hard exterior, for they glowed with intelligence and good humor, and with affection for the people before him.

His skin glowed a golden brown in the firelight, his white buckskin shirt and pants hugging his hard, muscular frame, enhancing its rugged strength. His hair, black as night, hung in braids and was decorated with two eagle feathers that he wore proudly.

There was no doubt in the minds of those who looked at him that he was the leader and the man from whom all about him could draw their own strength. If Rayne and Mack had been mesmerized by his appearance, they were startled more by the woman who stepped out of the tepee and stood behind White Eagle.

Lone Star and Night Sky also gazed in pride at the two people who had given them life, White Eagle and the beautiful white woman, Rebecca, who had chosen to make her life among the people of the man she loved.

As White Eagle strode toward the fire, Rebecca followed behind. He seated himself, and Rebecca found a seat behind him. Her position did not suggest a reduction in her status in the tribe or in White Eagle's life, for all knew she possessed completely the heart of the tall, handsome chief and had held it over the years. It was her obedience and her acceptance of their customs that had made her a well-loved member of their tribe.

The celebration resumed with a more vibrant undertone. After a few minutes, Sun Knife and Running Wolf appeared with Long Arrow. All three took their places

128

near White Eagle, and soon they were engrossed in a conversation that both Rayne and Mack would have given a great deal to have overheard. Both men knew they could not approach the chief unless he summoned them, and the formidable man did not seem about to do so. They both might have been even more nervous had they actually overheard the conversation.

"Running Wolf," White Eagle said with a half smile and a glow of wicked humor in his eyes, "I have been told the white trapper asks for Falling Water in marriage."

Running Wolf's grunt was a little less than pleased. "Yes, it is so."

"You have agreed?"

"I have told him I would think on this. He has offered much, but I would not give Falling Water to anyone she did not choose freely."

"You have wisdom, my friend." White Eagle smiled. "You have spoken to Falling Water about this?"

"I would speak to her tonight, when the celebration is over."

"Running Wolf, will you hold your answer for a short time?"

"Yes, but why?"

"I would speak with this . . . trapper." White Eagle said this softly, and the others exchanged looks.

"You doubt he is what he says he is?" Long Arrow questioned.

"I believe he is what he says he is." White Eagle laughed. "I also believe he is more than what he says he is, and I would like to speak to this man."

"I will do as you ask, White Eagle," Running Wolf said. "I would talk to Falling Water. It is not in my heart to give my daughter away so easily."

The conversation was interrupted when Little Eagle approached his father, Sun Knife, to speak to him.

Rayne had been watching the conversation and saw the handsome young warrior approach his father. It was only a sudden, instinctive turn of his head that drew his attention to the group of single women. One had become suddenly motionless and stood watching the same young warrior.

Deeply in love himself, Rayne fully understood the emotion he read in her eyes. It was clear to him in an instant that Lone Star, daughter of the chief, was in love with Little Eagle, son of the blue-eyed medicine man. He filed the thought in his mind in case he should need the information later.

He turned to speak to Mack and found his gaze traveling in the same direction, but his friend was looking toward a slim, dark girl who stood among the women. This time Rayne was taken completely by surprise.

Mack sensed his companion's awareness and turned his gaze away quickly. Wisely, Rayne let the incident pass without a word. Mack was too much of a friend to press. If he wanted to confide in Rayne he would; if he didn't, Rayne knew he would not tolerate curiosity.

"I think," Mack said softly, "the chief would like to speak to us."

Rayne's attention was drawn once more to White Eagle, who had motioned for them to come to him.

"Well, this is it, boy." Mack chuckled. "This is what we came for, to get close to this man and get the answers the senator wants."

"Let's go." Rayne smiled in reply. "I wouldn't want to do anything to upset him. That man beside him is Running Wolf, Falling Water's father. Maybe if we make a good impression on the chief, it might help with other things."

Mack laughed, and they both rose to walk the distance that separated them from White Eagle.

"Greetings," White Eagle said in a deep, resonant voice. "Welcome to my village. I have been told what happened to you, and I am grateful to the gods that we found you before your spirits left this world and walked the last great journey."

"We are grateful also, Chief White Eagle," Rayne replied. "Your people have been very generous with us. We would ask to be able to stay with you for the winter, to trap near your rivers. It would please us," he added, "to share what we trap with your people and to hunt while we are here to help sustain your supplies."

It was an excellent gesture, and it pleased everyone who heard, but Rayne was uncomfortably aware of the dark, piercing eyes of White Eagle, who seemed to read his thoughts, and of the sharp crystal-blue gaze of the man who stood beside him. Dark, obsidian eyes regarded him, and Rayne felt as if his very heart was being read. He also noted Running Wolf's intent regard. Again, it startled him to realize how important the reactions of these three—especially Running Wolf—were to him. He found himself holding his breath as he awaited a reply.

"You are welcome to stay with us, and what meat you can hunt will also be welcome. Come, sit and eat with us."

Relieved, Mack and Rayne took the spots offered and joined the chief and his friends to eat.

The tempo of the celebration picked up as the drums began to throb an insistent beat that brought dancers to their feet. Both Mack and Rayne were fascinated, even

131

while trying to keep their attention on all that was being said around them.

The women served platters of food, and Mack was, at first, unaware of the woman who knelt beside him. He turned to her and was met by wide, dark eyes and a quiet, sensitive smile as she offered him food.

He remained still, as if frozen in another time and place, and his eyes held hers as if he were searching for something valued, and something lost. Her eyes widened questioningly as she read the warring emotions that seemed to cross his features unbidden.

He forced himself to smile, but Little Dove was startlingly aware of something within him that seemed to cry out in pain. It was a specter, a vapor of emotion she could not name, yet she felt it in the innermost part of her.

Little Dove had reached toward no man, had not even wanted to until this moment. Something unknown called out to her, and her eyes filled with sympathy—the very last emotion that Mack's resistance could tolerate. His smile faded, and he thanked her quickly before turning back to the conversation.

She knew he was trying to shut himself away from her, and he might have succeeded if, in that one brief moment, she had not seen the pain and the need within him. She sensed something different, something special about this man, and somehow she felt it was connected to her.

It was impossible for her to push herself on him, especially in front of their chief, and most of all Running Wolf, the brother she worshiped. She would have sacrificed anything before incurring Running Wolf's displeasure, or worse yet, causing a blow to his pride.

She would wait until Mack chose to speak to her, if he chose to speak to her. If he did not, she would somehow find a way to solve the mystery she had seen in the depths of his eyes. Even if it came to nothing, she thought, it might solve the mystery of why her heart thudded so heavily and she seemed so short of breath whenever their eyes met.

The time moved by, and Mack tried his best to keep his mind on the conversation and his and Rayne's reason for being there, but unwanted memories had found a crack in his armor and had assaulted him. They roiled within him until he could no longer contain them. He rose from his seat, and the four men looked at him questioningly. With a light remark about the necessity of relieving himself, he turned and was gone.

Rayne watched him move slowly out of range of the fire, and again the feeling stirred in his mind that something was drastically wrong with Mack. He would have followed to speak with him, but White Eagle asked a question, and Rayne turned to answer. When he looked again, Mack was gone from his sight.

Little Dove, too, watched Mack walk away, and she suddenly felt responsible for his mood. Quietly, she left the fire and followed him.

Mack breathed deeply of the warm night air and half listened to the night sounds as he walked near a small creek. Beneath the tall trees, the sounds of merriment from the village were vague.

"Damnit!" he muttered. "Why don't you stay dead?" He cursed the memories that haunted him, feeling acutely the dull pain deep within him he had tried in vain to exorcise. He leaned a broad shoulder against the rough bark of a tree and for a moment closed his eyes against the memories too difficult to bear.

Little Dove's feet made no sound, and Mack, usually alert and able to sense the smallest noise, was unaware of her presence until she stood near him and spoke.

"Your heart is heavy this night," she said softly. Mack spun around in surprise. He groaned mentally. Of all things, this was the last he wanted to happen.

"Little Dove," he said as steadily as he could. "What are you doing here?"

She clasped her hands before her as if she were frightened, yet she remained.. "To speak the truth," she admitted, "I do not know. It is just . . . just that I felt . . . something. You . . . you seem so . . ."

"So what?"

"So unhappy," she whispered.

He stood in silence, staring at her for so long that she could have wept with nervousness. Then he walked to her side, sighing deeply. "Go back to the village, Little Dove," he said gently. "Do not think of me. My ghosts are my own problems."

"Ghosts . . . are spirits of the dead. The dead should not walk with you but should rest in the land of the Great Spirit. Do they stay because they desire it so, or," she added quietly, "do they stay because you refuse to let them go?"

He was angry, but it was not as strong as the truth with which she had struck him. "What do you know of ghosts?" he said sharply. "You are a child."

"You are not alone in pain," she said softly, "no matter what your years. Others have suffered." Quietly she told him how her mother had died at her birth and of the hunger she had always felt for a mother's love. Then she went on to tell him of the disastrous attack on their village, which had brought death to Michael Holliday and to so many others. She was giving him some of the information he and Rayne sought, but still he hesitated to question her for fear of letting her inside the barriers he had built so many years before. She saw his hesitation and knew she had touched a terribly painful spot. Shaken at the hurt she felt for him, yet filled with the need to somehow soothe his misery, she reached out a tentative, gentle hand to lightly touch his chest.

She was an innocent child-woman, and he refused to let her enter the dark place of grief he held. He could not. It had been too long since he had allowed anyone so dangerously close to him. He gripped her wrist firmly, and, though his voice had lost its harshness, his words were firm.

"Don't, Little Dove. You are kind and sweet, but you are too vulnerable. You can only get hurt. I have no intention of bringing grief to anyone else. Go back to the village and forget about me."

He saw her resistance, saw the gentleness within her and her desire to help him. He knew he would have to break and destroy it or open himself to her. "You don't believe me?" he asked gruffly.

"You are not such a man."

"No?" he questioned softly. He heard her startled gasp as he roughly jerked her against him. Expertly and quickly, he pinned her arms behind her. His mouth swept down and took hers brutally. He ravaged her soft mouth, forcing it open and drawing on her sweetness until he heard her moan. One strong arm held her with no difficulty while the other hand caressed, none too gently, the curves of her slim body. She writhed desperately in his arms as he set free all the violence and anger he had stored.

He heard her muffled sob, but he continued to play havoc with her gentleness. His open mouth savagely claimed her breath, and his hands roughly handled her until he knew she was terrified at his brutality. To complete what he had started, as roughly as he had grasped her he thrust her away from him. She stumbled back a step or two and stood looking at him.

He kept the bold look of lust on his face, openly showing her the avid hunger she had sensed in his kiss. He mentally drove her from him, or tried. Even in his violent touch she had felt the need buried deep within him. Sympathy filled her heart, and tears burned her eyes and fell unheeded.

"Go back to the village," he said harshly, "or I will take you here on the ground and you will not be able to stop me."

Now she knew. He needed her fear as part of his own defense, and even though her mouth was bruised by his kiss and her body throbbed with the violence of his attack, she rejected the fear he had tried so hard to induce.

She moved closer to him. Gentle hands reached to touch his face. On tiptoe she rose to sweetly touch her soft, parted lips to his. He could taste the salt of tears on her quivering lips. Her gentle touch spoke to him of her denial of his brutality, and, as no words could have, her actions reached within him to tell him of her understanding.

When she stepped back from him, their eyes locked in battle for a moment, and he felt the defeat her sensitive lips had brought. Without speaking again, she turned and silently walked away. In a few moments the darkness swallowed her slim form.

He closed his eyes against the agony of her gentle penetration of his well-guarded fortress. He braced one hand against the tree, as if all the strength had run from his body. He fought a grim, silent battle, and it was some time before he won.

Resolution filled him. He would not let this kind of thing happen again. He would keep a distance between them. Neither she nor anyone else would be allowed to cross it. He had lived with his pain too long to be able to let it go so easily.

When he had himself under as much control as he could accomplish, he retraced his steps, moving toward the sounds of the celebration from which he was now completely detached. But, despite his iron control, she remained a shadowy form in the corners of his consciousness.

Chapter 10

As the evening progressed, Rayne was becoming filled with a deepening admiration for White Eagle. Although they had talked much, Rayne was completely aware that White Eagle had told him nothing. At the same time, the chief had seemed to glean from what Rayne had said all that he had wanted to know. White Eagle questioned subtly and discreetly and very astutely.

After Mack had left, Rayne had gone to his tepee and brought out the gifts he had been able to salvage from the attack on the three of them. He was thankful that he had left a few bundles of gifts under a tree and that the attackers, in their haste, had overlooked them.

He returned and laid a large package before White Eagle. When he opened it, there were gasps of surprise from many onlookers, although White Eagle's face showed nothing.

Rayne gently lifted the long rifle he had brought specifically for White Eagle. He knew that a gift given with an open heart meant a great deal to these people. He watched White Eagle's eyes widen in appreciation and was satisfied with the results of his gesture.

Slowly, Rayne lifted the rifle so all could see, for it was an excellent one. Then he handed the rifle to White Eagle. "I bring this gift for the chief of the Cheyenne with my wish that it will protect you and bring good hunting."

It also pleased Rayne to see the glow of admiration in Running Wolf's eyes. Maybe, mused Rayne happily, it would make Running Wolf think a little harder about Rayne's request to marry his daughter.

White Eagle took the rifle in his hand, and, holding it gently with one hand, he caressed the rifle with the other as if it were a woman.

Among the gifts were several things Rayne had brought for Rebecca. He could tell in an instant that they pleased not only her but the man who loved her as well. White Eagle's eyes glowed with the pride and love he felt for her as she graciously accepted the mirror, hair brushes, and other trinkets Rayne offered.

"You are most thoughtful, Mr. Freeman. I thank you very much. You must come to our tepee soon and join us for an evening meal."

"Thank you, Mrs. . . . er . . . ah . . ."

She laughed softly, and he enjoyed the pleasant sound of it. He could see why the slim, golden woman had held the heart of this tall, powerful chief for so long.

"You may call me Rebecca, please, and I would add my welcome to my husband's."

"Thank you."

Rayne was quite pleased with himself as the evening became progressively more festive. The only question that concerned him now was where Mack had disappeared to, and what it was that had upset him so much.

139

He remembered the way Mack had looked at Little Dove, and it worried him. It was bad enough that Rayne wanted Running Wolf's daughter. He wondered how Running Wolf would feel if Mack should want his sister as well. He was sure Mack must have had the same thoughts.

Mack did not return to the celebration, but walked instead to the tepee he and Rayne shared. He lay down and, for the only time he would allow it, let Little Dove breach his strong defenses and glide through his mind.

After a while he slept, and Rayne found him thus when he finally returned. It was well after midnight, and still quite some time passed before the village at last grew quiet.

The next three days passed uneventfully, so uneventfully, in fact, that Rayne grew tense and impatient.

Running Wolf was a solid rock against which Rayne could not seem to make headway. He did not want to anger Running Wolf, but he also felt the urge to push him into some kind of decision about his offer of marriage. He just didn't know how to push this rock without harming his own cause.

To make matters worse, he saw very little of Falling Water during this period, and he was aware that she was being watched carefully by both parents. It did little for his peace of mind to have to be satisfied with the well-remembered dream of what they had shared.

He rode with Little Eagle and Night Sky to hunt and to keep himself occupied. He was a very able hunter, and his rifle brought fresh meat to the village, which he wisely shared with widows and tepees in which there were many children. He was also aware that what he did and all that evolved around him was reported to White Eagle and Running Wolf in accurate detail.

At the end of the third day, after he and Mack had shared supper, Mack sat back with an amused gleam in his eyes and watched Rayne fume impatiently.

"Isn't he a man of his word?" Rayne asked angrily. "He said after the celebration he'd make a decision. Well, the celebration is over, and he acts as if I never even asked."

"There's nothing you can do about it," Mack responded. "These people have their own way. They're infinitely patient, and they expect you to be the same. Besides"—Mack chuckled—"he didn't say how long after."

Rayne laughed reluctantly. "I guess you're right, he didn't. How long do you think he's going to keep me dangling like this?"

"I'll tell you what I've been thinking," Mack said quietly. "I think they're waiting for us to tell them the real reason we're here, because I suspect we haven't fooled them for a minute. They probably figure that if we lied about that, we'd lie about anything else."

Rayne sat down to face Mack. "And," he said softly, "he has no intention of giving his daughter to a man whose honesty and honor he suspects?"

"That's about it. After being here this long and getting to know White Eagle and his medicine man, Sun Knife, I think we'd be wise to come clean and tell them who and what we are and why we're here. I have a suspicion the senator is right about a lot of things. He suspects that Chevington's original attack report was false and that someone else also has plans for this valley. They know and value the truth, so let's tell them the truth. Maybe

141

we'll get all the answers we need. Then . . ."

"Then what?"

"Then you can have your bride and I . . . I'll take the report back to the senator before the snows come."

"Mack?"

"What?"

"Why are you so anxious to get out of here?"

"You know me, Rayne. I can't sit in one place a long time."

"Is that all it is, Mack?"

"What makes you think it's any more than that?"

"We've been together a long time. I think I know you pretty well. It's not like you to run from anything."

Mack rose and paced the floor slowly. "Sometimes, Rayne, it's better to run. Sometimes there're situations you just can't do anything about other than to run."

"Do you want to tell me?"

"Not now . . . leave it for now. I can't even look it in the eye yet, so how can I try to tell you or anyone else?"

"Mack, stay until fall. By then we'll have all our answers. Then you can decide just what you really want to do. The senator needs all the information we can get if he is going to find out who's behind Chevington and why they want this valley so bad. Stay until fall, Mack, and maybe something will happen to show you why you can't run from anything."

"What are your plans?"

"In the morning, I'm going to Running Wolf. I'll tell him the truth. Then, if he still allows us to stay, I'll ask our questions. Sun Knife might have a lot of answers too. We'll have the truth and work from there. Stay until fall, Mack."

Mack stood in silence for a moment, then he turned to

look at Rayne, whose steady gaze held his. "All right," he said resignedly, "until fall."

"Good. We'll go and talk to White Eagle this morning." Before Mack could reply, excited voices from outside drew their attention. Both moved to the entrance. Outside they stood and watched the arrival of a man they had not seen before.

He was a tall, broad-shouldered man, dressed in Indian clothing, yet he was white. He also rode Indian fashion— without a saddle. They were close enough to see the steel gray of his eyes and the ragged scar that ran the length of his cheek.

The stranger dismounted in front of White Eagle's tepee and handed the reins of his horse to a younger warrior standing nearby. From the way the warrior smiled, both Rayne and Mack knew the stranger was of some importance.

He requested permission to enter, and it was granted immediately. After a few minutes, White Eagle came out and spoke to another young man, who dashed rapidly toward Sun Knife's tepee. After another brief interval, Sun Knife left his tepee to cross the distance to White Eagle's dwelling and entered.

Mack and Rayne exchanged glances. Whoever this stranger was, he was someone of importance to both White Eagle and his blood brother, Sun Knife.

At the same moment the stranger was entering White Eagle's tepee, Falling Water was passing behind it. Suddenly the bundles of dried skins she was carrying tumbled from her arms. As she got down on her hands and knees to gather them, the voices from inside the tepee came to her clearly.

Within White Eagle's tepee, the atmosphere was

pleasant as three friends sat down to talk. Josiah Tucker groaned as he lowered himself to a sitting position. Then his laugh echoed among the others.

"God, I feel like I've got blisters on my butt. I've been on that horse so long I feel like I was part of him."

"You've traveled quickly." White Eagle smiled. "Did you find the answers you searched for?"

"I did. They've finished building the new fort," Josiah said with a touch of anger in his voice, "and it's called Fort Ramsey. It's due for a new commander soon."

"Do you know who he will be?" Sun Knife questioned.

"I have no idea, and nobody else at the fort does either or I'd have heard. I do know one thing that worries me."

"What's that, Josiah?" Sun Knife replied.

"It's got more men than any other fort in this part of the country and more coming every day. If it keeps up, it will have an uncommon amount of men, much more than this territory should require."

"What is it you feel, Josiah?" White Eagle asked.

"I don't know, White Eagle. I only know we'd better keep our eyes and ears open. There's something going on. I don't know what, but I've got this feeling it includes us."

"They can't touch this land while Lauren and her father own it," Sun Knife interjected.

"That's what scares me, Sun Knife. What if . . . what if something happened? There're only two people that stand between us and them—two people! Do you have any idea what kind of odds those are?"

"Not exactly the best, but they're all we've got."

"Well," Josiah said quietly, "they're not going to be much if they have to stand up against what I've found."

"What have you found?" White Eagle asked.

Silently Josiah reached into the pocket of his jacket and withdrew something. He extended his hand so the others could see what he held. White Eagle's expression was calm and unaware, but Sun Knife's face grew paler and he cursed softly. White Eagle looked at him in surprise.

"What is so important about this, Sun Knife? This yellow metal has been here for as long as I can remember. It is no good for anything; it is too soft."

"White Eagle," Sun Knife said worriedly, "it's gold. Josiah, is there much of it?"

"Enough to make a lot of men very rich if they found it."

"I don't understand," White Eagle interjected.

"It's gold, my brother," Sun Knife said. "For this, the white man would kill everyone in this village. I wonder . . ."

"Wonder what?"

"If this gold has any connection to our two white visitors. I wonder if the smell of gold has already gotten to them."

"Two white visitors?" Josiah questioned. He remembered well, as the others did, the reason he had first come to the valley and the near tragedy that had occurred.

"Yes," White Eagle replied. "They say they are trappers and want to spend the winter with us to trap along our streams. One has even made an offer for Falling Water as wife."

Josiah chuckled. "I'll bet that set well with Running Wolf. Did he get away with that and still wear his hair?"

Sun Knife and White Eagle both laughed. "Running Wolf will find what is in Falling Water's heart. But he will also wait and watch to discover what is in the white man's heart. Do you believe, Sun Knife, that these men have come to search for the yellow metal?"

"I don't know," Sun Knife replied. "But we will certainly watch them."

"The building of the new fort and the arrival of the two trappers . . ." Josiah began quietly. "It reminds me of another time. I remember well why I was sent here. I wonder if these two have been sent for the same kind of reason."

White Eagle's dark eyes grew cold and hard. Rebecca, who was seated quietly at the far side of their tepee, watched his face and remembered well the last confrontation with the people of her race. It sent a chill of fear through her.

"These trappers," Josiah said, "what are their names?"

"One is Rayne Freeman," Sun Knife answered. "The other is called Mackenzie Weaver."

"Weaver . . . Mackenzie Weaver," Josiah said slowly, his brow furrowed in a deep, thoughtful frown. Then suddenly his eyes lit with memory. "He's a big man, part Scot?"

"You know him?" White Eagle asked.

"I'm not sure. I'd like to meet them. If it's the Weaver I know, he's got a reputation for being a pretty honest man. He's been around these parts for a long time. If it's the same man, he's lived with one tribe or another since he was a kid."

"What do you know about him?" White Eagle questioned.

"Not too much; mostly rumor. But, if he is the one I heard of, he stood big in one of the tribes. I even heard he married into one. In fact, he was supposed to have had a

146

child. Maybe he isn't the same one. If he were, why would he be here?"

"There are many questions to be answered. I will speak with them tomorrow and again try to find the color of their hearts," White Eagle said. "If the one is who you think, he might be one who would know our customs well. He would also know how to live among us without causing any problems."

"Well, in the meantime"—Josiah laughed—"I am going to get something to eat and a little sleep. In the morning I'm going to stop by your tepee, Sun Knife. I have a gift for Snow Blossom. It's been a long time since I've seen her pretty face. I still can't convince her she chose the wrong man. I'd keep trying, but I'm afraid you'd mark the other side of my face; then none of the other women would look at me."

Sun Knife laughed in response. "I've not seen you having any trouble yet attracting any of the women. Why don't you get married and settle down?"

"Because, you half-breed heathen, I can't find another Snow Blossom."

"Well, you are right about two things," Sun Knife grinned.

"Yeah?" Josiah said suspiciously. "What?"

"You won't find another Snow Blossom, and I would surely mark the other side of your face." They laughed together and Josiah rose to his feet. Sun Knife rose also.

"I'll walk to your tepee with you," he said, and after they said good night to White Eagle, they left together. White Eagle sat in brooding silence, gazing, without seeing, into the low-burning fire.

Outside the tepee, Falling Water rose to her feet and left. The idea that the gold and Rayne might somehow be

147

linked bothered her greatly. Was it the real reason he was here?

Within, Rebecca quietly moved to her husband's side. She knelt beside him and rested her head against his shoulders. His arm slid about her waist, and he drew her close.

"First the trappers, then the yellow metal," he said quietly. "Why are the whites so greedy? Why can they not live on the land the Great Spirit gave them?"

"My people have caused you so much grief, my husband. I am truly sorry. If only all the white people could understand you and your people as I do, maybe then it would be different. Maybe then we could live in peace."

White Eagle turned to look at her, and his hand reached to touch her hair. Always, his fascination for her golden hair drew him out of himself, and he smiled down into her cornflower blue eyes. "I live in peace with all the whites I care to know. My only wish is that the rest of them would stay away."

"Lauren and her father have protected the valley so far," she replied hopefully.

"Then we will beg the Great Spirit to continue his protection through them."

"White Eagle?"

"Yes?"

"Would . . . would you seek peace elsewhere—go from this valley to another place—or would you fight?"

He was silent again as he studied her face. He loved her beyond reason, had fought to hold her, and knew in his heart he would fight again. Yet he didn't want to see pain in her eyes, and he didn't want to answer her question with the words that sprang into his mind.

"I would like to think that those choices will not have to be made. I know that Night Sky will be chief after me, and I want to leave him a peaceful village. Rebecca, I will do all I can possibly do to keep from fighting," he answered slowly. "To say those words now prove I am more chief than warrior."

Rebecca knew him well. She smiled, put her arms about his neck, and kissed him. "You are the strongest, wisest warrior, and you are a good, intelligent leader for your people. But do not try to fool me, my beloved husband. You fear no one, and I and all the others know it. White Eagle, I love you and I would fear for your life, but I would also understand and believe in whatever you decided to do. The gold—maybe they do not know of it. Josiah will tell no one. Maybe . . . maybe our fears will never be realized."

White Eagle drew her into his arms and kissed her, binding her close to him, and silently prayed her words would prove true.

Josiah and Sun Knife walked for a few moments in silence.

"Sun Knife," Josiah asked, "what will you do . . . what will White Eagle do if these two prove to be gold prospectors instead of trappers? Or worse yet, what if you find they have been sent by Chevington?"

"Well," Sun Knife replied, "to be honest, Josiah, I don't know what I would do. But I do know White Eagle is too strong and honorable to commit murder. Yet, he couldn't let word get to Chevington or to anyone else about the gold. I know another thing for sure. White Eagle will defend this valley with his life. If, by any

149

chance, Rayne is trying to make a fool of Running Wolf and hurts Falling Water in the process, he'll never leave this valley alive."

"They've been here for a while. What do you think of them?"

"If I were asked to judge right now, I'd say they were telling the truth. But there's too much at stake, and I might be wrong."

"This gold can bring a lot of trouble. I'd sure like to know if they have any idea it's here."

"Well, we have to try to find out somehow. You said you'd heard of this Mack, as they call him?"

"I've never met him."

"But you could get him to talk to you, just by telling him you've heard of him. You are a white man. They might think they've got a friend here and talk to you. At least it's worth a try."

"Anything I can do to help keep things peaceful here I'll try. What are we going to do about that fort?"

"There's nothing we can do right now but wait until the new commander comes and try to make peace with him. This valley is ours under the white man's law. As long as Lauren and her father own it, they can't do anything. The fort might make us nervous, and we might make them nervous, but we'll just have to work at keeping the peace and hope they do the same."

"Well, once we get things settled here and know what these two are doing, maybe we can wait a few weeks, then take us a little ride to the fort. The new man should be there by then, and maybe we can talk up some peace."

"Good idea, Josiah." They had reached Josiah's tepee and Sun Knife walked on, saying, "I'll see you in the morning."

150

Josiah said good night and entered his tepee. Sun Knife stood in the silence of the sleeping village and wondered why he could not shake the feeling that some disaster was brewing. He was filled with the frustration of not knowing from which direction to protect himself and those he loved.

Chapter 11

Inside their tepee, neither Mack nor Rayne could find sleep, yet neither seemed able to confide in the other. Mack was plagued with memories he was trying to fight and thoughts of the gentle woman who had stirred the embers of his past and had set them ablaze once more.

Rayne battled a hunger that gnawed within the depths of him—Falling Water. He could feel her slim body in his arms and taste her sweetness on his lips. He had spoken to her often during the days, but always she had been with someone else. He knew it was Running Wolf who had made sure one of the married women of his tribe had accompanied her whenever Lauren could not be with her.

For the hundredth time, he cursed Running Wolf for not answering his request to be allowed to marry. How much longer, he wondered, would he have to be patient. He laughed to himself as he began to conjure up fantasies of how he would go to Running Wolf and demand Falling Water, and Running Wolf would give her to him.

He was made aware of Mack's inability to sleep when

Mack rose. "I'm going to go out for a while," Mack stated. "I think I will go see if Little Eagle is awake. We're supposed to go on a hunt tomorrow. At least we can talk about it." He left, and Rayne realized he also couldn't be still and let his dreams control him.

Grimly, he rose and dressed. He intended to ride to the place he and Falling Water had shared. He would swim and maybe become tired enough to sleep. He took along a blanket. He decided that if he found he could sleep, a place with such sweet memories might be the best place to do it.

He moved quietly through the village to where the horses were kept. He used only a bridle and mounted without a saddle. He rode slowly, enjoying the warmth of the night and the beauty of the star-studded, black velvet sky, but the setting only made him want Falling Water more.

It was a long ride, and the moon was high and bright when he got to the river. The silver orb dappled the water with shiny speckles and lit the area about it with a soft, mellow glow.

He slid to the ground and tethered his horse so it would not drift too far away. Then he walked slowly to the edge of the water and stood for a while, enjoying the serenity. In his mind he relived the beautiful moments he and Falling Water had shared here. He laid the blanket on the ground, then pulled off his boots and tossed them upon it. He removed his shirt and threw it upon the blanket too.

The air was warm on his skin—an also-remembered pleasure. He removed the rest of his clothes and stepped into the cool water. He waded in to just above his knees, then moved forward rapidly and dove beneath the surface of the water.

He came up for air and swam away from the shore until he began to tire, then he turned and started back. When he reached the shallows, he stood up to walk ashore. Before he could reach it, he stopped. The breathtaking beauty of his dreams stood before him.

He couldn't quite believe she was really there, as for a time she stood motionless. Then her hands slowly reached for the ties to her dress, and in a few moments, it whispered to the ground about her feet.

The moonlight touched her body with fingers of mellow light, caressing her skin until it glowed. Her dark hair flowed about her. Never would he be able to forget this vision of loveliness that moved slowly toward him.

She stood only inches away, the water swirling about her slim hips. They needed no words. By the light of the moon, he could read in her amber eyes the glow of flaming need that matched his own.

He reached out and put his hands on her hips, slowly drawing her close. It sent a shiver of pleasure through him when her warm body touched his wet, cool skin.

He scooped up cool water and slid his wet hands over her shoulders and down her back, then he bent to sample the sweet taste of her wet skin. A low murmur came from within her as she raised her hands to slide up the hard muscle of his arms and caress his shoulders and back.

His lips traced a heated path across her shoulders and touched her slender throat as slowly he drew her tighter within the circle of his arms. Then his lips found her warm, parted mouth, and she clung to him as the fire of mutual need exploded within them both. He savored the moist warmth of her mouth, exploring, possessing, until he knew she was as lost as he.

Gently, he lifted her in his arms and held her against him. A light breeze blew her hair across them as again their lips blended in a fiery kiss that seemed to melt every sinew and bone within her, leaving her feeling as if they were flowing into each other.

He walked to the grass-covered bank of the river and very gently laid her upon the grass. Again, with an urgency she could barely control, she reached for him as he lay down beside her.

Her hands caressed his chest and slid up slowly to tangle in his hair and draw his head to hers. Their mouths locked in a blazing kiss, open and hungry for the flame that shuddered through them.

His hands moved slowly over her now sensitive skin, teasing her with their light, searching touch, while his mouth began a tormenting journey, touching, tasting, wandering, from soft rounded breasts to slim waist, finding spots that rendered her breathless with the wild sensations he produced. As he nibbled her velvet-soft flesh, he heard her passion call to him. It was an agony and an ecstasy she could not control. Sparks ignited in the center of her being and blossomed into a desire that left her mindless and gasping.

His hands now became possessive as he held her and his mouth found the center of her need. She cried out and writhed in his hands as every one of her senses exploded in a kaleidoscope of vibrant flame.

She wanted to touch him, to feel his hard, strong body, to have him fill the depths of her and end the fire that consumed her.

He rose above her, and their lips met again as her arms welcomed him against her. Her hands caressed his hard, muscled back, sliding down lean hips to urge him to answer the need that burned within her. And the answer she sought was there as he moved inside her, deeply possessing her. Hard and throbbing, he moved slowly, seeking both to give and to take the wild pleasure they shared.

With almost agonized groans, they reached a shattering culmination that left them wordless and spent. Still she clung to him, welcoming his weight and holding him close to her.

The sanctuary of her body was a haven he did not want to leave. He turned slowly, drawing her with him so that they remained together, and lifted her gently to lie half across him.

He closed his eyes and held her, tenderly caressing her hair until he could regain some semblance of control over his ragged breathing and the trembling of every nerve.

"How did you know?" he whispered softly against her hair. "How did you know that I needed you so desperately?"

"Because I needed you and could not bear another moment of being away from you," she answered quietly.

"Damnit, Falling Water, either I've got to convince your father that we have to get married pretty quick or do something drastic."

"Drastic?" She laughed softly. "What is that?"

"I'll grab you up and run and not bring you back until he agrees or you are with child and he has to agree."

Again she laughed. "My father is a brave warrior and a tracker better than others. He would find us." She rose on her elbow and smiled down into his eyes, hers sparkling with mischief. "Then he would tie your hair on his lodge pole. After . . . he made you suffer."

"He couldn't make me suffer any more than he already has. Sometimes"—he looked at her suspiciously—"I think he's enjoying it."

She bent to kiss him and again laid her hand on his broad chest, listening to the firm, steady beat of his heart. Gently, she let her hands savor the feel of his hard-muscled arms and chest, allowing them to stray down his lean ribs to rest on his thigh. He groaned softly and drew her tighter to him.

"God, I can't imagine what I'll do if he says no. The thought of ever leaving you, of being without you the rest of my life, is unbelievable."

"To me also," she whispered. "But I have spoken of you to my mother, Summer Rain. I have told her what I feel for you. She understands, and she is one my father will hear when she speaks to him, for they love each other as I do you. I believe, with all my heart, that one day he will agree. I have to believe, for I could not bear the blackness that would live in my heart if I did not. Rayne . . . I can believe? You . . . you speak the truth to me?"

He tipped up her chin and studied her face carefully, his eyes intently holding hers. "Believe," he said softly. "Believe with all your heart. Believe in me and in my love for you, because it is real and so huge I can hardly contain it."

He drew her head down to his and touched her lips with his own in a warm, melting kiss that drew a sigh of contentment from her as she relaxed within the circle of his strong arms. Complete contentment held them as they lay together listening to the soft lap of the water against the shore and the night sounds that surrounded them. It was some time before he spoke again.

"Falling Water, there are many things I have to tell you about me, and many things I must tell your father and your people so they will know I want to be honest with them. Maybe their suspicions are what is making your father hesitate. In the morning, I will speak to him."

Falling Water had never been so happy in her life as she was at that moment. Within Rayne's arms, held by the love she felt enclosing her, listening to his words, she was complete. She relished his strength as again she let her hands drift over his skin. With deep satisfaction, she felt his response.

One hand slid into her hair to lift her face so that he could touch her lips with his. The other slid down the curve of her back to rest on her buttocks and draw her even more tightly against him. Within her she could feel him stir and begin to warm.

It was a magical night, and they shared it as lovers blessed by the gods with love so deep that the miracle of it molded their two bodies and two souls together forever.

They rode back to the village reluctantly, knowing they would again have to be separated. Dreams occupied them through the balance of the night, dreams that the coming day would settle all their difficulties so that they would be able to share the rest of their lives together.

Despite the fact that he did not sleep most of the night, Rayne was awake very early in the morning. He dressed quickly, his mind set on talking to White Eagle and Sun Knife as soon as possible. Once he explained the truth to them, he intended to go to Running Wolf. One way or another he felt it was time for Running Wolf to make some kind of a decision, and he was prepared to argue with him if the decision were negative.

He left Mack still asleep, stepped out of his tepee, and found himself face to face with Josiah Tucker.

"Good morning," Josiah said. "I was just coming to speak to you and your partner." He extended his hand with a smile. "My name is Josiah Tucker, and I guess you might say I'm part of this tribe."

Rayne chuckled and took Josiah's hand in a firm grip. "I'm Rayne Freeman, and you don't exactly look Cheyenne to me."

"Not by birth"—Josiah laughed—"but by choice. I've been here for enough years that they've begun to think of me as Cheyenne."

"You said you were on your way to speak with me?"

"Well, actually your partner. I heard he's Mackenzie Weaver. I've heard the name before, and I'd kind of like to meet the man."

"Mack's still asleep," Rayne said. "I'm on my way to speak to White Eagle."

"Well, I hate to disappoint you, but White Eagle and Sun Knife just rode out."

"Where are they bound?"

"Not far, I don't think. Scouts came in and said they spotted a small herd of buffalo. Guess White Eagle and Sun Knife took an early ride to check it out. They'll be back with news soon. If there's a good-sized herd, they'll have all the village out for a hunt. Since you and your partner have guns, I'm sure you'll be asked to come along."

"Will the hunt start today?"

"Why?"

"Because I'd like to talk to White Eagle and Sun Knife. It's important."

"Well, even if they find buffalo, I don't expect we'd all

159

be ready to start out until late in the day. It'd give you time. Must be something real important."

"It's important to Mack and me," Rayne replied, but he offered no more, and Josiah knew the way of the frontier. A man did not question another too closely. A man's past was his own, and interference was not only unwelcome but could cause serious repercussions.

"Well," Josiah said, "I guess the whole village could use meat and robes for winter, so White Eagle will be pleased if there's a herd near. You might find him in a pretty good mood if he and Sun Knife come back and call for a hunt. I expect"—he laughed—"it would be the best time to talk to him . . . about anything."

Rayne smiled, but Josiah's meaning was very clear to him, as was Josiah's curiosity. Rayne wondered just what Josiah wanted to talk to Mack about. He realized that he had only known Mack a few years, and, although they were friends, there was a lot of Mack's past he knew nothing of. He was about to speak when the sound of movement from inside the tepee told them Mack was awake and moving around. Rayne didn't know what business Josiah had with Mack, but he respected Mack's privacy. If there was anything about his past Mack wanted to tell him, he would listen; if not, he had no thought of interfering.

"Mack," he called out.

"Yeah?" came the reply.

"You got company."

In a few minutes the door flap was pushed aside and a curious Mack came out. He looked at Josiah, and no sign of recognition crossed his face. If he knew him, he disguised he knowledge well, Rayne thought.

"This is Josiah Tucker, Mack. He lives with this tribe. I

guess he heard about you and wants to meet the great Mackenzie Weaver." Rayne grinned, but his smile soon faded, for, even as Mack extended his hand to Josiah, Rayne saw something in his eyes he had never seen before—a light touch of fear.

"Josiah Tucker," Mack said quietly. "I've never heard the name. How do you know me?"

"Don't exactly know you," Josiah replied. "I just heard your name before. Someone said you used to live with a tribe north of here a few years back."

Now Mack's face paled. "Yeah, I did. Why don't you come on in." He motioned inside the tepee. Josiah nodded and Mack turned to Rayne.

"It isn't necessary, Mack," Rayne replied quietly. "You don't owe me anything, especially explaining anything you don't want to."

Mack smiled his gratitude. "It's okay, Rayne. Maybe I need a friend . . . and maybe it's best you know from me rather than from someone else."

Rayne nodded and followed Mack and Josiah back inside. The three of them sat down on the buffalo hide mats that served as beds.

"You've been around here long?" Mack asked Josiah.

"Quite a spell. I had a place of my own down on the small river for awhile. Then . . . I left it. I've been with White Eagle's people for close to twenty years."

"You married into the tribe?"

"No, why?"

"Just thought maybe you had," Mack answered. "You staying with them because you like them or for the trappin'?"

Josiah wondered if Mack was fishing around for word of the gold he had found. "The trapping is good. But my

161

main reason for staying here is because these people have become sort of a family to me. I care what happens to them. I . . . I wouldn't want anything to happen that might bring trouble to them. White Eagle is a good, peace-loving chief, but I imagine he'd fight any one who tried to push him . . . for any reason."

It dawned on both Rayne and Mack that Josiah was not looking for information on Mack's past as much as he was warning them that they were to bring no problems to this village. Both men wondered if Josiah had any knowledge of the real reason they were in the village.

"You think White Eagle might have the idea we're planning to make trouble for his people?" Rayne asked.

"Are you?" Josiah questioned softly. Rayne and Mack exchanged glances. It was time for the truth, but Mack knew Rayne wanted to talk to White Eagle before they told anything to Josiah. They were both relieved, but as yet Josiah was not.

"Josiah," Rayne said, "from the look in your eye and from all you've said—and tried not to say—you've given me the idea that you think we're here to cause these people some kind of problem."

Josiah remained silent, but his silence spoke eloquently of his doubts. "I'd like to know, since other trappers have passed this way, why you're suspicious of us?"

"Didn't say that," Josiah countered.

"But you implied it."

"I guess," Josiah said softly, "maybe it's your timing. I'm sorry, but you two just seemed to have come at the wrong time. I didn't mean to sound so all-fired hard, but"—he shrugged—"I guess I get touchy where this tribe is concerned. All the friends I have in the

162

world . . . all the people I . . . love are here. It makes me kind of protective."

Before Rayne could speak again, Mack, whose eyes had never left Josiah's face, spoke quietly. "I can understand that. They're . . . they're kind of trusting, aren't they . . . and they're alone. Don't you think it would be a good thing if some strong leader were to try to pull some of the separate tribes together?"

Josiah held Mack's gaze. "They are trusting. To them, a man's honor means a lot. They don't lie, they don't cheat, and their word is their law. I've known some greedy whites, and sometimes they don't show much respect for those qualities, or for the fact that this valley belongs to the Cheyenne."

It was obvious to Mack and Rayne that if they wanted to find out if White Eagle were trying to draw the tribes together, then they would have to ask him, for Josiah did not intend to supply the information. It was just as obvious to Josiah that Mack and Rayne would have to be questioned by White Eagle and Sun Knife about their reasons for being in the village, for they had also refused to supply him with the information he sought.

The silence grew for a few minutes, then Josiah looked at Mack. Maybe he could touch a vulnerable spot, he thought to himself. Anger could reveal what one intended to keep hidden.

"You are the Mack Weaver who lived with Tall Bull's tribe a few years back, aren't you?"

"Yes . . . I am."

"That's why you asked me about marrying into the tribe. Because you did. I heard you became blood brother to Tall Bull. If I'm right, it was his sister you married."

"Yes, it was." Mack's voice was low and hard. "And if

163

you know the Cheyenne like you say you do, then you know that White Eagle does not need to doubt us. You know that to be made blood brother to Tall Bull, and to have him give his sister as a wife, meant that he and all his tribe had respect and honor for me."

Josiah's voice was just as cold and hard as Mack's. "Then," he said, "why did you leave them?"

"That may be White Eagle's business," Rayne interrupted angrily, "but it's sure as hell not yours." Rayne had seen the pain in Mack's eyes fleetingly and knew Josiah meant to rub a vulnerable spot until it exposed what Mack would have kept inside.

"We intended to go to White Eagle this morning and tell him everything about us. Any decisions he might make should have nothing to do with Mack's past, and they should be White Eagle's . . . not yours. I've been around the Cheyenne a long time too, and I know it isn't their way to judge a man on his past."

Again, there was a brief silence as all three digested the truth of what had been said. And all three knew that only White Eagle could decide what the final truth would be.

"I'm sorry," Josiah said. "You're right. It is not for me to question either of you."

He rose to his feet. "I can't question, but I can say this. These people live in this village in peace. They harm no one. If an outsider—any outsider—brings harm to these people, somehow I'll find a way to make him pay, even if I have to trail him forever. That's a promise." He turned and left without another word.

"God damn," Mack muttered softly.

"It's a good thing we decided to tell White Eagle the truth. The others must think the same way Tucker does. No wonder they've kept us hanging. They must have some reason for being so skittish, and they think we're a threat," Rayne said.

"Rayne?"

"Forget it, Mack. You don't have to explain anything to me. And," he added, "you don't have to explain anything to anyone else. We came for a reason, and that's all they have to know. As soon as White Eagle gets back, we'll go and talk to him. Then we'll ask a few questions of our own. After that, I'll go to Running Wolf. Maybe"— he smiled—"a wedding would smooth some ruffled feathers."

Chapter 12

Before the sun had risen to the center of the sky, Sun Knife and White Eagle rode back to the camp. They were both pleased, for they had indeed found a large herd of buffalo.

Rayne was drawn from his tepee by happy shouts from excited warriors and aspiring warriors. He watched as the chief of the Cheyenne called to his tribe and told them to make ready, for the hunt would begin with the next day's dawn.

White Eagle rode to his tepee, dismounted, and entered. Rayne felt that now would be the best time to talk to him. As he started across the open area between his tepee and White Eagle's, he saw Sun Knife walking toward the same destination from another direction. They met a few feet from White Eagle's door.

"Rayne," Sun Knife said, "would you and Mack care to come along? There is a herd of buffalo near, and every hunter is welcome."

"Mack and I would both be glad to contribute what help we can. I was just on my way to talk to White Eagle."

"All right," Sun Knife answered, preparing to turn and leave.

"No, don't go, Sun Knife. I think it would be a good idea for you to come in too. What I have to say concerns this tribe, and I think you will understand and maybe help me explain to White Eagle."

Sun Knife's startling blue eyes regarded him, and again Rayne was aware of the sensation that his very soul was being read. Then Sun Knife smiled and Rayne grinned in relief.

Sun Knife moved toward the entrance with Rayne close behind him. He called out to White Eagle, who immediately invited them inside.

White Eagle was seated against a wooden backrest, carefully examining the arrows he would use on the hunt. He motioned for Rayne and Sun Knife to sit near him.

"Rayne and his friend would come with us on this hunt, brother," Sun Knife said. He and White Eagle exchanged glances, then White Eagle's ebony eyes turned to Rayne.

The power and strength of this man again reached out to Rayne. There was no doubt in his mind that if any man among the tribal leaders had the charisma and leadership ability to pull tribes together with some kind of treaty, that man would be White Eagle.

"You are welcome," White Eagle said. "We will leave with the first light."

"White Eagle," Rayne said, "I would like to talk to you about something. I have asked Sun Knife to come because, in the end, I think he will add his words to mine."

If White Eagle was in any way startled by Rayne's

announcement, there was no sign of it on his impassive features. Since becoming chief many years before, White Eagle had learned to hide his thoughts and feelings behind a stoic expression.

Sun Knife was surprised at Rayne's words but said nothing. He waited patiently for Rayne to continue, wondering what he could have to do with anything Rayne had to say.

"Speak," White Eagle replied. Rayne took a deep breath and began. He tried to choose his words carefully, not because he believed White Eagle would not understand—he recognized the intelligence in the dark eyes that regarded him—but because he wanted no misunderstanding and he desired the trust of both men.

"Sun Knife, I don't know if you have any contact with what's going on in Washington."

Sun Knife smiled. "I get word from friends now and then."

"Then maybe you know of Senator Miles?"

"Yes, I've heard his name."

"Then," Rayne continued quietly, "I'll mention a few other names you might know: Alexander Brent . . . John Chevington." Both men stiffened at Chevington's name, and dark looks clouded their eyes.

"You know Colonel Chevington?" White Eagle asked.

"Yes, I know him . . . in fact, he is one of the reasons I'm here."

"Senator Miles is looking into several incidents," Sun Knife supplied.

"Colonel Chevington has had three commands since he was at the fort near your village. The fort," Rayne added quietly, "that you and your warriors burned." Both men were impassive and silent as Rayne continued.

168

"At each command there seemed to be the same problem with the Indians—misunderstandings . . . fighting . . . deaths." Neither man spoke, so Rayne continued. "There is a man, a powerful and wealthy man who swings a lot of weight in Washington. He's the one behind getting Chevington another command."

"Where?" White Eagle asked quickly.

"I don't know."

"What does this have to do with us and your being here?" White Eagle inquired with some impatience.

"Senator Miles wants peace out here. We have heard all kinds of rumors about what happened between this tribe and Chevington, but no one knows the whole truth."

"What truth?" White Eagle questioned. "Indian or white?"

"There is only one truth. Senator Miles believes that you . . . or perhaps someone else is drawing tribes together for the purpose of war. He wants to stop all this before it gets beyond stopping."

"Just how does he expect to do that?" Sun Knife asked.

"He needs to know the truth. Without it he has no way to stop Chevington from getting another command, making the same mistakes, and maybe setting the plains on fire—a fire we won't be able to stop."

"Who has sent you here?" White Eagle demanded.

"Both Senator Miles and Alexander Brent have combined forces to try to stop Colonel Chevington from creating a disaster. They asked me to find out just what is going on out here. Alexander has had no word from his daughter in over three years."

Sun Knife and White Eagle looked startled at this.

"But," Sun Knife said, "Lauren has been sending messages continually. She is rather upset that her father hasn't answered them."

"Maybe," Rayne said, "they've been intercepted."

White Eagle and Sun Knife became thoughtful as they digested the implications of his words.

Rayne was silent for another long moment, then he said softly, "Mack and I have been talking, and we both feel there are many things that are drawing Chevington's attention to this valley. Some things we don't know . . . but we think you might. There have to be reasons for men—any kinds of men, to do the things they do. We came . . ." he added truthfully, "to find out why, then to do something about it."

"And just what would you do?" White Eagle asked.

"Do our best to stop him, and do our best to keep the peace and to leave this valley in the hands of the people to whom it rightfully belongs."

"And we are to believe you?" White Eagle replied. "We are to trust as we trusted before? The white soldiers attacked my village, killed Sun Knife's father and many more. They stole my wife and Sun Knife's, and brought grief to many others."

"I am speaking the truth now, White Eagle. I speak it not only because I want you to believe, but because I want to become one of your people. After I have taken your words to the senator and Alexander, I would like to marry and live here."

White Eagle contemplated his words, and while he did, he gazed at Rayne, so closely that Rayne could feel the touch of it deep within him. He held White Eagle's gaze, trying to speak silently the same thoughts he had voiced a few moments before.

"I will think on your words," White Eagle replied. "I will speak at the next council and tell them what you say. When they have thought on your words, we will call you and give you our decision. Until then, you are free to live among us."

"Would it be possible for me to speak to the council also?"

"Yes, you may speak. Will you also listen to their decision?"

Rayne smiled. "I will not say that I will not fight for what I think is not only right, but necessary. And," he added, "I hope to acquire a wife from among you. For her, I will fight also."

A touch of humor lit White Eagle's eyes, and a soft smile transformed his firm mouth. "Running Wolf is not pleased to give his daughter away easily. You might find that your biggest fight is with him."

"Then," Rayne said grimly, "he will at least know he has fought the biggest battle of his life. I don't give up easily. After hearing what White Eagle endured in order to claim his white wife, I know that what one sometimes think is impossible can be found to be possible."

Now both White Eagle and Sun Knife laughed at Rayne, and he was pleased. Maybe, he thought, things would work out for the best.

Having gained the promises that White Eagle would think about what Rayne had told him and that Rayne could speak with the elders at the council, Rayne left. He told them both that he and Mack would join the hunt the next day. He had no idea that the hunt itself was to change everything for him and for the rest of the village.

After Rayne left them, White Eagle and Sun Knife sat in silence. Then White Eagle spoke, asking aloud what

171

Sun Knife was thinking.

"Can we trust again, brother? Does he know of the yellow metal . . . does the white soldier know of the yellow metal?"

"I don't know, White Eagle. If they all knew, many would be here already. Maybe it is just Chevington's evil. I have the desire to believe him, but I wish we could get some word from Alexander. It could be that all messages from Lauren have been intercepted. I also wonder if the wealthy man behind Chevington isn't Martin Preston. Revenge on Lauren and the rest of us would be to his liking."

"We will meet with the council after the hunt and talk of what we should do."

"A good idea. In the meantime, we'll keep our eyes and ears on our visitors."

"I have a feeling," White Eagle said with a chuckle, "that Running Wolf is doing that already."

Sun Knife laughed too. "I'll bet he is. Do you think he will agree to the marriage?"

"If he does, it will have to be because he trusts the white one, and I don't think he does yet, or he would have agreed before this."

"Well, I'm going to talk to Josiah. Maybe he has some ideas."

For the balance of the day the entire village was caught up in the excitement of preparing for the next day's hunt. Their crops had already been planted, and there was nothing to keep virtually the whole village from emptying out as men, women, and children moved onto

172

the land of shortgrass, grouping themselves into small hunting units.

A tribal hunt was a solemn affair, usually preceded by prayers and rituals. On the trail and during the hunt itself, Rayne and Mack were well aware that discipline was rigidly enforced by White Eagle. He made certain each hunter performed only his assigned task and did not attempt to hunt on his own. The group hunt was one of the few times a warrior submerged his own individuality.

Scouts ranged ahead, and Mack rode with them while Rayne joined Running Wolf and the group with which he rode. To compensate for poor eyesight, the buffalo had an acute sense of smell, and, because they were constantly sniffing the air for the scent of danger, the riders approached from downwind.

All warriors were stripped down to breechclouts and moccasins. Even Rayne and Mack had adopted the freedom of such clothing. The horses, too, were stripped of saddles and blankets. Bows and arrows and lances were used, and Rayne and Mack knew that during a buffalo hunt these weapons, in the hands of a strong warrior, were more accurate and effective than the guns they carried.

Such warriors were also personifications of grace in motion, and, when a herd was sighted, there was a classic beauty to the riders as they set their horses off at a gallop across rough country, guiding them by knee pressure alone.

Rayne felt the thrill of the hunt fill him when the shout came that the group of buffalo they sought was near. They charged, going after the buffalo, darting in and out of the herd and forcing the beasts into a circle

173

where they might be picked off. It was a risky undertaking, for a bull buffalo might weigh a ton and stand seven feet tall. Though large, such a buffalo had amazing agility and endurance. Even after being shot with arrows, it could run as much as a mile before collapsing. It was just such a situation that arose so suddenly that none involved had time to think.

Running Wolf had spotted a prime bull, a huge, shaggy beast that unexpectedly veered and moved away from the herd. Running Wolf went in hot pursuit and quickly disappeared over a small rise. Both the buffalo and Running Wolf were soon out of Rayne's sight.

He would never know what instinct told him to follow or why he obeyed it blindly. He quickly crested the rise. The scene being played out before him was horrifying, and it threw him into a situation in which he had to act quickly and carefully.

The wounded bull had tried blindly to run. Across a flat plain, Running Wolf rode after him. What happened next was so sudden that Rayne could hardly believe it.

The bull had put quite a bit of distance between himself and his pursuers, but he had nearly reached the end of his endurance. Running Wolf, sure of his own prowess as a hunter, raced toward him. Then his horse stepped into a hole, snapping its leg, and both horse and rider tumbled to the ground.

For a moment, Running Wolf was stunned with the force of the fall, then he stirred and was about to rise. The huge bull stood panting and gazing at the cause of his distress.

Running Wolf rose, and Rayne saw something that dumbfounded him. The huge bull lowered his head and pawed the ground in rising fury, and suddenly sensing that his aggressor had now become a victim.

Running Wolf knew that he could not outrun the bull and that he had no chance in the world of defeating him. All his remaining weapons were too far for him to reach.

Rayne was to witness the deep and almost religious respect the Indians had for all the creations of nature. There was a special reverence for the buffalo, who nurtured the Indian from birth to death, supplying him with all he needed for survival.

Running Wolf felt his life was about to end, and he resolved to die a brave and honorable warrior. He raised his arms and called to Wankentanken, the Great God, and thanked him for his life and the opportunity to die as a man by the very animal he revered.

The next three things happened in rapid sequence. Running Wolf ended his prayer and watched death approach, the huge bull charged, and Rayne raised his gun to his shoulder.

He would have one moment, one opportunity. If he missed, Running Wolf would surely die. The bull bore down on Running Wolf, who stood immobile. Rayne sucked in his breath and held it, then fired.

Within ten feet of Running Wolf the bull stumbled and fell. Running Wolf spun about, amazement on his face. Rayne rode slowly to his side. "Running Wolf," he said quickly, "are you all right?"

"I am fine. Thanks to you. You have saved my life, and I am grateful."

Rayne was now about to learn about another part of Indian nature—his regard for matters of honor and obligations.

"I owe you my life," Running Wolf added. "It is yours from this day. Your enemies are mine, and your honor is mine. There is nothing I possess that I would refuse to give you."

Rayne instinctively knew that Running Wolf would stand by his word, but he also realized that if he took Running Wolf's daughter in this way, the Cheyenne warrior would never forgive or forget.

"I want Falling Water more than I want anything else in this world," Rayne began. He saw Running Wolf stiffen. "But I do not want her at the cost of her father's pride and honor. I ask for nothing except that you consider our marriage. Think with your heart, and tell me when you are ready." He held out his hand for Running Wolf to mount behind him for the ride back. Running Wolf gazed at him with new respect in the depths of his dark eyes. Then he took Rayne's hand and, with a quick leap, was up behind him.

His pony had died from a broken neck after the fall, and this was hard enough on Running Wolf without the fact that he was forced to ride back behind Rayne like a young boy from his first hunt.

The end of a successful hunt was an occasion for joy. When the hunters returned to camp, followed by the packhorses and the women who had helped with the butchering, the few people who had remained behind shouted their approval. Fires were already burning and meat racks stood ready.

Exhausted from the hunt, the men rested for the few hours between the end of the hunt and the coming of evening. Then they were roused by the beat of the drum calling everyone to dance in celebration.

Rayne and Mack sat among the others about the fire and watched with amusement as stories of individual prowess were acted out by the young hunters. Both were surprised when Running Wolf leapt to the lighted center area. In a loud, authoritative voice, he called all to listen to his story, and all did, for Running Wolf commanded such respect. With a combination of chant and leaping dance, he told the story of how the white warrior had saved the life of Running Wolf. He spoke of the size and the power of the bull he had chased, the one he had been sure would take his life.

Running Wolf was a large, muscular man, and the play of firelight on his bronzed body made the story even more effective. There were calls of praise for Running Wolf's courage and joy that the gods had seen fit to give him his life.

Many eyes turned to Rayne with respect and awe. When the story of Running Wolf was finished, the older warrior stopped in front of Rayne. His strong voice carried to everyone. He spoke of his own courage and power, and of his abilities—not as though he were bragging, but as if he were stating facts.

"To this man, Running Wolf owes his life," he called out. "He will be my friend. I will defend his life with mine." Then he gave Rayne the greatest gift he could as he continued, "His pride is my pride, and his honor is mine."

Although Rayne didn't know it at the time, it meant that Running Wolf would answer for whatever Rayne did from that moment on. Rayne stood up, and Running

Wolf extended one hand, which Rayne took, and the other he placed on Rayne's shoulder.

Then loud, exultant shouts surrounded them, and, to Mack's amusement, Rayne was pulled into the dancing celebration. The women formed a circle outside the circle of men, and Falling Water watched with pleasure as the man she loved was honored.

When Rayne was pulled into the dance, she had smiled in happiness. Now, when the women were invited to join the men in celebration, she made her way close to Rayne, who was laughing and finding the stomping dance rather difficult to master.

The entire evening was an experience Rayne enjoyed completely, and both he and Mack were in a state of total exhaustion when they fell onto their sleeping mats much later that night.

Both men awoke early, and food was brought to them almost immediately. It was obvious to them that they were being watched and that all in the tribe wanted to make their stay enjoyable. Even when they moved about the village, they could sense a new regard.

A great deal of strenuous activity took place throughout the village as the buffalo that had been killed on the hunt were transformed into necessities for the entire tribe. For drums and rattles for ceremonial purposes to tepees, moccasins, and clothing, every inch of the buffalo was constructively used. The Indians truly revered the animal for the variety of gifts it bestowed upon them.

There was to be a gathering of the council that night, and Rayne mentally prepared to be questioned by the

178

men who governed the tribe. All the women were so busy that Rayne had no chance to speak to Falling Water alone. He was at a loss over what to do with the day until Mack suggested they ride out to examine the problem of the valley more carefully.

They rode slowly, unaware that they were silently being followed. Before them was a magnificent valley, one that would be able to sustain the people who lived in it for generations. Both Rayne and Mack could see why White Eagle's tribe loved it so. Its rivers were clear and cool, and fish and animal life abounded. Yet they could not understand why Chevington and the men surrounding him wanted the valley so badly. It was a small area in a vast land.

"Rayne, there's got to be a reason we just don't know. There're a lot of valleys out here. Why are they so bent on this one?"

"I wish I knew," Rayne said softly. "I'd do something to stop them."

"We've come a lone way. Let's stop and water the horses, take a rest, then start back," Mack suggested, and Rayne nodded in agreement.

They dismounted and let the horses drink. To stretch their legs, they walked companionably along the stony riverbank. Just before they turned back to remount and ride back to the village, Mack bent to grab up pebbles from the shore and began tossing them, one after another, into the water. Suddenly he froze.

"Holy God," he whispered as he studied the small pebble in his hand.

"What is it, Mack?"

"I'll be damned!" he exclaimed. "I've got a feeling I

179

know just why they want this valley."

Wordlessly he handed the small stone to Rayne, who studied it carefully. Then his face paled.

"Gold," he said softly. They exchanged apprehensive glances, unaware that the one who watched them had remounted his horse and was already heading back to the village.

Chapter 13

Both Rayne and Mack were stricken by the knowledge. For a moment, they gazed at each other in silence, as the full impact of their discovery filled their minds.

"Somebody somewhere has found out there's gold here," Mack said.

"Chevington," Rayne replied quickly.

"And whoever's behind him."

"I don't suppose they've told anyone else or this valley would be alive with gold-hungry prospectors."

"No, they probably want it all for themselves."

"Mack, that would mean . . ."

"That would mean that somehow they would have to get possession of this valley."

"You and I know he'd have to kill White Eagle and all his people to do that."

Their eyes held. "Do you believe he wouldn't?" Mack asked.

"No," Rayne replied. "Mack, do you think White Eagle and his people know this gold is here? Do you think that's why they don't trust us—because they think we're here because of it, too?"

"I wouldn't be surprised. They probably think we're here to spy out things for Chevington."

"But we told them we were sent by Senator Miles."

"Does that mean they have to believe us?"

"No," Rayne answered quietly, "I don't suppose it does. Mack, I've got to convince them. If I'm going to stay here, I've got to win their trust. I wonder if they're waiting for us to make some move toward the gold so they'll know for sure?"

"What are we going to do, Rayne?"

"Go back, go to that council meeting, and tell White Eagle and everyone else that we know about the gold and we don't give a damn. We've got to tell them that we are what we said we are."

"And if they don't choose to believe us?"

Rayne held Mack's questioning eyes. "I don't want to think about that. It would mean I'd never have Falling Water and I'd never be able to stay here. One way or another, Mack, I have to convince them . . . I have to."

"Then let's get started."

Rayne put the gold in his pocket, and they both remounted and started back toward the village.

Josiah, an expert at tracking, had followed Rayne and Mack. He had watched them leave the village, and his curiosity had been stirred. He had had no trouble following them and had watched intently as they had walked along the river. He had known at once what had drawn their attention. It was something he had felt Sun Knife and White Eagle should know immediately, and he had ridden back to the village quickly.

He dismounted in front of White Eagle's tepee and requested permission to enter. Once inside, he spoke rapidly to White Eagle, whose grim face told of his worry.

"I saw them pick something up," Josiah said. "It was very nearly in the same place I found the gold. I watched them talking, and, though I couldn't hear them, I'd bet they were talking about it."

"There's now no doubt in my mind that they know," White Eagle said. "The only question is how long they have known about it. Did they discover it just now, or did they know of it before they came here. Go, Josiah, and tell Sun Knife and Running Wolf what you have seen. Tell them we are to keep our silence until the council meets." He added quietly, "I am eager to see if they say anything about it. Now is the time we will learn the truth."

Josiah nodded and left, going to Sun Knife first and then to Running Wolf. The cloak of silence was in place, and no one would dare speak until White Eagle did.

Rayne and Mack rode back into the village. Rayne was impatient for the council to meet, and he would have given almost anything to be able to talk to Falling Water, even if only for a moment.

Despite what custom decreed, Rayne began searching for Falling Water. He had decided he must talk to her, no matter what it cost. He found her in the huge tepee that Sun Knife and Lauren had made into a hospital. She was working with her mother, cleaning it.

He stepped inside and looked about. There were sleeping mats lining each side of the huge tepee. Some were occupied, but many were not. Other than the few who reclined on the mats, Lauren and Falling Water were the only two present. They both turned to look at him

183

when he came in.

Lauren was quickly aware of the magnetism that drew her daughter's widening eyes to the tall, handsome white man. She saw their gazes lock and could feel him mentally reach for Falling Water.

"Good morning." Rayne spoke to both of them, but his eyes never left Falling Water, who remained silent.

"Good morning, Rayne." Lauren smiled. "Are you ill, or is this just a pleasant visit?"

"I'm fine. I'd . . . I'd like to talk to Falling Water for a minute if I may."

Both women were aware that Running Wolf would strenuously object to this, but Lauren read her daughter's face well.

"Go, Falling Water. I will finish here. There is not much left to do."

Falling Water's quick smile was reward enough for Lauren, and she watched Falling Water move quickly to Rayne's side.

"Can we walk for a while?" he questioned. Falling Water nodded, and they left the tepee. They strolled across the center of the village and out to the trees that bordered the area. Once beneath the trees and out of sight of the village, Rayne took Falling Water's hand in his, knowing quite well that public demonstrations between a man and woman were frowned upon. He held her hand possessively as they walked slowly.

"Is there something wrong, Rayne?" Falling Water inquired.

"Does there have to be something wrong for me to want to be alone with you for a while?"

"No . . . but I can feel it. Something worries you."

Beneath the shade of a tall tree, they stopped. Without

184

another word, he drew her into his arms. Their lips met in a deep, fulfilling kiss, and she lifted her arms to cling to him. He sighed deeply as she rested her head against his chest, and, for a few brief moments, he was content to hold her close.

Falling Water closed her eyes and allowed herself to be filled with the contentment Rayne's arms always held. She could feel their strength and safety and knew she always would.

Gently he lifted her chin, and his eyes smiled down into hers. He brushed her lips lightly with a tender kiss. "God, I wish you were mine," he whispered. "I wish I could take you to our own tepee right now and make love to you . . . hold you."

"I know," she replied, "for I feel the same. I think of you when we are separated, and I grow warm with the memories of your touch."

Rayne groaned, then laughed softly as he rocked her against him. "You don't do anything for my self-control, my love. Please remember I'm not the strongest man in the world. I need you. Every minute of every day the need grows stronger. I wish to God your father would make up his mind. I know if you were mine, I would not want to let you go, but I can't stand this waiting and wanting."

"Rayne?"

"What?"

"There is more troubling you. What is it?"

"Do you know me so well already?"

"I can feel what you feel," she whispered softly. "I love you, and love senses many things."

"I have to go in front of your council tonight."

"Does that worry you?"

185

"No, not exactly." He held her away from him, then reached into his pocket and took out the nugget of gold. He held it in the palm of his hand. "Do you know what this is, Falling Water?"

She looked at the object, then looked up at Rayne. "It is a very pretty stone."

"No, my love, it's not a stone. It's trouble for your chief, your valley . . . and maybe for us."

"What trouble can this stone cause, Rayne?"

"This is gold, Falling Water."

Gold! The word crashed upon her senses. She had heard the same words spoken within White Eagle's tepee. She had heard of the lust white men had for this yellow metal. She had also heard Rayne's name used in connection with this gold. Was it the real reason he was here? Was he looking only for what this valley could offer? And, worse, was he using her to get to these strange golden pebbles?

"Gold," she whispered. "Yes, I have heard of this gold. I have heard how it twists the heart of the white man until he would do anything to get it—anything!"

Her eyes sparkled with fury and mistrust, and his comprehension of her thoughts hit him like a physical blow. She believed he was using her to get at the gold! his mind screamed.

He reached for her, but she brushed his hand away.

"No! Don't touch me. You need not use me any longer. It is not necessary. You need only take the yellow stones and go." Her anger was her only shield against the pain that tore through her.

"You believe that is what I came here for?" he demanded. "You are a fool if that is what you think. I found the gold some time ago. I could have gathered all I wanted and left."

Tears stung her eyes, and he could clearly read doubt. He snaked out an arm and grabbed her before she was able to get away. She fought like a wildcat, but her strength was hardly a match for his. He pulled her arms behind her and pinned them effectively with one hand. The other tangled in her hair to hold her immobile.

"I will hate you always," she snarled. He grinned maddeningly.

"No, love, I'm not going to let you hate me. I love when you're loving me too much."

"I will not listen to your lies."

"Words lie," he said gently. "This does not."

He bent his head to capture her unwilling lips with his. She struggled desperately in his arms, moaning softly with the onslaught to her senses. Tenderly his mouth savored hers despite her attempts to pull free.

Her body refused to obey her commands. It came alive in his arms, and a boiling cauldron of desire within her made her weak.

His lips left hers to find more sensitive and vulnerable spots that swept a current through her like white-hot lightning. Every sinew and bone in her body felt as if it were melting.

"Rayne . . . no . . ."

"Oh, yes," he murmured. "I know what we have is too special to trade for gold. I need to convince you, it seems. Falling Water, I love you." He released her and caught her face between his hands, forcing her to look into his eyes.

"I love you, and nothing—nothing, not your valley, your gold, or anything anyone could offer, could take your place. Listen to me. I will stay here with you always.

The gold means nothing to me, but you mean my life. I can't lose you, because you would take with you everything worthwhile."

Again he touched her mouth with his, in teasingly soft kisses that stirred her need and breached any defenses that might have remained. She could not resist the power he held over her. She relaxed against him, and her arms circled his waist. A sigh of relief and pleasure came from him as he wrapped his arm about her and held her close, rocking her gently in his arms.

"Will you listen to me now? Will you let me try to explain what this means to us?"

"To us?" she whispered.

He chuckled. "Yes, my love, to us."

"Then explain to me," she replied, tipping her head to look up at him.

Rayne explained the white man's lust for gold. Then he made clear to her what would happen in her valley if the gold were discovered. He watched her eyes widen as the full impact of his words came to her.

"But no one need tell the white man that it is here. No one but . . ." She paused and her eyes sought his.

"No, I would never tell anyone," he stated, answering her unspoken question. "Do you believe me?"

"Yes, I believe you. We need not worry. If they are not told, they will not come here."

"Listen, Falling Water," Rayne said. He took her shoulders and held them firmly as he went on to explain what he felt her chief, her father, and Sun Knife suspected about his and Mack's presence in the valley. "They might be thinking we were sent, maybe to see if there is gold, maybe to find out if White Eagle knows it, maybe to see how strong he is and . . . just how they

188

could take this valley from him."

"No one would take this valley from us," she replied proudly. "It is ours, and we would fight to protect and hold it."

"I know that," he said quickly. "I've got to convince White Eagle and the council that I'm telling the truth. But I've also got to convince them just how dangerous this gold is and how they've got to keep it a secret and be prepared to defend their valley."

"White Eagle is a very wise chief, and Sun Knife and my father will understand. They will listen to your words."

"You have more faith in my ability than I do."

"You are a white man with a Cheyenne heart. I can feel that you care, and I am sure you will convince my chief and my father that you are true. Already my father is a friend. He feels he owes you much. He will listen with an open heart."

"Do you understand why I did not claim you as a reward for what I did?"

"My father's pride means much to me also. I would have been disappointed in you had you done so. Now he will be able to see, to believe, when you speak."

"I hope you are right, Falling Water. A lot depends on it."

She smiled. "I know I am right about you." She reached up and placed a hand on each side of his face. "My love for you is so great that sometimes I can hardly contain it and I want to shout it aloud so all can hear and know of my happiness. I wait only for the moment when I belong to you and we can begin our life together."

Rayne drew her back into the circle of his arms and bent to take her warm, moist lips with his. With a soft groan, half agony, half pleasure, he bound her close to him, and the kiss deepened until both were lost in its swirling depths. One hand held her head, his fingers tangling in her dark hair, while the other slid possessively down her back to her soft, rounded hips and drew her more firmly against him.

He savored her sweet, willing surrender as he felt her move against him, his heart singing with the knowledge that her need was as great as his. Though they both realized this was not the time or place to consummate their desire, they relished its sweet promise.

Reluctantly, he released her lips, but still he held her close to him. He felt the rapid flutter of her heart and the gentle pressure of her arms about him. He was engulfed by a feeling of completeness that left him without words.

He caressed her silken hair and closed his eyes. Silently they held each other, both hoping that the time would come when they would not have to separate.

"We must return," he whispered against her hair. "I do not want your father to have any reason to be angry with me."

He heard her soft laugh, and it took all of his self-control to move her away from him. He could see the laughter and the mischief in her eyes, and he had to laugh with her.

"Don't tempt me, my love. I'm nearly at the point where I could say, 'To hell with everyone else in the world,' and take you right here. Now, be a good girl, and let's go back." He took her hand in his and they laughed and talked together as they slowly walked toward the village.

* * *

Rayne and Mack were both chafing under the strain of the long wait until evening and the concern about what they would say. They ate the evening meal that was brought to them by the older woman who had been given the task of cooking their food. Then they waited for the beating of the drum that would call the men to council.

When they heard the sounding of the drum signaling the beginning of the meeting, they knew that soon White Eagle and the elders would speak, and then they would finally be summoned.

It was well over an hour before a young warrior came to tell them that they were to come, that the council awaited their presence. They walked toward the large council tepee without speaking, and silently prayed that what they had to say would be understood and accepted, just as they desired to be accepted.

They were motioned inside, and, once within, they stood and gazed at the grim and silent faces surrounding them. At that moment it looked to Rayne as if they didn't stand a chance.

White Eagle rose, and, to Rayne, he had never looked larger or more imposing. Sun Knife, Running Wolf, and Josiah sat nearby, their faces as impassive as all the others.

"You have asked to speak at this council," White Eagle said. "You have things in your heart you wish to say. Now speak."

Rayne took one last look at Mack, then resolutely began to speak. He told them the reasons for his being sent by his white chief. He told them he had learned to respect their ways and their people and wanted to live among them. He told them he wanted to take back word that the people of White Eagle desired peace, and that afterward he wished to return to the valley and make it his home. All this met with a very impassive silence.

Silently White Eagle prayed that the white visitors would be honest and tell the truth about the gold. Sun Knife and Josiah mentally echoed his prayer, for they knew that, without the truth, Rayne and Mack would find themselves firmly ejected from the village.

"I must speak to White Eagle and his people of another thing, a thing which I just discovered and a thing that could bring disaster to this village. Sun Knife, you will understand more than any others the greed of some whites. We are not all the same, but, just as among you live some black hearts, so among us live some."

He reached into his pocket and took out the gold nugget. He held it up for all to see, not knowing that White Eagle and Sun Knife had already informed the council of his discovery. There was an audible murmur, and Rayne was aware that a strange emotion seemed to be sweeping over them—as if they were breathing a collective sigh of relief.

"This is gold. To you it means little, but to the greedy white man it means wealth and power. They would come here, fight you, kill you and your women and children if necessary, to get this. I am trying to warn you to protect yourselves, to keep the white man from your valley. I can only do that if you trust me. I can tell the white chief what he needs to know, so that he can keep the white invaders from coming.

"I ask for your trust. I will keep my word as will my white chief. When I have made your valley safe, then I will ask permission to marry and live among you. My heart is here, and I would help you fight any danger that comes. I am a strong warrior, and I would add my strength to the tribe of White Eagle . . . and I would add my strength to the family of Running Wolf."

Rayne looked about him, noting that the faces seemed more friendly; yet no one spoke. Then Running Wolf stood.

"I will speak for this man, for I know his strength. He has given me my life, and I will defend his honor."

It was a significant speech, for Running Wolf was a highly respected warrior, and the fact that he had added his voice to Rayne's carried a great deal of weight in the council. Now all eyes turned to White Eagle, who rose slowly to face Rayne.

"Josiah brought us word of the gold in our valley. He also told us what it would mean to the white man. We listened to your words before and wanted to trust you, but trust does not come easily, for we have been betrayed before. Josiah followed you this morning. He knew you had found the gold. We waited to see if you would speak the truth to us."

"You were testing us?"

"Yes."

"And if we had said nothing about the gold?"

"Then we would have known you lied, and we would no longer have listened to your words. We would have sent you from our valley."

Rayne stood frozen and speechless, realizing how close he had come to losing everything he wanted. He could even feel the perspiration on his skin. "White Eagle, I speak the truth. Mack and I want only to help you. Word of this gold will not come from us. But we are afraid there is someone who already knows. We must be prepared to protect the valley . . . and we must be prepared to protect the woman who owns the valley, the wife of Running

Wolf, for surely these greedy men desire her death."

"Who?" questioned White Eagle quietly, and Rayne knew the naming of names was the final test.

"John Chevington, Martin Preston, and any they might have hired to carry out their dirty plans."

White Eagle nodded, and a satisfied smile touched his face. He looked at every man and received a slight nod from each. Then he turned to Rayne. "Stay in our village. You are welcome to live among us for as long as you like."

Rayne couldn't remember when he had felt so happy about anything in his life. White Eagle gripped his shoulder in a sign of brotherly friendship. It signaled the end of the council, and all rose to go. Just outside, Running Wolf turned to speak to Rayne.

"I am very pleased you have become one of us. You have asked for Falling Water, and I have made a decision."

"What is it?" Rayne asked, hoping the fear and anxiety he felt wasn't obvious in his voice.

"It is only right that what I say should be between us only. Come to our tepee tomorrow and we will speak."

Rayne wanted to curse at the delay, but instead he smiled as best he could. He missed the sparkle of amusement in Running Wolf's eyes at being able to make Rayne squirm for another day.

Mack joined Rayne, and they went back to their tepee. It was a long, dream-filled night for each of them, and Rayne was quite happy to see the rising of the sun.

It was after the midday meal that Rayne walked to Running Wolf's tepee. When he had gained permission to enter, he was welcome within. Lauren and Falling Water were not present, and Rayne's heart sank, for he felt sure this meant that Running Wolf had decided against them. He sat opposite Running Wolf, the small fire between them.

"I have watched you since you have joined us. You are a good hunter, a good horseman, and a strong warrior. Last night I also found out you are an honest man," Running Wolf began. Rayne didn't speak; he did not even know if Running Wolf expected an answer. "My daughter is a good woman. She," he said quietly, "will make you an excellent wife."

Rayne wasn't sure he had heard right and sat immobile for a moment while surprise and amusement touched Running Wolf's face.

"You . . . you agree?" Rayne finally asked, his smile of sheer pleasure making Running Wolf laugh. "Running Wolf," Rayne inquired happily, "how soon can the wedding be?"

"You are not a very patient man," Running Wolf remarked with a grin.

"Not in this case. I'm afraid something will happen, and she'll be gone."

"The wedding will be at the next full moon."

"Running Wolf," Rayne said seriously, "I will be a good husband to Falling Water. I swear, neither you nor she will regret this."

"I hope not, Rayne," Running Wolf answered just as seriously, "for if you are not . . . if my daughter suffers any pain at your hand"—His voice became firm—"you will answer to me."

There was no doubt in Rayne's mind that Running Wolf meant exactly what he said. "Can I see Falling Water?"

"She is not here now. When she returns, I will

tell her."

Rayne knew that he was being dismissed, and he left. He was deliriously happy, and he wanted to share his joy with Falling Water, but he couldn't find her.

The afternoon passed into night. Rayne walked the path to the meeting place he and Falling Water had often shared. He hoped she would sense his feelings and come to him. He had just arrived when he heard her voice calling to him. He turned and saw her running toward him.

He scooped her up in his arms, and they both laughed and kissed each other as he spun her around, letting her dark hair flow about him. He kissed her over and over until she was breathless, then he set her on her feet. As he captured her face between his hands, he saw the tears of joy in her eyes.

Such a surge of love filled him that he could barely speak. He touched her lips gently with his own once more. "You are mine, Falling Water," he whispered, "mine—and I will love you forever."

Chapter 14

The throbbing of drums generated as much vital spirit as an Indian's heartbeat. To mark the wedding of the daughter of one of their favored subchiefs, the drums beat in a rhythm of celebration. Songs also accompanied the wedding preparations, songs that did not necessarily need words to convey their meanings. Sung by the women, these high-pitched, trilled melodies inspired joy throughout the entire tribe.

Rayne wanted to be part of the Cheyenne, so he insisted that the marriage ceremony be performed as if he were. He was instructed, and he followed each direction carefully. This too brought him the tribe's respect, for the Cheyenne were impressed that he accepted their ways. Yet he did so more for Falling Water than for anyone else's benefit. He sincerely wanted a happy wife.

He sat in the sweat lodge and felt the cleansing steam from water poured over hot rocks. He had been told that Falling Water would do the same. Afterward, he bathed in an icy stream. Then he dressed in the clothes Falling Water had made for him in the days before the wedding.

It was a custom that had pleased him, and a smile lit his face as he recalled how she had shyly come to him and given him the shirt and pants over which she had labored.

The clothes were fashioned of well-tanned buckskin, soft to the touch, fringed, and beaded in beautiful designs. He wore them with pride as he walked to the tepee of White Eagle, where they would be married.

He waited outside for Falling Water, and his eyes filled with the pleasure he felt when he saw her being brought to him.

Her father led the dark horse that Rayne had given her. Though it would be returned to him with his bride, Rayne had insisted that the stallion would always be hers.

Falling Water stood beside him, and he looked down into her dark eyes and felt a deep sense of gratitude toward whatever powers were responsible for bringing them together. She was so beautiful it took his breath away. They were called inside to face the oldest medicine man of the tribe, who would join them. Most of the ceremony was chanted in the Cheyenne language, very little of which Rayne understood, yet he could feel Falling Water beside him, and her presence was all that mattered to him.

Then the ceremony was over, and the celebration began. Rayne had seen some ceremonies, and Mack had explained certain others, but this was something special. It was loud, colorful, and exciting. More food was served than he had ever seen offered at one time, and the good will and happiness everyone shared with the new bride and groom caused all to draw closer together.

The moon was high, and Rayne had begun thinking of the tepee he and some newly acquired friends had built in a secluded spot, where he and Falling Water would spend the first few days of their married life. Rayne was wondering just how soon he could get his bride away from the crowd to be alone with her. Time passed and his patience wore thin. He resolved to take the first opportunity that presented itself. A few minutes later it came. He took her hand and drew her into the shadows. His horse had been saddled and stood with hers. They mounted in silence and rode away from the celebration toward a place of peace and love that was theirs to share.

She stood beside the tepee, watching him while he cared for the horses. He is so handsome, so strong, she thought, and I love him so much. She inwardly prayed for the ability to keep him happy.

He walked toward her, and suddenly she felt shy and just a little frightened. It surprised her, for they had been together often. Yet this was somehow different, and she wondered if he would sense the difference too. He stopped closer to her, and she smiled, for the tenderness she saw in his eyes told her he did.

He reached out and gently caressed her long, dark hair. "You're so very beautiful," he said softly. "It is still hard for me to believe that you chose to marry me. I will never cease to wonder at my good fortune and"—he smiled—"I will never cease loving you . . . never."

She came into his open arms willingly, now unafraid. It was the natural place for her to be, and they both knew it. Their lips met in a gentle, promising kiss that slowly warmed as his arms tightened about her. "I have followed all your customs," he whispered, smiling down at her. "Now I will show you one of mine."

"A white man's custom?" She laughed. "Here?" He nodded, then he bent and lifted her in his arms.

"It's a custom for a groom to carry his bride over the

threshold of their first home. It's to assure good luck. I don't intend for us to share anything but good luck, so I'm taking no chances."

He easily carried her slim body inside. Once there, he held her while he pressed his lips against the soft skin of her throat. Her arms clung to him as slowly he let her feet touch the earth floor.

The world was lost to them. They felt no need to hurry, for they had a lifetime to share. With gentle touches and lingering kisses, they helped each other remove restricting garments. Both were eager to learn everything about the other. Sensitive fingers reached to touch, to explore, and they moved to the soft fur sleeping mats without realizing where they were.

Falling Water knew only the magical way he touched her senses. She reveled in the masculine scent of his warm body, the touch of his large hands that seemed to find every vulnerable spot until she moaned with the ecstatic need that demanded she draw him to the depths of her. His lips found hers again after a heated journey that set her body trembling. It was a deep kiss that muffled the sound of her pleasure as he entered her, filled her, and possessed her completely. It was a mutual possession, for he no longer knew anything but the flame that ached inside him to be quenched. There was no thought except that this joining was the ultimate fulfillment.

He moved hard and powerfully, and she met each thrust with the sweetness of her own giving. Higher and higher they flew until a joyous and violent culmination left them with only the ability to cling to each other until jagged breathing ceased and thundering hearts quieted.

He spoke gently, tender words of the wonder they had

shared, all the while caressing her trembling body. Again his lips were soft and warm against her skin as he calmed her and drew her close to him. His words and exquisitely gentle touch relaxed her, and, after a time, she slept.

Rayne lay awake long after, content as he had never been before, and unable to relinquish his treasured pleasure to seek sleep. Finally the night waned, and, in the early dawn, with the soft sound of light-falling rain, he too slept.

The following week would remain engraved within his heart for all time. Falling Water came to him with laughter and with moods that changed with the moments, and each mood became special to him as he watched her blossom before his eyes into a woman of rare beauty and insight.

They were in their own world, untouched by others, and they wanted to hold each moment. They swam in the rivers and frolicked like children in the bright summer sun.

Sometimes she would be involved in preparing his meal or some other chore and look up to find his eyes upon her. Their smiles would reach out to each other. He enjoyed watching her graceful, golden body and the way the sunlight touched her hair, turning it a glowing ember.

Rayne prayed that all would be well in their world. He planned to return to Washington, tell Senator Miles all that had transpired between the Indians and Chevington in the past, and report that White Eagle was drawing some of the tribes together for their own protection. Also, he would assure the senator that they had no plan to attack the whites.

The gold would be a secret between him and the Cheyenne tribe, and he would never speak of it. He only hoped that no other whites, especially Chevington or Preston, knew for certain the gold was there. The fact that so far they had sent no one seemed a good sign.

He would ask Senator Miles to somehow protect these Indians who only wanted peace and the opportunity to live in their valley with no outside interference.

The week drew to a close much too quickly for both of them. Reluctantly, they packed everything and went to rejoin the tribe.

Life eased into a slow-moving routine, and Rayne and Falling Water were more than happy. So content were they with each other, that only gradually did they become aware of the fact that a few others about them were not so satisfied. One was Mack and the other was Lone Star.

Mack refused to say anything, and Rayne would not push him to talk of what he chose to keep to himself. Mack had again stated his plans to return to Washington before the snows fell and he was forced to remain in the village for the duration of the winter. Rayne could get no more information from him, despite many subtle attempts.

Ever sensitive to Mack's feelings, Rayne also became aware of Lone Star's plight. He remembered the first time he had noticed her eyes watching Little Eagle, and similar situations that he had witnessed enforced his suspicion that Lone Star was in love with Little Eagle. He wondered how much longer it would be before the handsome son of Sun Knife realized this himself.

New riders came to the camp, bringing word that no sign of Thomas could be found in any of the other villages or along the trails they had followed. It was a thing that puzzled both Rayne and Mack. "Alive or dead, there should be some sign of him. A man doesn't just disappear," Rayne said. "And if he wasn't killed or hurt when we were attacked, then I've got a lot of unanswered questions."

"Yeah, and I do too," Mack agreed. "You don't suppose the boy knew who attacked us?"

"God, I'd hate to think that, Mack."

"He's Preston's son. Maybe he's not the kid you thought he was. Maybe that was his father's reason for suddenly letting him go along with us."

Rayne contemplated this for a moment, then he shook his head negatively. "I don't believe it. I'd stake everything on the fact that the kid was honest. There's some other reason why we haven't found him. He's just not the kind of person his father is."

"Family runs deep, Rayne. Maybe he didn't always agree with his father, but they're still the same flesh and blood."

"He wasn't the kind that could set us up to be killed, Mack. He might have gone so far as to spy for his father, but not murder—I just don't believe that."

"Well, maybe that's true. White Eagle says he'll send another search party out for the boy. I hope you're right, Rayne, but, just in case, you'd better consider one other thing."

"What?"

"You know how important your family is in Washington. Suppose that kid goes back and tells them Rayne Freeman was ambushed and killed by bloodthirsty Indians. What sort of a thing do you think that will brew up?"

"They weren't Indians."

"We know that, but the kid probably doesn't. It would give Preston and Chevington one hell of a good excuse to come out here and start a fight in this valley. You and I both know how that would end."

"Well, Mack, we've got to try to find Thomas, and, when you and I get back, we'll tell the truth. That should take the wind out of their sails."

"I hope you're right."

"Mack?"

"What?"

"Are you coming back here with me?"

"Well, I've been thinking of riding up to the Platte to check out the trapping up there for the winter."

"Why not trap right here? There's a lot of beaver and—"

"Rayne, I . . . I just think it would be better if I go."

"I don't understand, Mack. We've been trapping together a lot of years. It's a trapper's paradise here, the villagers want you to stay, and I sure don't want to split up."

"I guess . . . I guess I can't explain. You'll just have to understand, Rayne. It's going to be the best thing if I go now. I'll drop by after the snow goes"—he grinned—"maybe in time to be godfather to any kids that might come along. That little girl looks pretty happy with you."

"I hope so." Rayne chuckled. "I hope I can keep her happy."

"Yeah." Mack laughed in response. "You're outnumbered here. She starts to cry and you might start to bleed. I've had a good look at her daddy's way with a lance, and I wouldn't want him unhappy with me."

They laughed together, but Rayne knew that Mack had

deftly dodged all the questions in Rayne's mind, questions he had no intention of answering.

Three men on horseback accompanied a wagon as it rolled slowly along a dry, rutted road. In the back of the wagon, on a thick pad of blankets, Thomas groaned and struggled to open his eyes. For a moment such an action seemed nearly impossible, for the pain in his head made looking at the sunlight almost too much to bear.

He was completely disoriented, unable to pull any thoughts together coherently. Where was he . . . and why did he feel so much pain and little else? He reached up to feel his throbbing head and found it bound with cloth.

One of the men who rode alongside the wagon saw Thomas's movement. "Hey! Stop Jess! The kid's awake," he shouted.

The wagon came to a jerky halt that prompted a groan of misery from Thomas. Again the conveyance rocked as the man called Jess climbed up and knelt beside Thomas. "You awake, kid?" he asked.

Thomas groaned again. "I'm afraid so."

"I'm glad. You had us scared. We thought you weren't going to make it. You've been in and out for over three days."

"Wha . . . What happened? I . . . I don't understand or remember much."

"Your guardian angel must be tired." The man laughed. "You just survived an Indian massacre."

Suddenly the memory made Thomas's eyes grow wide, and he tried to sit up. "Rayne . . . Mack!"

The man's hands pressed against his shoulders to

gently push him back on the blankets. "Easy boy, easy."

"Where are they?"

"I'm afraid," the man said softly, "both of your friends are dead."

His words plunged through Thomas's misery and left a hot, new pain of their own. In the weeks he had known Rayne and Mack, they had treated him as a younger brother, and he had grown to care deeply for them both, especially Rayne, who had laughingly taken Thomas under his wing.

He had listened to their words when they had told him just how peaceful the Indians really were and how he would enjoy spending some time in their village. He had listened and believed, and now that belief came crashing down about him, leaving him with an anger to fill the empty space.

The man who knelt over him was quite satisfied with the look he saw in Thomas's eyes. It was exactly the look he had wanted to produce. Now, as they moved closer to home, he would fan that anger with false descriptions of Rayne's and Mack's violent deaths and other atrocities committed by the Indians, until Thomas's anger turned to hate. Once he had done this, he would release Thomas into a believing Washington society that would accept his "eyewitness" report without question.

Jess was quite familiar with the Freeman name, and he knew that reports of Rayne's violent death would stir up both anger and the results he and his associates in Washington wanted.

"Dead," Thomas replied softly. "It's . . . it's hard to remember."

"Take it easy. In a few days you'll feel better. Then maybe you'll remember. I . . . I can tell you how we

206

found you . . . and them."

"Tell me."

"Later, when we stop for the night. You need to eat and get some strength back. When we stop, we'll talk about it. Here, drink some water, then we'll ride on. We want to get close to some kind of civilization as soon as we can."

Thomas was too weak to argue, and the pain in his head had again reached such unbearable proportions that all he could do was close his eyes and pray silently that it would soon diminish.

Jess and the other men exchanged glances, satisfied that so far their ruse had gone as they had planned. Jess mounted his own horse again, and the group continued on their journey.

The rocking of the wagon made the pain worse for Thomas, and, after a while, he lost his hold on reality and once more drifted into a state of semi-consciousness.

It was long after dark when he awoke again. Now he was lying close to a crackling fire, and he discovered it had been the odor of food that had awakened him. After the three days he had been told he had been unconscious, he was ravenous.

Jess brought him a tin plate of food and helped Thomas to a sitting position, though not without a grunt or two of pain from Thomas.

"Good to see you awake again." Jess smiled. "How are you feeling?"

"I've felt worse." Thomas tried to grin. "It's just that I don't remember when."

Jess laughed as he handed Thomas the plate. "Eat. Maybe it will help."

Thomas began to eat slowly, and, as he did, he studied

Jess. He was an average-sized man, slim and, Thomas estimated, somewhere in his forties. He had thick, sandy hair and a mustache to match. His eyes were blue and seemed warm.

"What's your name, kid?" Jess asked amiably. "We didn't have the opportunity to ask you before."

"Thomas . . . Thomas Preston. I guess I owe you my life. I'm grateful."

"It's all rght. I'm glad we happened along when we did."

"You said . . ." Thomas began, thinking of Rayne and Mack.

Jess nodded, regret on his face. "There was nothing we could do for them, Thomas. They were already dead when we got there."

"Why didn't they kill me?"

"They probably thought you were already dead. I guess they would have taken your hair, except they must have heard us coming and ran."

"Taken my hair?"

"It's a way they have. When the Indians kill, they butcher a man by taking his scalp. It's a sign of bravery or something."

"Did they . . . ?"

"Get to your two friends? I'm afraid so."

"God . . ." Thomas muttered, then his eyes met Jess's. "Tell me what happened."

This was the opportunity for which Jess had been waiting. In a low voice, he described to Thomas the most brutal and bloody scene he could conjure. He added details of bloodthirsty tortures that greyed Thomas's face and filled his eyes with the kind of horrified terror he wanted Thomas to carry back to Washington with him.

Thomas set aside his empty plate. "Jess, Mack told me how he had lived with these Indians, how they were . . . generous, kind, sort of family. Neither Rayne nor Mack was ever afraid. I don't understand. Why did they do it?"

"Thomas, I guess your friends never took it into consideration that these red bastards are unpredictable and sneaky. They say one thing and do another, and they'd just as soon kill if it's convenient as they'd extend a hand in friendship. Rayne and Mack—your two friends—they just got fooled by them. I guess . . . I guess they got fooled one time too often."

Thomas, too young and naïve about the ways of the frontier, believed Jess's explanation. It was difficult for Thomas, and Jess didn't want to push him. He knew he would have plenty of time to feed him similar ideas on the way to Washington.

It was time to back off and let Thomas consider everything that had happened. "You need all the rest you can get," Jess told him. "We're going to get an early start in the morning. I want to find a town as soon as possible and get you to some kind of doctor. Then me and my partners are on our way back to Washington."

"Washington?"

"Yes, Stark, my friend, and Russ have business there, and I'm going back to settle some things, then travel on up to Canada."

"Would you mind taking me along with you to Washington? My father's very wealthy—he'll make it worth your while—and I'd be grateful . . . again."

"Hell, kid, you don't have to pay me. If you want to ride along with us to Washington, come on."

"Thanks, Jess."

Jess nodded and stood up, prepared to return to his own blanket for some well-deserved sleep.

"Jess?"

"What?"

"My friends . . . did you . . . I mean, did you bury them?"

"Yeah, kid, we buried them."

"They were . . ."

"I know, kid. I've lost a few people I care for to these red heathens."

Thomas nodded, too crushed by his loss to see the look in Jess's eyes as he lay down to sleep.

Chapter 15

Thomas felt much better the next day, though he still had to ride in the wagon. Sitting on a horse would require more effort than his wounded head could handle.

After another two days, he began to see a definite improvement in his condition. Four days later, he claimed he was well enough to ride. For the first time, they saw signs of civilization as they approached a military fort, Fort Ramsey. There Jess made arrangements for Thomas to obtain a horse and the traveling equipment he would need. They spent three days at the fort, then headed east.

Several more days of rugged travel brought them to the first town that offered the luxury of the railroad. They took two adjoining rooms in a building that only remotely resembled a hotel. The next day they would board a train for the trip to Washington.

Jess and his friends were in the saloon drinking. Thomas had had a few drinks and had decided to go to bed. He lay across the bed and did manage to sleep for a while.

When he awoke, the room was dark except for the pale light of the full moon that filtered through the curtains to make weblike patterns across the floor. He turned over and looked around the room. The door between his room and Jess's was closed, but he could see a thin bar of light beneath it and knew Jess was still up.

Of late, he had been plagued by uneasy feelings and unexplainable nightmares. He sensed they were caused by the descriptions he had heard of the way Rayne and Mack had died. He needed to talk to Jess.

He rose and walked slowly across the room, his bare feet making no noise. He reached for the door handle and was stopped by the sound of voices on the other side. He would have turned and gone back to his bed but for the words that froze him in his tracks. He knew one voice was Jess's and the others were those of the men who had ridden with them.

"The kid believes every word you said, just like Chevington and Old Man Preston said he would."

"I don't understand"—Jess laughed—"how a snake like Old Man Preston got a kid like that one. He's a nice boy."

"Yeah . . . a boy. Preston has got a lot at stake out here. Once he has what he wants, he'll probably buy the kid anything he needs to take his mind off his problems."

Thomas was so overcome with crushing reality that he could not move. The conversation continued.

"At least he thinks it was Indians that killed his two friends and not us. Can you imagine how satisfied his old man will be when he starts telling his stories about those—what did you call 'em, Jess?—those bloodthirsty red savages. It will sound good in the papers, and it should stir up a lot of hate for those Indians."

212

It was almost impossible for Thomas to believe what he was hearing, and his thoughts were jumbled. These men—not the Indians—had killed Rayne and Mack. Now they planned to use him, his name, and his father's influence, to stir alive the red coals of hatred. His father . . . *his father* had deliberately planned this, had allowed him to be maneuvered—used—to destroy others, others who had been friends.

He didn't want to hear anymore. He was sick with the knowledge he had already obtained. As quietly as he could, he went back to his bed, but in doing so he made a noise that attracted the attention of the men in the next room. He was barely in bed when he heard booted feet approach the door. He closed his eyes and tried to breathe evenly. He could sense the man who stood in the lighted doorway, and it took every effort he had not to display the rage he felt at their deliberate use of his emotions.

The man stood for so long that Thomas was afraid he knew he was awake. It was with deep relief that he finally heard the door close softly again.

He folded his hands behind his head and tried to think. Everything within him was in turmoil. No matter what he had heard in the next room, he had no proof. He felt a black need rise within him to destroy all their well-laid plans and, in the process, the ones who had been responsible for the deaths of two he had learned to care for and respect.

It was too late to do anything for Rayne and Mack, so he decided to let them continue believing they had fooled him and to go on to Washington with them. At that moment, he wished he could look into his father's eyes. He wanted to see if his father was truly the kind of man who could do such a thing. He had to know. It seemed to him now that he had never really known his father.

Old, half-forgotten memories flashed through his mind, and slowly the Thomas he had been died. A new Thomas was born who saw with deeper insight, not only what he was now, but what his father had tried to make him. He also found the answer to why he had so desperately wanted to go with Rayne and Mack. He realized now that he had been running away from his father's influence, from the fact that his father had always bought him, never giving of himself but instead pushing Thomas in any direction that would best serve his own lust for power and money.

Thomas took a true look at himself and found himself wanting, found himself incomplete and hollow. Mentally he slowly began to pour into that hollowness all that he wanted to be. He knew there was only one way to complete himself. He had to finish what had been started, finish it so that he would be able to live with the deaths of Rayne and Mack. It was only after many more hours of deep, painful thought that he slept.

They rose for an early start the next morning. Thomas had regained his equilibrium and was able to keep his emotions and his anger to himself. If Jess and the others noticed any difference in him, they attributed it to the fact that he was nearing home and probably thinking of all he would say to the newspapers, the military, Congress, and his father.

Thomas stood before his father's mansion and looked

at it. He realized he had lived in this house all his childhood days and had never known a sense of loving peace that home was supposed to give a person.

Jess stood beside him and suddenly clapped Thomas on the shoulder. Thomas had to grit his teeth in order to keep smiling and not shrug away the friendly gesture.

"Your father will sure be pleased to see you alive and well," Jess remarked.

"Yes, I'm sure he will. It must be the last thing he expected," Thomas replied dryly.

Jess wasn't sure how to take this remark, so he simply shrugged. It didn't matter how Thomas felt. Jess had brought him home and eliminated the two with whom he had gone. He had done as Martin had told him, and he wanted payment. At Thomas's direction, they walked up the steps and through the huge doors.

Martin and Thomas's mother awaited them as they entered the large drawing room. Ruth Preston rose and ran to her son, who took her in his arms and embraced her warmly. She was a small, slim woman, and one person in the world who loved Thomas with no designs, no restrictions, just pure, giving love.

He held her close, knowing she was the only one present who was completely innocent of all that had happened. He looked down into her tear-filled eyes, kissed her gently, then turned to look at his father.

"Thomas, my boy"—his father smiled and walked toward him—"it is good to have you home. After that close call, I'm happy to know you're safe."

Thomas kept his arm about his mother's waist, not only because she was his only source of love, but also because he did not want to extend his hand to his father.

215

"Thank you, Father. It is good to be home."

"You must rest and get yourself together."

"I don't feel any need for rest. I'm fine."

"Nevertheless, you had better. You have a lot to do in the next few weeks."

"Oh? What do I have to do?"

"Thomas!" his father said in surprise. "You don't intend that those filthy savages get away with killing your two friends, do you?" Thomas threw Martin Preston a look that Martin could not understand, yet it made him uncomfortable.

"No," Thomas replied, "I don't want the killers of Rayne and Mack to get away with what they've done. I'm going to do everything in my power to stop them." Thomas's gaze was level with his father's, and Martin was surprised at the cool, composed look in the eyes of a man he had thought was merely a boy. For a moment, he thought he read some new, elusive purpose in the depths of Thomas's eyes, but the look was quickly replaced by nothing more than cool regard.

"That is good . . . that is good," Martin said. "I have arranged for you to talk to a few influential people tomorrow. If we get things started, we can facilitate a quick reprisal for their brutal, unwarranted attack upon you and your friends."

Thomas watched his father closely. He could see the almost fanatical gleam in his eyes, and he recognized the well-rehearsed words. "I cannot tomorrow, Father. I have some plans of my own to take care of. Besides, the pain of it is too fresh. I need a few days to organize myself and figure out just what I'm going to say . . . and to whom."

"Now, Thomas," his father said with cool authority. He was not used to anyone contradicting him, much less the boy he had raised in the shadow of his ambition. "You will know what to say. Just tell them how those savages attacked you with no reason. They will understand and know exactly what to do about it. I've made all the arrangements. The men will gather here and—"

"Father," Thomas interrupted firmly. Martin looked at him in surprise. "I'm not talking to anyone until I'm ready. I hope you understand that. I wouldn't want you embarrassed by inviting all those . . . influential people here when I refuse to talk to them. In a few days, I will know what I want to say, and that will be the only time I will say anything."

"Thomas, I don't understand you. The time to strike in any conflict is quickly. Now, I think—"

"But Father," Thomas said calmly, "this is not your conflict. It *is* mine, isn't it?"

Martin was temporarily shocked into silence.

Thomas continued. "I don't believe that what happened out there would concern you unless I had died. But I did not. I am here, safe and sound, and I will handle the telling of what happened at my own convenience and when I think the time is right."

There was rage in Martin's eyes at Thomas's thwarting his plans, and his face darkened in his effort to control it. He smiled his professionally cool, manipulative smile and shrugged his shoulders. "All right, Thomas. Maybe it is best that you relax for a while. That way there will be no part of what happened that you might forget. It was a destructive, brutal, bloody thing they did, and the right people should be told every detail so that they will

217

understand completely."

"Don't worry, Father." Thomas smiled, and again Martin was shaken by something new, strange, and even deadly in Thomas's smile. "When it is time for me to tell a story, I will tell it all, and I will tell the truth. I will also do it when I am sure the ones responsible will pay in full for what they have done."

"Very well," Martin replied. "I await your word."

"Good. Now, I think I will go up to bathe and change. There are some people I must meet this afternoon, and I don't want to be late."

Thomas started toward the door but was stopped by his father's voice, which seemed to be rather strained. "Who are you going to meet?"

Thomas turned about with a half smile on his lips. "Why, Mr. and Mrs. Freeman. I think they should know how their son died, and how much I cared for him . . . Don't you agree?"

"Yes . . . yes, of course," Martin answered. Thomas left the room, closing the door behind him. He did not immediately go upstairs. Instead, he walked to the room adjoining the one he had just left. Stepping inside and closing the door, he walked softly across the room to another door that opened into the room in which his father, Jess, and his mother remained. Gently, he turned the handle and pushed until a small crack allowed him to clearly hear their conversation.

"Ruth," Martin said smoothly, "why don't you see to a room for our guest. He will be staying a few days—" he turned to Jess—"won't you?"

"Yes, I'd be pleased to stay," Jess answered. Ruth rose from her chair, and Thomas could hear the soft murmur

218

of her voice and the rustle of her dress as she walked across the room. Then he heard the flick of the door as it closed behind her.

"Jess, did you let anything slip on the way back to give him any idea of the truth?" Preston blurted.

"You know me better than that, Martin. I didn't slip in front of him. He's no wiser now than he was when we found them."

"Damnit, he sounds as if he doesn't believe it. You're sure they were both dead?"

"They were dead, all right. Don't get so jumpy, Martin. The kid has no idea we killed them, and we filled him with enough butcher stories about them Indians to scare the hell out of him. When it comes time to talk, he'll tell them a story that will rile every one of them. That valley and the gold are as good as ours."

"I don't want anyone spoiling my plans now, especially my weak-hearted son. I want that valley, and I want that gold . . . and, most of all, I want Cade Holliday, his wife, White Eagle, and his family to be buried there before this is over. I also want Lauren Brent. I want the word spread that she and that half-breed daughter she had are to be brought to me. She has a debt to me, and I'm going to make her pay."

"Don't worry. Lauren Brent and her daughter—her name's Falling Water—will be brought to you. You can do whatever you want with them, because no one will know they were left alive or put in your hands."

"Good."

"Martin, talking about the Brents, what are you going to do about Alexander Brent's hold on that land?"

"You don't think I'm going to let that man interfere in

219

my plans, do you? Chevington has already arranged the future demise of Mr. Alexander Brent. Then the entire valley will belong to Lauren . . . and Lauren will belong to me."

"Did Chevington get the post at Fort Ramsey like you planned?"

"Did you doubt it? Despite the fight Senator Miles put up—and that damn shadow of his, Grant Jamison—we did it."

"What's Grant Jamison got to do with it?"

"He was once a good friend of Michael Holliday. He helped get that valley into the hands of the Brents. I can't reach him yet, but one day the opportunity will come along, and I'll crush him, just like I intend to crush his friends."

"Well, all we have to do now is wait a little while," Jess said. "Thomas will say what you want him to say, and, when he does, Chevington will be in a good position to take care of the rest. From here, we'll make sure Alexander Brent is out of the way and you can personally concern yourself with Lauren and her half-breed. Looks like we've got a pile of gold all tied up."

"Yes, there's a fortune out there, and it's not only in gold."

"Gold sounds pretty good." Jess chuckled.

"Jess, look ahead. We'll push those Indians out of that valley—kill them, all of them. The land will be worth another fortune, and one day . . . one day the railroad will extend, and, when it does, I want to own enough land to make millions. We can build our own private empire if we keep our heads and make our plans work."

"A fortune," Jess breathed softly, "a whole damn

fortune, and all that stands between it and us it a bunch of half-naked savages."

"Don't worry, if Thomas tells the story you fed him, those savages will soon be gone." Martin rose then, and Thomas could hear him walking across the room. There was the tinkle of glass and the sound of liquid being poured. Then he heard Martin retracing his steps, saying, "Here, Jess, have a drink. Let's drink to the end of that red nuisance and the beginning of our empire." Their glasses clinked together and Thomas could hear the sound of soft laughter.

Bitterness and black rage filled Thomas to the point where he had to restrain himself from breaking into the room and committing murder with his bare hands. It would do no good, he told himself, for he still had no actual proof.

But he had overheard one piece of information that gave him courage. Now he had names, names of his father's enemies, people he could contact who would understand and hopefully help. He knew Senator Christian Miles, and he vaguely remembered meeting Grant Jamison at one time. He would begin with them, and he would go as far as necessary to stop the vile plan that had been set in motion by the deaths of his friends.

Slowly, silently, he turned and tiptoed across the room, opened the door, and slipped out soundlessly. Then he turned and came face to face with his mother. He was shocked, but before he could say a word, Ruth put her finger to her lips in a silencing gesture and beckoned him to follow her.

He was surprised, yet he followed her, for it was obvious that she did not want her husband or their guest to overhear them. They climbed the stairs, and he followed her into his own room. After locking the door, she turned to face him. Her face was pale, and he could see she was trembling.

"Mother, what is it? What do you want to say to me?"

"Oh, Thomas, I'm not sure of anything anymore. I only know someone has to stop him. He is insane. He will kill—has already killed—so many."

"Father?"

"Don't call him that! I am sorry that I bore that man a child. It is only because I can see how you've changed that I talk to you at all. I was afraid for you, Thomas, afraid of what he might make of you. Now I see the light of compassion in your eyes, and I think it is your two dead friends who put it there. You must avenge their unnecessary deaths, my son, but only by seeking the men who are truly responsible."

Thomas walked to her, put his arm about her shoulder, and led her to his bed. "Sit down, Mother, and we'll talk. I have a feeling you can tell me many things I need to know."

"Yes. Oh, Thomas, you must listen to me; you must understand what you are dealing with. He is a cold, unfeeling man. He has robbed me of my life, and I will not let him do the same to you. I will not let him turn you into what he is."

Ruth Preston may have been a quiet, unassuming woman, but she was much more intelligent than her domineering husband thought her to be, for he had taken her shyness as stupidity. She had been a sweet, innocent girl of seventeen when the rumors of Martin and Lauren Brent had swept Washington. Then Cade Holliday had come along, and Lauren had followed him into Indian country.

Martin had then turned to Ruth, for her family had an excellent name. She had been frightened to death of him and had never known that he had used blackmail against her parents in order to make her his wife.

Her wedding night had been a horror, for he used her brutally and carelessly. He continued his despicable abuse, knowing there was no way out for her. She was forced to be his hostess and a bedmate he could beat and subjugate, all of which gave him a great deal of pleasure. Her pride caused her to remain silent even after she found out about his many mistresses.

She had loved Thomas completely and had been overjoyed when he returned her love. Yet she had begun to fear when he was younger that he would never be able to fight his father. Now, as she looked at the tall, handsome man before her and at the new strength in his steady gaze, she knew it was time he heard the truth.

Quietly, she began to speak, and Thomas listened until there were no more words to be said. He could now believe all she had said, for he had seen and heard first hand his father's iniquities. When she was finished, they were silent for a few moments. Then Thomas turned to her.

"Mother, we must do nothing for a few days. When I decide to make my move, is there a place you can go? I don't want you here where he can get to you."

"I have a sister in England. She married a sea captain. I could sail there and stay with her."

"Good. Make very quiet plans. When I tell you, I want you to be ready to leave. Can you do that?"

"Yes, I can. And I will. But what about you?"

"I'm going tonight to see Grant Jamison and ask him to go with me to Alexander Brent. The three of us will do everything in our power to stop what is happening."

They talked for a while and solidified their plans. Then Thomas left the house. First, he would go to see Rayne's family, and then he would begin to undo the tragedy his father's poisonous hatred and greed had begun.

Chapter 16

Thomas's carriage stopped in front of one of the largest and most elaborate homes in Washington. As he stepped out, he told the driver to wait for him.

He was reluctant to see Rayne's parents, but it was something he felt he had to do. He supposed it was part of his penance for being alive when their son and his friend were dead.

He walked up the steps to the front door and knocked. In a few minutes it was opened by the butler.

"Are Mr. and Mrs. Freeman at home?" Thomas inquired.

"Yes sir, they are. May I have your name, sir?"

"Thomas Preston."

"Come in, sir."

The butler ushered him into a cool and inviting reception area. The floor was tiled in black and white, and the black staircase curved out of Thomas's sight. White lace curtains, strategically placed red velvet chairs, and several green plants were the only touch of color. The butler instructed him to wait, then he disappeared through a set of double doors that opened into another room. The muted sound of soft voices reached Thomas's ears, then the butler reappeared. He bowed slightly, announcing, "Mr. and Mrs. Freeman are in the library, sir. They will see you there. Will you come this way?"

Thomas followed the butler to the doors, stepped inside the room, and saw four people gathered near the low-burning fire. He assumed that the older man and woman were Rayne's father and mother, but the tall man who stood by the fireplace startled him completely. It took a few moments for Thomas to realize that the man was not Rayne, for they could have been copies of each other judging from the breadth of the shoulders and thick, wine-colored hair.

The older man rose, and Thomas could see the source from which Rayne had acquired his looks. Rayne was only a younger version of the man who stood before him.

"Mr. Preston." Mr. Freeman smiled. "Come in. Won't you join us in an after-dinner brandy?"

"Yes, thank you." Thomas's courage was shaky, and he felt he could certainly use a brandy. During the time it took for Mr. Freeman to pour the brandy, Thomas gathered his thoughts. Then Rayne's father held out his hand to Thomas.

"I'm Steven Freemen. This is my wife, Amanda, our son, Greg, and his wife, Cassie."

Thomas took his extended hand in a firm grip, then shook Greg's. He bowed toward the two women.

"Please sit down, Mr. Preston." Amanda smiled.

"Thomas, . . . please."

"Thomas, I believe I know your father, Martin Preston," Steven said.

Thomas took a sip of his brandy. "Yes, I believe you do."

"Is there something I can do for you?"

"This . . . this is very difficult for me," Thomas began.

"It's Rayne, isn't it?" Greg questioned quietly, and Thomas's eyes rose to meet his. They were so much like Rayne's that his stare left Thomas shaken.

"Yes," Thomas replied. "It is."

Amanda seemed to stiffen, and her eyes grew wide. Steven reached over to take her hand in his. "Tell us," Steven said.

Thomas took another sip of brandy and began to tell his story. No one moved, no one seemed to breathe, and no one questioned him until he finished and the last words echoed hollowly in the now quiet room.

Tears touched Amanda's eyes and rolled down her cheeks, but she made no sound. Cassie too wept silently.

"Would you excuse us for a moment, Thomas," Steven said.

"I'll go . . ."

"No, stay," Greg said. "I would like to talk to you."

Thomas nodded and watched the two women as the men took them to another room, where they would share their pain and attempt to comfort each other. It was a little over half an hour later when Greg returned. He sat down opposite Thomas.

"I think," he said softly, "that you have more to tell me."

"Yes, I do."

"I'll get us another brandy," he said. He took Thomas's glass and his own and refilled both from a decanter. Then he returned and handed one to Thomas.

"My brother's death was no accident?"

"No."

"Who's responsible?"

"Will you listen to the rest of the story and to my plans if I tell you?"

"I'll listen."

Again, Thomas sipped the warming brandy, then he looked at Greg, who saw the pain in his eyes. Thomas sighed and said, "My father . . . Martin Preston." Greg sat perfectly still as disbelief appeared in his eyes. "It's true. I am ashamed and disgusted, and if you will let me continue, I will tell you just what I intend to do about it and why."

"Continue," Greg demanded, speaking through stiffened lips.

Thomas began at the very beginning and revealed all he knew, from the first day he had met Rayne and Mack to the present. "I know it will not bring back your brother," he told Greg, "but at least it will bring to justice the one who's responsible."

"This must be very difficult for you, too," Greg said. "I ask you only one thing."

"What?"

"Keep me informed of your progress. I want to know your plans, maybe take part in your justice."

"Of course I will keep you informed," Thomas said as he rose. "I have to leave now. I intend to see Grant Jamison tonight and start from there."

"I'll be waiting for word from you."

"I'll send word as soon as I know exactly what we're going to do."

228

Greg extended a hand and Thomas took it. "I'm sorry for any grief I've caused you and your family," he said.

"I believe that none of this was your fault, and if we can see to it that the guilty parties receive some kind of justice, then at least Rayne will not have died unavenged."

"I'm grateful for your understanding and forgiveness."

"Thomas, don't be so hard on yourself. I loved my brother, but I understood that he was a man who knew what he wanted. I think maybe," he said softly, "he died where he wanted to be. Go easy and forgive yourself. Don't let this hurt you."

"Thank you."

Greg escorted Thomas to the door and watched as he entered his carriage and it disappeared down the dimly lit street.

In the dark carriage, Thomas was finding it difficult not to weep as he struggled with the combined emotions of anger, hatred, gratitude, and guilt. The carriage moved down the quiet streets to a new destination. Thomas had just enough time to regain his composure before it stopped again.

Grant's home was a more modest edifice, though it seemed to Thomas both large and inviting. Thomas again told the driver to wait as he walked to the door and knocked.

It was Grant who answered the door, with a cigar in one hand, the evening paper in the other, and a welcoming smile on his face.

"Mr. Jamison, Grant Jamison?" Thomas asked.

"Yes, is there something I can do for you?"

229

"I'm Thomas Preston. Could I come in and speak with you, sir? It's of utmost importance. I have news of friends of yours, which might interest you."

Grant studied him for a moment. The Preston name was not a strange name to him, and he knew it only meant trouble. "Come in."

Thomas was ushered into a comfortable parlor. It was a cheerful room, and Thomas could sense the warmth of the family that lived in the house. The woman who sat near the fire was very beautiful. Grant came in behind Thomas and motioned for him to take a seat. "Mr. Preston."

"Thomas," he corrected, smiling hopefully.

"Thomas, this is my wife, Martha. Martha, my dear, this is . . . Thomas Preston." Thomas watched her eyes grow wary even though she smiled. "Won't you sit down, please. Can I get you anything . . . a drink?"

"No, no thank you. I . . . I would like to speak to you both of something very important to you as well as to me."

Grant sat beside Martha. "All right. Go ahead."

Again, Thomas stumbled through the entire story, watching Grant's face darken with anger at each word. When Thomas finished, a furious Grant rose to his feet.

"That damnable bastard! I'm sorry, Martha."

"It's all right, Grant. I think I feel the same."

"I'm sorry, too," Thomas said softly. "He is my father, and I feel the guilt he should be feeling. I cannot live with what he's planning to do. I must stop him."

Martha bent forward and touched his hand. "Every man carries his own guilt. You cannot carry his. The fact that you want to right his wrong shows us the kind of man you are. Do not condemn yourself for his deeds."

"You are most gracious," Thomas replied. "But . . . you do understand . . . I must do something. I cannot live with what he has done, or allow what he intends to do. I cannot." Thomas could see the sympathy and understanding in their eyes, and it only served to make him feel more guilty.

Grant sat down in a chair near Thomas. "Thomas, we will do all we can. In the morning I will go to Senator Miles. He is the one who has been suspicious of Chevington and your father all along. We'll all get together with Alexander Brent. One of us alone might not be very effective, but all of us together just might be able to stop them. I know it's a lot to ask, but can you keep your silence for another day? Tomorrow night we will all meet here. Then we can figure out the best way to proceed."

"My father wants me to talk to the newspapers and to some of his . . . friends," Thomas said bitterly.

"I'm sure he does. Can you hold off?"

"I can do anything I have to do. If he thinks I am going to be manipulated into provoking a massacre, he's sadly mistaken. A lot of lives depend upon my actions, and I have already been stupid enough to cause the deaths of two people I cared for. I don't intend to be responsible for any others."

"I don't think Rayne or Mack would blame you for what has happened. You were expertly set up. Don't berate yourself. Together we might be more effective than your father and his friends think possible."

"I hope so . . . I pray so."

Thomas rose, and both Martha and Grant walked with

him to the door. They watched as he waved and disappeared into his carriage.

"I feel sorry for him, Grant. It was bad enough that he lost his two friends, but to find out that his own father is responsible is a tragedy."

"Yes, it is," Grant agreed. "But I've an idea the boy is going to find that he has more iron inside than he or his father thought. It might be one of the biggest surprises Martin Preston has ever had."

Thomas entered his home quietly. The last person he wanted to see was his father. He walked up the steps and entered his room. The lamp was burning very low, and the room was filled with shadows. He closed the door and crossed to the lamp, turning the wick higher so that the room became bathed in mellow golden light. He turned about and froze, with shock and a touch of fear. His father sat in the wing chair by the window. He sat motionless, his eyes on Thomas's pale face.

"You've been out late," Martin said mildly. "I have to talk to you—have wanted to ever since your arrival—but it seems you've been extremely busy all evening." He smiled, and, for the first time in Thomas's life, he noticed that his father's smile went no further than his lips. It never touched his cold, penetrating eyes. "Of course, I expect your friends have been celebrating your return."

"Yes." Thomas returned the smile with a similar amount of sincerity. "They were anxious to find out what the frontier is really like."

"And of course you told them of the heathens that live there and their blood-thirsty ways."

"I really wasn't there long enough to be able to tell anyone what it was really like . . . You wanted to talk to

232

me about something?"

"Yes, I want to discuss some plans with you."

"Plans?"

"For what you intend to say about your . . . experience."

"I've time to think about that."

"I would like to call a meeting tomorrow. The sooner this matter is taken care of, the better. After all, those savages butchered a man who comes from a very influential family. I am sure they would want to see their son's death avenged."

"I have been thinking of what I must do and say," Thomas replied. "I need another day or so to organize my thoughts and decide just what must be done."

"Then you do plan to do something about this situation?"

"Did you think I wouldn't?" Thomas questioned.

"I wasn't sure. I thought perhaps you were so pleased to get home safely that you had decided to forget the others who did not."

"No . . . I haven't forgotten. I will do what must be done. Just give me another day or so to . . . to think."

"Don't think too long. It is always wise to strike when such things are fresh. Emotions will run high, and it will be easier to convince some reluctant politicians that something must be done about the murderers of such fine men."

Thomas was well aware that Martin intended to stir these emotions until a valley's innocent inhabitants were killed—and until the riches of that valley belonged to him. This sickened Thomas, and he desperately wanted his father to leave him alone.

"I know what I must do," he replied firmly. "If you don't mind, I'm very tired. I'd like to get some sleep."

"Of course. I shall make the arrangements for . . . shall we say day after tomorrow? Will that give you enough . . . rest?"

Thomas could read his father's disdain at his seeming softness, but he no longer cared. "Yes, that's fine."

"Good night, Thomas."

"Good night," Thomas replied, unable even to say "Father" again, for the whole idea of it was unbearable.

The door closed behind Martin, and Thomas began slowly to undress. A new kind of tiredness filled him. He removed his jacket, tie, and boots and lay back across his bed, staring at the ornate ceiling. After a while, he drifted into a light sleep filled with agonizing dreams.

He relived the stories Jess had told him of the massacre, only this time he could actually see Rayne and Mack dying as Jess had described. He cried out and tried to help them, but in his dream he was being held by someone. When he turned, he could see his father's twisted features as he laughed diabolically at the deadly scene. His father seemed to possess the tentacles of an octopus, which twined around him and held him immobile.

Rayne called out to him as Mack did, begging for his help as again and again they were beaten and stabbed by faceless men.

Thomas called out in agony and suddenly sat erect in his bed. His face was wet with combined sweat and tears, and he was trembling and sick at heart.

He rose from the bed and staggered to a table nearby to pour himself a healthy glass of whiskey. Downing it in

234

three rapid gulps, he choked as its fire touched his throat.

He poured another and went to sit on the window seat, knowing quite well he could not return to his bed, for that would mean facing once again the inevitable nightmare.

Thomas did not bother with breakfast the next morning. He left the house early and went to see Greg Freeman, to tell him of the planned talk with Grant and the senator. He knew that Greg, clever and as strong as Rayne, would be an important ally to have here in Washington after he made his way back to the valley.

When he had spoken to Greg at some length, he left the Freeman house and went to a good restaurant, where he ate a quiet lunch. Then, knowing his father would be occupied, he returned home to see if his mother had taken care of her own plans for leaving Washington.

They spoke in the garden where no one could hear, for both of them knew that the household servants might be tempted to carry word to Martin of their plans.

"I have gone to the ticket agent and purchased my ticket," Ruth said. "When you tell me all is well with you, I will leave. I am taking nothing but a few clothes with me, so I expect it will be some time before . . . he misses me."

"Mother, I am sorry for all of this, but he has to be stopped."

"You have no choice, Thomas. I know that. What you are doing is the right thing. I am proud you have become the man you are. After . . . after this is over, will you write and let me know?"

235

"Of course I will, and I will come to you as soon as it is possible. Try to find some happiness, Mother. You deserve it." He kissed her cheek and held her close for a moment. There was nothing more to say.

Thomas left the house again that night just after dinner. He took a carriage and went to the Jamison house. It was well lit, and three other carriages were sitting in the driveway.

He went to the door and knocked, and it was opened so quickly he knew they had been waiting for him. He walked into a room where Grant and four strangers sat.

"Thomas," Grant said. "Come in. We've been waiting for you." He took Thomas's elbow and drew him toward a tall, rugged-looking man who smiled slightly. Thomas knew him, or of him, and was impressed, for the reputation of Senator Christian Miles would impress any man. "This is Senator Miles," Grant confirmed.

Thomas extended his hand, and it was gripped in a firm, strong handshake. "Senator, I'm pleased to meet you."

"I would not have said that to Martin Preston's son a month ago, but I say it now," Senator Miles replied.

"I know, Senator. It is a thing I regret."

"We have much to talk about."

"Yes."

"Sit down and explain everything to me."

Thomas did, and the senator remained silent for the entire time. Even after Thomas was finished, no one spoke for several minutes.

"Chris?" Grant spoke quietly. "What's wrong?"

"I'm afraid we've one big problem already. John

Chevington was granted his post. He left for Fort Ramsey almost two weeks ago. In fact . . . he should be there by now."

All those present exchanged looks of worry and fear as they contemplated the damage that could be done before they had a chance to stop it.

Chapter 17

"If White Eagle discovers that Chevington is that close," Grant said, "I don't know what will happen. White Eagle hates that man. Chevington was responsible for the death of his best friend's father. I'm sure you, Senator, and some of you others remember Michael Holliday. There is not much forgiveness for John Chevington in the hearts of White Eagle's people."

"And," one of the men said, "there is not much of anything in John Chevington's heart for anything . . . or anyone."

"Gentlemen, we have to determine just what we can do to stop Chevington and prevent an Indian uprising," another man suggested. Thomas knew neither man, and Grant quickly came to his aid.

"Thomas, this is Richard Mulvey"—he motioned to one—"and Carl McBride. They are part of an organization that tries to protect the rights of the Indians."

"Mr. Preston," Senator Miles said, "did Rayne Freeman mention my name to you on this journey?"

"No sir, he didn't."

"I sent Rayne and Mack out there to get the information I needed."

"What information?"

"I had been informed that someone—perhaps White Eagle—was attempting to bring together all the tribes in the area. I wanted to know who and why. From what you have told us, it would seem that Chevington and your father are the reason why, and White Eagle is the one drawing the tribes together. Now . . . we've got to find a way to keep the blood from flowing out there, and to protect that valley."

"The valley belongs to Alexander and his daughter, Lauren," Grant said. "No matter what happens, I don't see how Preston expects to take hold of it with them owning it."

"I'll tell you," Thomas said regretfully. "I do not doubt for a minute that plans have been made to remove the obstacles of Alexander and his daughter. Once those two people are gone, who is to stop him? By our own law, no Indian can own land . . . and no white man will be there to claim it—except Chevington and my father."

Senator Miles nodded, and there was a moment of silence. Then Grant spoke. "Suppose . . ." he said thoughtfully, "just suppose that valley was not owned by just two people, but by several more."

Senator Miles laughed. "Then all someone would have to do would be to find out I owned land out there. I'd be out of office in a flash and in no position to help at all."

"Not you." Grant grinned. "Me, Thomas, and a couple of friends I have in mind. Chevington couldn't do a thing about it, and killing Alexander and his daughter wouldn't help one bit. They'd be up against a stone wall."

"You're right." Thomas smiled for the first time. "As

239

a group, we could protect the Indians more effectively than Alexander and Lauren can."

"Then we've found a solution to that problem," Senator Miles said, "and I will let Chevington know that if an incident occurs out there, I will demand a full investigation . . . and Martin Preston—excuse me, son—will not help Chevington seek revenge if there is nothing in it for him."

"I agree with you, sir," Thomas said quietly.

"Thomas," Grant said, "Alexander must be informed. Suppose we ride over to see him, tell him what we think, and see if he'll agree to deed the land to us."

"Good idea."

"And I shall also send a message to Chevington," Senator Miles said.

"Then, Senator," Thomas said, "I am going to hire a guide and go back to that valley. First, I will talk to Lauren Brent and see if she agrees with our plan. And . . . I want to tell White Eagle's tribe the story. That way, Chevington cannot push them into some kind of fight."

"Another good idea," Grant replied. "Lauren and I are friends. I will go along to help you convince her and her people. Cade—Sun Knife, their medicine man—is the son of Michael Holliday. He will know the truth when I tell him, and know what must be done."

They all agreed to this.

"When do we get this started?" Richard Mulvey asked.

"I can be ready to go in a few days," Grant told them. "Thomas and I will meet with Alexander tonight."

"What of your father's preparations for your presentation?" Carl McBride asked Thomas.

"I'll find a way out of that. I'm not his puppet, and I

won't speak his words." Thomas could sense a respect in the eyes of the men whose respect he desired most. It helped to ease the other dark emotions that still plagued him.

Satisfied at the evening's progress, the senator and his two friends shook hands with Grant and Thomas, then left. It was then that Martha came down the steps.

"I suppose you heard most of that," Grant said with an amused chuckle.

"Of course I did." Martha laughed unashamedly. "When do we leave?"

"We? No, Martha, you put that out of your mind."

"Grant Jamison, if you think you are going to travel out there and have the fun of spoiling Chevington's plans all by yourself and leave me here with nothing to do but listen to gossip and go to teas, you are sadly mistaken. I'm going with you."

"Martha, this is nonsense. What about Savannah? Our daughter is a social butterfly. She'd hate to leave Washington."

"Grant, I've been meaning to talk to you about that. I think it would help to settle our wayward daughter if she weren't fawned over by every soul she meets."

"She's a beauty." Grant smiled. "She deserves to be fawned over. I admit we spoiled her, but she's a very sweet girl."

"When she gets her way, as she always does with you. Grant"—her smile faded—"she is seeing Paul Gregory."

"Who?" Grant asked in a shocked tone.

"Paul Gregory."

"That . . . rake, that womanizer! She can't be that ignorant of his reputation!"

"Grant," Martha replied, "a man's reputation is

241

sometimes a challenge to a woman."

"I won't have this!"

"And resistance often breeds more resistance."

"Martha—"

"Let's go and take her with us. She'll be angry, but she'll be out of his reach long enough to allow her to regain her common sense."

Grant wasn't sure he wasn't being manipulated by a very clever Martha, but he loved his only daughter too much to take the chance. "All right, you win. We leave in three days. But you tell her—I don't want to be around when the fireworks start."

"I'll tell her . . . you enforce it."

"Done! I'm going to see Alexander. I should be back in a few hours."

She nodded. Grant bent to kiss her lightly, then he and Thomas left.

Alexander Brent was lonely. He missed his daughter very much, but for her protection he stayed in Washington, though he would have liked to visit her. He had learned, in the few short weeks he had spent with her and her Indian husband, to respect the man called Running Wolf and to understand the love he and Lauren shared.

He had seen his granddaughter only three times in the past years, but he knew she would grow to be as beautiful as her mother. Now, sitting before his fire, he reminisced about the old days, when his daughter had blessed his house with love and laughter.

He was annoyed when the butler interrupted his reverie to announce visitors, but his annoyance quickly turned to happiness when he found that one of his visitors was Grant Jamison.

He rose, dismissed the butler, and walked to the door himself to greet his friend. He extended his hand to Grant with a smile. "Grant, my dear friend. How are you, and what brings you here at this hour?"

"Alexander, I'm sorry for the lateness of the hour, but I have something very important to discuss with you."

Alexander's eyes had darkened when he gazed at Thomas. He knew Martin Preston too well, and he recognized Thomas as his son. Grant too saw the look.

"It is not as you think, Alexander. Let us talk to you. Then you will understand the urgency of our visit." Alexander nodded and motioned for them to accompany him to the room in which he had just been sitting.

It was over two hours later when a stunned Alexander spoke in a soft, ragged voice. "It is so hard to believe. I thought we had made that valley safe once and for all. I thought my daughter and her child were safe. Now I find it is not so." He turned from the window through which he had been looking. "I shall make out the papers and give them to you tonight. May God speed you. Bring my daughter my love and tell her I will follow soon." He sighed. "I would like to live my last days with her. This"—he waved his hand at his surroundings—"cannot compensate for her absence."

"We will tell her," Grant said. "She will be very happy to know you are coming."

Alexander went to his desk and wrote for some time, while Thomas and Grant sat silently sipping the brandies he had given them. When he finished, he handed two

243

folded packets to Grant.

"This is what you need," he said. "You must obtain Lauren's signature; and then we can file for a transfer of the property when you return. The other is a letter for my daughter."

"I'll see that she gets it, Alexander," Grant promised.

Alexander walked with them to the door and bade them god night. When he walked back into the house, he felt it had become even colder and lonelier than before.

He took a cigar and went out into his garden to walk and smoke. As he strolled along the moonlit path, he thought of his daughter, and a smile touched his face. Soon he would leave this large, lonely house for an Indian village and spend the last of his days hearing the sound of his daughter's voice and the laughter of his grandchild.

The assassin struck his fatal blow so quickly that Alexander never knew. He died thinking pleasant thoughts of Lauren and the beautiful valley in which she lived.

John Chevington rode arrogantly through the wide-open gates of Fort Ramsey. He was well pleased with what he saw as the bugle signaled his entry and rows of stiffly erect soldiers stood at attention to herald his appearance. He hated this country with a hatred no one could read on his face, but he felt it with every breath in his body.

He did not plan to be here very long. A malevolent smile came to his lips as he looked toward the southwest. Soon he would ride to that valley. When the word came, he and his troops would attack, and all within would die. Then it would belong to him, and all the gold it contained.

244

He dismounted and was greeted by his second-in-command, who had been governing the fort until his arrival. After he had been shown his quarters, he took over the command of his troops.

Thanks to Martin Preston, he now controlled a much larger force than any other fort in the territory, and Chevington set out to train his men to fight Indians, and to kill them. It became his obsession.

Soon, he believed, news of the attack on Thomas's party would inspire anger and hatred for the Indians. Then would come the death of Alexander Brent. Once these things were accomplished, he would receive word from Martin, and then he would move—quickly and with deadly intent. He would deliver Lauren and her daughter to Martin and cleanse the valley of all who now lived there.

"I will not go!" Savannah Jamison cried. Her eyes were red with the tears she had been shedding most of the morning. "It is too far; it is uncivilized . . . I would die out there."

"Hardly," Grant said calmly as Martha hid her smile. "There are many young girls in the village, and they survive quite well. You are going with us!"

"Father, please. The Stevens party is in two days. I've been asked to go. It's the biggest ball of the season!"

"Who asked you?" Grant demanded.

Savannah closed her mouth quickly. She realized it would not be wise to mention a man she knew her parents did not like. She sobbed softly, hoping to arouse her father's sympathy by a show of tears. Her ploy was to no avail.

"Who?" he asked sharply.

"P—Paul," she murmured, letting her tears flow freely.

"Paul Gregory. Did you believe for one minute I would let you go anywhere with that poor excuse for a man? No, Savannah, you will go with us. Maybe if you learned a little compassion, you would be a wiser person. Right now, you are selfish, shallow, and vain. I helped make you that way, but I'll be damned if I'll let Paul Gregory take advantage of it. You will go with us, and, if you intend to cry, go upstairs and cry while you pack."

Savannah turned to her mother. "Mother!" she wailed.

"It's not as bad as you think," Martha said. "Do as your father tells you."

Savannah turned and ran to her room. Once inside, she slammed the door behind her and gave way to frustrated tears. After a while, she stopped crying and sat up on her bed. Then she rose, and walked slowly across the room, and looked into the large mirror over her dressing table. A very upset Savannah Jamison stared back at her.

She was a tall, slender girl with a well-rounded form she was quite pleased with, for it had attracted the catch of the season, Paul Gregory. Her face was oval and dominated by slanted, sea blue eyes and a full, ripe mouth. A thick mane of bronze-gold hair was coiled elaborately on her head, and her skin was peach kissed and soft as velvet. She was innocence crying to be enlightened, and Paul Gregory, expert seducer of young women, had not missed the invitation she was unaware she had offered. Her father had just saved her from the seduction Gregory had planned for the night of the party.

Savannah knew she had been defeated, but she was hurt and angry. She placed her hand against the cool mirror and promised herself that she would not surrender completely. She would go with her parents, but it would be a battle all the way.

Grant and Martha had begun to pack, as had Thomas. Thomas let his father go on believing that he would do what was expected of him, knowing that by the time his father finished the preparations, he would be gone.

It was midday when word of Alexander Brent's death reached those involved. It was obvious to them all that no one knew Alexander had given his share of the land to Lauren. But one thing was certain; Lauren's life would be in jeopardy if they did not get to her quickly. It was decided they would leave the next morning, and their departure went unnoticed. Another day passed before word was brought to Martin Preston of all that had happened, and he was furious that his prey had escaped the net. Then he sent a message to John Chevington, instructing him not to do anything before he arrived. He knew they would have to do something to stir the Indians into action, and he would use the time spent traveling to plan his strategy.

He decided to make a statement in his son's name, explaining that Thomas was too distressed to speak about his ordeal. Thus the bloodthirsty story was told, and enough believed it to kindle the flames of hate.

The small band of travelers progressed slowly, for Savannah made every mile as difficult as possible.

Thomas and she became immediate enemies. She felt guilt at his looks of frustrated rage over their slow pace, and he felt he happily could have strangled her for her obstinancy.

She looked upon everything about her with disdain, from the inconvenience of travel, to what she called the "dirty" land to which they journeyed.

Grant did not want to go anywhere near Fort Ramsey. Thought of Alexander's death still festered within him. He knew he could not face Chevington on his own ground without trying to kill him, and that would play right into Chevington's hand. Instead, when they reached the end of the stage line, he waited three days to find a half-breed guide who would take them to White Eagle's village.

The first night out they camped, and the evening was made miserable for all by Savannah's nasty remarks about the quality of everything she laid her eyes on.

Thomas could stand her offensive attitude no longer. He set aside his plate of food and went for a short walk, hoping that she would soon retire for the night. When he did return, he was annoyed to find that the only person seated at the now low-burning fire was Savannah.

He would have passed her without a word and gone on to his sleeping area, but her voice stopped him.

"Even in this godforsaken wilderness you could be enough of a gentleman to say good night, or does such courtesy cease when one comes out here to join the savages?"

Thomas had taken as much of her snobbish arrogance as he could bear. With slow, deliberate steps, he walked to her and hunkered down beside her. His smile was a cool sneer. "One has to see a lady before one can remember his manners. I don't see one. As a matter of fact, Miss Jamison, you are about the most inconsiderate, selfish, arrogant bitch it has ever been my misfortune to meet. Your wonderful parents are rushing to save the lives of an entire village, a village, I might add, in which the most ignorant slaves have more compassion than you. If you are not blind, you will look about you and find more beauty than your eyes have ever seen before. I hope your parents do take you home as soon as possible, for this very beautiful place does not need one who seeks only to gratify her spoiled whims and doesn't care a damn for the lives of people. Tell me, Miss Jamison, have you ever really given a thought to anything but yourself?" He rose and walked away from her, because the urge to slap her was so strong that he could hardly restrain it.

He didn't see the tears in Savannah's eyes as the sting of his harsh words struck her harder than any blow his hand could have inflicted.

She knew by now, from her parents, just why they had come. But she was frightened of this large, wild place, and she yearned for the security of the things she knew. She also could not face the fear that she was incapable of coping with the demands this untouched wilderness might make upon her.

She looked about her, at the moonlit sky with its millions of diamond-bright stars sparkling against the black velvet night. She felt so small . . . so insignificant. She could not fight the feeling that some drastic change was about to take place in her life.

Unable to cope with these thoughts, she went to her bed, and, after a time, she slept. The taunting sound of Thomas's angry words echoed through her dreams.

When she rose the next morning, both her parents and Thomas were surprised at her silence. They were getting

249

ready to travel when Thomas approached her.

"Savannah . . . I'm sorry about last night. I'm a little tense, and I didn't really mean what I said. I guess a girl like you just doesn't belong out here." His words made her feel as if some important truth were slipping by her, and they seemed to create a strange sense of need, but for what, she did not know.

She smiled. "It's all right. I suppose you are right, Thomas. I guess I don't belong out here." She turned away from him as questions formed in her mind. She thought to herself, Where do I belong? Am I truly a pampered plaything of a woman, needing to be cared for like a child?

They were preparing to depart when the sound of approaching hoofbeats caused the guide to hold up his hand in a signal for them to wait.

"What is it?" Grant called.

"Two riders," the guide answered.

"Do you know them?"

The guide gazed at the figures of the two riders as they grew nearer, then he smiled. "Yes," he said. "One is Josiah Tucker, and the other is Night Sky, son of Chief White Eagle."

Grant was pleased and eagerly awaited their approach. All eyes in the small party were on them as they rode up.

Chapter 18

White Eagle stood in the entrance to his tepee and watched the return of a successful hunting party.

Rayne and Mack rode among them, as did Little Eagle and most of the young warriors of the tribe. White Eagle admired the scene before him, for all of his warriors showed their strength and good spirits. They laughed often, and there was a sense of camaraderie among them as they rode into the village.

Their skin bronzed by the sun, Rayne and Mack could easily have been mistaken for warriors of the tribe.

Each man rode his favorite horse, and some led another. A breechclout, leggings and moccasins were all they wore. All other clothes had been left behind to facilitate easy movement on the hunt.

What held White Eagle's attention for the most part was the figure of his son, Night Sky. White Eagle smiled in pleasure when he saw him, for his pride was infinite. Night Sky rode his horse with ease, as did all the warriors, for he had ridden almost from the time he could walk. He sat his horse proudly, and sensing his father's eyes upon him, he raised his arm and gave a triumphant cry that reverberated through the village, alerting all who were not yet aware of their arrival. White Eagle chuckled and raised his arm in reply.

Sunlight glistened on Night Sky's muscled back and arms, making him glow with a bright sheen as he rode toward his father's tepee. Tall and well built, he was a youthful expression of his father's massive size. He had strong features. His face of granite-hard planes and angles was softened by dark eyes that could be sensitive and understanding or could harden with a chill that had already weakened the hearts of many of his enemies. His thick, black hair sparkled with a blue cast in the afternoon sun. As he halted his horse beside his father, he smiled with the open, white smile of Rebecca Wade.

"The hunting was good, my father. We bring much meat and hides."

"Good," White Eagle answered. "It has been four days since you left. The village will feast tonight to celebrate your return."

With a lithe movement, Night Sky slid from his mount. He stood by his father, and only then was the immense size of both men obvious. Night Sky would follow in his father's footsteps as chief of this village, and White Eagle had been very careful in training his son. He wanted Night Sky to learn to be a wise, cautious, yet strong leader when he was gone.

His only concern at the moment was the fact that Night Sky seemed to have absolutely no inclination to marry. White Eagle had subtly suggested, quite often, that it was the duty of a strong leader to marry and have sons to follow him. At this, Night Sky would laugh and tell his father that when he found a woman who pleased him enough that he would choose to marry her he would take a wife. Until then, he would wait. Whenever White Eagle chose to belabor the point, Night Sky would slyly remind him that he, White Eagle, had not even chosen a woman from among his tribe but had awaited the arrival of the one with whom he most desired to share his life. Even then he had gone against all tribal rules to have Rebecca Wade as his wife. White Eagle would remember, as would Rebecca, and they would laugh together and let the matter drop, which satisfied Night Sky, for, at the moment, marriage to anyone was the last thing on his mind.

"While we were on the hunt, my father, I scouted the far end of the valley. The water is good, and the land is ready for us."

"We will move when the first leaves begin to fall. I would prefer to winter there, for Father Wind is not as bad there as here." Night Sky nodded his agreement, then he grinned and sniffed the air. White Eagle laughed again. "As always, you are hungry," he said. "And, as always, your mother saves you the choice pieces of meat and the thickest soup." His voice sounded grieved and Night Sky laughed. It had probably been at his father's insistence that Rebecca had saved the best for their son's return.

Night Sky ducked his head and entered the tepee with White Eagle behind him. Both men were met by the loving smile and wide blue eyes of Rebecca. They exchanged quick looks, and each knew the other would gladly lay down his life for the slim, golden-haired woman who knelt by the cooking fire.

"I heard your noisy arrival, my son"—she laughed—
"and I knew your hunger would be drawing you home
soon. Come, both of you, and eat."

The men silently moved to the fire where Rebecca
served them, White Eagle first and Night Sky after. Night
Sky's astute gaze did not miss the way his parents smiled
at each other and the way their hands often reached to
touch. It warmed Night Sky's heart when his father
absently called Rebecca "Golden One" instead of by
name. He sensed the tenderness in the love they shared,
and its manifestation had been one of the consistent
pleasures in his young life. If he married, he mused, she
would be a woman like Rebecca, one who wanted and
needed him before anything else. She would not be afraid
to make sacrifices for that love. Brushing aside these
serious thoughts, he ate, completely content in the
warmth that surrounded him.

Rayne loped easily across the open area, moving from
the space where the horses were kept toward his tepee.
He chuckled to himself. Gone only four days, and he felt
as if part of him were missing. His hunger for food was
secondary to his hunger to see Falling Water, to hold her
and taste her sweetness. He had dreamed of her the three
nights he had lain alone under the stars. His arms had
known the emptiness of not having her with him. During
the few weeks of their marriage, he had learned to cherish
the quiet time of early morning, when he could gently
draw her sleeping form into his arms and hold her.

He pushed the flap aside and was disappointed to find

the tepee empty. Evidence of her presence filled it, and he smiled; he could almost feel her here. He would wait, for he knew she would return soon. He sat down toward the rear of the tepee, resting against a backrest covered with fur.

The fire burned steadily and slowly cooked two rabbits that were impaled on sticks and hung over it. They were nearly done, so he assumed she was not far away. He looked about him at the place he now called home. His tepee was large. He and Falling Water had wanted it so, and it had taken many buffalo hides to build it. He knew it was considered an ideal dwelling place in this village. He thought of the luxury he had known in his parents' home, yet he had never been as happy there as he was in this tepee he shared with his wife.

It was comfortable and filled with many things. Parfleches—the closets and drawers of the Indian—contained many of their possessions and hung on the walls with the balance of Rayne's weapons and the shield Running Wolf had given him when he and Falling Water had married. The buffalo skin bed was across the tepee from him, and his blood warmed at the memory of the nights he had shared with Falling Water there.

He rose and moved about, anxious to see Falling Water, but having no idea where to find her. He knew it would be best to wait, but when it came to Falling Water, patience was not one of his virtues.

Falling Water, who had been at the stream getting water, heard the approaching warriors and Night Sky's cry. "Rayne," she breathed softly. Her heart pounded as her feet flew. She ran as fast as she could, uttering a soft laugh as she saw his weapons outside their tepee.

Immediately she bent and entered, but before she could even say his name, she was caught up in his strong arms, and his mouth silenced any words she might have said.

It was a long, deep, heady kiss, and she felt her blood warm and her bones grow weak at the depth of it. He held her, rocking her against his broad chest, enjoying the way her arms enclosed him and her parted lips molded to his.

Very reluctantly, he let her feet touch the floor, but one arm still held her bound against him. "I never thought I would miss anyone as much as I've missed you," he whispered against her hair. "Four days seemed an eternity."

He drew her with him to the fur bed. They lay together for a moment, just holding each other and letting their lips play upon each other's. The tunic she wore was no restriction for him, and he rid her of it easily. Slowly, his hard hands caressed her tingling skin, drawing a ragged sigh of pleasure from her.

He looked down into her upturned face and saw the reflection of his own passion in her half-closed eyes. Then he bent his head to again plunder her willing mouth. His lips slid slowly away to touch her throbbing breasts, teasing and taunting them to make her cry out in pleasure.

He moved within her with gentleness and began a very slow, rhythmic movement. It was enough to make her yearn, but not enough to satisfy her. She stirred to vibrant life, telling him with murmured words and with her body that her need for him was more than she could bear.

His kisses burned against her now sensitive skin, yet

256

she desired more. The flame of desire leapt to volcanic life, and their passion-filled whispers urged each to more giving.

There were no restraints, no reservations in their mutual surrender as they came together with an almost frantic violence. He was hard and throbbing to life within her, and she reveled in the ecstatic pleasure she received as he drove again and again to the depths of her. She lost all hold on reason and cried out words that filled his heart. Her eyes were closed, and her hands caressed and urged him to a possession beyond imagining.

In the afterglow of heated passion, they lay holding each other in a silence that spoke more words than they could have found. Their bodies, joined together, slowly regained their balance, yet still they could not seem to separate.

He held her against him, and, with gentle hands, he soothed her quivering flesh. With eyes closed, she rested against the breadth of his chest and listened to the slowly easing thunder of his heart.

"I do not think"—he chuckled softly—"that I will like long hunting trips anymore. There are some hungers I can cope with and some I cannot."

He heard her throaty laughter. "You say such things now, my husband, but one day you will tire of me, and your hunting trips will grow longer and longer."

He tipped her head up and smiled down into her teasing eyes. "I shall be an old, gray, withered warrior before my need for your passes. In fact," he added with a laugh, "you would probably still be able to set a fire within me if I were on my deathbed." They laughed together, and his arms tightened about her.

257

"Rayne?"

"Yes?"

"I heard you speaking to my father just before you left on the hunt. You have decided not to go until the new season, after the snows are gone?"

"That's right. I'm having a difficult time thinking of leaving then. I'll bet it will be the fastest trip I ever made, and"—he grinned—"it's not the snows that hold me here. If there were any other way to give the senator the information he needs, I'd do it. Besides, I want to be here after the village is moved. White Eagle says he is going to attend another meeting of the chiefs. I would like to attend it with him. That way, I can speak the truth to my chief, and we can help keep things peaceful out here. I want our children to be raised in this valley in peace, and I'm going to do all I can to make it happen."

"I am glad. I would have you to myself for as long as possible before I must make room in our world for others."

He turned on his side and laid his hand against her cheek. Her eyes smiled up into his, clear and open, so that he could easily read her feelings. He brushed a light kiss on each cheek. "Don't you know yet, my love, that there is a place within me that no one else could ever touch. It is a place where only you live. No matter where I am or what I am going, I hold you there. No matter how far I have to wander, my heart is here." He pressed his hand gently against her breasts. "I feel your heartbeat and the rhythm of mine is the same—you . . . you . . . you. You're every breath I take. I love you, with all I possess. I love you."

He watched the tears form and escape down her

258

cheeks, saw her tremulous smile, and again he bent to touch her moist lips and draw her within the circle of his arms. They floated on the soft wind of mutual love that lifted them beyond who, where, and what they were into a world that knew nothing but the entwined emotions that bonded them one to the other.

Mack had dismounted and watched Rayne's excitement as he cared quickly for his horse, then went to his tepee. A feeling of something akin to jealousy had touched him for a moment, and an old memory had nudged him for a place in his conscious mind. He refused it entry.

He walked slowly toward his own tepee, knowing it would be empty. He stopped in surprise as he saw the thin wisp of white smoke emanating from the smoke hole.

Maybe, he thought, one of the older women had seen fit to build his fire for him. He continued to walk toward the entrance. It was empty, but he could see that it had only recently been vacated. Someone had spent a great deal of time there while he had been gone. He looked about him. The buffalo robes he slept on were spread neatly. His clothes were not only hung up but had been mended. The rest of the tepee had been arranged and cared for.

What surprised him the most was the meat that was slowly roasting over a low-burning fire and the soup that bubbled and smelled so enticingly good.

He was hungry and tired. He would find out who he had to thank for all this care after he had eaten. He sat down and scooped some of the soup into a bowl that had been placed near the fire. It was excellent, and he ate it quickly and took another helping, which he accompanied with pieces of the roasted meat.

Satisfied at last, he took clean clothes with him to the river, where he bathed and dressed in a soft buckskin shirt and pants. He walked back slowly through the village and thought about the contentment he had found here. He knew such thoughts were dangerous. He did not want to allow anything inside of the solid walls he had built between his emotions and the things he knew would bring unwelcome pain.

The tepee next to his belonged to one of the older men of the tribe and his wife. Their children were grown and married, and, since Mack's arrival, the older woman had often done little things for him to make his stay in their village pleasant. Sometimes she had brought hot, good-tasting food. This, he thought, must be another such occasion. He felt it was time he rewarded her in some small way for her care. He had had good luck in the hunt, and he would make sure a prime hide and some meat went to her.

He stopped in front of their tepee and requested permission to enter. Once granted, he went inside.

Swift Horse and his wife, Calling Wind, smiled their welcome. They were pleased at his visit, for in some way he reminded them of their oldest son, who, as was custom, had gone to a nearby village to make his home with his wife's family.

"The gods were generous this day to give me good luck." Mack smiled. "I would share it with you both. It is small thanks for what you have done. I was very tired, and it was a welcome thing to come home to a good meal and a warm, comfortable tepee."

"We are grateful," Calling Wind replied, "but it is not me you should give your thanks to. I would have cared for your meal, but there was another who chose to do it for you."

Mack was surprised. "Tell me then, whom do I thank for a comfortable tepee and warm food?"

"Little Dove. She spent much time there while you were away. She is a good girl with a kind and gentle heart, and I'm sure she was pleased to take care of your possessions while you were gone."

"Little Dove," Mack said quietly.

Mack had made it a point to keep his distance from Little Dove. She was a weakness he couldn't afford. She alone had the ability to open too many closed doors. Yet, it would be considered extremely rude for him not to acknowledge such kindness.

He thanked Swift Horse and Calling Wind and told them he would bring them the promised gifts anyway, for he appreciated all the generosity they had shown him in the past.

Again, he walked slowly back to his tepee. He stood outside for a moment and gazed at another tepee that stood some distance from his.

He had to go there, had to look into her dark eyes that seemed to see more of him than he wanted seen. He had to gift her with something, and he had to thank her. Anything less would be considered bad manners.

Again, he bent and entered his tepee. He walked to a bundle that hung on the wall. He took it down and unrolled it. He picked up a necklace of blue beads. They were pale blue and very pretty. Little Dove was young, and Mack knew she probably would never have seen anything like it, for White Eagle's tribe did not often trade with white trappers. He put the beads in his pocket and left the tepee to walk with determined steps to the dwelling of Running Wolf's father, Great Cloud. There he would speak to Little Dove and thank her, give her the gift, and leave as soon as he could. These were his thoughts, but thoughts and actions are sometimes barely related.

Little Dove sat in her father's tepee alone. She had heard the arrival of the hunting party, had heard Night Sky's exuberant call, but she could not leave her tepee.

In her mind she could see Mack walk into his tepee, see the surprise in his eyes. She felt pleasure knowing he would enjoy what she had done. It was enough for her. She felt he would assume Calling Wind had cared for his things, and therefore she would not have to face him. It was a thought that quickly died when she heard his voice from outside requesting permission to enter and speak to her.

Fear struck the pit of her stomach, making it seem hollow, and she could feel her legs trembling as she stood up. Why should she be afraid? she demanded of herself. Yet she knew the answer, she did not want to see rejection in his eyes; she did not want to see them cold and empty, as if some part of him were gone.

In a voice that shook, she called out for him to enter. He came in, and it seemed to her he filled the tepee with his presence.

They looked across the small area at each other and their eyes met. There was no doubt she was beautiful, but he did not allow that beauty to reach him. He didn't dare. He was too vulnerable for that.

"Little Dove, I would speak with you."

"Speak then," she replied softly.

"I want to thank you."

"It is not necessary."

"I think it is. You have been very kind to me. I am grateful for the care you have taken of my possessions and for the food you prepared for me. To come home from a long hunt to find such welcome things is very satisfying."

"Then it is enough for me to know that it has pleased you."

"Why did you do it?" he asked gently. Her eyes lifted to his, and, for a moment, they stood in a silence that was eloquent.

"Because," she said quietly, "you were hungry, and I would feed you. You were in need of comfort, and I would give you that comfort." She did not say that she felt his loneliness and wanted desperately to fill it with kindness, if not more.

"I will bring to your father's tepee gifts in return for your kindness."

"Thank you," she said, fighting the tears that threatened to choke the words in her throat.

He walked to her side and reached into his pocket to withdraw the glittering necklace. "But to you, Little Dove, I would give a small gift with my thanks. It would gladden my heart if you would take it and wear it."

He held the necklace before her. She had never seen such a beautiful thing. The blue was like the river on a sunny day. No woman of her tribe had anything as beautiful as this. With a trembling hand, she reached out and took the necklace from him. She put it about her neck and touched the beads gently.

"I will be proud to wear it. It will show what a great heart the white hunter has and how generous he is with his gifts."

He reached out and touched the necklace lightly. Of its own accord, his hand went, for an instant, to her dark hair. Then, without another word, he turned and left her gazing after him.

There was a light of knowledge in her eyes that it was better Mack had not seen.

Chapter 19

The celebration that night was a wild and happy affair. Once again, the drums called the people together to send their thanks to the gods for providing them with their sustenance.

There was more than enough food and drink, and the exuberance of the successful hunters was responsible for dancing demonstrations that brought happy laughter to all. Through the dance they told the stories of their feats, and some tales were found to be outstanding as each brave revealed his personal success.

Rayne watched with some awe. After this, there was dancing among couples who formed undulating lines. The rhythmic dance was enjoyed by all the young people, especially those for whom it provided a rare opportunity to be close to the one they loved. Rayne found it exciting for it pleased him to be given an opportunity to be near Falling Water.

He was filled with happy laughter until suddenly he looked across the fire to see Mack walking toward his tepee. Something about the set of his shoulders or the way he walked startled Rayne for a moment. It was as if Mack were suddenly carrying a load too heavy to bear. Rayne was about to follow him, when White Eagle spoke.

"With the rising of the sun, the council will meet. Josiah will go to the new white man's fort to learn the name of the man who is chief there and see if we can smoke the pipe together and speak of keeping the peace between us."

These words drew Rayne's undivided attention. Keeping things peaceful here was an ideal close to his heart. "It is a wise idea, White Eagle, if Josiah can get the white chief to meet us halfway; then maybe we can keep things under control. It will certainly make my job easier. I'll just report that you are combining some tribes to keep the peace, and the white chief will do the same."

"It is good," White Eagle said softly. "I am only afraid that it seems too easy."

"The only thing that can cause a problem is if word of the gold gets out. I'm praying no one knows."

"Josiah says the same. The yellow metal is the only thing to cause trouble."

"White Eagle, you said I could go with you when you next go to the big council. I would speak for the white man and try to help both sides understand each other."

"Yes, but you don't disagree with what I am trying to do. Combining, and being able to call for others for help, will make us strong enough to prevent war."

"War," Rayne said softly. "The word has such an ugly sound."

White Eagle was about to speak again, then his eyes sparkled with amusement. Standing several feet from them was Falling Water. It was unthinkable that she would approach them while Rayne was in conversation with their chief, but, even at this distance, White Eagle was well aware of the emotions playing in her dark eyes.

"I will speak to you later of this matter. If I am not mistaken, your woman would enjoy the rest of the celebration with you. The morning is soon enough to talk of this matter."

White Eagle walked away, and Rayne turned toward Falling Water. His concern about Mack had temporarily slipped his mind, and Falling Water's warm smile as he strode toward her was enough to push aside thoughts of anything but her.

Mack had no idea why he was so uneasy and discontented. He only knew that sitting amidst the celebration was becoming unbearable.

He rose, unaware of Rayne's eyes upon him, and tried to leave unobtrusively. He went straight to his tepee. Once inside, he noticed that the room was semi-dark, for the fire had burned low. It was fine with him, for he was in no mood for brightness or cheer.

He lay down on his mat, folded his hands behind his head, and listened to the noises from the celebration. He had been to so many such celebrations and had always enjoyed their uninhibited joy. Now he felt choked with an alien emotion he could not name or would not name.

He heard the excitement build as the hours grew, then heard it recede as the festivities slowly ended. Rising from his mat for a moment, he discarded his clothes, for, unless it was winter, all the people of the tribe slept naked. Mack had adopted this custom many years before.

He slid beneath the fur robe and wondered if tonight he would be lucky enough to sleep without the disoriented dreams he had been having of late. Slowly the silence grew, and slowly he drifted into sleep.

The village lay quiet as the high golden moon bathed it in pale light. A lone figure moved slowly and silently between the tepees. Sure of the destination, the form moved with deliberation to stand before the closed flap of a tepee.

Little Dove knew what she was doing, and that it was strictly forbidden. She also realized that after this night she would never be able to marry any other brave, for none would have her. Yet she understood, in her heart, that the black thing within Mack needed to be set free, and she loved him enough to do it, no matter what price she might pay.

Her hands shook as she reached to push the flap aside and enter. She stood for a moment until her eyes adjusted to the darkness that was brightened only by what moonlight came through the smoke hole.

She could see his large form beneath the fur robe, and, from the steady rise and fall of his chest, she knew he was asleep. She moved to stand closer to him, then slowly she untied the neck of the tunic she wore. It slid silently to the floor. Then she knelt and moved the fur robe aside, and, very gently, she crawled beneath it and lay close to his hard body.

Mack struggled in the depths of his dream. She was there, Sweet Water, the woman he had loved so deeply. He saw her laugh up at him, and he reached to draw her close. Her cool body molded to his as he bent to take her sweet, giving mouth. She was there, and he felt a forgotten joy as she reached within him and soothed the pain that had lived there for so long.

His hands, hard and aggressive, moved over her slim body, seeking the knowledge he had possessed so long ago. The hunger built within him as his lips tasted the smooth texture of her skin and began to move over her in the heat of growing passion.

He felt the cool touch of her hands as she caressed him with a gentleness that almost made him cry out. They swirled together in the mist of the dream—she, so alive and warm, and he, so filled with his need that he could no longer contain it.

Little Dove bit her lips to silence the cries of ecstatic pleasure that threatened to break free. But she lost control when he pulled her beneath him and pressed himself deep within her. Her cry and the spasmodic grip of her body pulled him into instant wakefulness.

He gazed down at her, stricken to the depths of his soul. "Oh, Holy Jesus," he groaned as he realized what was happening.

He was part of her body, and she was a part of his, and the flame of desire that possessed them both was now far beyond the control of either of them.

With gentle hands, Little Dove reached up to draw his head down to hers. A low, groaning sob marked the destruction of the last barrier between them as his open mouth descended to ravage hers.

What had passed between them before was a brilliant and memorable thing to her, but it was nothing compared to the rapturous magic he performed as he seemed to drain her very heart from her. His mouth was hungry and hot, his hands hard and demanding, and his body a part of hers—moving, seeking, and demanding all. It was violence, but a sweet violence. It was passion, but the sweetest of passion. It was need, and the very sweetest of needs.

They moved together, clinging to each other, their gasps and senseless words urging them to dizzying heights. His throbbing maleness deep within her and the overwhelming power of his possession drove her to mindless abandon, and she lost any hold she might have had on reason. He wanted it so. He was lost, and he yearned to have her soar in the void with him.

Her eyes closed and her head rolled from side to side as her hands clutched the rippling muscles of his back and hips. She cried out as they tumbled together into oblivion.

His breathing was ragged, and he could not speak for some time, but neither could she. He held her in silence until they both regained their sanity and their ability to reason. It was only then that he withdrew himself from her body, and she felt the void as if some part of her was gone. She was afraid of the silence as he lay beside her, yet she knew she must answer his yet unspoken questions.

Mack rose slowly and went to the dead fire. Within a few minutes, he had built another, and it was burning crisply. It was only then that he turned to look at Little Dove.

She sat on the dark fur of his robe, her copper skin aglow in the firelight, aware of the graceful beauty of her body and unashamed of the fact that she had given to him everything she was, both in body and spirit. His eyes held hers, then he reached a hand toward her. "Come here, Little Dove," he said gently.

She came to him and sat beside him. With an infinitely tender touch, he caressed her hair. "Why, Little Dove . . . why? You know what might happen if you are found here. You know what a sacrifice you have made."

She nodded her head. "Yes . . . I know."

"Then why?"

Her eyes rose to his, and she reached to press her hand to his broad, muscular chest. "I only saw that you were empty here, and in pain," she said softly. "I only know that I feel a great love for you, and I would fill that emptiness so the pain will no longer be there. I only know," she went on, "that I understand your loneliness, and, for a while, I would drive it from you and see you smile and see happiness in your eyes."

He took hold of her shoulders. "Little fool," he said without anger. "You would give so much and not even ask why?"

"I do not need to ask," she replied. "Do I not have eyes to see? A woman can understand pain and loss sometimes more than a man. I love you, and love does not have to ask why . . . it is enough."

"And you ask nothing of me?" he said in wonder.

"No, I do not ask what you cannot give."

"And yet, you give . . . your life. You know you cannot marry within this tribe now."

"Yes, I know," she answered quietly. "I do not . . . I do not choose to marry."

"Liar," he said gently. She did not deny this, as her tears confirmed the word. "Listen to me, Little Dove. I married once into the tribe. I loved her very much. We had a child. I had been victorious in a battle between tribes, and, in retribution, the enemy struck our village one day when I was gone. I lost them both—Sweet Water and my child. I have been drifting back and forth between the white and Indian world for a long time. I can't find a place or an anchor. There's nothing you or anyone else can do."

"No," she replied softly. "There is much someone can do. It is just that you won't let anyone close enough

271

to help. I . . . I think you are afraid to love again. You are afraid to be hurt."

He sighed heavily. "Maybe so. Maybe you're right, but I don't want to hurt you either. If you do not marry, you will be forced to care for your own tepee. You and I both know just where that will put you in a few years. You could not stand a life like that."

He took her in his arms and held her as one would comfort a hurt child. She rested her head against his breast and closed her eyes. "Little Dove," he said softly, "tomorrow I will go to your father and offer a bride price. We will be married as soon as possible."

She suddenly sat erect, her eyes aflame. "No! I do not need your sympathy or your gratitude. What I did, I did because I love you and I would not see you caught in old memories, dying inside from the hurt. But I would marry no man just because he is grateful!"

She moved from his arms and bent to pick up the dress she had discarded. He watched as she stood in the glow of the fire, and something deep within him stirred to life, something he had thought long dead and buried. The desire to have someone close . . . someone to love . . . someone who loved him . . . As she slipped the dress over her head, he smiled at the trembling hand that tied the strings.

He was shaken by another thought. He had possessed her completely, yet he had the desire to hold her in his arms again and love her gently, pull her within the depths of his emptiness, where she had been a short while before.

He went to her, and, despite her protests, he held her close to him. "You and I know your father thinks I am a strong and able warrior. We also know he would honor

272

my request for marriage if I told him we had already shared a bed and that I desired to marry you."

"You . . . you must not do this to me! I would die of the shame."

"Then agree to marry me without those words being spoken."

"I cannot." She sobbed, then asked, "Don't you understand?"

"Yes," he replied softly. "I do understand. We will give this some time . . . we will both think."

"Unless you truly want me," she said in a low whisper, "do not do this. My love for you will die. Don't leave me with hatred for myself for loving you. Let me have this to remember when you are gone."

She broke from his arms and ran from his tepee to her own, where she lay on her mat and wept until she slept from exhaustion.

Mack returned slowly to his bed, but it was a long time before he slept. Her violent sacrifice still astounded him. She had given him all a woman could give and had asked nothing in return but that he honor their joining by keeping silent and letting her go. She was willing to go on with a life that would be empty.

The next morning, when he looked for Little Dove, he could not find her in the village. He knew quite well that she was still running from him. He would give her the days she needed, but his resolve was firm. She would marry him if he had to fall back on an old custom that had somehow slipped her mind. He would tell Rayne to inform her father. Then he would kidnap her and take her from the village to a place where he could keep her. When enough time had passed, they would return. In the eyes of the tribe they would be married, and there would

273

be nothing she could do about it.

He hoped that in this way he could show her the difference between gratitude and other, much deeper emotions.

The council was to meet in less than an hour. Rayne dressed and walked to Mack's tepee. Together, they started toward the large tepee in which the council would be held.

On their way they were joined by Little Eagle and Night Sky, who seemed to be in excellent spirits.

Any words spoken in the council would be spoken by the elders. Little Eagle and Night Sky were expected to learn from what was said.

Rayne, Mack, and Josiah sat together, for they were white and had no voice in what was decided. As long as Josiah had been in the village, any words he had wanted to say were spoken to White Eagle or Sun Knife first, so they could present them to the council, the group of men who decided the fate of all things that concerned the tribe.

Many things were discussed and decided before the subject of the white fort was raised. Sun Knife stood and addressed the council, telling them it was not necessarily true that the white fort meant trouble for the tribe. It was possible, he said, that the tribe of White Eagle and the whites at the fort could live and trade together in peace. He asked if the council would consider sending an envoy to the fort to speak to the white chief.

When Sun Knife sat down, White Eagle rose to speak. There was absolute silence, which indicated the phenomnal respect and admiration all those present felt for this

274

huge man who had led so well for so many years.

"My father, Chief Tekata, spoke often to me and to you of the white threat. I do not know if he saw a danger that was not there, or if the new white fort is another step toward that danger. You remember well the last fort that was so near our valley, the fort whose chief tried to force us into battle." He went on to retell a story most of the men present already knew, but he wanted that story fresh in their minds. He also wanted them to remember other events, among them the attack that had been made on their village, the deaths of their loved ones, and the way he had sought revenge.

They did not really need any reminder of White Eagle's power or his intelligence. But he wanted them to know, in the very depths of their hearts, that anything he said or did was not done from fear, but from wisdom.

"I do not fear them," he said, "but I do not trust them either . . . with the exception of a few," he added with humor. A soft laugh came rippling over the group and touched the lips of the white exceptions to which he referred. "If they want to trade in peace with us, we will let them be. I must know what is in the heart of the white chief at the new fort. I must know how he thinks. I would send one of their own to talk to the white chief. I would send Josiah Tucker to speak words with him. Then he will return and tell us, and we will know whether to trade or to defend ourselves."

There was a murmur of discussion among the elders. It was soon agreed that White Eagle was wise in what he suggested. Josiah Tucker would go.

According to custom, the request was made formally, and Josiah immediately agreed. There was a moment or two of silence then, to the surprise of all, Night Sky rose and faced his chief, his father, whose obsidian eyes regarded him as he would any other young man who rose to speak in the presence of the elders.

Night Sky would not speak until his chief chose to acknowledge him. It was a moment or two before he did, a moment when their eyes met and held.

Nothing made Night Sky prouder than the fact that he was the son of White Eagle. He stood tall and straight, his eyes unflinching. White Eagle's face showed no sign of the pleasure he felt knowing he had sired the imposing, handsome, and very brave young warrior.

"You wish to speak to the council?" White Eagle questioned.

"I would speak both to the council and to my chief, White Eagle."

"Speak," White Eagle said, his voice telling his son in no uncertain terms that what he had to say would be held in the same light as words from any other warrior.

"It is good that we have the white one go to the fort, for Josiah is our friend." There was no answer to these words, for neither White Eagle nor the council felt they needed the agreement of a young warrior. "But would it not also be helpful if one of us went with him? Then two will know, by the way the white chief treats us, how he will treat the rest of our tribe. It might be easy to deceive one of their own. They will let him walk freely in the fort. But will they do the same for one they do not know . . . and perhaps do not trust?"

There was silence again. White Eagle regarded his son, trying to contain the pleasure the young warrior's intelligent observation had stirred within him. Then White Eagle turned again to the council, who quickly agreed that Night Sky had made a very astute judgment.

276

"You will go," White Eagle said. "You will walk among them, talk to them, and, most important, you will listen. Then you will return and tell me what you find."

The sparkle of pleasure in Night Sky's eyes did not go unnoticed by his father. Night Sky clenched his fist and pressed it over his heart to show his complete obedience to his chief.

"Yes, my chief," he said. White Eagle nodded. Soon after, the council ended.

Outside, Night Sky's youthful exuberance could not be contained. He raised his clenched fist and gave vent to a loud war cry, which brought a smile to all lips, even those of his stern-faced father, Chief White Eagle.

The next morning, Night Sky and Josiah left the village and rode toward the new fort. It would be a five day ride if they traveled easily, and since there was no need to hurry, they would hunt for food as they traveled.

As they rode, Josiah could not help but admire the strength and ability of the handsome young warrior at his side. This man will one day rule the tribe, he thought and prayed silently that Night Sky would have the same abilities his father had shown.

Three days on the trail passed quickly and easily for Josiah, for Night Sky was a good companion. He had no trouble finding all they needed to eat, and his easy laughter and intelligent mind made conversation comfortable and interesting.

They were riding along slowly, when suddenly Night Sky drew his horse to a halt.

"What's the matter?" Josiah asked. Although Josiah had lived in this area for many years, he still did not possess certain abilities that seemed innate in all Indians, senses that had naturally developed.

277

"Strangers," Night Sky said. "They are beyond that ridge."

"How do you know they are strangers? They might be some of our warriors."

"No." Night Sky grinned. "They are strangers."

Josiah chuckled. "All right. Suppose we go and see who it is."

They rode rapidly ahead and soon approached the group of travelers. As they were welcomed into the camp, Josiah was quick to realize that he was in the presence of Grant Jamison, one of Sun Knife's closest friends. All were soon in animated conversation, all except Night Sky, who sat in silent admiration of the sun-haired beauty called Savannah.

Chapter 20

Savannah knew she had never seen such a wild, fierce-looking man as the handsome Night Sky. He frightened her to death, yet she could not seem to take her eyes from him. He sat his horse as if he owned everything that surrounded him.

Despite the fact that she trembled in fear, she found herself mesmerized by his dark, piercing eyes. She promised herself that as soon as her father's business in this wild country was finished, she would beg him—on hands and knees if she had to—to allow her to leave this place.

With conscious effort, she tore her eyes away from Night Sky. He was almost an animal! she raged inwardly. She would not let him upset her. Soon they would be gone. She longed for civilization, where men did not look at her as he did. Despite the fact that she refused to look again in his direction, she could feel the heat of his gaze upon her.

Josiah shook hands with Grant. After introductions were made, he realized immediately who Grant was.

"Sun Knife will be glad to see you."

"Not half as glad as I will be to see him. How are Lauren and White Eagle? Running Wolf and Rebecca?"

"They are fine. And I'm willing to bet they throw the biggest celebration this area has ever known when you get there."

Grant laughed. "This is my wife, Martha, and my daughter, Savannah."

"I'm pleased to meet you." Josiah smiled. "And this young man with me is Night Sky."

"Night Sky," Grant said. "He looks familiar to me."

"He should; he's the image of his father, White Eagle."

"You're White Eagle's son!" Grant exclaimed happily. "I'm more than pleased to meet you. Will you be going back to the village with us?"

Josiah answered for him. "No, we have something to do first. But we will rest here for a little while with you. I want to tell you what's happening."

"And I've a lot to tell you," Grant replied.

With alacrity that made Josiah laugh to himself, Night Sky slid gracefully from his horse.

He stood too close to Savannah to suit her, and she moved closer to her father. The overpowering virility of this half-naked savage had shaken something within her.

Night Sky read her fear easily, but what upset him was the fact that her eyes were ice. It was as if she could not bear his presence. He did not understand this, for many of the pretty girls of his tribe would have been more than pleased had he looked their ways. He knew two things for certain: he was glad she was going to his village, and he intended to return home quickly. He wanted to speak to her, to see her smile. He remained silent, but his dark eyes missed nothing about her, from her copper-gold hair to her slim, yet rounded, woman's body.

Josiah and Grant spoke for a few minutes, exchanging information. They knew there would be time to talk at length when Josiah and Night Sky returned from the fort.

Savannah remained uncommonly silent, and the tension of keeping her eyes from returning to the huge bronze man had frayed her nerves.

Night Sky remained silent also, but in his mind visions formed that would have shattered Savannah's control completely.

She breathed a sigh of relief when Night Sky and Josiah remounted. They waved and rode away, but her eyes followed the tall Indian. She was startled when he suddenly reined his horse to a halt and turned to look back. In a quick motion that no one saw but her, he doubled his fist and placed it against his chest, then raised it, open palm toward her. She had no idea of what it meant and stood motionless.

As suddenly as he had turned, he whirled about and was gone.

She turned away. Savage! she thought. To look at me like that . . . it's . . . uncivilized! She was angry at what he had done to her equilibrium, and angrier still at the effect he had had on her. Grimly, she set her mind. She had to get out of here. She would not tolerate the hot gaze of that savage again. She was a lady used to civilized luxury, and she would not let an ill-mannered wild man change her ideals. He never even spoke to me, she mused. What kind of a man treats a lady so?

Though she determined to forget him, his lean,

bronzed body and dark eyes lingered in her mind despite all she did to exorcise them.

Josiah and Night Sky rode in silence for a long while. Josiah laughed to himself, wondering how long it would be before the gentle inquisition would begin.

"These people," Night Sky began. "They have been to our village before?"

"Before you were born," Josiah answered.

"They are friends of my father?"

"Both your parents owe Grant a lot. He is also blood brother to Sun Knife."

Night Sky smiled. "You think they will remain in our village for a time?"

Josiah shrugged. "I've no idea how long they plan on staying. If it's up to Sun Knife and your father, they will stay for a while."

"I have heard some of the stories of that time, but"— Night Sky laughed—"I did not always pay attention. Will you tell me again of my parents and these people."

"These people?" Josiah laughed now. "Are you interested in stories, in Grant Jamison . . . or in his pretty daughter?"

Night Sky chuckled in response. "The white woman," he affirmed softly. "She has the same golden hair as my mother. Are there many with this color hair in her village?"

"Yes, there are a lot of women with light hair."

"And her eyes are like the cornflowers in the fields or the sky at midday. It is a strange thing, these eyes like Sun Knife's."

"You're a poet, too," Josiah said with a laugh.

282

"A poet? What is that?"

"One who makes words like the songs for celebrations, pretty words that tell what one feels inside."

"She is a pretty—no, a beautiful woman. Do you think she belongs to someone in her village?"

"No, I don't suppose she does, or she wouldn't be with her parents."

"Good."

"Don't count on it. She didn't exactly look happy to be out here. I think maybe she misses the place she calls home. Her heart is there, and she does not have eyes for this place . . . or anyone in it," Josiah warned.

But Night Sky's mind ignored his warning and fled back to the one who had stirred a new emotion within him. He could not imagine a woman who would not want to be the woman of a chief.

"We must move quickly to the fort and finish what we were sent to do. I have a great desire to return home," he admitted.

Josiah laughed with him, but after seeing the look in Savannah's eyes, he felt Night Sky was in for a rude awakening.

John Chevington had taken command of Fort Ramsey with an iron hand. He had slowly formed the large group of men into a tightly bound fighting force, a force he intended to use to make a fortune and to eliminate all those in his way.

He stood on the porch in front of his quarters now and watched the wide gates of the fort swing open and the messenger approach. The rider entered and spoke to the guard at the gate, who pointed toward Chevington. Then the rider rode toward him. He dismounted in front of Chevington and saluted.

"Colonel Chevington?"

"Yes."

"I have messages for you, sir."

"Good, let me have them."

The man handed a packet of letters for Chevington, who promptly dismissed him. His attention was immediately drawn to the first letter in the bundle, for he recognized the writing. It was that of Martin Preston. He took the letter to his office and read it carefully.

John:

There has been a change in our plans. Don't do anything until I arrive. I should be there within a month.

Alexander Brent is dead. But we cannot proceed as planned. Before he died, he gave the land to his daughter. We were too late there.

We have to change our methods. What plans I had for Thomas have failed. He refused to speak out. We have no help here, so we will have to do it someway ourselves. Be careful.

Martin

"Damn," he muttered. Thomas would have made everything so easy if he had just done as his father wanted. He wondered why their plan had failed, but he would wait the month for Martin to arrive. Together they would make new plans. He knew Martin was as determined as he and that they would be able to achieve their goals on their own. And they would not have to share the golden valley with anyone else. He calmly destroyed the letter and for the next two weeks, drove his men even harder.

Seated behind his desk early one morning, Chevington was interrupted by the corporal outside his door. He knocked once, then opened the door.

"Colonel Chevington?"

"Yes."

"The guard says there're two men outside the fort. They want to come in."

"Well, why shouldn't they?"

"Sir, you said there were to be no Indians inside the fort."

"Indians?"

"One of them's a white man; the other's a Cheyenne brave."

Chevington rose from his seat slowly. The only Cheyenne tribe close enough to be visiting was White Eagle's. He wondered if White Eagle knew he was here. He remembered quite well the last time he had faced White Eagle, Sun Knife, and his braves. It was not a memory that gave him any pleasure.

He walked across the room, through the anteroom, and out to the porch, followed by the corporal. The guard stood outside awaiting orders.

"There are two of them?" Chevington questioned.

"Yes, sir."

Chevington thought for a minute, then he smiled. It might as well be made clear to them now, he mused. He was here, and he was here to stay. This time, White Eagle and his braves would not drive him out. This time he would win.

"Let them come in," he said.

"Both of them, sir?"

"Yes . . . both of them."

Josiah and Night Sky sat outside the closed gate. This was a new experience for Night Sky, to be kept waiting and treated as if he were an enemy. A strange unease touched him. He had never seen a white fort, and he wondered how men could stand being closed in behind such great walls. He was so used to the freedom of the open plains and valleys. He knew he could never stand being closed up in such a place.

The wide gates swung open, and both men were motioned inside. Josiah stopped to speak to the guard.

"We would like to see your commanding officer. Who is he, and where can we find him?"

"He's Colonel John Chevington," the guard replied. "And he's over there on the porch."

Josiah was stunned at hearing the hated name he knew so well. Chevington was back, and there would never be a chance for peace with any Indians. He knew Chevington too well. He turned quickly to Night Sky, who was gazing about him in open wonder at the inside of the fort.

"Night Sky, listen to me," he said quickly. Night Sky was surprised at his intensity, but he had been trained to respect his elders. Josiah was considered a strong man among Night Sky's people, and he would not ignore what he had to say. "Turn and go now to the stand of trees on the hill. Make camp and wait for me. I will explain everything to you later."

Night Sky's smile faded. "But I would speak to them. I would see the inside of their strange wooden tepees."

"Night Sky, please do as I say. It's important. I will explain everything. Believe me, a great deal depends on it."

His eyes were worried, and no smile touched them. Night Sky did not question him any further. He turned and rode away, and only then did Josiah ride slowly toward John Chevington, who smiled coldly as he saw his old enemy approach.

Night Sky hobbled his horse so it would not stray too far. On the crest of the hill he built a small fire and sat beside it to look down on the fort. He didn't know why Josiah had sent him away, but he knew Josiah would tell him later. He would wait, and while he did so, he would let his mind drift to other, more pleasant thoughts . . . thoughts of the golden-haired girl with the cornflower eyes . . . thoughts of Savannah Jamison.

The interest he had had in the white man's fort was secondary to his interest in the woman who refused to acknowledge his presence. It had startled him, annoyed him, and now challenged him. He would go back to his village and look again into her eyes.

The day began to lengthen, and Night Sky slipped off to hunt something to eat. Within an hour he had a rabbit roasting over the fire, impaled on a stick pushed into the ground.

He ate, drank from his water bag, then again sat by the fire to watch the fort. Though sometimes carried away by excitement, by nature he was a calm man, and his training as a warrior had taught him the value of patience. Still, he was beginning to wonder what had upset Josiah so and what was going on between Josiah and the white chief within the walls of the fort.

Josiah rode slowly toward the porch. Once there, he stopped and gazed at the man who had been the cause of so much pain to the ones he now called family. He remembered too well the man who stood before him, had known him many years before, and now felt in his heart that John Chevington was here for an evil purpose. He wondered, as an apprehensive chill touched him, if Chevington knew that the valley held a treasure in gold. Silently, he prayed he did not.

"Well, Josiah." Chevington smiled. "It has been a lot of years since I've seen you. Are you still living with the savages?"

"I'm living with White Eagle's people as you well know," Josiah replied quietly. "What are you doing here, John? I would have thought your last visit would have been enough for you."

Chevington's face flushed as the memory of his defeat at the hands of White Eagle and Sun Knife came flooding back to him. He also remembered how Sun Knife had beaten him before the entire tribe of warriors and his own men. Hatred leapt into his eyes, then, seeing Josiah's concern, he quickly veiled it, using powerful self-control and an icy smile.

"An officer does not have control of where he is sent or the nefarious jobs he's forced to do," he replied coolly. "I was sent here to keep the peace."

"Keep the peace? There have been no problems out here since the army left. There will be no problems if the army stays away. These people are peace loving already. They do not need you or your army."

"*Left!*" Chevington spat angrily. "They burned the fort and nearly killed me and my entire force. You call that peace loving? I am here to see that such a thing does not happen again."

"John, for God's sake, leave these people alone. They

288

cause no trouble. They stay in their valley and move only to its far end in winter."

"I have been here for some time." Chevington smiled. "They will not have a problem with me unless they start it."

"Start it," Josiah said softly, "like they started it the last time, when you stole Snow Blossom and Rebecca and drove their husbands to fight you. Do you expect there will be another . . . incident like that one?"

"Rebecca . . ." Chevington said in a low voice, "a white woman who chose to live with such dirty savages. I imagine she has lived to regret such a move?"

"Hardly." Josiah smiled. "She is loved not only by her husband but by the entire tribe. She is also loved by her children—twin children—Lone Star and Night Sky. Night Sky is growing to be a man like his father. I would not want two such men angry at me . . . again," he said.

Chevington chose to ignore his quiet jibe. "And Snow Blossom, White Eagle's sister?"

"Very happy with Cade. They also have two children. There's the boy, Little Eagle, but of course I can't call him a boy. He's a grown man, a man with as much courage as his father. They also have a girl, Spring. You see, John, they're all where they belong, with whom they wish to be. No one in that valley wants a war with the whites. I will remind you again, as I did once before, that they are braver and stronger than you know. Don't start anything. If you do, this time White Eagle might finish it for good."

"Is that a threat?"

"No . . . more of a promise. They will not be pushed from their valley."

"Their valley?"

"It's owned by Alexander and his daughter, Lauren, who is now Summer Rain, wife of Running Wolf. Legally you can't do a thing about that."

"I'm sorry to give you bad news."

"Bad news?"

"I just received some dispatches. Somehow I am to send word to Miss Brent . . . or Summer Rain."

"What word?"

"Her father is dead."

Josiah could only stare for a moment as the shock of the news washed over him. It meant that Alexander was not in Washington to do anything to protect them. It also meant that Lauren was the sole owner of the valley. Josiah knew Chevington quite well. This news put Lauren in the gravest danger.

"This makes no difference," Josiah said. "The valley is still Lauren's. No one can change that—no one had better try. She is well protected. All of us—me included—would give our lives to see these people and their valley safe."

"Josiah, you are unfairly accusing me of many things. We have been here for some time now, and I have done nothing. If those people behave, there will be no trouble. As I said . . . I am only here to keep the peace."

Josiah had no argument for this, but he did not believe a word of it.

"By the way, when they told me you were outside, they said there were two of you. What happened to your heathen friend? Was he afraid to come inside?" Chevington smiled an irritating smile.

"No, I was afraid to let him."

"Oh?"

"I know the men under you too well. He's the son of

White Eagle. I don't want him to be accused of breaking the peace. Anything happens to him here and that whole tribe will explode. No, I sent him to wait for me. When I leave, I will have time to explain the truth to him on the ride back.''

"Then I suggest you go back to these people and tell them to be careful."

"Oh, don't worry, John," Josiah said calmly, "I'll see to it they're not pushed into anything. But if they are, I and some new friends I have will see to it that everyone in Washington knows exactly who is responsible. It's not going to happen again. The last time Cade lost his father and the tribe its medicine man. Their memories run very deep. They have not forgotten the death you brought."

"You are a fool, Josiah," Chevington said quietly. "Neither you or your friends can stop what's going to happen."

"Cade knows what's going to happen, but he intends to help this valley keep peace with the change, so the white invaders can't take it from them."

"Just how is he doing that?" Chevington scoffed.

"You'd be surprised. I'd invite you out to see, but you will never be welcome in that valley, so I'll tell you. He's teaching them much about the white man's ways, including reading and writing. But most of all, he wants them to learn not to be tricked by the white man's treachery as so many of the other tribes have been in the past. This valley is theirs, and he is determined that they will keep it . . . no matter what."

"With Alexander Brent dead, it will be difficult for a woman to hold it. Her husband is Indian, so once it passes from her hands, where will it go? I will tell you. It will be sold in Washington. Once it is, then the tribe will have no choice. It will move . . . or all will perish."

There was so much more Josiah wanted to say, but he was afraid, now that he was angry, that he would say too much. "I will leave now," Josiah announced. "It is time I returned."

"You are welcome to spend the night here," Chevington offered.

"No, it is best I am on my way. Besides, like Night Sky, I prefer to sleep out under the stars." He did not want to say that he did not trust him not to have some accident occur to him. Then he'd need only catch Night Sky unprepared and he would hold the chief's son hostage. He knew quite well that Night Sky would perish in a place like the fort.

He examined the fort closely as he walked to his horse. It was twice the size of any he had ever been in. He guessed that fifty to sixty families made their homes here on their way through to California. There was also a tremendous number of military men, surpassing any force he had ever seen outside of those preparing for battle. He was certain then that Chevington was up to something. He only wished he had some idea what it was.

Night Sky was surprised when Josiah told him they would leave the area now and travel a short distance before they camped. It would have been easier, since it was already early evening, for them to camp where they were and leave in the morning. He suggested this, but Josiah replied, "No, believe me, Night Sky, it is best we leave now."

In these few words and in the shadows that moved behind his friend's eyes, Night Sky could see that Josiah did not trust the white men at the fort. He questioned no longer, but began gathering his things. Soon they were on

292

their way. He did not argue for another reason. It suited his purpose to go back to the village as soon as he possibily could.

He wondered if the white friend of Sun Knife had reached the village yet. Many questions filled his mind. Would the whites stay long? Was she promised to any man? What kind of a life would she want? And, most of all, would she look upon him in the way he desired?

The questions could only find answers in his village, but they lent speed to his journey, so much so, in fact, that it took Josiah no time at all to figure out his thoughts. It worried him. He didn't think Savannah would be the kind of girl to be pleased with Night Sky's suit or eager to live in his village any longer than she had to. He assumed that when Grant left, Savannah would go with him. He wondered just how Night Sky would take his first defeat.

Chapter 21

It had been an interlude in Rayne's life that would become the source of his dearest memories—those warm days of late summer that had blended into unforgettable nights. As he lay awake thinking of all that had happened, Falling Water was curled close to him, and he could hear the steady breathing that told him she slept.

The fire was only a red glow, yet it bathed the tepee in a pale light. Rayne rose on one elbow to look down on Falling Water's sleeping form. Very gently, so as not to disturb her sleep, he moved the robe away that covered her.

He would never cease to be stirred by her beauty. Tenderly, he placed his hand on the soft skin of her hip and slid it up the curve of her waist. As he cupped one rounded breast in his hand, he felt its warmth seep into him. He bent his head to touch his lips lightly against the curve of her shoulder, loving her with a depth that even he could not understand. It swelled through him like a crashing wave, and with it came the strange fear that had been filling his dreams lately. It was one fear he would not be able to face—the fear of losing Falling Water.

It came in dreams, dreams so real that he would awaken from sound sleep trembling with sweaty fear. He knew quite well the Indians strongly believed in dreams, so he had told no one, not even Falling Water. Such a dream had awakened him now, and the memory of it was so vivid that he had to reach out to touch her, just to reassure himself she was all right.

The dream always began the same way. They were in the woods, and he didn't seem to be with her as much as he was watching her. There were others with Falling Water, and he could hear their laughter. At the beginning, they were more sounds than faces, but slowly the faces took form and he could recognize Lone Star and Little Dove.

Suddenly the laughter turned to shrieking and he found himself running toward them. Now he could see that they were trying vainly to fight against dark forms. Falling Water saw Rayne and cried his name. Then a huge form grabbed her up. She fought valiantly but was helpless against the strength of her opponent, who began to move away with her.

Rayne tried to follow, but suddenly his legs seemed to be caught in a thick substances that prevented him from moving. He struggled, but he was held fast and could not get to her. He heard her cries grow weak, could hear her weeping, then the sounds were gone and he was left with a silence he could not bear. He cried out her name as he was suddenly released from what had held him, but it was too late. He searched wildly, but he could find no trace of her. Falling to his knees in complete exhaustion, he heard harsh, demoniac laughter and a heavy voice.

"She is mine and I will make her suffer . . . I will make

her my slave!" The laughter continued, but Rayne had fallen to the ground, crushed by the weight of his utter desperation. He felt it and believed it to be the truth—that he would never see Falling Water again.

Even awake as he was now, the thought of it could make him shake. He lay back down and drew Falling Water into his arms, as if he could erase the dream by holding her.

"Rayne?" she questioned sleepily, struggling up from sleep.

"Shhh, love," he whispered as he kissed her hair. "Go back to sleep . . . everything's fine."

"What is it, Rayne?" she asked. "Can you not sleep?"

"It's nothing." He chuckled. "I've been thinking of you, and that's enough to keep any man from sleeping."

She sat up and looked at him, aware of his mysterious apprehension. He knew she recognized his fear, but he could not answer her questions. It would only upset her more, he realized, for, to her and her people, dreams were voices and instructions from the gods. He stopped her questions the only way he could. He sat up beside her, reached out to slide his hand into the thick mass of her hair, and drew her to him.

His open mouth slanted across hers. If she was startled by the near violence of his kiss, her shock was lost in the fire of her response. Never would she be able to control the flame he could light within her—and never would she want to, she thought. She was breathless when he released her. She looked at him with a half smile on her parted lips, and the passion in her dark eyes flashed back at him.

He traced her lips with a gentle finger and let his hand move slowly down her slender throat. He heard her soft intake of breath as his hand first touched gently then captured her breast in a searing caress.

She did not understand, nor did she care to understand, the wild emotions he loosened within her with just his touch. She only knew that she wanted him to continue to build this warmth to the blazing fire she remembered so well.

He took her shoulders and gently laid her against the fur robes. Then she closed her eyes as she felt the hard strength of his body and the searching need of his possessive mouth. She sensed a new and deeper urgency in his lovemaking, and her arms held him close as she sought to give whatever he might need to ease the tension within him.

"I love you, Falling Water," he said huskily, his lips against her skin. "More than my own life, for life would be an endless nothing without you."

She caressed the hard muscle of his back, letting her fingers trail down his lean length to his hard buttocks. She savored the feel of such strength, strength that could render her mindless and ecstatic. He closed his eyes and groaned softly as her hands continued their intoxicating exploration. It set fire to his blood and stimulated his desire. When she found the source of her pleasure in the hard throbbing shaft of his manhood, her light touch made his heated flesh leap with life in her hand.

His hands, hard yet sensitive, gently stroked her flesh, and she moved beneath him, eager for more of this burning rapture. She wanted more, needed more, but he intended that they undertake a slow journey to the summit he desired.

His mouth hungrily claimed hers, then moved from one flame-touched spot to another. He nibbled gently on the corner of her lips, her ear lobe, and down to one rose-crested breast, where he sucked until she cried out from the intense pleasure. He tortured her body with his mouth until it tingled in response. He stirred the caldron of molten desire within her until she wanted to scream out for their union. Still, he restrained himself.

His hands slid up the soft flesh of her inner thighs to the moist, throbbing valley, where his fingers explored the soft peak nestled within. It was almost more than she could bear, and she arched to meet him, seeking release from this spiraling and overpowering need. She was utterly lost now, and he heard her call to him, felt her hands urge him closer, and saw her eyes close in passion and her head turning from side to side as if seeking the final peak of rapture.

Only now, when she was completely lost to passion, did he press himself within her. Thobbing deeply, gently, inside her body, he slowly began to move, withdrawing the length of his shaft, then renewing his path in slow, steady rhythmic movements that forced her beyond any control. He heard her cry out and felt her body tremble as she slowly began cresting the peak of passion.

Only when he knew she was reaching fulfillment did he begin his own search. As he drove himself deep and hard again and again, his need became a volcanic eruption. They seemed to explode together into a star-touched oblivion, then they slowly fluttered back to reality, drifting, sinking, and clinging to each other as the calm overtook them.

He did not want to rest his weight on her, yet he couldn't let her go. He rolled to his side and drew her with him. She curled close to him, and a new tenderness touched them both. They had been blended into one breath, one passion. He was warmth and protection, and she was peace and contentment, and, for a time, they lay together in silence. There is no peace like this, he thought, nothing more precious than this touching of souls and bodies that melted both. For a time they treasured the silence that bespoke all.

Falling Water rose to one elbow and looked down into his smoldering gaze. He could read well the look of love in her eyes. She reachd out to caress his brawny chest, then bent to kiss the warmth of his flesh. "You are satisfied, my husband?" She laughed softly. "Your body will not seek any other trails to follow?"

He chuckled. "'Satisfied' is a temporary word, my love. I have only to touch you, to feel your touch, to know again the desire to possess you."

Her lips played softly across his flesh, and she could feel him quiver, though he made no move to stop her. Her lips crept up to his strong chin and touched his own. Her tongue traced their outline, then gently sought admittance. His mouth parted to draw the warmth of her within, and they played a gentle game for a moment, then she moved again to taste his skin and smell the heady scent of him. He closed his eyes, and his hands gently held her while she began to explore more bravely. She nibbled softly and was thrilled with the sensations being created within her, as well as with the power she felt when she realized the tumult she was causing him.

Her lips sucked gently on a nipple, then moved down to taste the warm, salty flavor of his skin. She heard his breathing increase, and he stirred beneath her questing hands and mouth.

She felt the firm, vital strength of him as her hands slid

over his broad chest, to his waist, then further down to caress the heat of his passion that throbbed at her touch.

She was dizzy with the pleasure of possession. He was hers; he belonged to her as much as the breath in her body. She heard him murmur her name and felt his hands grow more insistent as he tried to draw her closer. But she was not ready to set him free from the exquisite torment yet.

Slowly, purposefully, she set a flaming trail to passion that he could only follow. It was a path whose end was the goal they both craved. With gentle hands and branding lips she drove him to near-mindless pleasure.

He could hear the sound of her throaty laughter as his ability to control his wayward emotions reached its limit. Hands that would tolerate no more drew her beneath him, and a low moan of passion escaped his lips as he entered her and sank into the depths of her pulsing warmth. His slow and gentle movements gave way to more demanding passion, a passion that could no longer be contained. The pace of his rapid breathing was matched by the force of his possession. He drove with hard, tormenting strokes that were almost savage, and her body met his thrusts with an answering intensity that signaled both triumph and surrender. Together they climbed to the volcano's crest and found their goal in the white-hot lava of consummation.

Drained and exhausted, they lay side by side for a time. Then, very gently, he drew her close to share the warmth of the aftermath of their powerful and joyous joining. It was a silent time, a peaceful time, for both knew that words could never fully describe the rapture they had found in the sanctuary of each other's love.

In all the times they had been together, never had a

union been so intoxicatingly complete, never had she felt as much possessed by him, and never had she felt as much one with him and loved by him as she did now.

She curled close to his warmth as deep contentment and delicious exhaustion drew her into the valley of sleep. "I love you" were the last whispered words she heard along with the warmth of his soft laugh as he realized she slept. He held her tight, kissing her soft hair, then closed her eyes to let sweeter dreams claim him.

When Rayne awoke the next morning, the sun had already risen and Falling Water was gone. He knew that since sunrise she would have been about her daily work, and it was his usual habit to be up early also, but his comfort and physical exhaustion had kept him abed.

He rose and dressed, then left the tepee to go to the river to bathe. Afterward, he returned to the village to see what the day promised. He thought of his life here and knew this was the only place he would ever really be happy. He liked the leisurely ways of the Cheyenne and their warm, accepting attitude.

As he entered the outskirts of the village, he saw White Eagle and Sun Knife deep in conversation in front of White Eagle's tepee and he walked toward them. They greeted him warmly and even teased him a little about his recently extended sleeping hours. He laughed, enjoying the friendly camaraderie they both offered.

"White Eagle," Rayne said, "would you mind if I asked you a question?"

"No, ask what you want," White Eagle replied.

"I have heard small bits and pieces of the story of what happened between your people and the whites some years ago."

White Eagle nodded, waiting for Rayne to continue.

"Would you tell me the whole story?"

White Eagle and Sun Knife exchanged glances, then White Eagle smiled. "Come to my tepee. We will smoke and talk. It is a long and interesting story."

They went in and sat before a low-burning fire. White Eagle filled pipes with tobacco and handed one to each. They lit their pipes and smoked in silence for a few moments.

"The story begins many years ago, when Sun Knife and I were boys," White Eagle began. Sun Knife laughed.

"Don't make it sound like so many years. You will have him thinking we are old men."

Rayne smiled as he watched these two close friends. Their eyes sparkled with humor, they were tall, strong, and handsome, and he found it impossible to apply the word "old" to either.

White Eagle grinned in response to these words, then he continued his story. There were no interruptions or any other sounds as White Eagle related the tale.

"Then this John Chevington actually tried to destroy your entire village?" Rayne questioned.

"He very nearly succeeded."

"And Lauren and her father are the only ones who actually have the power to hold this valley?"

White Eagle scowled. "I will hold this valley no matter what the whites decide to do."

"I did not mean that you could not hold it, White Eagle. I respect your strength. I was speaking only of the law of the white man."

"Under their law, it is so. But their law is not mine. Their ways are not ours. And I say again, this valley

302

belongs to my people, and I will hold it—despite white man's laws or anything else."

Rayne remained silent. To insult a chief as strong and powerful as White Eagle was unthinkable, and he had no intention of doing any such thing. He noted Sun Knife's silence and determined to find a way to discuss the situation with him later, for Sun Knife understood the ways of both the whites and the Indians. He knew their strengths and weaknesses, and he also realized the whites' inexhaustible numbers.

"Maybe you can," Rayne finally said. "It would seem that only Josiah, Mack, and I know about the gold in the valley."

"It is a possibility," Sun Knife replied. "As far as I know, there have been no other whites in the valley for several years. If they had known, we would be flooded by now."

"The only things that puzzle me are the identities of our attackers, why they disguised themselves as Indian, and where Thomas went."

"Perhaps they took him away so he could tell the tale of your attack to others," White Eagle offered. "If he was as young as you say and had never been here before, he might have been fooled. If so, he would spread the word of an Indian attack. For some whites, that would be more than enough reason to retaliate."

Rayne sighed. "There are too many questions and not enough answers."

"The answers," White Eagle reminded gently, "lie in the white man's village. We do not wander from our land; we do not hunt their food; we do not want to take what is theirs. Why do they insist that they must possess what is ours?"

"It is not all whites, White Eagle," Rayne said. "I know many who could live in peace with you and your people."

"Yes"—White Eagle chuckled—"but those people are not the ones we have to think about."

Sun Knife laughed softly. "Those are the people who come out here and decide to live with us. Some"—he grinned at Rayne—"even marry into the tribe."

Rayne smiled. "Yes, some are lucky,"

"Speaking of your bride, does she know you must leave when spring comes?"

"Yes, I've told her. She's not happy about it, but I promised her I would be back before long, before the summer grows hot."

"I have spoken to your friend, Mack," White Eagle said. "He says he will not return with you."

"No, I don't think he will."

"He carries a heavy heart," White Eagle said thoughtfully. "I think some old memories linger in his mind to cause him much unhappiness."

"Yes, but I do not know what they are," Rayne replied in a firm voice that told both listeners he had no intention of questioning Mack about such things.

"I will tell him when he goes that he will always be welcome here. Maybe some day he will choose to return."

"I hope so. Mack has been a good friend."

"There are others in this village that carry the same hope." White Eagle smiled. Rayne looked at him questioningly.

"Others?"

"At least one."

"Who?"

"Little Dove, the sister of your wife's father."

The revelation took Rayne completely by surprise.

"Little Dove! I never realized . . ."

"Maybe your friend has not realized either." Sun Knife laughed.

"I wonder," White Eagle speculated, "how Running Wolf would take it if he chose to ask for her. He had some trouble in giving away his daughter to a white visitor. Giving away his sister, too, might not make him a happy man."

Rayne was about to answer when a voice called out to be allowed to enter. White Eagle gave his permission, and a young warrior stepped inside. He was a scout whose job it was to protect the village from surprise intruders. White Eagle questioned him. "There is trouble?"

"No, my chief," he replied. "There is a small party of whites less than a day's ride from the valley. They travel slowly, but they come straight. They know where they are going."

"How many?"

"Five or six."

"Bring my horse and Sun Knife's. We will go to meet these strangers. It would be best if no other whites came here. The yellow metal must be kept a secret."

"I will ride with you," Rayne said.

"No," White Eagle replied. "They should not know that other whites live among us."

The scout left to bring the horses, and the three men stepped outside to wait. He returned quickly, then mounted agilely, proud to ride with his chief. Every young warrior prayed for any opportunity to bring himself to the attention of his leader.

Rayne stood and watched them ride away. Both Sun

Knife and White Eagle rode as men accustomed to horses, and, with a relaxed and easy pace that was meant to cover much ground, they left the village.

They rode in silence for a long time, each deep in thoughts that were in many ways similar and in some ways completely different.

They stopped twice to rest their horses and to drink from their water sacs. After over four hours of steady travel, they stopped to watch the riders approach.

Slowly Sun Knife began to sense something familiar in one of the riders. Then he smiled and turned to White Eagle, who had also become aware of the identity of at least one in the party.

"Grant," Sun Knife said. "It's been a long time. I'll be glad to see him again. Maybe he'll have some answers."

"I would not be surprised." White Eagle smiled.

They kicked their horses into motion and rode to meet the welcome visitors.

Chapter 22

It took the guide with Grant's party only a minute to spot the two approaching riders and to identify them. It took Grant only a moment or two longer. Old, familiar memories tugged at him, and his eyes shone suspiciously as he swallowed deeply before he spoke.

"Martha! Savannah! It's Cade and White Eagle. We've got an almost royal welcoming committee."

"Papa," Savannah asked, "how did they even know we were here?"

Grant laughed. "White Eagle knows everything that goes on in this part of the country. I expect they spotted us a long time ago. I'll be glad to see those two again."

Savannah looked at her father. It still surprised her that he could be so excited about being in such a place and meeting two half-naked savages. She watched them approach, and it did not take her long to see the obvious similarity between the huge chief of the Cheyenne and the Indian that had met them on the journey and had looked at her so fiercely. She knew without asking that they were father and son.

Her father dismounted as the two stopped and slid from their horses. Sun Knife held out his hand with a wide smile, and Grant grasped it in a firm, hard grip.

"Cade . . . Damn, it's good to see you," Grant said.

"It's been too long, Grant." Cade grinned. "Old friends should see each other more often. What brings you out here? I hope"—he laughed—"that you plan to stay for a long time."

"I'm staying for a while, and it's a long story why I'm here. First, I'd like you to meet Martha, my wife, and Savannah, my daughter."

"Mrs. Jamison," Cade with with a smile.

"Martha," came the quick correction.

"Martha, welcome to my part of the country. You're not too far from our village, and we'd love to have you stay with us for a while."

"Thank you." Martha was captivated by the charm of a man who looked like an Indian and spoke in such a cultured manner. His blue eyes held her attention. Then Grant took her arm and turned her to the tall, handsome man who stood by Cade.

"This is White Eagle," he said and Martha and Savannah could hear the deep respect in his voice. "Chief of the Cheyenne."

This time there was no denying that he was fierce, but, when he spoke, both women were completely startled by his command of their language and his good manners. Their conceptions of the savage Indian began to dissolve in their minds.

"You will be welcome in our village," he said. His dark eyes glittered with humor. "My wife has been the only golden-haired woman my people have seen. Your daughter will surprise them."

Savannah did not speak, but she now wondered if this man's son was quite as savage as she first had thought.

Thomas had stood quietly, but now he stepped forward, and Grant quickly introduced him.

Both Cade and White Eagle had heard Rayne refer to a Thomas as their lost friend, but neither associated this Thomas with Rayne's.

"Come, join us for some food," Grant said. "Then we will ride back to the village with you."

Both men agreed. The guide took their horses, and they sat about the fire with Grant, Thomas, and the women. They ate and talked, and soon the conversation turned to White Eagle's village.

"Thomas has quite a story to tell you, Cade—you and White Eagle. I think there are a few problems in store for your people. We're here to see that nothing comes as a surprise, and you have some time to find ways to protect yourselves."

"What do you know of our village and any problems we might have?" White Eagle questioned Thomas.

"Let me tell you the story from the beginning," Thomas said. "It is one I still don't really understand myself, and," he added, "it involves the deaths of two of my very best friends."

"Go on with your story," White Eagle replied.

Thomas began to speak slowly, and no one asked a question or tried to interrupt until he came to the point in the story when he was about to start toward the plains with two companions. He had not yet mentioned their names, but he had spoken of his father and his greed, and of John Chevington. He spoke of the twisted way in which they had planned to use him.

"I left with my two friends, and we were attacked by

what I thought for a long time was a band of Indians. My two friends were killed, but I was kept alive"—he laughed harshly—"kept alive for a reason."

When he said these last words, Cade's eyes at first grew wide, then glowed with pleasure. He turned to face White Eagle, who had already begun to think the same thoughts.

"Your friends, Thomas, what were their names?" White Eagle asked quickly.

"Rayne Freeman and Mackenzie Weaver. Why?"

Both men smiled. "Well," Cade said, "you'll be pleased to know that your friends are not dead."

"Not dead! But I was told . . ."

"They were left for dead, but we found them and cared for their wounds. You will find them in our village, alive and well. They also thought you dead. They will be overjoyed to see you," White Eagle replied quickly.

Thomas's eyes grew suspiciously damp, and, for a moment, the lump in his throat choked back any words he might have said. "God," he finally gasped. "Alive! This is wonderful. I could not have heard better news. I cannot wait to see them."

"Well, we do not have far to ride," Cade said. "By nightfall we should be in the village."

They all rode swiftly, especially Thomas, who could still hardly believe the good fortune that had kept Rayne and Mack alive.

Rayne and Mack were as impatient as the others in the village to know of the whites whom Sun Knife and White Eagle had ridden out to meet. It was now long after dark, and the scent of food coking over the evening fires drew all to their tepees.

Rayne stepped inside his tepee to find Falling Water on

her knees beside the fire. She looked up at his entrance and smiled.

"Ummm." He grinned. "Whatever that is, it smells good. I'm hungry."

"I knew you would return when the scent of food reached you," she teased. "No doubt it is the surest way to draw a man home. The echo of his empty stomach will always bring him when nothing else can."

He chuckled in reply and went to kneel beside her. "And you think the rumble of my empty belly is what drew me here?"

Her eyes sparkled with mischief, even though she did not smile. "Were those not your first words?"

"I said it smelled good. I didn't say it was the answer to my hunger."

"Oh," she replied softly, "and what is the answer to your hunger?"

His arms enclosed her, and he drew her against him to kiss her firmly, slowly, and very thoroughly. "You will always be the cause and the satisfaction of my deepest hunger," he whispered.

Falling Water reached up and placed her hands on each side of his face. Unshed tears of happiness glistened in her eyes. "Truly, husband, I love you more than my own life."

Their lips met, and he enfolded her in his arms. Slowly they sank to the fur mat. The kiss grew deeper as her lips parted to accept him. He groaned softly as his arms bound her to him and his hands began a slow, delightful exploration of her curves. The next groan was one of half anger, half misery as Mack called to him from outside. Falling Water's muffled giggle could be heard as Rayne sat up. He turned to look at her suspiciously, but she

311

retained her innocent look. Again Mack called to him from outside.

"Rayne?"

"Yes, come in," Rayne shouted. He moved closer to the fire and hoped his physical condition wasn't as apparent to Mack as it was uncomfortable for him.

Mack bent and entered, smiling inwardly. He knew what kind of situation he had interrupted, but he felt the news he carried would at least temporarily make up for it, and, from the soft smile and glowing eyes of Falling Water, he knew the moment would soon be recaptured.

"What is it, Mack?"

"Come outside."

"Why? What's going on?"

"You're not going to believe it. You'll have to see it for yourself. Sun Knife and White Eagle are back with the white visitors."

"Someone we know?"

"Just come on out. You have to see this for yourself."

Rayne got to his feet with a grunt. "Well, if you're not going to tell me, I guess I'll just have to find out for myself."

Together, he and Mack left the tepee, walking toward White Eagle's dwelling. There was a large gathering of people that made way for them as they approached. Then suddenly Rayne came face to face with Thomas. He stopped in his tracks, unable to believe what he was seeing. Thomas was grinning.

"Hello, Rayne, kind of surprised to see me?"

"Thomas! How the . . . damnit, kid, we thought you were dead."

Thomas held out his hand. "I'm very much alive, and I've got some things to tell you."

Rayne gripped his hand with such force that Thomas winced as he laughed.

"I'm glad you're glad to see me, but you don't have to break my arm to prove it."

"I'm glad to see you." Rayne too laughed. "And I'd sure like to know what happened."

"Come inside," White Eagle said. "The others have been cared for, but this one would speak to you and your friend."

"Others?" Rayne questioned.

"An old friend of Sun Knife's has returned with his family. They are with Sun Knife and Snow Blossom, and they will meet you tomorrow. For now, let us talk."

Rayne nodded, and White Eagle, Rayne, Mack, and Thomas went inside. They sat about the fire and Thomas explained to Rayne exactly why he had been allowed to go with him and what his father's plans had been. Rayne was silent and filled with anger for a man who would callously order the deaths of two innocent people and allow his own son to be put in such danger.

"Don't worry about it, Rayne," Thomas said gently. "It doesn't matter to me anymore. I guess I always knew he valued a lot of things more than me. I know him for what he is, and at least I didn't fall into his scheme. He'll have to think of some other way."

"Yes," Rayne said, "but I'm quite sure he is already doing that."

"I guess he probably is," Thomas said sadly.

"Thomas, are you staying for a while?" Rayne asked.

"Grant plans on it. He wants to talk to you about a few things. Senator Miles sent some messages, and I expect he wants you all to get together to help figure this out."

"Well, we'll talk in the morning. For now, you'd better

313

get some rest. Do you want to share a place with Mack?"

"Sure. That would be fine."

They rose, said good night to White Eagle, and started back to Mack's tepee.

"How come you two aren't sharing a tepee?"

Mack grinned. "'Cause Rayne went and got himself married, that's why."

"Married!" Thomas cried in delighted surprise. "Who did you marry, Rayne?"

"Falling Water. She's Running Wolf's daughter. If you remember, we told you that Running Wolf's the one who is married to Lauren Brent, Alexander Brent's daughter. She and her father own this valley."

"That was a pretty little thing you brought with you," Mack said. "Grant's girl, what was her name . . . Savannah?"

"Well, she may be pretty," Thomas replied in disgust, "but she's a silly, spoiled little rich girl who thinks she's too good to be out here, away from her fancy society. I was tempted several times on the way out to turn her over my knee and give her what she was asking for."

Both Rayne and Mack laughed. "Some people just don't belong here, Thomas," Rayne said softly.

"I suppose you're right." They stopped by Mack's tepee and said a quick good night. Mack and Thomas went inside while Rayne continued on to his own tepee. He moved quickly, for thoughts of the dark-eyed beauty that waited for him had suddenly invaded his mind. He pushed aside the flap and bent to enter, closing the flap behind him. Then he gazed across the space into dark, welcoming eyes.

* * *

Inside the tepee, Mack showed Thomas where he could sleep and told him to make himself comfortable. "I'm going out for a few minutes," Mack said as he gathered some things in a bundle.

He left the tepee and walked to the dwelling in which Little Dove and her father lived. He called out and requested permission to enter. It was immediately given. He went in, and Little Dove's father made him welcome, but Little Dove could only stare at him in surprise.

"I would speak with you," Mack said.

"Sit and speak," Little Dove's father replied.

Mack was fully aware of Little Dove's silence. "I come to offer gifts," he said. He heard Little Dove's soft intake of breath. "I offer you horses and buffalo robes," he continued.

"And you seek something here?" he demanded.

"Yes. I ask for Little Dove as a wife."

Little Dove made a soft, inarticulate sound and lowered her head. He knew there were tears in her eyes, tears she would refuse to weep before him or before her father, and her father was too wise not to sense the unspoken emotions between them.

"I will think of what you ask," he said. "I will let you know what I decide."

"I am a strong warrior. She will have all she needs. I will care for her well and use my strength to keep her safe."

The old man nodded silently. Mack knew he could say no more. With one last look at Little Dove, he rose and left. He walked slowly, and, in a few minutes, he heard what he had expected to hear—the sound of her footsteps approaching. He stopped and stood still, waiting for what he knew was coming. She stopped beside him, and he turned to look at her.

"You cannot do this," she whispered.

"Can't I?"

"I do not want your pity," she choked out.

"I do not ever think of pity when I think of you. I think of a gentle woman who touched a place inside of me that has been dead a long time. I never thought that could happen."

"I came to you because I cared that you were in pain. I do not hold that as a debt for you to repay. I will not marry you. I will not marry a man who comes to me with gratitude instead of love. Go to my father and tell him."

"I will not," he said with determination.

"I will not marry you!" she said firmly, then she gasped and he roughly grabbed her wrist and dragged her to the shadows behind the nearest tepee. Suddenly, she was pulled into his arms and bound against his iron-hard chest. His firm, possessive mouth captured hers, halting her words and her breath. Slowly he took command of her senses. She could not move until he chose to release her, and he took enough time to let her know that he understood this. He loosened his hold and she stepped back from him. He would have said the words then that would end all the pain; he would have told her of the love that was slowly seeping into the dark places of his mind and heart. He would have spoken, but, with a soft cry, she turned and ran from him. He would tell her soon, he thought. He would take all the time in the world to care for her and build her belief in him. Slowly, he walked back to his own tepee.

Inside Sun Knife's tepee, it soon became apparent to

both Snow Blossom and Sun Knife that Savannah was less than pleased to be where she was. Snow Blossom and Martha were getting acquainted while Grant and Sun Knife were deep in conversation.

"Cade," Grant said, "it's pretty obvious from Thomas's story that Chevington and Martin know about the gold here. I can't believe they haven't done something by now. At least Senator Miles and Alexander are trying to protect our backs a little." He went on to tell his friend about the document Alexander Brent had given him that he would ask Lauren to sign.

"Both Alexander and Senator Miles are good protection to have. I'm sure we would have had many more problems a long time ago if they hadn't been there."

"I would certainly be afraid for Lauren's life if her father hadn't seen fit to trust us with the land. Once the deed is filed, she and Alexander will no longer be the only ones standing between this village and a disaster."

"It would be so, for White Eagle will not give up this valley without a fight. They will know they have met a strong force if they come up against him. He destroyed a fort once. He'd do it again. He won't be pushed any further."

"And they'll build them and build them and build them, so what good will it do?"

"It will give us time, and time is what I need to help bring these people to a point where they can understand the white man."

"That's pretty hard," Grant said grimly, "when you and I can hardly understand some of them ourselves. Men like Chevington and Preston are beyond me."

"I'm teaching, or rather, Lauren and Rebecca are teaching the children to speak the white man's tongue.

317

One of the differences between them and the whites is that they cannot understand the white man's possessiveness about land and their destruction of it. They have learned to live with nature. The white man has learned to subjugate nature. There's a big difference. The white man tends to want to conquer everything he comes in contact with. These people will not be dominated. They have a kind of pride the white man will never understand. They just don't see all the danger yet."

"Yet White Eagle says this valley is his."

"But he means it in a different way. White Eagle and all the others believe that they must live in harmony with all that nature created, making room for all things to live. He does not believe that the trees, the water, or the animals are his to destroy; they are his to live with in peace as the Great Spirit has planned. They do not even kill an animal for food without praying to the gods and speaking for the animal itself, and they never kill for the sake of killing. That is another of the white man's accomplishments."

"You sound bitter, Cade," Martha said softly.

"Not bitter, Martha," Cade replied. "A little disappointed maybe. My father's people include a lot of good men. It seems almost impossible to get them to understand what's happening here, but it so easily comes to the attention of the evil and treacherous ones."

"But we cannot stop trying," Martha said.

"No." Cade smiled. "We won't."

"You all must be very tired," Snow Blossom broke in. "Since your arrival, I have had some women preparing a comfortable place for you to sleep. I know our tepee will be too uncomfortable for everyone. If you will come with me, I will show you."

"You are very kind, Snow Blossom," Martha replied. "I am tired."

They rose and followed Snow Blossom, who led them to a rather large tepee. Inside furs had been spread to make comfortable beds. A low fire burned in the center. After asking if they required anything else, Snow Blossom left.

"Mother," Savannah complained, "we're practically sleeping on the ground . . . again."

"Well," Grant said with a chuckle, "I can't see your four poster in a tepee, and besides"—he sighed as he lay back on his bed—"this is very comfortable."

Savannah gave an exasperated sound and went to the other pile of furs, where she plopped herself down. "I could be at the ball and having fun with all my friends, and I'm forced to sit in this disgusting place. When can we go home?"

Grant was tired—physically and mentally tired—of Savannah's continual pouting. "Young lady," he said, "I'm tired of your complaining. Be the lady you are supposed to be. These people are warm and friendly and you might find yourself having a good time if you only allow it. Now, I intend to stay here for a while, and you will stay with us, so you might as well make the best of it!"

Savannah's eyes flew to her mother's, and she found them just as angry. She turned her back to them, and lay on the dark fur, trying to contain her tears of utter frustration.

Within an hour, most of the village was asleep. Only well-placed guards remained awake to protect the sleeping inhabitants, and only those guards saw the return of Josiah and Night Sky.

319

They rode slowly into the village. First they cared for their horses, making sure they were rubbed down and well fed and watered. Then they walked toward the chief's tepee.

"Should we not wake Running Wolf and his wife and tell them?" Night Sky asked softly.

"No, let's go to see White Eagle first. It's going to be damn bad news no matter whom we tell first."

Night Sky sighed deeply. He knew as well as Josiah the problems their news could bring. He also knew the grief it was going to cause in their village.

In front of White Eagle's tepee they called out softly. Within moments White Eagle, who slept very lightly, was at the entrance with a questioning look on his face.

"White Eagle," Josiah said softly, "we have to talk to you."

"There is something wrong?" White Eagle questioned.

"Yes . . . very wrong," Josiah replied.

White Eagle motioned to them, and they walked a little away from his tepee so that Rebecca would not hear their words. They stopped, and his dark eyes studied both men. "All right," he said quietly, "tell me your news."

Chapter 23

White Eagle's face was grim when Josiah finished talking. He stood for a moment in silent thought, then he spoke.

"Night Sky, my son, Josiah, my friend, go to your beds. Such news would be better left until tomorrow. Grief seems to be much blacker at night. I will tell them in the morning."

Both men nodded. They were extremely tired, and breaking such news to people they loved was not something either of them had looked forward to. They moved away silently, and White Eagle stood for some time, thinking. Then he turned and retraced his steps to his tepee. He was disturbed to find Rebecca sitting by the fire, to which she had recently added fresh wood. She studied his face for a moment, then spoke softly.

"Come, sit by me, my husband, and tell me what disturbs you so in the middle of the night." From the time he had reached manhood, Night Sky had had a tepee of his own, so it did not surprise Rebecca that her son did not accompany his father. What did surprise her was the dark look in White Eagle's eyes. "There is trouble?" she questioned softly.

"I don't know. Night Sky and Josiah have brought news. The chief at the new fort"—his eyes met Rebecca's—"is John Chevington."

Rebecca gasped and closed her eyes for a moment as visions of past tragedy flashed before her. She remembered John Chevington far too well.

"Why?" she whispered softly. "Why does he have to continue to haunt us? Why can he not just let us live in peace?"

"Because he hates," White Eagle replied. "And his hatred is so deep he cannot see any other thing. Golden one"—his voice grew firmer—"there will come a day and a time when I will have to kill that man, for only his death will stop his hatred."

But Rebecca, being white, knew what this would bring. "If you killed him, they would send a flood of white soldiers here. They would destroy your whole village . . . all your people . . . and your children."

Utter frustration and futile anger were reflected on White Eagle's face. "We have to put a stop to him, because if we do not, he will come."

"Not if we do not provoke him."

"He will come anyway," White Eagle said grimly.

"Why are you so sure?"

"Because Josiah found the shiny yellow metal your people love so much."

"Gold?"

"Yes, and the white chief, Chevington—he also knows it is here."

"They cannot touch this valley! Alexander and Lauren own it. They cannot do anything about this gold."

"Golden One," White Eagle said quietly, his eyes filled with sympathy, "Summer Rain . . . Lauren . . . her father is dead."

Rebecca gasped as real fear began to seep into her heart. "How . . . how do you know?"

"The white chief at the fort, he told Josiah. It seems he was very pleased to do so. He must think that we are helpless to stop him now, but he is wrong."

He stood up, and Rebecca gazed at him. In the light of the fire, he was a bronze giant of a man. His eyes were fierce and darkly cold, and his granite face was firm as he clenched his jaw and restrained the desire to go to the white fort and kill their chief this very night. Only Rebecca understood the pain and the worry that had brought forth this reaction, for Rebecca was the one who knew the depth of his love for his people, for her, and for their children. And only Rebecca knew the gentle man beneath the rock-hard exterior. Her eyes now filled with fear, real fear, the fear of losing him. He was the rock of her world, and she did not believe there could be an existence without him.

He looked down and saw the fear and uncertainty in her eyes. Slowly he came to her, knelt beside her, and, without words, took her in his arms. She closed her eyes, hoping she could give him as much comfort as he did her.

Night Sky lay awake. He wondered what effect the news he had brought his father would have on his family and his village. He also let his mind drift to the white girl he knew lay asleep in a tepee not far from his. He struggled to control the desire to go and see if she were awake. He wondered what she would do if he did. He closed his eyes and battled for sleep, and, when it came, it brought dreams. What he could control when awake was not so easily controlled when he slept.

Only the few—Night Sky, White Eagle, Josiah and Rebecca—remained awake. The others, contented, were asleep. The village was quiet and remained so until the first rays of sun touched the horizon.

When the dawn was still a grey mist, the village began to stir. Soon fine wisps of white smoke signaled early-morning fires.

Within their warm tepee, Falling Water lay very still. She was curved against Rayne's hard body, and one of his arms rested possessively about her. Across the lower part of her body he had flung a leg, and she knew she could not move without waking him.

The tepee was half in shadow, yet she could see his face clearly. What was strong and mature when awake became almost boyish in sleep. His thick, auburn hair was growing longer and tumbled across his forehead. She studied his face, knowing already every emotion that could cross it. She could still feel the tingle within her that his smile or sparkling eyes could evoke. She felt her body grow warm and the deeper places of her womanhood grow moist with even sweeter memories.

She reached up and gently pushed his hair away from his face, letting her fingers thread lightly through the thick mass of it. She enjoyed its clean, soft feel. There was nothing about him she would alter. She could still taste that firm, hard mouth as it had brazenly ravaged hers. She followed the line of his jaw to his throat, where the pulse beat rapidly. Very gently, she moved aside the robe that covered them and let her eyes touch where they chose: a broad, fur-matted chest, a slim, lean waist, and hard, muscular hips that tapered down to long, heavily muscled legs.

She saw the maleness of him, and, though softened, it could still excite her. Very gently, she reached to lightly touch the flesh of his belly, then slip down to gently hold him. She felt new warmth come alive in her hand and looked up quickly to see his eyes intent on hers.

"Don't let me stop you, love," he said softly. "Whatever you planned to do is fine with me."

Their eyes held. "I want to know you," she said quietly.

"Do you not know me now?" He smiled.

"I . . ."

He chuckled softly and drew her close to him. "I know, love, I know. Sometimes I just want to look at you, to sort of pull you inside of me and touch every part of you until every part of you is part of me. God, loving you is something so fine and wonderful that I can't believe it." He looked down into her eyes. "We have a lifetime to learn together," he whispered. "Let us learn everything there is to learn, and, after that, we will create a love that is only ours, that no one else can share as we can."

His voice died to a soft whisper as their mouths parted and blended in a soul-shattering kiss. They touched, their hands seeking to discover every beat that this wild emotion drove through their blood. He stroked her sleek, soft body, cupping her breasts and kissing them, sucking gently on each hardened nipple, nipping with strong teeth the tenderness of her flesh until she cried out in passion. His hands slid down her slim waist to grip her buttocks and draw her even closer against him.

325

She felt the heat of him, hard and striving to reach to the center of her, and she welcomed him within her with a moan of pure ecstasy. He filled her to the limit she could contain, and she gasped at the sheer joy of possessing him. It was a thunderous, overpowering joining, and they were caught in a maelstrom from which they could not escape—and from which they did not want to escape.

She engulfed him, and the white-hot pleasure of it forced a cry from her lips. Bracing himself on his elbows to release some of his weight from her, he began to thrust more rapidly. Her head rolled from side to side and her body writhed beneath him, arching to accept each thrust. She was mindless now, knowing only the strength of him as he moved faster and faster, harder and harder, until she felt she could stand no more. Like a brilliant, cataclysmic explosion, completion left them gasping and clinging to each other. Wordlessly, they clung tightly while the careening world righted itself.

He held her, knowing the value of this moment that they shared. Though still dizzy with rapture, he knew that if she left his side now, something very precious would be lost. He caressed her hair and spoke quietly of his love for her.

The sun was well over the horizon before they rose and dressed. Rayne left the tepee with the intention of going to see Thomas again, but outside he met Lauren walking by.

"Good morning," she said cheerfully.

"Yes," he said with a quick laugh. "It is a very beautiful morning, isn't it? Where are you off to so early?"

326

"I am on my way to see White Eagle. He sent for me. I hope Rebecca is not sick."

"It's too beautiful a day to be ill, but with you about, I'm sure whatever it is will be dealt with quickly."

Lauren laughed and continued on her way. She had no idea why the chief would send for her unless someone was ill, but she had seen Rebecca the day before and she had seemed quite well then. Running Wolf had risen very early and she assumed he had gone hunting.

She reached White Eagle's tepee and called out for permission to enter. It was immediately granted by White Eagle. But when she stepped inside, she was surprised to find a grim-faced Running Wolf there. What upset her more was the fact that Rebecca had obviously been crying. The smile on her face faded and she turned a questioning gaze to Running Wolf, who rose and came to her side. It was very rare for a warrior to show affection in front of anyone, for such displays were usually reserved for the privacy of his own tepee. It actually frightened Lauren when he put his arm about her and drew her close to him. With sinking heart, she realized that something tragic had occurred to someone close to her. She clutched Running Wolf and looked up into dark, sympathetic eyes.

"Running Wolf," she whispered, "who . . . what— not my daughter, Falling Water?"

"No, my love," he said, "yet I am filled with pain for you. It is your father."

"Father?"

"He is dead, Summer Rain," he replied softly. "There has been an accident, and he is dead."

"Dead," she whispered raggedly. The words stunned

327

her, and for a moment she could not believe them.

"Josiah and Night Sky brought word," Running Wolf said sadly. "It happened over four weeks ago."

"Four weeks," she repeated. "He is already buried . . . buried, and I was not there."

"I know how you must feel, my love." The pain on his face was for her, and it was evident in his voice. The three of them yearned to comfort her because they loved her, but she turned blank eyes to them. It was as if she were frozen. No tears touched her eyes, and she stood motionless for what seemed an eternity.

"I . . . I must go," she whispered and, to the surprise of all of them, she turned and left.

"Running Wolf," Rebecca began, wanting to go after her.

"No, Rebecca, I will go. She is frightened and holds it within herself. I must help her, or the shock will do her harm," Running Wolf replied. He quickly left.

Lauren had walked to her tepee with unseeing eyes, and now she stood inside, still, as if she did not know any longer what to do. She clasped her hands before her to quiet their trembling.

Running Wolf entered behind her, and, for a few minutes, he silently studied her, knowing she did not even know he was there. Then he walked to her and turned her about.

"I . . . I must . . ." she began feebly.

"He is dead, Summer Rain," Running Wolf said firmly.

"I have things I must do," she said, turning her head away from him as if looking at him now would make her pain unbearable. He refused to let her do so. Gripping her shoulders in a strong hold, he forced her to see him.

"Weep, Summer Rain," he said. "You cannot keep such pain unshared."

"It is too late to weep. I . . . I have not seen him for so long. He never saw Falling Water grow. I did not bury him as a good daughter would. What can I do to justify my tears?"

He knew that the pain and guilt were bottled up within her. They needed to be released if she was to be able to cope with it. He shook her violently and snarled sharply. "He is dead, Summer Rain—dead. Do not do this. Let his spirit go. He is dead!" He shook her with each word, and suddenly they seemed to reach her. She moaned softly and sagged limply to her knees.

"No . . . no . . ." she whimpered. Still the hot tears refused to come. He drew her to her feet and looked into her shocked eyes.

Regret filled him as he clenched his teeth. Then he reached out and struck her sharply, first on one cheek and then the other. He heard her startled gasp and struck her again. Then what he had hoped would happen finally did. She struck back. She began to fight, and he caught her and held her. She struggled angrily in his arms, unable to fight the pain. Her tears began with a low, ragged sob.

He held her trembling body against him and shared her pain, rocking her tightly in his arms. She cried in helpless agony, clinging to his strength.

He let her cry until she could cry no more and had washed the pain and guilt from her bruised heart. After a while, he began to speak to her, telling her gently of the love all in the village had for her and of the need he and their daughter had for her. He spoke of the Indian belief that after his death a man would walk a great road to a happier place, where he would be contented to wait for loved ones until their own time came.

"The Great Spirit will care for him in this place, for he was a good man, a strong man, and a brave warrior. He lived in honor, Summer Rain, and his memory will never leave us. Still, his spirit will not let it be," he whispered softly. "Let him go, my love. Let us share this grief. You must know that we would not let you feel your pain alone. I love you, my wife, even more now than the first time I saw you. Take my hand, and we will face whatever we must . . . together."

Slowly she struggled to regain herself. She looked up into dark, compassion-filled eyes and could feel him reaching for her. Gently and silently she put her arms about his waist and laid her head against his chest. She closed her eyes as she felt his arms close about her.

Running Wolf sent word to Rayne and explained what had happened, and it was Rayne who told Falling Water.

"I hardly knew him," Falling Water said softly. "The last time I saw him I was a little child. I only remember that he was very gentle and kind."

"Your mother must be feeling great grief at the loss."

"Yes, Rayne. I should go to her."

"Come"—he smiled tenderly—"we will go together."

They walked to Running Wolf's tepee, and when they called out to him, Running Wolf came outside.

"Father?"

"Go inside and stay with your mother, Falling Water. I

330

would like to speak to Rayne." Falling Water went inside.

"Come, Rayne, walk with me. We must talk to White Eagle and Sun Knife. We must make some plans."

"You are really worried, Running Wolf?"

"Yes, I am. With Summer Rain's father dead, the only person who stands between Chevington and this valley is Summer Rain. Grant says that with her father's death the document he wanted her to sign is useless. I fear for her life. He is a bloodthirsty man, and I do not doubt for a minute that he would kill her if it would bring what he wanted."

"How can he harm her? We surround her and we will protect her."

Running Wolf stopped and faced Rayne. "That is nearly impossible. Summer Rain would not let us be beside her every minute. One day she would make a mistake. She would go too far to gather wood or berries. She would go to the river to swim. One mistake . . . one. It would be fatal. No, we have to find another way." Rayne walked beside him, but even though he kept his silence, he could not think of any real way they could protect her. It sent a shiver of fear through him. Through Summer Rain they struck too at Falling Water, and that was one thing he could not bear.

Inside White Eagle's tepee, they were met by two grim-faced men. White Eagle motioned for them to join him at his fire. Once seated, they waited for him to speak first.

"We share the grief of you and your family, Running Wolf, but we must take this time to make plans. Summer Rain is in great danger, and, with her, our whole village faces a great trial. Sun Knife and I have been speaking of what might be done."

331

"We would listen eagerly, White Eagle," Running Wolf said quickly. "I have been trying to think of a way to proceed, but none has come to me."

"Listen to my words," White Eagle said. He bent forward and brushed smooth an area of the dirt floor. With his finger, he drew two oblique lines that were close to each other at one end and widened out at the other like a V that was open at both ends. "Our valley is somewhat like this," he said, "and we are now camped here at the wide end, a position very difficult to protect."

"Yes," Running Wolf said quickly. "It is too wide here. They could come at us from any direction."

"This is what we will do," White Eagle said firmly. "We will move the village to the narrow end, then we will place small camps at this end. The space in between will be safe, and if any danger comes from this end, we will be warned quickly enough to be prepared."

"And," Running Wolf said with a smile, "I will not have Summer Rain or my daughter angry with me because they have no freedom. They can wander where they choose in the valley, and they will always be under our protection and within our reach."

White Eagle chuckled softly. "Which do you fear most, the attack of the white soldiers or the anger of your women?"

Running Wolf's eyes twinkled with amusement, and Rayne joined in the laughter as Running Wolf replied, "With the white soldiers, I can strike and I know my power. With Summer Rain, I am not sure how to strike, and, in the face of her anger or tears, I have no power."

"When the sun rises tomorrow, we will begin to move. It should take us no more than four days of travel to reach the other end. I will speak to the ones who will stay. They will form three camps across the wide area, and, if anyone tries to come this way, they will send warning."

"I would suggest," Rayne said, "that in addition to these precautions, we try to keep Falling Water and her mother under our eye. I'm sure if we are careful, we can make it seem innocent. We'll just try to be somewhere about whenever they leave the village."

Running Wolf chuckled deeply. "And that will probably last for about one sun."

"We have to try. If they are made aware of what can happen, they will also have to realize that it is a thing we must prevent." He looked steadily at Running Wolf. "No matter what they say, they will have to understand just what they mean to us . . . to all these people."

"Yes," Running Wolf added quietly, "they must understand . . . and we must do whatever is necessary to protect them."

White Eagle nodded. "Go and have the word spread through the village. Tomorrow we will begin. I shall go to inform the ones who are to stay."

Further conversation was unnecessary. The men rose and left the tepee. Running Wolf returned to his dwelling to find Summer Rain once again in control of her emotions. She listened to the plans for the moving of the village, and she knew from his unspoken words the reason it was being done. They were afraid for her life. She did not want her perception to disturb Running Wolf, so she remained silent as he related the news.

Rayne went to Falling Water and also did his best to explain the necessity of moving the village. "This is going to be an interesting procedure for me. I don't understand

333

how you can move a whole village in a few days."

She smiled, "It has been done often. When the sun rises, we will begin, and within two hours the packing will be done and we will be on our way."

"Well, I'll still have to see it to believe it."

For a moment she was silent. Then she looked at him, and he could not retain the smile on his lips. "Rayne?"

"What?"

"Do you believe they will come here and try to kill my mother?"

Rayne sighed. He knew that she was far too intelligent to accept a lie and that she would resent his trying to protect her. "Yes," he said. "I honestly believe—from what I have heard of Chevington, and from what I know of Martin Preston—that they would stop at nothing. In the white world, the marriage of your mother and father means nothing. To them, she is a white woman who is the sole owner of something they want. If they could get to her—even if it were through you—they would do it. They would capture her if possible, but they would not hesitate to kill her if necessary."

"Then we must do all we can to protect her."

"White Eagle and your father are doing just that."

"Rayne . . . do you think my grandfather's death was really an accident?"

"I doubt it," he replied honestly.

Falling Water rose slowly and went to him. She knelt before him and rested her arms on his legs. "I am so grateful for your strength, my husband. At such a time as this, I would be frightened if I were alone."

"You will never be alone if I can help it. Don't be frightened, Falling Water. There are many whites who are kind and generous and wish you and your people no

334

harm. As for those few others, such as the ones we face, we will show them we are united and strong. We will stand and defend what is ours, and someday, somehow, we will rid ourselves of their threat."

He held her, silently praying that the words he had so confidently spoken would come true.

Chapter 24

The gates at Fort Ramsey opened wide to welcome the new arrivals. Six men rode through the portals. John Chevington stood on the porch in front of his office and watched them ride up. He smiled as Martin Preston dismounted and walked up the few steps to stand beside him.

"Martin," he greeted, "I was expecting you about now. Come in and have a drink with me. We have a lot to talk about."

"Good. I'm dry. My God, it is hot out here. I could use a drink."

He motioned to the other men to come with him, and they all walked into Chevington's office, where he poured each one a drink. While he did, he examined each man. Jess he had met once before, but the others were strangers. At first glance he thought that three were Indians, but when he looked closely, he realized they were half-breeds, for their white blood was evident.

They drank in silence for a few minutes, then Martin smiled at John. "You have quarters where my men can rest while we make some decisions?"

John realized that Martin preferred to discuss their plans alone. He raised his voice and called to the man who occupied the desk outside his office door. "Sergeant Peters!"

"Yes, Sir," the sergeant replied, entering the room quickly.

"Take these men and find them a place to bed down. Get them something to eat and see to their horses."

"Yes, Sir."

Martin motioned to Jess to remain, and they did not speak again until the door closed behind the others.

"That's an ugly crew, Jess," John said.

"But, they'll do anything I tell them to do, and that's what you were after, wasn't it?"

"Exactly what we were after," John answered. "I see you got Alexander out of our way." John turned to Martin as he spoke.

"It was a necessity, so I took care of it," Martin replied as he sipped his drink. "But now there are a lot of other problems that need to be taken care of."

"Jess," John said, "those men you brought—they're experienced in the ways of these savages?"

"Completely," Jess answered. "They could go in and move among them without a problem. It would not take them long to get the information you wanted—from the gold to the chief's plans."

"Good. Get one of them to drift into their village and bring us back word of what is going on there."

"All right."

"What about your son, Martin?" John questioned.

"The ungrateful pup! As much as I have done for him, he didn't have enough gratitude to help me. We could

337

have been wealthy enough to buy the state."

"What did he do?"

"Nothing is what he did. I laid these plans so well and went to all the trouble of arranging everything so that we could have scooped up all that gold. All he would have had to do was tell the governor and the newspapers what he saw and everything would have fallen into place. What he did was nothing—just nothing. Ungrateful pup!"

"Still, you managed to get rid of his two friends. I had a feeling they were going to cause us some trouble."

"Oh, we're rid of them." Martin laughed. "Now, if we can sit down and get comfortable, we can make some plans."

They did so, and both Chevington and Jess waited for Martin to continue.

"I know, John, that ultimately we want to rid ourselves of that entire village, and we will, but first we have something else to do, something much more important."

"Nothing is more important than that. They were the cause of my embarrassment once. This time they will pay the long overdue price. I want to stand in the center of that village and watch it burn to the ground. I want their chief, White Eagle, and their half-breed doctor, Cade Holliday—or Sun Knife, as they call him—to crawl to me on their knees and beg for mercy—beg! Then I will have the final satisfaction of killing them both."

"You'll get all that, John. But what good will it do us? We need Lauren Brent to sign a paper that gives that valley to us. If she doesn't, and you kill them, Senator Miles will see to it that the valley falls into someone else's hands. It might be someone we can't get rid of. Then

338

where will we be?"

John sat down abruptly behind his desk. He picked up his drink and gulped it down. The hand that held the glass still shook from his rage. Martin bent forward to emphasize his next words.

"John, first we've got to find a way to get either Lauren Brent or her half-breed daughter. If we get Lauren, we can force her to sign. If we cannot get her, we will get her daughter. Either way, she will have to sign that paper. After that, we can arrange a reason to clear *our* valley of all that interferes with our plans."

"Just what are these plans, Martin?"

"We must wait until our spy reports to us. When we know what they're doing and what they know, then we can proceed."

"Do you want me to go with him, Martin?" Jess asked.

"Not this time, Jess. They might be a little shy around white visitors. I think our friend can slip in and get all the information we need. We'll just have to wait."

"It shouldn't be too hard to slip in and grab either one of those women," Jess said.

"I want you to find a place somewhere away from this fort, Jess," Martin said. "You and the rest of your men make a camp. When you get the woman, take her there. This is the first place they will come, and we don't want them to find anyone here."

"All right. I'll go now. We'll find a place, and I'll send a man in. When we get a report, I'll come back here. Then you can decide where we go from there."

"Good idea," John replied. "Travel cautiously. These Indians can track smoke across a rock. I don't want them to find you."

"Don't worry, they won't. The ones I'm with don't

leave tracks. They're too good for that."

Jess rose, drank the rest of his drink, and left without another word. For a few moments the two men were silent.

"There have been more complications than I expected, thanks to my son," Martin said. "I've no idea where he has gone. Once this is over, I will have to teach that young man a lesson. There will be no share of the gold for him. I . . . don't like to be crossed, not even by my own son."

"Have another drink, Martin," John offered. He rose and poured two more drinks. He lifted his. "Here's to the completion of our plans. My revenge . . . and all the wealth we'll ever need."

Martin raised his glass to lightly touch John's, then silently they both drank.

Jess walked across the compound to the area in which his men were staying. There was no love for Indians in this fort, Jess thought, and not much consideration either, for he saw that the men had been given a corner of the stables in which to sleep. After looking them over, Jess had to admit that they were indeed a hard-looking group. "Fox," he called to one, who slowly left the group and walked to Jess.

Fox was a tall, slim, almost handsome man of less than thirty years. He was quiet, hardly speaking unless necessary. Jess knew he held no love in him for anyone. He had never inquired about his past, for Fox's dark, cold gaze kept most people from asking questions. Jess knew only that Fox's father had been white and his mother Cheyenne. He knew also that Fox was an expert at tracking and could vanish into the wild like an animal. He could also live off the land and had a phenomenal way of surviving on very little. He was a good man for what Jess required.

"I want you to find a way to join White Eagle's tribe. Once there, I want you to listen and report to me as soon as you find out what their plans are and what they are doing. I want to know everything that goes on in that camp."

Fox nodded. "Where will you be?"

"I'm thinking of camping near the twin rocks by the bend in the little river. It's high, and we can see anyone who comes."

Fox nodded. "It is a good place. I will send up smoke when I am coming."

"All right. Maybe you'd better head out in the morning. It's a few days ride, and you'll have to think up a good story before you get there. I don't want them getting wise to you, Fox, so be careful. White Eagle is nobody's fool. One slip, and he'll wear your hair."

Fox grinned. "Fox is no fool either. I will be careful."

"Do you need anything?"

"No, I have my weapons and my pony. That is all I need to travel."

"All right. We'll move in the morning."

Fox nodded and returned to take care of his horse, which seemed to be the only valuable thing he owned and the only thing he really cared for.

The men kept themselves separated, mostly to make sure there were no arguments, and they ate their evening meal gathered about a small fire. When the moon rose high, they rolled in their blankets and slept.

Fox, like the others who had been raised in the wild,

had a way of waking at the time he chose. Jess had asked him about this once, and Fox had laughed. "Drink a lot of water before you sleep," he said. "That will wake you early."

Long before dawn broke Fox was already preparing to leave. The sentry watched him quietly move past and go through the gates, which were promptly closed behind him. Another sentry standing above at the lookout post watched his shadowed form disappear into the night.

Fox rode slowly, with the easy grace of the Indian. He was a solitary man, and he preferred his life that way. He trusted no man, white or red, and he allowed no man close to him.

Midday found him seated before a low-burning fire, eating a swiftly prepared meal. As soon as he finished, he resumed his traveling. He would not stop to eat again until very late at night.

During the next three days he followed the same routine. The day after, he rode with more alertness, and he also began to form in his mind the words he would say to any scouts of White Eagle who might be in the area and run across him.

He was being watched. He knew it even though he could not see the watcher. His instincts told him with subtle, yet sure reminders. His dark, knowing eyes scanned the horizon, but there was no sign of life or movement of any kind. Yet he knew someone was watching every move he made.

He came to a deep ravine with slanted slopes on each side. The situation presented no problem to him, for he was an expert horseman. His own self-assurance and lack of preparation was the cause of the accident that followed, yet he would be grateful, for it would serve his purpose.

He started down the rough, rugged slope, his mind concentrating on what he would say and not on what he was doing. The horse stumbled over something—he would never know what—and suddenly they were tumbling down the slope, rolling over and over. When he reached the bottom, he was stunned momentarily, then he regained his quick wits and lay still, waiting for his observer to come and see if he were dead. He felt it had to be a scout from White Eagle's village, and realized that his fall would provide the best opportunity to be taken to the village. He knew well the generous nature of most Indians, and he was certain that White Eagle's people would care for any injuries he might have sustained.

He lay still for what seemed to him an interminable time, mentally feeling his body to see if he had any real injuries. He did not feel any severe pain, yet he felt bruised. Assured that nothing was broken, he kept his eyes closed and remained silent.

Suddenly, he sensed the stealthy approach of whoever had been watching him. He came on feet so silent, that only a man like Fox, accustomed to listening for unnatural sounds, could hear his approach. He knew when the man stood over him, and only then did he groan and open his eyes.

The man over him was very young, and Fox felt he would be more easily fooled than one with more years. Fox allowed himself to appear dazed and unable to move. The dark eyes regarding him lost their worried look, and it was replaced by one of concern.

Quickly, he knelt by Fox, but Fox was well aware that one hand still rested on the knife sheathed at his side. He changed his opinion of the boy from foolish to cautious.

He knew the kind of training each boy underwent and assumed this one was not only quite able to defend himself, but to kill him as well.

"You are badly injured?" the boy inquired, speaking in Cheyenne, and Fox answered in the same tongue. It was enough to make the boy relax a little more. No Cheyenne was his enemy, he thought.

"I do not know," Fox said. He pretended to attempt to rise, then groaned again and fell back.

"I will get your horse and help you. You must come to our village and let our medicine man look at you. If you are injured, he can help you. He has great medicine."

"Whose village," Fox questioned in feigned innocence, "and how far is it? I do not know how far I can travel."

"I am from Chief White Eagle's village," the boy said proudly, "and it is only a short ride from here."

"Get my horse. I will try," Fox said.

The boy studied him a few minutes more, then obviously made a decision. He rose, and, mounting his horse that was grazing nearby, he rode some distance to find Fox's horse, which had run in fear after the fall. He brought the horse back, then slid from his pony to help Fox mount.

Fox made it obvious that he was deliberately trying to control pain. He actually felt very little, but still he leaned heavily on the younger man, who had a difficult time holding his weight. They made their slow, laborious way to Fox's horse, where the boy used all his strength to get Fox up on the horse's back. Once he was up, he bent low over the animal's back, as if still in pain. The younger man took hold of the horse's reins and led him behind his own mount. He set a very easy pace, his brow furrowing

344

with concern.

They made their way very slowly, and the younger man knew they would not cover too much ground before night. He decided to make camp and help the stranger as much as he could, hoping a good night's rest would enable him to travel more comfortably the next day.

He dismounted and went to Fox to help him down, gently spreading his blanket and helping Fox to lie on it. He saw to the horses, for they were still the most valuable things they had. Although he knew he could make it quite easily on foot, he was quite sure Fox could not.

Once the horses were rubbed down and tethered, they contentedly grazed while the younger man went back to Fox. He built a fire and cautioned Fox to lie still. There was little light remaining, and he meant to find food before night covered the land.

"Do not move," he said. "I will place the water sac near you in case you are thirsty. I will return soon with food . . . I hope." He grinned boyishly.

Fox returned the smile. "Do not worry. I am in no condition to go any further."

He watched the boy disappear in the dim light, then he lay back on the blanket. He was quite sure the boy would watch him from the shadows for some time, just to make sure Fox wasn't trying to trick him.

He was right in his assumption, for the boy did remain in the shadows, with enough distance between him and the fire that Fox could not see him. After a while, he silently left and began to hunt for food.

Less than an hour later, he returned with two rabbits he had cleaned. He speared them on two sticks and braced the two sticks in the ground near the fire to let the game cook. The smell of roasting meat soon filled the air.

They did not speak for some time, but their silence was habitual, for they had been taught from childhood that silence was necessary, both for hunting and for their protection against enemies.

When the rabbits were done, he put one on a flat stone he had cleaned and placed it close to Fox. Then he took the other for himself and began to eat.

They finished the meat and drank from the water sac. Then the boy stretched out on a blanket close to the fire and prepared to sleep.

"What are you called?" Fox asked.

"I am Buffalo Calf."

"I am grateful to you for helping me."

"I am sure you would have done the same for me."

"Perhaps, but you did it for me, and I am grateful. Maybe one day I can repay you."

The boy did not answer. Fox had known he would not. "You said you belonged to White Eagle's village?"

"Yes."

"I have heard much of White Eagle. He is a very brave warrior and a strong leader for his people."

This was a subject about which the younger warrior was most willing to talk. He was proud of both his chief and his village. He began to speak, and Fox, with a slight smile, lay back and absorbed everything.

The boy questioned Fox also, and he was given a well-prepared story of the village from which he had come, which was quite a distance away. He hoped none of the people in White Eagle's tribe had relatives in or knew much about the village of which he spoke. He also explained that he had been hunting and had left his party to scout further for more interesting game. "You spoke of a medicine man with powerful medicine," Fox asked suddenly.

"Yes, Sun Knife," Buffalo Calf answered. He went on to tell the often-told story of the light-eyed medicine man. He had no idea that Fox had already heard of him and was somewhat excited that he was about to meet and be cared for by a man who was already a legend among the tribes.

"You said it would be another half a day before we reach your village."

"I think it could be more than that."

"Why?"

"First, you cannot travel fast."

"What else?"

"I spoke to a friend a few days ago and was told that the village might be moved. If what he said is true, it will be more days."

"How are we going to know, and why are you out here alone?"

"Why I am here concerns my chief only, and I will know in the morning." He then added, "They will send me a signal and tell me where the village will be."

"But why—"

"For a man who is hurt, you ask a great many questions. It would be better for you to sleep and regain your strength. If it is more than a day's travel to the village," he remarked with some humor, "you might not get there."

Fox knew he had gotten all the information that Buffalo Calf intended to give. He drew the blankets about him and, after a few minutes, he slept.

Buffalo Calf lay quietly and watched Fox for a time. He could not push the thought from his mind that somehow he had made a very grave mistake in helping this man. He didn't know why, for Fox had said or done nothing out of the ordinary, yet, as he drifted off to sleep, the thought nagged him that all was not as it appeared.

Fox awoke very early and lay quietly, waiting for Buffalo Calf to rise. He was clever enough to know that if a medicine man looked at him closely, he would realize instantly that Fox had no severe injuries. He had to recover before they reached the village, but first he had to discover just how far the village was and if indeed it had been moved.

Just the fact that the village was to be moved was significant. He would find the reason for the move eventually, and he would send word to Jess. He felt sure Jess would be interested and that it had some connection to the fort and the men who inhabited it now.

Buffalo Calf awoke and rose immediately to restore the fire. His dark eyes studied Fox, who still feigned sleep. He moved silently away to relieve himself, then returned to the fire. Fox stirred and pretended to come slowly awake.

"How do you feel this morning?" Buffalo Calf questioned.

"I am stiff and sore, but I do not think any part of me has been seriously damaged. I would still like to see your medicine man. Sometimes there are injuries we cannot see."

"Can you stand . . . or ride?"

Fox rose slowly to his feet. "Yes, I think I can ride. Will your chief allow me to stay in his village for a time before I travel further?"

"Of course. He will expect you to stay as a guest until you feel that you can travel again."

"How long must we wait until you know if your people are moving?"

"I watch for smoke now."

"From where?"

Buffalo Calf pointed to a ridge of hills a few miles away. "It should come from there."

"Then we must wait," Fox said in cheerful resignation.

Buffalo Calf drew from his bundle some dried meat and a handful of dried corn. He walked to Fox and handed him some, then returned to his own blanket. They ate silently, each involved in his own thoughts, unaware that those thoughts were related.

The sun began to rise higher and the small fire slowly dwindled and died. Still they sat.

It was Fox who first saw the faint wisps of gray smoke that touched the horizon. He rose, and Buffalo Calf's eyes followed his. He stood also as the gray and silent message was written for a moment on the wind, then dissipated and was gone, but not before it was read by the hawk-eyed boy who watched.

"They will be at the village for another day. It is good. It will give us time to join them." Buffalo Calf turned to Fox. "Come, we must travel faster than I had at first thought. Can you ride with greater speed, or must I send someone back for you?"

"I will ride fast enough." Fox grinned. "Come, let us go. I am very anxious to meet White Eagle and your light-eyed medicine man."

They gathered their things swiftly and mounted. In moments, they were well on their way. Buffalo Calf set a slow, yet very steady pace that was meant to cover miles.

They stopped for a short time at midday, so short a

time that Fox only had time to stretch his muscles and chew a bit more dried beef. He drank deeply from the water sac, for he knew that, except to rest the horses for a very short time, this would be the last stop.

The lowering sun rimmed the horizon, setting into relief the hundreds of tepees they saw before them as they crested the last hill. It was a beautiful and peaceful sight, the tepees resplendent with bright-colored paintings upon them and the wisps of smoke from the smoke holes bespeaking comfort and the warmth of a friendly, peaceful people.

Chapter 25

It was quiet within Rayne's tepee, yet he was awake and had been for half an hour. It was his favorite time, early morning, when he could savor the rare pleasure of simply feeling content in all he possessed. In the dim light of early dawn, he could vaguely see the inside of his dwelling. In comparison to all he had had before, it seemed he owned very little. Yet he felt wealthy, and he knew his most precious possession lay warmly curled against him. He would not have traded this contentment for anything in the world.

When the sun was high, the entire village would move. He still could not quite believe that the whole village— the entire five hundred tepees and all the tribe's possessions—could be moved as easily as Falling Water had told him.

The move was very important to the entire tribe, and Rayne knew it, perhaps better than most, for Falling Water would be in as much danger as her mother and had to be protected.

They had gone, he and Mack, with White Eagle and

Running Wolf to the far end of the valley to decide on the most strategic location. The valley was shaped like a funnel with both ends open. The end toward which they would travel was more narrow and easier to protect. Scouts would be placed across the wide end, where they were at present. No one would be able to pass into the valley without several days warning for the tribe.

He knew that the new camp would be much easier to protect, but still he could not seem to ease the nagging worry that some unforeseen event might occur over which he would have no control. Some dark thing seemed to fill him with fear, and he drew Falling Water close to him as if that would keep her safe.

She stirred restlessly and murmured his name. One of her arms was about his waist, and her legs were tangled with his. She snuggled closer. Very gently he turned so that he could encircle her with both arms and look down on her sleeping face.

"So sweet," he murmured as he bent to kiss the corner of her soft, vulnerable lips. They stirred under his and very slowly responded to his kiss as she rose to wakefulness. Her arms tightened about him, and he could feel her come to warm throbbing life in his arms.

"You awaken early, husband," she whispered.

"It seems a shame just to sleep, with something as warm and soft in my arms as you, love," he replied. She made a halfhearted attempt to leave his side.

"I must be up and moving. It will be a long, hard day."

He chuckled, but his arms held her firmly against him. "I cannot let go so easily," he whispered softly against the tender skin of her throat. "You must pay the price for your freedom."

"And what price would please you?"

"I'm afraid, my sweet, that nothing short of complete surrender would set you free."

"What makes you think," she replied mischievously as she reached up to draw him to her, "that I would ever choose to be free of you?"

It filled him, the hunger he would always have at her touch. The taste, smell, and feel of her created a warm need that began in the center of his being and blossomed into a flame he would never be able to control. His open mouth slanted across hers in almost violent possession, and her fingers twined in his hair to make his capture more complete. Her lips parted beneath his questing ones, and their tongues warred with equal need. She made a soft sound of pleasure as she felt his hands begin a journey that set her blood ablaze and made her tremble at the twisting, turning path of his touch.

He cupped the softness of one taut breast and left the sanctuary of her lips to taste the sweetness of her flesh. Gently he sucked, slowly increasing the force of it until she moaned softly with the shattering pinpricks of pleasure that moved through her.

With slow, leisurely caresses that drove her frantic with blazing desire, he stroked her warm, soft skin. His long, sensitive fingers found even more sensitive places. Hot and moist, she welcomed their probing touch.

She gasped as he began a slow massaging of the vulnerable softness of her burning flesh. His own urgency held in check, he heightened her senses until she wept with the need for fulfillment.

He was hard and heated as he surged within her, slowly drawing away to again thrust to the limit. Again and again he withdrew and reentered her with slow, driving force.

She gripped his waist, running her hands up the

convulsing muscles of his back, then down to his driving hips that forced within her the answer to her need. She wanted all of him, wanted to possess and be possessed, wanted him to drive within her and assuage the fury that overwhelmed her. Yet still he moved with slow, steady strokes until she could control herself no longer. She lifted herself to meet him, holding his force with surrounding thighs, and cried out her desire. Words unheard by her were a joy to him as she begged passionately for completion.

He was rapidly becoming as lost as she, and he began to thrust with magnificent, overpowering force. Her moaning cries mingled with his as they crested the mountain of passion together and stood on its peak for that single, consummate moment before tumbling into complete oblivion. It was an overwhelming experience, and they had barely enough strength remaining to hold each other until they could regain their senses.

He rested on both elbows and gazed down into her half-closed eyes. She welcomed the weight of his body as he still remained within her. Neither wanted to separate, for both felt the magic in this special moment.

He bent his head and took her mouth with a new, peaceful warmth, sucking gently on her moist lips and tracing their outline with his tongue. Then he spoke gentle, loving words to her as he brushed her damp brow with his lips.

"Beloved," he whispered, "heart of my heart. What a complete and beautiful thing we share. I love you, Falling Water . . . with all I am and all I will ever be."

"Oh, my warrior," she said as tears of happiness slipped down her cheeks. "I am so grateful to the gods who brought you to me. What joy I would have missed if you had not come."

Their eyes met and held, and each smiled with the utter happiness they shared.

He did not want to leave the warm sanctuary of her body, nor did she want him to, but the sound of movement outside told them both that their moments of privacy were over. Reluctantly, he withdrew from her and rolled away.

They rose slowly and began to dress in preparation for the day. He watched her, taking great pleasure in her graceful beauty. As she began to move toward the door, he reached to stop her and enclosed her again in a warm embrace.

"I do not want to leave, but I must," she said.

"I know. But I might not see much of you today in all the bustle, and I need another kiss to keep me going."

She laughed softly, but his arms encircled her waist and she pressed close to him, raising her lips for his kiss. It was long and leisurely, and it swept her breath away. He was delighted to see her reluctance to leave him and cursed the necessity that drew her from his side.

After she left, he gathered the things he would need for the journey, for he would not be stopping for anything until the day's travel had ended.

Still he could hardly believe that this whole village would soon be in bundles, and that they would be camping miles away from here as they rode toward a new location. It seemed an impossibility to him, yet everyone had assured him it would be done.

He stepped out into the early morning sun in time to see Little Eagle walking toward him. He greeted him cheerfully, still somewhat awed by the light-eyed warrior.

355

"You will ride with me this day?" he asked Rayne.

"Yes, I'd be glad to. How far will we travel today?"

"The women and children will travel slowly, so it will take us nearly three days to reach the new camp."

"It is a good thing we are moving. I will feel much better in a spot we can protect more easily."

"Maybe we will ride ahead to see what lies before them. It would be a very bad thing to be caught without warning while we are moving. The women and children would be helpless, and we would be too scattered to do any good."

"Your chief should be very proud of the warrior who will lead this tribe when he is gone."

"I would not like to think of him ever being gone, but I hope never to shame his name."

Before Rayne could answer, they both became aware that everyone else's attention had been drawn to the two who rode into the village. Buffalo Calf they knew, but the other rider was a stranger. Little Eagle and Rayne exchanged a quick glance, then both started to walk in the direction of Sun Knife's tepee, where the two arrivals had stopped.

Buffalo Calf and Fox slid from their horses in front of Sun Knife's tepee. Buffalo Calf called out, and immediately Sun Knife came out to see what was happening.

"Sun Knife," Buffalo Calf said, "I found this man injured and brought him to you."

Sun Knife's eyes moved quickly to Fox, who—like anyone else who had never before seen his blue eyes— was at first startled then shaken by their effect on him. They seemed to pierce his flesh and read his heart.

"He does not look too damaged." Sun Knife smiled.

"Buffalo Calf was generous enough to help me when my horse threw me down a ravine. His good care has been of much help, but he insisted I see the medicine man. I am stiff and sore, but I do not think I am badly hurt. Still, I would make sure, and if you and Chief White Eagle do not mind, I will ride with you for a few days."

"Come in, I will look at you," Sun Knife said. "But as for staying with us, you will have to speak to White Eagle about that."

Fox nodded and moved to accompany Sun Knife inside. Sun Knife immediately began a swift, but thorough, examination.

Buffalo Calf stood talking to Rayne and Little Eagle for the short time it took for Sun Knife and Fox to reappear. No one was surprised to learn that Fox had no serious injuries.

"Before it is time to move, I will take Fox to speak with White Eagle," Buffalo Calf said. "He might be pleased to know we have another warrior to help supply food for the winter."

"I'm sure he will," Sun Knife agreed, "but you had best go see him now."

As Rayne, Little Eagle, and Sun Knife watched them walk away, Rayne was again filled with the same strange inkling of danger he had felt that morning. He turned and was about to talk to Sun Knife and Little Eagle of his feeling when he saw Little Eagle's attention being totally diverted by something else. He let his eyes follow Little Eagle's to see where they led, and he saw Savannah Jamison walking slowly across the open area between the tepees. Little Eagle could not seem to take his eyes from her until she disappeared into her own tepee.

357

Rayne smiled to himself. He would not say a word or tease a warrior like Little Eagle until he understood the situation, but it seemed obvious to him that Little Eagle was quite interested in the fair-haired girl.

Little Eagle watched her with his thoughts in his eyes, though he did not know it. He had tried to speak to her, to tell her of his admiration and perhaps ask to be her friend—a relationship he hoped could lead to more. But Savannah had not been receptive to the friendly advances of any of the young people of the tribe, especially those of his friend, the handsome, vibrant Night Sky . . .

"We had best see to our horses," Little Eagle announced, forcing himself to rid his mind of thoughts of Savannah. "It will be time to move soon, and we want to be out ahead."

Sun Knife nodded in agreement and returned to his tepee to complete preparations that had been interrupted by the arrival of Buffalo Calf and Fox.

"I'm sure we have a lot of time before they begin moving, and even more before they have a chance to catch up," Rayne speculated.

Little Eagle grinned. "If we do not move soon, they will not only catch up, but they will also run over us and pass us by."

"That's hard to believe," Rayne remarked with a laugh.

"It is so. I have seen it done many times."

Rayne and Little Eagle quickly found their horses. They had just mounted when they were joined by Mack and several other warriors. Together they left the village and rode toward the far end of the valley.

*　　*　　*

358

The encampment consisted of over five hundred lodges. It was struck, packed, and on the move in less than twenty minutes. At the announced time, the lodge of White Eagle was seen flapping in the wind, several of the poles having been taken out from under it. This was the signal, and, in a few minutes, five hundred tepees could be seen similarly flapping and waving in the wind. In a few minutes more, all were flat upon the ground. The horses had been readied, and were speedily loaded. The lodges were rolled into bundles and placed on poles behind each horse along with all the other possessions of the family. The horses then formed a grand procession.

Each horse had a conductress, someone who led the horse, and even she carried a small pack on her back. Children and women were given the choice of riding or walking, but most often they chose to walk. It gave the children a chance for freedom, and they took it.

The amount of ground this procession could cover was remarkable. Trained in such moves, the villagers walked at a free and easy pace that ate up the miles. Their hearty constitutions were well suited for the strenuous task.

Rayne and his group stopped to rest at midday. After he ate, he rose and looked back at the trail over which they had come. He was completely startled and could hear Little Eagle laugh as, in the distance, he saw the long line of travelers that followed them.

"I'll be damned," he exclaimed. "I don't believe it."

"Do you think it would be best to be on our way, or should we wait to be trampled?" Little Eagle teased.

"I guess we'd better," Rayne answered. "How far will they be able to come today?"

"They will probably cover more ground before nightfall than they did this morning. Come, let us go."

Rayne watched the long, trailing procession. Falling

Water was there, and he would have loved to have returned to take the strain of this hard march from her, but he knew quite well that such an act would shame her in front of her people and that she would see herself as weak if he forced her to ride with him.

He conceded to their custom, knowing how much it meant to her, but he didn't like it. He would try to make things easier for her in any way he could when they were together again.

They rode on, spreading themselves in a long line in order to scout the area carefully. It became a long, silent ride, and Rayne began to wonder when it would cease.

They rode far ahead of where the procession would stop, and it was growing dark when they had assured themselves that the area was safe for the night and had turned back to meet the balance of the villagers who had already made camp.

They crested a small hill and saw the tepees already erected below them. It was a breathtaking sight. The night was dark, and the many tepees glowed faintly red from the fires within. Shapes moving inside could occasionally be seen. The tepees seemed alive, almost breathing with the blue-white smoke rising from their smoke holes. Slowly, the small group rode toward the village, each man feeling the same sense of coming home.

First they reported to White Eagle, telling him that the area was clear for several miles ahead. Nevertheless, White Eagle sent guards to strategic points to make certain it remained so.

Rayne and Little Eagle walked to the place where the horses were kept and made sure theirs were properly cared for. Then they turned to walk back into the village, each to his own home.

After saying good night to Little Eagle, Rayne quickened his steps, for his desire to be with Falling Water had burned within him until he could think of nothing else. From the distance he could see that his tepee was lit from the fire within, and this would have filled him with pleasure, but for the scene he beheld as he drew closer. Falling Water stood before their tepee, and the man standing near her, speaking to her, was Fox, the stranger who had come to the village because of an accident.

An accident . . . he thought. A tingle of suspicion crept through him, though he had no idea just what he should be suspicious about. He was also aware that he was jealous, and he mentally attempted to reject that blinding emotion.

He moved quickly toward them and was pleased by the sparkle of love and welcome that danced in Falling Water's eyes when he reached her side.

"Welcome home, husband," she gushed with a sunny smile. "I have kept your food warm. I am sure you must be hungry."

Rayne grinned, not missing the double meaning in her words. "Yes," he replied, "I am very hungry." He turned to Fox, who smiled pleasantly. "I'm glad to see you were not too uncomfortable on the long, hard ride, Fox."

"I am fine," Fox answered. His eyes quickly turned from Rayne to Falling Water. "You are a very lucky warrior to have such a woman. I am sure every warrior in this tribe envies you."

"Thank you," Rayne replied. "I'm sure they do."

"Good night, Falling Water," Fox said. "I thank you again."

"You are welcome, Fox. Good night."

Fox said a quick good night to Rayne and walked away, and Rayne's eyes followed him. This man had done nothing wrong, yet he could not shake the feeling that he wished he were anywhere else than in this camp.

He turned back to Falling Water, realizing she was watching him with a quizzical expression on her face. "Why was he thanking you?" he questioned.

"I gave him water today. His water sac was empty, and he was thirsty . . . Rayne?"

"What?"

"What is the matter?"

"Nothing really. I guess I'm just tired."

"You do not like this warrior, Fox?"

Rayne put his arm about her waist and drew her close to him. "I don't know why. I just have the feeling he means trouble. He has said and done nothing, yet I do not trust him. I would like it better if you kept your distance from him."

Her smile sparkled, and her body pressed against his. "Are you maybe just a little upset because you found him with me?"

"Do you mean, am I jealous?" He grinned.

"Are you?"

"You bet your life I am." He laughed. "You are the most precious thing in my life, and I don't like another man looking at you like he did."

"He was just being friendly."

"Let him be friendly elsewhere."

She laughed softly, and her arm tightened about his waist. "I could not look with favor upon any other warrior with you here. My eyes can only see you."

"I love you, Falling Water, and I'm sorry for being a grumpy bear. But even if you did not look at him, he was

362

thinking of you. If he continues to do so, I may have to speak to him . . . firmly."

The tinkle of her laughter touched the night air, and he could not help but laugh with her.

"You spoke of feeding me, woman," he said softly. "I'm very interested in a meal."

"Come," she whispered seductively. "I would feed your hunger . . . and I would have you feed mine, for it has been growing all day."

"Then," he replied with a tightening of his arms, "let us feast."

They pushed aside the door flap and entered, closing it behind them as they proceeded to share a night of ecstatic pleasure in the privacy of their own special world.

Chapter 26

Savannah walked slowly across the open area in the center of the tepees, exhausted from the day's ordeal. She thought back over the period since they had arrived. Obstinately, she had refused to become a part of the group of young people who had tried to offer her friendship. She was angry with Thomas for being so susceptible to their ways. He had turned savage, she realized, the thought playing angrily upon her mind, and she refused to do the same.

She was a lady of wealth and position, and she did not intend to swim half-naked or ride astride like a man. She even refused to adopt the comfort of their clothes and clung to the petticoats that caused her to swelter in the heat. It frustrated her further that her parents seemed to be so happy here.

Tomorrow they would travel again. She had ridden on a travois behind the horse her mother rode and, when she could not bear it anymore, had chosen to walk. She did so because she saw the smiles of the young women and felt she had to prove she could. Despite the fact that she nearly hadn't made it, the achievement had given her a sense of accomplishment that was new to her.

As she walked, Night Sky had ridden up beside her. He looked down at her with deep admiration of her beauty. Perspiration on her brow had forced her hair into curls that framed her face. Her soft, rounded breasts rose and fell rapidly at her exertion, and the defiance in her eyes held him nearly spellbound. If only there was a way to breach her defenses, he mused, and let her know the depth of my feelings. There might have been many ways, but Night Sky chose the wrong one.

"You are hot and tired," he stated matter-of-factly. "Would you like to ride with me?" He was taken aback by the look of anger and defiance that lifted her chin and blazed in her eyes.

"Why?" she snapped. "To prove to everybody that I cannot do what they can? That I am weak because I am white? No, thank you, I will walk."

"I did not mean . . ." he began, but he astutely saw the beginnings of frustrated tears in the corners of her eyes and the flush in her face. He began again. "No one would dare laugh at you if you rode with me. I am Night Sky. No one questions what I choose to do."

She choked back the tears that threatened to stop her words. Insufferable savage! she thought. Does he believe I need his protection? "I do not need any help," she said aloud. "I can and will do what any of the others do." She would have said more, but tears hovered too near, and her pride refused to allow her to cry in front of him. She had no idea of the respect and love for her that surged through him. He had seen that she was a proud and stubborn woman; that she was also strong and self-controlled, and these were qualities he greatly admired.

Yet, unwittingly, he continued to make matters worse.

She stopped and gazed up at him. Pushing aside her anger, she had to admit he was a vision of masculine perfection. Perspiration glazed his hard, muscular body, clothed only in a breechclout. His rigid muscles gave him a look of ultimate strength and power. His black hair was held in place by a band of beaded leather, and his strong, chiseled face seemed to be symmetry itself. He exuded a virility so overpowering that it stormed her senses no matter how hard she tried to refuse it.

He was caught and held by her fragile look. The delicacy of her features and her slim body tugged sharply at his masculine sense of protectiveness. "Come . . . let me help you," he offered gently.

"You can help me best by leaving me alone. I will walk as long as the others do. I do not need your help or anyone else's." She was desperately close to tears. "Go and leave me alone. I do not choose to ride with you or with anyone else." She turned and walked on, and, for a few moments, he sat and watched her slim, retreating form. He wasn't quite sure whether or not to be angry, for he had never been rejected so fiercely before. He knew one thing for certain—he wanted her—and Night Sky was a man of equal stubbornness. He would not give up until he had penetrated her fortress and reached inside to touch the woman he knew existed within. He gave a soft laugh and rode on, but his eyes never left her for a moment during the balance of the day, and his admiration grew at her grim determination.

Savannah's reverie ended as she moved past Running Wolf's tepee, and she would have continued on to her own, but Lauren called out to her. She altered her course and went to Lauren. "You wanted to speak to me?" she asked.

Lauren could see that she was nearing complete mental and physical exhaustion. She, too, admired Savannah's pride and determination, mostly because it reminded her a little of herself when she had first come to the village. She remembered well the lessons life had taught her, and she wondered if she could help Savannah by telling her the story of her own arrival and her fateful meeting with Running Wolf.

Lauren had watched Savannah and Night Sky and had seen the mutual attraction. She also understood that with Savannah's present attitude neither of them would be able to meet the other on neutral ground.

She knew Running Wolf would be late, for he had to make plans and meet with White Eagle. She had an opportunity that might not come again for a long time. "I do not like to eat alone," she said, "and I thought you might share a meal with me."

"Why will you be alone?"

"Running Wolf will be meeting with White Eagle and the council. I doubt he will return for quite some time."

Savannah would have preferred going to her own tepee just to sleep, without thought of food, but she was too well mannered to refuse a woman such as Lauren Brent. Besides, she realized it might be her only opportunity to ask all the questions that had plagued her since their arrival.

"Will you join me?" Lauren pressed.

"Yes, of course," Savannah replied. She walked ahead of Lauren, who held the tepee flap open. She studied Savannah closely and felt the girl had strong fiber within. Maybe, she thought, Savannah had more than she realized herself. They sat by the warmth of Lauren's fire

367

and ate what was, to Savannah, a well-prepared meal.

Savannah ate little, and Lauren observed this also. When the meal was finished, Lauren put the bowls aside to clean later. What was more important now was this half woman, half child who sat before her. Savannah, she knew, was afraid. And she felt she might be the only one who could dispel some of that fear.

"Savannah," she began tentatively, "are you enjoying your stay among us?"

"I . . . I, well, I . . ." she stuttered, suddenly overcome with the emotions that had threatened to shatter her since her arrival. Tears with which she had struggled all day finally could be contained no longer. She wept raggedly, and Lauren moved to her side to put her arms about her and rock her gently.

"Cry, child. It will make you feel much better." Savannah wept until she had no more tears. Then Lauren held her away from her and smiled down into her swollen features.

"Savannah, I think it would be helpful if I told you a little story."

"I don't need a story!" Savannah hiccuped. "I need to go home!"

"And," Lauren said gently, "where is home?"

"Home . . . but . . . you know where my home is."

"Yes, I do. But I don't think you do."

"Wha—what?"

"I said, I don't think you do."

"Of course I do."

"Well then, why don't you go to Washington without your parents?"

"I can't do that."

"Why?"

"They're . . . they're the only family I've got."

"What difference does that make if you are home? After all, isn't the place more important than the people you are with?"

"N—N—No," Savannah said hesitantly, though Lauren's ploy was slowly beginning to register in her mind.

"What," Lauren asked gently, "do you really want? Are you a child who needs pampering and toys to play with? Or are you a woman who can challenge life and take from it what you want?"

Savannah's head dropped. "That isn't fair."

"Isn't it? Isn't that what you are crying over?"

"No," she said quickly. Then, after a moment of poignant silence, she softly whispered, "Yes."

"Listen and I'll tell you a story of a spoiled little rich girl who was wise enough to choose what would really make her happy. Listen and I will tell you how Lauren Brent became Summer Rain and found a whole new rich life." She began to speak, and for some time Savannah listened in silence. At first she could hardly believe the extent of what Lauren had given up, but the light of happiness in Lauren's eyes and the look of peace and contentment on her face caused her thoughts to change.

"People you love and people who love you are all the world you need. If you are in that wonderful city and no one cares about you, or if you are surrounded only by people who want to take from you, then what do you have?"

"But you love him . . . Running Wolf."

"I didn't always. When I came here, I was pursuing Cade . . . Sun Knife. I thought I loved him. I was blind to love for a long, long time. Savannah, the young people

369

here are very loving and sharing. They would welcome you as a friend if you would let them. There are even some who would offer you more."

"They laughed at me today, and Night Sky taunted me, asking if I would like to ride with him."

"He asked you that?" Lauren said in surprise.

"Yes, why?"

"Let me tell you something about these men. They have the most fierce and fragile pride I have ever seen anywhere. Few men would ask women to ride with them at a time such as this. A warrior would be teased unmercifully by the others. He would have suggested you ride on a travois, but never behind him . . . unless he cared about your welfare so very deeply that he would accept the teasing in order to help you. And the son of the chief would have been the last of all. He must have wanted your comfort more than his pride, and that, my girl, is something remarkable."

Again Savannah's head fell, and Lauren could hardly hear her next words. "I—I'm frightened of him."

"Frightened . . . of Night Sky?"

"Yes."

"Do not be taken in by his rough exterior." Lauren laughed. "I have known him since his birth. He is a very open hearted and, I suspect, very gentle man. His father, White Eagle, is such a man. Rebecca has never been unhappy since she chose to stay with him. I have a feeling his son walks in his path."

"Oh, Lauren, I am frightened of everything here."

"That is because you don't understand these people. Open your heart and try. Be friendly to the young girls and see what happens. Maybe you can even spare a smile for Night Sky. You might be pleased with the result."

Savannah brushed away her tears and straightened her shoulders. Lauren had the sudden feeling that Savannah was finding herself and was going to be surprised at the woman she met in her search.

"You are very tired, Savannah. Go to your tepee and sleep. Think of what I have said, and maybe tomorrow and the following days it will not be as difficult for you."

"I will try," Savannah promised. She rose and walked to the door. There she stopped and turned to Lauren. "Thank you," she said softly and was gone before Lauren could reply.

As she made her way to her own tepee, Savannah was unaware that the sharp eyes of Little Eagle followed her movements. She was also oblivious to the look of intense interest that radiated from their blue depths.

Lauren smiled to herself, then she put new chips on the fire. She would not sleep until Running Wolf returned, for she still enjoyed the way he held her close in those warm moments before they slept. She sat reminiscing before the fire, reliving old memories that had been awakened by her talk with Savannah.

Suddenly the flap of the tepee was pushed aside and Running Wolf entered. Lauren looked up with a smile, then rose and went to him, watching his always quick smile and the light of warm pleasure in his eyes as she approached.

For Little Dove, the past few days had been equally difficult. She had managed to evade Mack and keep a distance between them. Still certain that his request to marry her had been made out of sympathy, she remained upset. She had not spoken to her aunt or to her father since Mack had made his offer, and had kept far away from the astute eye of her brother, Running Wolf, who was always aware of her problems.

She had chosen to walk all day because she wanted to be exhausted enough at night to sleep without dreaming of Mack, whose image kept invading her sleeping hours. Her father had spoken to her of Mack and had told her that he considered him a good and sincere man with the strength to provide well and protect her. She remembered well the conversation they had had.

"The white warrior named Mack has asked for you as wife," her father had said without warning as they sat by the evening fire. Her heart thudded painfully as she tried to appear unconcerned.

"Yes, Father?"

"I have told him I would think about it."

"Yes, Father," she whispered, dreading what might come. She had bent her head so their eyes would not meet, and she did not see the worry or the gentle love in his eyes.

"Little Dove," he said, "look at me." Reluctantly, she lifted her head and met his gaze. "I would have you speak, my daughter. Tell me what is in your heart. Do you look on this man as a husband? Would you choose him so?"

Her heart cried out yes, but her pride would not let her marry a man who looked at her only with pity. It was something she could not bear for all the years they would have to share. But could she say the words that would keep him forever from her side. She remembered well the glory of his possession and would have given her soul to be in his arms at that moment.

"Father," she began, "if I did not want to marry this

man . . . you would not force me?"

Her father flinched as if he had been struck. His brow furrowed and he frowned deeply. "My daughter, do you believe I would force you to do this? If you do not choose this man, then we will tell him to look elsewhere for a wife. Neither Running Wolf nor I would see you married to a man you did not want."

"Then," she whispered, "I do not choose to marry now . . . I do not choose to marry this man." She had said the words, and she could have cried for the pain it caused her.

She did not see the way his eyes penetrated her words and read the lie in them. But why did she speak falsely if she truly wanted him, he wondered silently. He would not speak now, but he would wait and watch. Maybe the truth would come. He knew that Running Wolf's love for his young sister matched his own. Neither would want her unhappy, and yet she was . . . and he wanted to know why.

As she concluded her reverie, exhaustion once again took hold, and she wanted nothing more than to sleep. She still had a few things to do, one of which was to fill the water sacs for the following day's journey. It was dark, yet she knew her way to the small stream near which they had camped.

She walked slowly, for her weariness would barely allow her to lift her feet. Her senses were also somewhat dulled, for she did not hear the one who followed her. She bent and filled the sacs, then turned back to the darkened path. Suddenly, a huge, dark form appeared before her. She cried out, dropped the sacs, and would have run if he had not spoken.

"Little Dove, don't be frightened. It's Mack."

She stood quietly, for a greater fear enveloped her now, the fear that she could not resist the power he had over her. He walked close to her, so close she was surrounded by the masculine scent of him and the power he radiated.

"Let me pass," she whispered softly.

"Running away is never a good thing, Little Dove," he replied gently. "I have only recently found that to be true."

"I am not running away," she insisted, but her voice quivered, and she grew even more tense at her inability to deceive him.

"Are you not? I have just spoken with your father. He has told me I should no longer seek our marriage. He knew I was angry, and to keep problems from forming, he let me know it was your choice."

"Yes," she whispered softly. "I do not wish—"

"You lie, Little Dove," he said softly. "You know it and so do I. It is your foolish pride that stands in our way." He stepped close enough to touch her, but he did not. "Little Dove, when I was blind and could not see the truth, you gave me all you had to give in order to lead me out of the dark. Why do you take back what you gave? Why do you intend to walk away and leave me in the darkness again?"

"Don't," she sobbed. "You say these words because you think you must."

"No."

"Yes, you—"

He gripped her shoulders and shook her. "Look at me, Little Dove, look at me and tell me honestly that you believe anyone or anything could force me to do what I choose not to do. If I wanted to go, I would; if I wanted to be free, I would be free; and if I wanted to be lost in that pain again, I would be lost. But you have found me, and I cannot let you run away."

He released her shoulders only to capture her face between his hands. Faint, pale moonlight cast shadows on her face. She could see their reflection in his eyes. "Stop listening to me with your pride," he whispered. "Listen to me with your heart. I want you for no other reason than that you are a woman of beauty and gentleness. I want you because you destroyed a pain I thought would follow me all my life. I want you," he said softly, "because I feel for the first time in a long long time, and I like what I feel. I feel love, and it is a good thing. Don't take it away . . . not for a foolish reason like pride. It will cost us both far more than we can pay."

She wanted to believe, wanted it with a desperation born of love. But still a trace of fear lingered in her wide eyes and trembling lips.

He bent his head and took those trembling lips in a deep kiss that was meant to purge the last of her doubt. Slowly, gently, her lips parted beneath his, and his tongue searched the sweetness of her mouth as he drew her against him.

Hard arms bound her to him until she thought she would stop breathing. The world of doubt began crumbling about her, and she succumbed to her heart's desire. Slim arms crept about his waist, drawing him even closer. Her mouth went from surrender to possessive need. Hunger engulfed her, the hunger to again belong to him, to be enfolded in the warm magic she knew he would share with her. When the kiss ended, they stood for a moment in breathless silence, overpowered by a force neither of them could ever hope to control again.

"So you see, love," he said gently, "no matter how either of us has fought, there is nothing we can do now but admit the truth. At first I did not recognize it for what it was, but now I can say it . . . freely. I love you, Little Dove. I want you to marry me. I want to stay here. Rayne and Falling Water are happy, and we will be as well. It can be a whole new life."

Words she might have spoken were choked into silence by the flood of happiness that filled her. For the first time, she could feel the truth of his words.

"Little Dove," he said desperately, mistaking the reason for her silence, "Do you still doubt that what I feel for you is love? It is the truth . . . believe me." He waited for her reply.

"Yes," she murmured, "I believe."

He gave a whoop of joy, snatched her up in his arms, and whirled about with her. She clung to his neck, and their mutual laughter rang out in the darkness. When he placed her back on her feet, he kissed her again.

"Go to your father and tell him you've changed your mind. Tell him we want to be together. I think"—he smiled—"a new village should be blessed by a new marriage, don't you?"

"Yes," she said softly as his mouth claimed hers in a kiss that sealed their promise.

Chapter 27

The march toward the location of the new village began again before dawn the next day and lasted until long after the sun had set. When they finally did make camp, no one had the ability to do more than eat a rapid meal and fall on his mat to sleep.

The next morning, the rising sun found them again on the move. One more day and one more night—that was the thought in everyone's mind. Then they would be able to make a permanent camp before autumn turned into winter.

On their arrival, everyone could see that it was a perfectly chosen spot, both for protection and for its ability to sustain the village. It was near water, an essential prerequisite for the location of any Cheyenne village. They had reached their destination just before time for the midday meal. It was eaten quickly and followed by a bustle of activity as the villagers began to settle themselves into a familiar routine.

Five hundred tepees were reassembled, and soon smoke rose from cooking fires. Children laughed and played as mothers lost the tension of travel and began to smile again.

Hunters moved in and out of the village, and women prepared for the snows that would come. Mack had urged Little Dove to speak to her father quickly, for he wanted the marriage to be part of the ceremonies of celebration honoring their new village.

Little Dove's father was not surprised at his daughter's change of heart, for he had never quite believed the words Little Dove had spoken. Now he was quite pleased to give his permission, and to receive the abundance of gifts Mack offered. He was certain in his own mind that this man would keep the smile of happiness on his daughter's face.

Rayne was the one who was more surprised than anyone else.

"If you had not been so blinded by your own happiness," Mack teased, "you might have seen more. What a scout you will make, when you cannot even see the forest for the trees."

"It's only because you're a damn sly man. I had no idea you even wanted to stay here. The last we talked of it, you were going to leave before the snow fell."

"Well, a lot has happened since then. You looked pretty happy, so I began to realize I might be missing something."

"You have been." Rayne chuckled. "I wonder if Running Wolf is as happy. We've been here only a matter of weeks, and already we have taken both of the single women in his family."

Mack smiled. "Don't worry. We'll keep him happy. I, for one, wouldn't want to provoke his anger." They laughed together.

"I think it's damn fine, Mack. I'm glad you're staying. We've been partners too long to let it go now."

"Thanks, Rayne."

"Mack, it will only be a few weeks before it turns cold. In another month or so, we'll see snow."

Mack's astute gaze reached him. "You're thinking about Chevington and that fort."

"I'm just kind of surprised he's so quiet. He knows he can't do anything after the snow falls but wait until spring."

"Rayne, you think maybe he doesn't know about the gold? Maybe he's just doin' his job and won't bother us at all?"

"No . . . I don't think that for a minute, and neither do you. He's got something in his mind, and I just wish I knew what it was."

"Well, he sure as hell can't get to Lauren or Falling Water."

"Not if we stay careful."

"And you plan to."

"Yes . . . but all he needs is one mistake."

"Rayne, we're all in this together. We just won't make any mistakes. We won't give him the opportunity to do anything. For sure we won't let in any strange whites to trap. That way, the gold will stay put."

"You're right. The scouts should warn us if any strangers try to come in."

"And we'll move about the area and keep our eyes open. Once the snow falls, we can rest a while. Nobody can move in the winter out here. We can sit back and make plans."

They were walking in the open area between tepees, and they stopped there so that they would not be overheard.

"Mack?"

"What?"

"What do you think about Fox? Do you believe he just wants to spend the winter with us, then go his way?"

"You suspicious about something?"

"Nothing I can put my finger on. It's just a hunch, I suppose. I don't quite trust him."

"What's he done to get you suspicious?"

"That's the trouble." Rayne shrugged. "Nothing."

"Rayne, you aren't just out of joint because . . . he's been talkin' a lot to Falling Water, are you?"

"Mack, if I thought he meant to put a hand to her, I'd kill him, and I think he knows that. It's more than that. He's been talking a lot with Lauren also."

"What's that prove?"

"He wants them to be comfortable with him, to be off guard."

"So?"

"Mack, who stands between Chevington and this valley?"

"Lauren."

"And if Falling Water were in the hands of Chevington, what do you think Lauren would give to keep her safe?"

"Christ," Mack muttered. "Rayne, maybe we ought to do something about him."

"What? The man's done nothing. Hell, you know how these people are about being polite to guests. They'd think we were rude and crazy."

"Not Running Wolf."

"No, maybe he'd understand. It's his wife and daughter. But what do we tell him? We can't show him any proof, so he might believe we're imagining things."

"Well, it's still worth it to tell him."

"You're right. There's a big celebration tonight to mark our safe arrival. I'll talk to him then . . . when I can get him away from Fox's eyes. If Fox is up to something, I want him to believe he's got us fooled. I don't want him suspicious. He'll get too careful, and I have a feeling he's a man who doesn't make many mistakes."

"Good. I'll occupy some of his time tonight, and you get Running Wolf away and talk to him."

"All right." Rayne grinned. "There should be some happy people tonight when White Eagle tells his people that you and Little Dove are going to marry soon. They look for just about any reason to celebrate, and, in my opinion, this is about the best I know." He extended his hand to Mack, who took it in a firm grip. "Congratulations, Mack," he said softly. "I can only hope you're as happy as I am."

"Thanks, Rayne. I'm sure I will be."

"I'd better move on. I haven't seen Falling Water all day, and if I don't watch, she'll be working with every woman around after she's finished her own chores. She's kind of like her mother—always has room for someone else."

"Good thing for you she takes pity on strays," Mack reminded him, "or we'd be lying out in the brush somewhere."

"Right, but now she's mine, and I don't want her taking in any more strays. I'll see you later tonight."

"All right."

They separated, and Rayne moved toward his tepee

and Mack toward Little Dove's.

Fox was up before dawn, telling those who had also risen early that he planned to spend the day alone. He intended, he said, to search for some spirit message that would indicate the way he should continue his life. All Indians respected such a quest, and none would think of interfering with his plan or following him.

He had ridden carefully, backtracking many times to make sure no one was near. Then he rode toward the little river. Before he reached his destination, he dismounted and built the small fire with which he would send the prearranged smoke signal to Jess, who would then be watching for his arrival.

Once he had extinguished the fire, he rose, mounted, and rode on. In less than an hour he saw Jess riding from a stand of trees to meet him. They dismounted and tethered their horses so they would not drift away. Then they walked to a large boulder, where they could sit and talk and still watch for any approaching riders.

"What can you tell me, Fox?"

"Many things," Fox announced with a grin.

"So, tell me."

"The men at the fort are in for several big surprises."

"Such as?"

"Preston's son—he's here with the tribe."

Jess was surprised. "How the hell did he get back out here?"

"Grant Jamison brought him. Thomas must have told him a lot, because the whole family's up and moved here. I'd say White Eagle is wise to a lot. He's moved the village to a place where it would be pretty hard to catch them unprepared."

"Well, if things work out the way we plan, we won't have to attack. They will be forced to give it up and move on."

"Preston and Chevington should live in this village for a while," Fox said grimly.

"Why?"

"Then they'd get a little wiser." He turned to look at Jess. "I heard about his last tangle with them. He hasn't learned anything since. These people are not going to run just because he expects them to, and White Eagle is one smart man. Besides that, he's surrounded by men that are brave and clever. They'll fight. Believe me, they'll fight."

"Once we have our hands on Lauren Brent and her daughter, there won't be any fight left in them," Jess replied.

Being half Cheyenne, Fox knew the people better than Jess. He smiled. "It's going to be a lot harder than that. You might—and I said *might*—be able to force them out of the valley, but you're going to have White Eagle, Running Wolf, and a couple of men you hadn't planned on right on your tail. They'll trail you to hell if they have to."

"What men are you talking about?"

"You remember the party Thomas was with when we hit them, the ones that were supposed to start this thing rolling?"

"Yes. Why?"

"They are alive and well and in White Eagle's village. Not only that, but one has married Running Wolf's

383

daughter, and the other is going to marry his sister soon."

"Jesus! I thought they'd died then. Who saved them?"

"Falling Water," Fox replied. "I guess she was swimming not too far from there and ran across them while they were still alive. She had them brought to the village, and Sun Knife took care of them. Anyway, they're a part of the village now, and they're wise to what happened."

"Do they know about the gold?"

"I've never heard it mentioned, but that don't mean anything. They can be closed mouthed if they want to keep a secret. I'll keep my ears open and try to find out. What are you going to do now?"

"Right now I'm going to the fort and dump this in their laps. I should be back here with some kind of plan in about two weeks."

"I'll be here in two weeks," Fox replied. "Jess?"

"What?"

"You're paying me good for this job, but I'd like to make another deal with you."

"What do you want?"

"I'll only take half the pay you promised."

"But you want something else to balance out the other half."

"Yes."

"What do you have in mind?"

"Falling Water," Fox said quietly. His dark gaze told Jess he was very serious.

"You're crazy!" Jess replied in surprise.

"After they get what they want, they're going to kill her and her mother anyway. What's the difference if I take her with me? Who will know? You know damn well

384

they don't intend to leave anybody alive who can dispute their claim to the valley. I want her Jess . . . I want her alive."

"All right, Fox, all right. I'll talk to 'em. If they don't have any plans that include her, I don't see what difference it would make. Where will you take her?"

"I'll head for the high country. There isn't a man alive who could follow my trail over those rocks."

"She isn't going to be willing to go anywhere with you, especially after she finds out you've been spyin' on them."

"I'll take care of taming her. In a couple of weeks she'll find out who's boss. She'll come around."

"Well, it don't bother me none, you havin' her, but what the hell do you want with a half-breed squaw?" Jess said the words without thinking, then suddenly realized that Fox was a half-breed also. "I didn't mean it that way, Fox." Jess saw Fox's eyes grow dark and cold. "What I meant was, what do you need with her when the money we promised you could buy you all the women you want?"

"I don't want that kind," Fox said coldly and spat upon the ground. "You haven't seen her, so you don't know what you're talking about. I aim to keep her permanent."

"Permanent . . ."

"That's right. She'll understand one day. We're two of a kind—both half-breeds. Besides, I have my own plans for the white bastard who calls himself her husband. When I'm through, she'll think he's deserted her. She'll be willing to stay with me by then, especially if her parents and most of her village are dead. Where else would she be able to go?"

"I'm sure Preston and Chevington will be glad to see

385

him out of the way, no matter how you do it. I expect there won't be any problem. They'll give her to you."

"Jess," Fox replied softly, "I'll have her . . . one way or another."

Jess realized now, for the first time, that this man was extremely dangerous. He would tell Chevington and Preston that it would be best not to cross him. And what difference would one squaw make? he mused. "Okay, Fox. Consider her yours." He rose and walked to his horse. Once mounted, he raised his hand to Fox. "See you in a couple of weeks."

Fox nodded and watched him ride away. His eyes were cold and he smiled grimly. "Of course she is mine," he said softly, "and I would kill even you if I had to."

He watched Jess until he was out of sight. The thing that Jess didn't understand was that, to Fox, Jess was just another white man who had made the days of his childhood a hell. Fox had no qualms about Jess. He would kill him if he stood between him and what he wanted . . . and he wanted Falling Water. It enraged Fox that Jess felt he had the power to give Falling Water to him. If he wanted to, he would take her without giving a thought to Jess. It just suited his purpose for Preston and Chevington to help him eliminate the people who stood in his way.

He mounted now and rode back toward the village. He rode slowly and leisurely, allowing his thoughts to roam. He hated his white blood, had fought against it all his life, and had never quite been accepted by either race. He had felt a deep affinity for Falling Water from the moment he had first known of her. Who but someone such as she would know and understand how he felt?

Once he had seen her, he had been totally captivated.

He would rid her of the white man who had convinced her father to let them marry. He was sure it was because Rayne had offered the coveted gun and many other gifts. Once he got her away, she would realize they were two of a kind and meant by the Great Spirit to be together. He would take her to a place he knew, and there he would teach her what love meant. She would soon forget her white husband.

He rode on, conjuring visions of how it would be when they were together. It stirred his blood until he could almost feel her in his arms and taste her sweetness. The visions were so vivid and real that when he was beginning to cross the stream that led to the village and saw her at its edge he thought for a moment she was part of his dreams.

The sun sparkled off her hair, making it look like a dark flame. Her slim, graceful body jumped to new life in his mind. She was lifting clothes from the bushes where she had hung them to dry.

He rode across the stream to her side. Unaware of his thoughts, she smiled up at him.

"Hello, Fox."

"Hello, Falling Water." He smiled. "You are alone here?"

"I am not supposed to wander far. But I had to clean these clothes, and I could not ask a warrior to guard me while I did. It would please me if you did not tell Rayne that I was here alone."

He slid from his horse and stood beside her. She had no idea what real danger he represented, for he was sorely tempted to take her then. He only restrained himeslf by great effort.

"If you allow me to talk to you for a while"—he

grinned to hide his dark thoughts—"and to walk back to the village with you, I might be convinced to keep my silence about it."

She laughed. "I am sure a warrior such as you has many more important things to do than to spend his time watching a woman wash clothes."

He would have liked to have taken her in his arms and to have told her that nothing could be more important than the moments he could share with her. "It is better that a warrior is here to protect you. I do not have necessary duties at this moment, and I'm sure your husband would be relieved to know you are not alone. He is a very foolish man to leave you so." He added, "If you were my woman, I would guard you every minute. You are much too beautiful and desirable to risk losing."

All at once, Falling Water became aware of the intense look in the dark eyes that regarded her so seriously. It was as if he expected something from her, and for the first time she felt a faint touch of alarm. He was smiling and had said nothing wrong, yet she could not deny the strange feeling that flooded her.

"My husband is not foolish," she replied softly. "He is a warrior of great strength, and he will give me all the protection I need. I am his woman, and he will let no harm come to me."

"And yet," he reminded her, "if I were an enemy, I could have taken you away and no one would have known for many hours. By the time they discovered you were missing, I could have had you many miles from here."

"Why do you try to frighten me, Fox? I have done something that I should not have done, but it was not the cause of any problems. What enemy could get past the guards of White Eagle?"

"Are you frightened?"

"No, I am not," she stated firmly.

He chuckled. "You are brave. I knew you would be. I am sorry. I was only teasing you. Listen to me, Falling Water. I admire your courage and your beauty. I would be a warrior to protect you, too. Know this: no one will ever harm you while I am alive."

Again she felt a touch of apprehension, yet her nature refused to allow her to show anger, for she had heard only words of kindness from him. Yet were they words of kindness . . . or a threat? she wondered inwardly. Why, she thought, did she suddenly feel like running . . . like hiding in the safety of her tepee? "Thank you, Fox, but I am sure Rayne is all I need."

"I just wanted you to know. Now I will walk with you to make sure you have no problems." He held the bridle of his horse and drew it along behind him as he walked beside her. He knew that she was still uncertain about him, so he spoke of many other things. He wanted her to relax with him. He also wanted her to get used to his presence so that when the proper time came he could move quickly and she would be caught unaware.

They entered the village, and it took a very pleased Fox only seconds to spot Rayne and to know that Rayne had also spotted him. He smiled and spoke a few last words to Falling Water, then left her side. She continued on to her tepee alone.

Rayne had been standing on the other side of the valley when he saw Falling Water and Fox enter. Again the feeling twisted inside that this man meant them harm. This time the feeling was stronger, and this time he was determined to talk to Falling Water about it.

He walked across the clearing slowly, forming words in

his mind so he would not sound merely jealous. She had to realize that her danger could come from many directions—even from people she considered friends.

He stepped inside the tepee and found her on her knees, busily checking his shirts to see if they needed mending. She looked up when he came in, and her smile weakened his words. Still he had to say them. He went to her and knelt beside her. Questions seemed to be forming on her lips, and he intended to answer them all.

Chapter 28

"Falling Water," Rayne said, "where have you been?"

"I . . . I was just cleaning some clothes."

"At the river?"

"Yes."

"Alone?"

"Rayne . . . I . . ."

"Were you alone, Falling Water?" he asked firmly.

"Yes, I was."

"Falling Water, I don't think you take the danger of your situation seriously," he began. "Please don't be upset, but I must make you understand that you and your mother are in danger every minute of every day."

"Rayne, we are safe here. White Eagle has said so. The guards watch the village carefully. No one can come and go without us knowing of it. What is it that really bothers you?" she asked, astutely guessing what the real problem was.

"Sometimes the people near are dangerous too," he said softly. "Falling Water, I do not want you to spend any time with Fox. I don't want you to be near him. Will

391

you do as I ask?"

"What upsets you, husband?" she questioned.

"I do not trust him," Rayne admitted, "and I do not like the way he looks at you."

"And how does he look at me?" She smiled. He had to smile in return, for he knew how he must sound. "All right, so I am jealous. But he looks at you as if you were a possession, someone he could reach out and touch if he chose. I cannot stand it. I do not want to do him any harm, but I shall do whatever is necessary."

Falling Water put her arms about Rayne's neck and kissed him gently. "I will do as you wish, because I love you and I do not want your anger. But you must also understand that Fox may reach all he chooses, but Falling Water is not there for him to touch. There is only one warrior in my heart, only one warrior I can see, and the only one I will ever want is you. I will stay close to the vilage, no matter how painful it is."

"Painful?" He grinned.

"Yes. It is hard not to be free, not to ride across the valley floor like wind, not to swim as we did before."

"If you want to ride or swim, say so," he said. "I will ride with you."

"Now?" she queried mischievously.

"I think I've just been tricked," he admitted with a chuckle.

"Must I trick you into riding with me?"

Now he laughed loudly and drew her into his arms to rock her against him. "You need no tricks, my love. You have only to ask. If you wanted the stars from the sky, I swear I would try to get them for you."

He captured her face between his hands and kissed her. It was a long, leisurely kiss that drained the strength from

392

both of them. Gently he tasted, nibbling at her soft mouth, savoring the honeyed sweetness of her giving.

"God, I love you, woman," he whispered. "Stay close to me, love. I couldn't bear it if anything ever happened to you."

"I will not stray from the warmth of your love," she vowed. "I will do whatever you wish of me. I would not cause you worry, my husband, but I would ask that you share more time with me. Let us ride and swim again." Then she whispered, "I want to be with you."

"Can I say no to such a thing," he said. "We will go tomorrow, for tonight . . . I would share more than your time."

"It is not yet sundown." She laughed softly. "If we have visitors, what will they think if they call out and no one answers?"

"They will think I'm a damn lucky man, and they will certainly envy my good luck." She could no longer protest, for his insistent hands and relentless kisses drove all words from her mind.

The wedding of Little Dove and Mack was the highlight of the first celebration in the new village. It was a joyous affair, celebrated wholeheartedly by everyone, for Little Dove was well liked by her people.

Mack, though nervous, fared well despite the teasing he received. The entire tribe had taken him into their hearts, and, without doubt, they felt he was one of them.

Savannah, trying to take Lauren's advice, had made tentative overtures to several young girls. To her surprise, she found she was enjoying herself. They had tried to communicate to her that they admired her golden

393

hair and the blue of her eyes. And Savannah had laughed when they told her she should be in the sun more so her white skin could tan.

"I will never be as tan as you," she said with a giggle. "I am afraid I will always be white no matter what I do."

"You are very pretty," one shy girl ventured.

"Thank you," she replied modestly.

"But," another added, "why do you wear so many clothes? Does it not make you too warm?"

"I am warm, but it is all I have."

They had gathered in Lone Star's tepee so they could chatter together before the celebration as all young girls enjoyed doing. Savannah had touched on an area close to their hearts—generosity.

"You may wear one of mine," one offered. "Or mine," another quickly added.

"I have a dress here you can wear if you like," Lone Star said, and she quickly jumped up to get it. It was a tawny color, and even the inexperienced Savannah could see that it had taken a great deal of labor to make it. To Lone Star's delight, she quickly accepted it. With the help of her new friends, she quickly changed into it.

Her hair had been twisted into a knot upon her head because of the day's heat, and now they coaxed her to release it and let it fall free. She laughed as she undid it and they insisted on brushing it until it hung free of tangles and sparkled in the glow of the fire.

Another girl offered a band of beaded leather, and they tied it about her forehead to hold her hair.

"How do I look?" she asked, smiling at them.

"You look like one of us," Lone Star replied with a chuckle. "I am sure all the young men will be looking in your direction this night."

394

This was one thing for which Savannah was still not prepared. During the past few days she had felt Night Sky's eyes upon her often, but she was still a little frightened of him. She could not admit it in front of his sister, but the thought of the fierce-looking young warrior made her weak.

"Come, let us go and join the dancers," one girl cried. They left the tepee and walked toward the bright, glowing fire that marked the center of the celebration.

Some were dancing to the throbbing drums, and others were gathered in small clusters, talking and laughing. The scent of cooking food filled the air and mingled with the sounds of a happy gathering.

Thomas, quick to find a shy young girl, was thoroughly enjoying himself. He was astounded when he saw Savannah walking in his direction in the company of several young girls. He still could not believe the changes in her that had occurred in the last few days. He would now be the first to admit she was a remarkable beauty, and knew that both Grant and Martha would be pleased to see the transformation taking place in their daughter. Thomas moved to meet the arriving girls. He greeted them all, then turned to Savannah.

"Savannah, how beautiful you are. That dress certainly becomes you."

"Thank you, Thomas," Savannah replied, sensing the shyness of the other girls. Custom usually kept young men from saying such things so easily when they were in groups. The girls were not used to such flattering comments. They were somewhat in awe of a girl who seemed capable of accepting such words as if they meant nothing.

"Come, Savannah," Thomas invited. "Come, all of

you. Let's enjoy Mack's wedding."

They all moved closer to the fire and greeted those they knew. Savannah went to Mack and expressed her good wishes as coolly as if she were in a Washington drawing room. She was conscious of the strong emotion that existed between this large man and the slim girl standing beside him. His love for her was obvious, and he could barely keep his eyes from her.

Savannah left them and started toward her parents, who were sitting and chatting with Sun Knife. She moved slowly, enjoying the scene being played out before her. She could feel the warmth that pervaded the entire group and realized that it was really the first time she had ever looked at them without anger and resentment.

Her eyes were drawn to a group of young warriors who were laughing together. Among them was Little Eagle, the blue-eyed warrior. Lone Star, walking up to Savannah, had stopped when she did, and her eyes too were drawn to the same figure.

Savannah turned to speak to her, and, before Lone Star could mask her emotions, Savannah had read them easily. She did not speak, for she had been shown kindness by Lone Star, and she wanted her for a friend. But she wondered if the medicine man's son had any idea of what Lone Star felt for him.

Savannah pretended ignorance. "He is a very handsome warrior, isn't he?" she asked softly.

"Yes," Lone Star murmured. "He is the handsomest one in this village."

Savannah could have laughed. Little Eagle stood in a group of warriors, yet Lone Star had only spoken of him, without realizing Savannah could have been referring to any one of the young men.

They continued on until they joined Grant and Martha. Savannah sat down beside them, and Lone Star decided to move about a while longer. "You are enjoying yourself?" Martha asked Savannah.

"Yes, Mother, I really am." She laughed. "They are . . . so generous. Look, they gave me this dress to wear. It's Lone Star's. Isn't it pretty?"

"Savannah," Grant said, "of all the gowns I've seen you in, I believe you look your prettiest tonight in that one."

"Thank you, Father."

"I hope you enjoy the rest of your stay in our village, Savannah," Sun Knife said. "You need only ask if there is anything you want."

"I'm sure I will," Savannah said politely. Sun Knife's astute gaze and vivid memory told him of her adoption of a more open and sensitive attitude. He, above all others, could remember Lauren in the first days he had known her. He hoped Savannah would be as wise and fortunate as Lauren had been.

While Grant, Martha, and Sun Knife continued their conversation, Savannah let her eyes drift among the merrymakers. She almost gasped with shock when her gaze touched the dark, intent eyes of the man who stood half in shadow and half in firelight. He must have been watching her for some time, she realized. Her breathing grew shallow, and a strange tightness filled her until she could barely breathe.

She knew he would come to her, and a feeling akin to terror touched her. He seemed so immense, so overpowering, that she was left with only fear.

Slowly he began to move in her direction, and she could feel her heart begin to race. Her fear lifted her to

397

her feet. Without a word to her parents, she turned and almost ran from the celebration.

She stood by her tepee, gasping for breath and shivering. She was angry at herself for being such a child, and slowly the anger began to overcome all other emotions. Why should she be so upset at his presence, she thought. She would face him, and the fear would be gone. Once she had spoken, she would find he had lost the power to upset her. She would know he was just an ordinary man, no different from any other. She closed her eyes for a minute to regain her equilibrium, but her determination was promptly shattered at the sound of his voice coming from behind her. She spun around and came face to face with Night Sky.

Neither seemed to be able to speak for a moment as each was shocked by nearly overwhelming emotion.

"Savannah." He said her name as if he were caressing it. "Why are you frightened of me? Why do you run away?"

"I . . . I am not frightened of you."

"But you run from me. Why? I would only speak with you. I would only be your friend."

"It is just . . . you're so . . . so . . . immense." She flushed at his amused chuckle.

"And you expect a warrior to be small and weak? Would you speak to me then?" He laughed aloud. "If so, I could get on my knees. That would make me much smaller than you."

She had to laugh at such a thought, and he enjoyed the sound of her laughter. "I doubt that," she said. "I think that on your knees you would still be as tall as I. Besides," she said gently, "I could not envision a man such as you on your knees for any reason."

The moon was high, and she could see his face clearly. Suddenly it seemed to soften, to lose its harshness. His obsidian eyes seemed to glow with a glittering flame. He reached out a hand and very gently touched her hair.

"Your hair is like the light of the moon. It pleases me to touch it. You are a very beautiful woman, Savannah. It is a great wish of mine that you choose to stay with us for a long time."

She was surprised at the gentleness in a man she had thought so formidable. "I believe my parents have decided to stay for a while."

"Good. If you stay, perhaps you will share some time with me."

She could not help but question him. "Why?"

"So you would understand this place, my people . . . me," he added softly. "Will you ride with me tomorrow? I would show you that you can find much beauty and pleasure here."

Whatever fear she might have harbored before slowly melted away in the warmth that seemed to enfold her. "Yes . . . yes, I will."

His smile was quick and bright, and it immediately changed his face from one that was stern and fierce to a countenance she thought was sensitive and extremely handsome. "Good. Would you like to walk back to the celebration? I would walk with you, for I would like to ask you questions about your world."

She nodded, and they turned to walk slowly back. He did question her, and listened with sincere attention to all she said. In her innocence, Savannah did not realize that this was not a warrior's way. It was a most unusual thing, and she would not understand this for a long time.

Still, Savannah was not prepared to let this overpowering man come close or breach any of her defenses. She laughed and joined in the festivities but kept Night Sky at as much distance as she could. Her behavior did much to frustrate Night Sky, who was quite used to the shy, inviting glances of the pretty, dark-eyed girls of the village. By the time the wedding ceremony was over, he was quite tempted to grab her and carry her away.

He watched as she walked away from the now-dying fire with her parents. He was gazing at her so intently that he did not realize his sister, Lone Star, was standing beside him until she spoke.

"She is pretty, this white one," she said softly. He turned and looked into eyes that were like a mirror of his own. He knew the words she spoke were not meant to injure him.

"I do not understand her," he mused. "One minute she smiles at me, and the next her eyes are for someone else."

Lone Star chuckled softly. "And you would keep her eyes for you alone?"

"Yes," he answered. "If I could."

"I would not like to see you hurt, Brother," she said gently, "but one cannot always have what one wants. She will leave this valley one day, and her thoughts will never return to this village . . . or to you."

"Her parents will stay for a while yet."

"But in time they will go," she reminded him.

"Perhaps," he muttered.

"Night Sky," she said softly, "I know what you feel." Her eyes grew dark and sad. "Sometimes I feel the gods play with us. They show us the things we desire, but keep them out of our reach."

"The gods do not play," he said gruffly. "A warrior

400

must be strong enough to fight and take what he wants. I am not a boy. I know what is in my heart, and I will not blame the gods for failure because I will not fail. She is here, and as long as she is here I can still try to convince her to stay. Did not Summer Rain and our mother stay? It is not an impossible thing."

Lone Star sighed. She knew her brother well. He had set his mind on a goal, and he would fight in every way to achieve it. She knew the hurt of caring for someone who did not seem to see her. Slowly she began to wonder if her brother was right. But how could she, a woman, fight for the love of Little Eagle? It would scandalize the entire village, and her whole family would be shamed.

For a moment, she wanted to confide in her brother, to tell him her feelings for Little Eagle. She did not know that Night Sky already knew. If his mind had not been so caught up with Savannah, he might have seen the hurt in Lone Star's eyes.

For several minutes they walked slowly toward their tepees, through a slowly quieting and darkening village. They stopped in front of the one she still shared with their parents. Again she turned to face him. Lone Star loved her brother completely. As twins, they had shared a happy childhood. She put her hand on his arm and felt the strength there. "I wish you only good things, Brother," she said softly, watching the reappearance of his dazzling smile.

"And I you," he replied. "I would give you some words of advice, young sister."

She laughed. "I am only minutes younger than you."

"But," he insisted happily, "you are still younger." His eyes grew more serious. "You are the daughter of a very great chief. Remember that any man should be greatly honored to have you as his wife. Maybe," he said gently and with a grin, "if you chose someone and lifted your shy eyes to smile at him, you might find a surprise."

Lone Star was quiet, wondering just how much her brother knew of her feelings. She remembered well how they had always shown concern for each other and had understood each other all the time they were growing up.

"Maybe, Brother," she said softly, "it is not in the hearts of the gods to give either of us what we want."

"I will never blame the gods for what I am too weak to take," he said firmly.

Among their people it was the custom that when a man found a woman too shy, he would grab her up and ride away with her. If he could manage to keep her for some time, the tribe, her parents, and his family would consider them married. Mack had known this and would have taken Little Dove if her pride had continued to stand in the way of their happiness. But Lone Star was quite sure that this procedure would not work with Savannah and her parents, and she wondered if her brother could be contemplating such an act.

"Their ways are not our ways, Brother," she reminded him gently.

His impassive face told her absolutely nothing about his thoughts, but the fact that he did not answer alarmed her.

"Brother?" she questioned anxiously. He turned opaque eyes to her, then he smiled.

"Do you remember," he said, "many years ago when the river that was close to our village was suddenly changed from its path to another? The hands of the gods made it so. It only proves that what the gods wish to be will be so. I will go to seek a vision. Perhaps," he added

402

softly, "the gods will decide to change the courses of lives, for I do not wish to do battle against them."

He turned from her and walked away. As she watched him go, she felt an ache deep within her. She closed her eyes for a moment, praying silently that he was right, and that the gods would listen not only to her brother, but to her as well.

The village grew quiet; the celebration was over. Slowly the fires died and tepees darkened. A lone rider rode from the village. He rode without weapons, without food or water. He was naked except for a breechclout and moccasins. Following an ancient tradition, he went to find a place to seek the gods. He would lay his heart and his will before them.

It would be a long and difficult trial, but, in his mind, the quest for answers would be well worth whatever he might suffer.

Chapter 29

He rode through the balance of the night, rested his horse, and rode again until the sun was high. He stopped only to allow his horse to rest, then continued on. Night found him at the top of a bluff that overlooked a deep box canyon. Into the canyon he rode until he felt enclosed by the hills. He hobbled his horse and let him graze, then sat wearily on his blanket.

He studied the stars above him as he lay back on the blanket. Slowly he emptied his mind of all thought, hoping the gods would fill it with the answers to his questions.

The night passed. He did not sleep but lay still in his silent search.

The bright morning sun found him again seated. He built no fire, ate no food, and drank no water. The day ended, and again the stars looked down on him. Another day was met and another night.

Now he was lost to the world in which he sat, his mind an empty void waiting to be filled. Hunger and thirst made him weak, yet he remained motionless.

A soft breeze slowly turned into a whispering wind that caused him to lift his head. The early sun was just cresting the horizon. In its dim light he saw a huge hawk slowly circling gracefully. He watched it soar, and a strange floating feeling filled him, as if the hawk and he were one. Then his eyes caught a glimpse of movement, and a second hawk joined the first.

They spiraled and floated in the sky, sometimes brushing wings. Night Sky knew they were mates. A slow smile touched his lips. This, he thought as his heart leapt with joy, was his answer from the gods. He would find his mate. He would have the woman he wanted. He rose, gathered his blanket, mounted, and rode back toward his dreams.

Savannah rose early the morning after the wedding. Night Sky had asked her to ride with him. She was surprised at the feelings this thought evoked. But those feelings quickly turned to anger when she discovered, after waiting for some time, that Night Sky had left the village the night before. She fled to her tepee as her fury began to grow at his lengthy absence.

"He is a savage!" she stormed aloud. "No gentleman would do such a thing. Did he think I would be standing there waiting until he decided to return? I shall never speak to him again! Savage! Beast!" She almost wept with her frustrated anger.

Martha watched with a half smile on her face. She did not speak, but she realized that Savannah felt a new emotion, one she could not name and of which she was afraid. Savannah had met a man she would never master, a man she wanted in a way she did not understand. It was

405

a new experience for Savannah, not being able to control her own emotions.

Savannah tried to mask her disappointment by joining the young girls in their work and in their play, but Martha and Grant were very much aware that her eyes continually fled to the horizon, filled with the hope of seeing a lone rider approaching.

"I do believe," Grant said with a grin, "that our daughter has met her match."

Martha chuckled. "She'll be the last to admit it, but I believe she finds the young man attractive."

"I believe it's something more than that for him. Martha, do you think she would ever seriously consider him? He is a good man, and I think he's more than a little in love with her."

"I don't honestly know, Grant. She has changed a great deal since she came, but I don't think she'll let him through that wall she has built for protection."

"Protection?"

"Well, at least in her mind. She's afraid, Grant."

"Afraid of what?"

"Well, at home she was pampered and cared for. She was spoiled. I think she has just begun to realize that. She's afraid she wouldn't make a good wife for Night Sky. After all, one day he will be chief. She really doesn't know yet"—Martha smiled—"that she's made of the same fiber as her father. You love it here. You're happy here, but she's still afraid."

"Well, how the devil can she find a future if she's afraid of it?"

"Leave her alone, Grant. She has to read her own heart and find her own way. If it is meant to be, it will happen. Besides," she added with a laugh, "I don't think Night

Sky is the kind to court too long or to take no for an answer."

Grant chuckled, for he had his doubts about this also.

Savannah saw Night Sky from some distance away. She was shocked at the feelings that filled her as she gazed at him. Something stirred within her, leaving her weak and trembling.

She was kneeling with two other girls before a stretched buffalo hide and tried her best to appear unaware of his approach.

She knew his horse had stopped beside her, yet she refused to acknowledge his presence. He was the son of a chief and used to obedience. He instinctively knew her act was deliberate, and done out of fear. The other two girls had become silent, looking up at him with wide eyes.

"Go," he said firmly. "Leave us."

They took only a moment to climb to their feet and disappear behind the tepee. Night Sky looked down on her golden head as she still continued to rhythmically scrape the skin.

He did something he would have done for no other. He dismounted and dropped to one knee beside her. He reached out and stilled her hands. He could feel her trembling and saw the frustrated tears on her cheeks.

"Do you weep from anger or from joy at my return?" he inquired softly.

She turned to face him. "You are a conceited one. I did not even realize you were not here."

"Did you not?"

"No, I did not."

"Did you think for a moment I had forgotten you? I

407

have not, but I had to seek a vision, and answer to my question."

"A vision?"

"I will explain to you one day. Believe that it was very important."

"Of course," she snapped. "Anything is more important than I am around here. I wish my parents would decide to go home. I would like to leave."

She stood up and, he rose to stand beside her.

"Everyone is important," he replied. "And you are more so. Your family is happy here. It would please us to see you smile. I know that you have found some pleasure among us. I am sorry if I made you angry, but it was not intended. I would not have you believe that I would deliberately hurt you. You promised to ride with me. We could talk then."

Savannah summoned all her pride and lifted her chin. "I will think about it. Ask me tomorrow. Maybe I will agree."

He was too stunned to speak. He had never been addressed in such a manner by a woman before. He watched her spin about and walk away from him. Then, after a few minutes, a slow smile crossed his face. Such pride! Such arrogance! This was the woman he wanted.

He turned and walked toward Grant's tepee.

Both Grant and Martha were surprised when he requested permission to enter. They gave it and waited in silence as he strode inside.

It was not customary for a woman to participate in important discussions. Understanding this, Martha moved to the back of the tepee and waited for the words she and Grant knew were coming. She looked at the strong, handsome young man who stood before them.

She was surprised to find herself hoping that Savannah would look at him without false ideas. He was a man, a man who would give her the love and security she could not seem to find.

Night Sky sat before Grant, who already knew why he was here. Grant waited, surprised again when Night Sky, the proud warrior, seemed to search for words.

"I come to speak to you of something important," Night Sky began.

"Speak, Night Sky," Grant replied. "I will listen."

"I am a man of great wealth and well honored in my tribe."

"I know that." Grant smiled. "It is a thing you did not need to tell me."

"It is important to me for you to understand."

"Then go on."

"I can provide well for the woman who would be my wife. There would be warmth and plenty of food in our tepee."

Grant nodded.

"I come to offer you whatever bride price you decide. I would make your daughter my wife. To me she is worth much, even all that I possess."

Grant was silent for several minutes. He wasn't quite sure he could explain to Night Sky that their customs were not the same and that the choice of a husband was Savannah's alone to make.

"Night Sky," he began, "we cannot accept a bride price."

Night Sky stiffened, and Grant could see his misinterpretation. He thought that Grant was refusing him. Pride sparkled in his dark eyes.

"No, Night Sky," Grant said quickly. "We are not

409

refusing you. It is just that our customs are different from yours. It is our way to let our children choose whom they would marry, and once that decision is made, we honor it. But a bride price is not part of our custom. It is not necessary for us that a man prove anything but his honor and his love for his bride. That, to us, is the most important thing."

Night Sky had a very difficult time digesting Grant's words. He had thought to influence Savannah's parents and thereby put some pressure on her. Now they were telling him that his attempt had been useless. He could reach Savannah only by confronting her and making her admit their mutual attraction. It created within him a grim determination and the seed of another thought.

"I must ask you one more question. Think before you speak. I want to know your true heart."

"Ask," Grant replied. "I will be as honest as I can."

"For this I would ask you and your woman both to speak."

Martha looked up in surprise. This was something she knew was never done. A man might ask his wife's opinion in private, but it was never requested before others. Grant looked at her, and she nodded silently.

"Would you look upon me with favor? Would you be displeased if your daughter agreed to remain here and be my wife? Would the thought be an honor or stir your unhappiness? I must know this."

Martha and Grant had only to exchange a glance to know what the other was thinking.

"Can I speak for you, Martha?" Grant questioned softly. She nodded, and Grant's eyes returned to Night Sky.

Night Sky contained himself only by great effort. The

words Grant was about to say meant more to him than anything else, so much more that he was shaken by the fact that he found himself holding his breath in suspense.

"The thought pleases both Savannah's mother and me. I have known your father, and I think I know you. It would honor us, indeed, if Savannah chose to marry you. But, you must understand, it must be her free choice. We will never force her."

"I would not take a woman I had to force," Night Sky replied quickly. "She does not understand my words. She does not listen. We must talk. And because she has a place to run and hide, she will not speak to me. I must take her from here."

Martha looked startled. Grant grew grim. Night Sky quickly realized that again they did not understand.

"I would only have time to speak to her. You have my word, my honor, that I would not touch her or do her any harm. I would lay my life at your feet if any harm came to her. I only wish to make her hear my words. Then, if she does not choose to stay with me, I will speak no more. I will return her to you safely and unharmed. I swear."

He watched their faces intently, wondering if they could really understand. In his heart, he knew he was going to do something they would find difficult to condone.

"Night Sky, if your words convince Savannah of how you feel, we both agree. We accept your word of honor that you will not harm her in any way—in *any* way," Grant added softly. "I would be the first to claim your life if you did so. I want you to understand also that she means everything to us."

"I understand that." Night Sky smiled. "She means as much to me as well. It is just that I cannot convince her

411

this is so."

Grant laughed and Martha smiled. "I believe," she said, "that Savannah has inherited a streak of stubbornness."

"I don't know from where." Grant chuckled. "I am a very reasonable man." Again Night Sky watched the sparkle in Martha's eyes as she looked at Grant. He had the strong desire to see Savannah look at him in such a long way.

He rose to leave before too many more questions could be asked. He'd rather they did not know the details of what he planned to do. With a quick exchange of words, he left and went to his own tepee to carefully prepare for what he would bring. Then he went to where the horses were kept, took his own, and led another. He left the village and returned at dusk.

The next morning Savannah awoke early. Despite her previous complaints, she liked the first touch of dawn. She decided to walk to the spot on the riverbank where all the young girls bathed. She knew she was likely to be the last one there if she did not hurry, and she did not want to miss the fun. She drew the tawny-colored tunic over her head, again realizing how comfortable it was compared to her other clothes. Her hair was tangled from sleep, and she decided to let it hang free until she could wash it. She drew on her knee-high moccasins and tied them firmly about her calves. Then she quickly moved outside.

The path from the village to the river was one she had walked several times before, and she knew it well. She breathed deeply of the fresh morning air. Autumn was near, but still the touch of summer lingered. The smell of pine mixed with other things she could not yet recognize hung in the clear air. Only to herself would she admit that she enjoyed the beauty of her surroundings, and she walked slowly, humming to herself.

The sound of hoofbeats from behind her caused her to turn about. For a moment she did not recognize the rider who was approaching from the village. The morning sun was behind him, and it made him a dark, shadowed form.

As he drew nearer she recognized Night Sky. At first she smiled with admiration as she noted his ability to control the still half-wild stallion he rode. But he was riding fast—too fast. Her smile faded as she began to think that perhaps he did not see her and would ride her down.

He was almost upon her, and she automatically threw up her arms to cover her face. She could feel the thunder of the horse through her feet and could almost sense the massive power of the animal as it bore down upon her.

She did not even have time to cry out. Night Sky had learned to ride before he could walk, and with ease he bent forward and caught Savannah about the waist, drawing her up before him in one fluid motion.

Her heart pounded in fear, and she was at first grateful that he had saved her. Then she realized they were still thundering away from the village. The situation suddenly became clear. He was taking her further and further away. Real fear coursed through her.

She fought wildly, striking out at him, but it was useless. His superior strength was much more than she could handle. He laughed softly as she ceased her struggles and remained still.

"You are wise as well as beautiful," he remarked.

"You are an arrogant beast—an animal! What do you

413

think you are going to do? This is ridiculous. Take me back to the village at once!"

"I will take you back to the village, and even though you think I am not a man of honor, I am. I want to talk to you."

"Talk! You drag me from the village across your horse like a deer you have killed. You don't even ask if I choose to go."

"If I had asked you would have refused," he said, amusement in his deep voice.

"Yes, I would have!"

"Then," he said reasonably, "it is of little use to ask. Now I have your attention. You will listen."

"Oh," she groaned raggedly. She wanted to be free of the strong arms that so easily held her bound to him. She was becoming alarmed at the fiery response of her wayward body. She refused to lean against him until the rhythm of the horse and the strain on her muscles were too much for her. She sagged back against the hardness of his chest.

"Very wise," he said with a laugh. "I thought you would never tire."

"Beast!" she snapped.

"You have called me that before. Can you not think of anything new? Soon," he whispered against her hair, "soon you will call me many other things."

Terror filled her. Was he going to rape her, or leave her here in the wilderness? What was his plan?

He knew she was afraid, yet did not speak. He would allow her thoughts to wander. Maybe she would be more gentle and prepared to listen to what he wanted to say.

They had gone many miles, and he knew she was tired, yet by her stiffness she was refusing to acknowledge this.

414

With ease he turned her to rest more easily against him. He could feel the curve of her breast against his chest, and her slim waist in the crook of his arm. It was where he would always want her to be.

Savannah could hear the steady beat of his heart, and, despite what her mind commanded her body to feel, it resisted and chose to acknowledge its own wayward feelings.

She had no idea how long he was going to travel. They had already gone so far from the village that she knew it would be impossible for her to find her way back without his help. She was completely and entirely at his mercy, and she had never felt so helpless in her life.

It seemed to her many hours—and many miles—before he drew his horse to a stop. He slid easily to the ground and lifted her down to stand beside him. Her legs were so weak she nearly fell. He kept his arm about her waist until her legs became more steady.

It was only then that she looked about her to discover they were in a previously prepared camp. A tepee stood near, along with other evidence that he or someone else had already spent some time here.

A new fear filled her. Would he ever take her back? Did he intend to keep her here, maybe even leave her here . . . alone?

The fear transformed her features, and he read it well. She looked up at him with genuine terror in her eyes.

"No," he said softly. "I will not hurt you, and I will not leave you alone. Besides"—he laughed—"you would be too easy a meal for a hungry bear."

She turned to face him. "I am more afraid of you at this moment than any bear. Please, tell me what you are going to do to me." Though she had mustered all the control she had, her voice still trembled, and she felt dangerously close to tears.

"I want you to rest for a while. You must eat and drink. Then we will talk."

"Talk now!" she demanded as her fear gave way to anger.

"You are a stubborn woman," he said and chuckled, "but this time you will do as you are told. You will eat and drink," he said firmly. "Then you will rest and we will talk. I am stubborn also," he continued, the amusement again in the depths of his voice. "And you will need all your strength, for I do not surrender very easily either. I"—his voice softened—"have too much to lose."

He handed her the water sac, and she snatched it angrily from his hand. She drank, realizing then how tremendously thirsty she had been.

He spread a blanket on the ground and told her to sit. She obeyed only because she realized that until she ate, she was going to get nothing from him.

He built a fire, and, from a sac he had placed in the tepee, he brought food. Sitting beside her, he handed her some. In silence they ate. She had no idea that he was even more nervous than she. His impassive face told her nothing. To her, his face looked like a granite wall, and his huge body a formidable obstacle she could never overcome.

She was physically aware of his presence, even though she was not looking at him, and he was even more aware of hers. He was trying his best to resist taking her in his arms. He knew it would only frighten her more, and he did not want her to be frightened. It was the last emotion he wanted to elicit.

The silence deepened, and he turned to look at her.

416

She was gazing out at the scene before her, caught up in her thoughts. His heart quickened its beat. How beautiful she was and how desperately he wanted her to understand! The sunlight caught her hair and made it sparkle like burnished gold. His hands twitched with the desire to be buried in the thick mass of it, and he yearned to draw her to him to taste her slightly parted lips. These thoughts were reflected in his dark eyes, unguarded, when she suddenly turned to look at him. The result left her breathless and for a moment she was stunned.

"You are so beautiful," he said softly. "I would not hurt you. I would not see fear in your eyes when you look at me."

"Then take me back," she whispered. "Let me go."

"I will. If you will give me the time to make you understand. If you will listen to me. Talk to me."

Again she remained silent for a moment, then she smiled. "I have been told so many times that I am too stubborn for my own good. Even Thomas still finds it difficult to talk to me. I guess . . . I guess I just didn't want to hear. Am I really so bad?"

He chuckled, and she enjoyed the sparkle of laughter in his eyes. It made him seem so much younger and so much more vulnerable.

"I would not change anything about you," he said, "except"—his smile was broad and white—"to make you a little more interested in me."

They both laughed, and he felt a surge of pleasure. At least she was less afraid and less guarded. She leaned back on both elbows and smiled up at him, which did much to upset his equilibrium. With as much self-control as he could maintain, he moved closer to her.

"Then," she said, "tell me about you."

His people had always made good use of story telling. They did so when they returned from the hunt or did something to merit praise, often with some exaggeration.

Night Sky was astute enough to know that Savannah would not be impressed with bravado. Therefore he spoke with honesty and simplicity and knew a great deal of pleasure when she seemed interested. It began so, and his hopes grew. Would he be able to make his way into her heart? he wondered. These few days he intended to keep her would give him his answer.

Chapter 30

Fox squatted in the camouflaging depths of the brush and watched the curve of the river. It was the place where the women went each morning to gather water and to bathe. Several were there, but his eyes dwelt only on one—Falling Water.

Rayne had attempted to make the river a well-guarded area. Outlying guards had been set. Rayne had laughingly said that if he couldn't keep Falling Water from the water, at least he would try to make it safe. He remembered vividly the slim girl who had appeared over him, glistening with water in the bright sun. It was his favorite memory, and he didn't intend to share it with another. He had asked White Eagle for guards, and they had been supplied. But they guarded against the enemy from without, not the one within.

Fox licked his dry lips as he fought the heated desire that stirred in his loins. It was not the time yet, but he found it very difficult to wait.

She stood in the water, laughing at something someone had said. The sun glistened on her dark hair, and long

419

tendrils of hair clung to her body.

He watched as most of the others dressed and began to make their way back to the village. Falling Water remained until the last. Fox observed her closely while she dressed, squeezed the water from her hair, and braided it. Then she bent to pick up her water sacs and turned toward the village.

Fox was about to reveal himself, for he wanted to be near her, speak to her, maybe even touch her. He had no chance to do so, however, for, at that moment, both he and Falling Water heard the approaching horse. He remained in hiding and was filled with jealous rage when he saw Falling Water's quick smile as her gaze turned toward the approaching rider.

Rayne drew his horse to a halt beside her and dismounted. Fox heard Falling Water's soft laughter as Rayne caught her up in his arms.

"Umm," Rayne whispered against her hair. "You smell good." He laughed softly. "You feel good, too."

"You have only been gone for one day and one night," Falling Water remarked, laughing with him.

"Sleeping out under the stars with nothing warmer than a buffalo robe is not my idea of comfort. At least not when I remember so vividly what is waiting at home."

"You missed me?" she teased.

"From the moment I rode out of the village. I'm sure Little Eagle and his friends were well aware of my haste to find some meat and get home. I should have dragged Mack along to teach him a little lesson."

"You would drag a man away from his woman so soon after their marriage? You are a heartless man."

"I still feel as if it is the day we were married. Let's go home and revive some memories."

420

Falling Water looked up into his eyes, warmed by the desire that flamed in his gaze until she felt it tingle through her. As he always could, he melted any resistance she might have had. The idea of work was forgotten. She felt her legs grow weak and the warmth seep through her veins until she could only cling to him for support. He held her in a possessive embrace and bent to take her parted, inviting mouth with his. A half sob-half sigh escaped her as his possession questioned deeper and her answer matched his.

He held her against him with one arm while his other hand caressed well-remembered curves. Gently he nibbled her lips, then left them to travel over the soft flesh of her throat only to return to the sweetness of her mouth. His tongue bravely explored its depths, and hers savored the heady masculine taste of his. She was caught up in his maleness, in the scent of tobacco and leather and in the overpowering strength that held her bound against him.

It was with reluctance that he freed her lips. The flame that ignited their passion leapt between them and she stood resting against him while she greedily enjoyed his touch. He was hers, as completely and truly as the sun belonged to the sky. She felt elated at the powerful feeling that her possession gave her. She allowed herself to dissolve in the heat of his gaze and could only nod her agreement.

He smiled, then turned to remount. He reached down and drew her up before him. They sat so for a moment, while he leisurely kissed her again and let his hands roam to more sensitive spots. It was all either of them could bear. He turned his horse about and headed back to the village, the water sacs completely forgotten by both.

421

Fox rose slowly from his place of concealment. His dark eyes burned with hatred and lust.

"White man," he muttered, "I will see you dead."

Fox's hatred of the white man festered within him. His half-white blood had always been a curse to him. He had fought both worlds—his Indian mother's because she had chosen a man of white blood to love, and his white father's because he had returned to his world and left his half-breed son with no love and no one to fight its loss.

Why was it that the only woman he had ever wanted had turned to a white man? She still believed that the white man could bring love, when Fox knew they brought only greed, hatred, and deceit. He would convince Falling Water that this was so once he got her away from the white man's influence.

Fox returned to the place he had hidden his horse. In one lithe movement he mounted. Slowly he made his way from the valley, speaking a smiling greeting to each guard as he rode by and marking the position of each one for his return.

He rode for a long time, dwelling on both his jealous hatred of Rayne and his need for Falling Water. He dreamed of the moment she would see the mistake she had made and would come willingly into his arms. He allowed the dream to fill him until he could almost taste the sweetness of her lips and feel the slim length of her body against his.

He reached a familiar place, dismounted, and built a small fire. In a moment a fateful signal rose and faded into the sky.

Fox waited with inherent patience, as he ate the small amount of food he had brought along.

The sun had reached its zenith and was slowly

beginning its descent as he sensed the approach of the rider.

Jess dismounted and walked toward the fire and a waiting Fox. He sat down beside Fox with a grunt.

"Fox, you took your good old time getting back to me."

"I was busy," Fox said shortly, pointing out without words that what he had been doing had nothing to do with Jess.

"You have everything lined up?"

Fox turned to look at Jess. "Did you tell Martin and Chevington what I said?"

"About Falling Water?"

Fox nodded shortly.

"Yes. Let me tell you the plans. Chevington and Martin want us to make a move now. Since Lauren Brent now owns the valley, they have to make her sign it over to them. The only hold we'll have over her is her daughter. Chevington is afraid White Eagle will put on his paint if we snatch the girl, so we've got to have some protection from him."

"How are you going to do that?"

"Simple." Jess grinned. "We snatch his girl, too. With Falling Water and Lone Star in our hands, Lauren will sign what we want, and White Eagle won't lift a finger." Fox digested this in complete silence. "You don't think it will work, Fox?"

Fox turned again and his eyes held Jess's. "Now tell me," he said softly, "what is he really planning to do with them?"

Jess's smile faded. "Kill them," he said slowly.

"Both of them?"

Jess nodded. In a swift movement, Fox stood up. He looked down on Jess.

"I'm not going to help you."

"What? You've been paid. You said—"

"I said I wanted Falling Water. I want her, and I want her alive. If he plans on killing her, he gets no help from me. Is that clear?"

Jess knew Fox meant what he said, and he also knew that without Fox to get the men into and the women out of the village, they didn't stand a chance. He was sure that Chevington and Martin wanted the valley badly enough that they would agree to anything Fox demanded. Jess rose to his feet.

"Okay, Fox. I'm supposed to offer you anything you want. We need to get into that valley. The girl is yours. Once you get us in and out you can take her and go."

"And Lone Star, the chief's daughter?"

"The two Crows get her. They are working for Chevington just to get hold of her. They have a score to settle with White Eagle. I guess his girl will even up the score. Anyway, they'll both be out of the way."

Fox grinned, and Jess was not quite sure why he felt shaken by the grin or why he felt Fox was laughing at him.

"White Eagle," Fox said softly. "He is a very strong chief. They had best put a lot of distance between themselves and White Eagle. His arm will reach far."

"Don't worry. They'll ride with her a long way before they stop to play their little games. Fox, what are you going to do?"

"I'll get them in. We'll grab the two and run, but I'll go my way and they'll go theirs. You won't see me again until all this is settled. Then I'll get word to you once that tribe is gone. I want some of that gold, too."

"All right. I'll go get the others. I'll be back around sundown."

Fox nodded. "I'll wait."

He said no more but dropped to the ground beside the fire. Jess looked at him for a moment, and the same uncomfortable feeling touched him. No one ever really knew what Fox was thinking. After a while he turned and walked to his horse. Fox watched him go, and the smile on his face became cold and malicious. If Jess had known his thoughts, he would never have faced Fox again without readily acceding to his demands.

"Fool," Fox whispered before turning to contemplate the fire and the dreams that twisted his mind. In silence he waited for the ones who would help him get what he wanted.

Jess rode slowly and steadily. He did not have to ride to the fort, for Chevington and Martin waited for him some miles away. They waited with military troops who would ride with them when they entered the village to put their ultimatum before White Eagle and Lauren Brent.

He passed the guards and rode into the camp and up to the large tent that stood in the center. There he dismounted. Before he could enter, Martin and Chevington came outside to greet him.

"Well, is everything arranged?" Chevington demanded.

"Yes," Jess answered. He pointed to two Crow Indians who sat nearby. "They'll go in with me. When we come out, they can have Lone Star and go one way. Fox can take Falling Water and go another, and I'll come back

425

here. You can ride into the village and tell them what you want. Once she signs the papers, get out. It will take a few days before they find out what really happened. By that time, you'll be back at the fort. With the troops you have, they won't be able to do a thing. All you need to do is enforce the orders to move—enforce them, and don't leave enough of them alive to cause you any trouble."

Chevington grinned. "Well done, Jess. In a matter of days, we'll have everything settled."

"You planning on really letting Fox have Falling Water, or are you going to kill her?"

"I don't really care. If Fox wants her, let him have her. By the time he's tired of her and sells her off to some other buck, it will be too late anyhow. Why?"

"Fox doesn't seem to be the kind to cross. If we tried to kill her, we might find more trouble than we bargained for."

"Fox? One man? What the hell can he do?" Martin laughed.

"I'll tell you," Jess said quietly. "You take that woman he wants away from him, and he'll trail you and kill you one dark night. He'll slip in and gut you with that knife he's so good with. You ever seen an Indian gut a man? He'll run that knife into you and cut you from groin to throat. It ain't pretty."

Martin gulped heavily, and his face paled. "Well, let him have her. We'll get what we want. What do we care about one squaw? I want that valley, and I want Lauren Brent. I have to repay an old, old debt."

"Well, me and the Crow will get going. We should be in and out of the village in less than a day. Give us three days from now before you ride in with your demands."

"Agreed," Chevington said, the light of fanaticism in

his eyes. "I will finally wipe that valley clean of those abominable savages. I will make them remember well every step I had to take when they forced me to walk from their village."

Jess looked at him for a moment. He was pleased he did not belong to the village of White Eagle, for he could see the desire for death and bloodshed in Chevington's eyes.

"I'll be leaving," he said. With a slight gesture he motioned to the two Crows, who silently rose, mounted, and followed him. Chevington and Martin watched them ride away.

"Martin," Chevington said, "that man almost sounds as if he has respect for those heathens."

"Yes, he does, doesn't he?"

"He might be a nuisance one day."

"He also"—Martin chuckled—"might want a bigger chunk of the gold than we are ready to give."

"I had thought of that. A two-way split sounds much more lucrative to me."

"Yes, I agree."

"What do you suggest we do about it?"

"I suggest that when he rides back here to tell us of his success we . . . eliminate the problem."

"Maybe we can have him ride with us to wipe the valley clean. Strange things happen in battle. You never know who might get killed."

"You're right. You never know."

"Come inside. We'll have a drink. We must discuss future plans."

"You don't plan to build and remain in the valley?"

"In this godforsaken wilderness? Never! I will go back East, retire my command permanently, and those who helped me will again help to mine this valley and take from it enough for us to live in comfort for the rest of our lives."

Martin nodded in agreement.

"Martin," Chevington added, "just what do you intend to do with Lauren Brent? Will you take her back East?"

Martin chuckled. "Yes. I think it would do much to cure her arrogance if she were brought back as my Indian squaw. I will find it very amusing to make her a showpiece, a toy for some of my close friends. Oh, she will pay so dearly for what she has done. And I shall remind her daily of what Fox and his friends are doing with her daughter. It should bring her to her knees. I shall enjoy very much hearing her beg. Yes, I shall enjoy that very much."

They walked into the tent, and Chevington drew a bottle from his pack. They sat down and drank while they continued to discuss the plans about which they had long dreamed; plans which included the destruction of White Eagle, his village, and every sign that it had ever existed.

Falling Water nestled close in Rayne's arms. Gently she caressed the hard muscle of his chest. He held her close in silence, enjoying her possessive touch. He had found a peace and contentment here, within Falling Water's arms, that was greater than any he had ever known. Sometimes it amazed him how they could seem to become part of each other.

Within his arms she felt so slim and delicate, yet only minutes before he had been hard and pulsing within her. Rayne was an extremely large man in every way, generously endowed by nature, and he was often somewhat afraid to possess her with the depths of his desire. Yet once within her he was lost and could not control the fire that consumed him. What thrilled him even more was the way she seemed to draw him within her, to want with the same urgency as he the sometimes violent, yet always beautiful blending that left them as they were now, bereft of any words that could describe the thing they had just experienced.

He closed his eyes to savor more with his other senses, relishing the delicate odor of her skin, the touch of her hair that lay like silk across his arm, the feel of her warm body with its curves that fit his own as she nestled close to him. He wanted to say so many things to her, but he knew that even if they lived lifetimes together he would never be able to find the words to tell her what he felt. She was now as much a part of him as his breathing or the beat of his heart. He knew he would rather die than live without her.

He felt her lips gently brush the skin of his throat, then drift, like butterfly wings, to another spot. He tightened his arms about her.

"I must go," she whispered. "There is much to be done. You would not want them whispering about your wife's laziness, would you?"

He chuckled. "If you leave my side now, I shall shrivel up and die like the grass in the hot sun."

He was pleased with the soft sound of her laughter and more so with the fact that, despite her words, she made no attempt to leave.

He rose on one elbow and turned to look at her. He studied the lines of her face, reaching a gentle finger to trace them.

"I had never known there was anything quite as beautiful as you in this world, my love. From the first moment I looked at you, dressed only in water, my heart and all my thoughts were lost."

"It was the same with me, husband. When I found you lying there, I thought you to be the handsomest warrior I had ever seen. I had never thought of belonging to any man until you."

"And now?" He smiled.

"And now I would never be able to live without you. I cannot bear the thought of your going away, even if it is only for a little while."

"I have been thinking about that. Since the winds of good fortune saw fit to send Martha and Grant out here, I don't see why I don't write Senator Miles a letter and let Martha and Grant take it back with them when they go."

He watched her eyes grow brilliant with excitement.

"Then you will not have to go? You will be able to stay with us—never leave?"

"Never," he whispered as he drew her closer. He kissed her deeply and hungrily, surprised that although he had just possessed her he could feel the fire of desire like burning liquid flow through him once more.

The kiss grew in depth and intensity. His tongue lay claim to her moist inner places, and hers sought to taste the wine-sweet depths of his. Passion reigned, and they both gave no battle.

He rolled on his back and lifted her over him, drawing her down to impale her on the hardened, throbbing shaft of his desire.

She moved now, in possession of his body and soul. She tossed her head with the almost painful pleasure of her need as she writhed with him, and she moaned as his movements matched her own. He gripped her slim waist and thrust upward, driving from her all thought but this agony of passion.

The words she cried out in her rapture filled his heart.

For a time—long, golden moments—they were lost to all, then they clung to each other as their passion crested to a consummation that left her weak. She collapsed upon him, and he held her until they could right their world. His heart sang. He would never leave and always they would share this exquisite ecstasy.

Chapter 31

Fox and the two Crow who accompanied him left their horses in a safe place and moved stealthily on foot. If they hoped to reach the village without provoking shouts of warning, they would have to eliminate the guards who protected it.

On the path Fox wanted to take, there were at least three, and they were moving close to the first guard.

They could see him standing, his eyes intent on the paths from the village. Fox and the others circled behind him.

It was a young warrior to whom Fox had often spoken. Fox motioned the two with him to sneak past while he kept the young warrior busy.

They nodded their agreement, but there was a glow in their eyes that told Fox they would have rather killed him. There was still deep enmity between the Cheyenne and the Crow, and they would have preferred to have taken his hair for their lodge poles. Fox shook his head negatively. A dead body would rouse the entire village and warn them of trouble long before he was ready.

He held the young warrior in conversation while the other two slipped silently past. Speaking pleasantly, he bade the warrior a good night and left him completely unaware that the enemy had entered the village he was to protect.

The same procedure was used just as successfully with the next two guards, and, a little over an hour later, they were hidden and watching the village.

Using sign language, Fox told them to keep hidden and wait for him. Slowly and silently he returned to the village. He was stalking the two unsuspecting women, looking for a way to get them alone long enough to capture them without noise.

It would prove to be an easy thing in Lone Star's case. Fox watched as Little Eagle rode from the village. He knew of the feelings Lone Star carried for this warrior. It would be an easy thing to reach her by saying Little Eagle was hurt and needed her help.

He watched to see if he could get her alone, and the moment she walked a little away from the village to gather some firewood, he approached her. He ran so that he would take her by surprise and keep her from thinking.

"Lone Star," he said breathlessly.

"Fox! What is wrong?"

"It is Little Eagle. He is injured and needs your help."

He was pleased with the fear that leapt into her eyes. Panic made her careless, and love made her make a very serious mistake.

"Little Eagle! Where is he?"

"Come, I will take you to him. Hurry. I think he might be injured very badly."

She followed with no thought except of Little Eagle. It

never occurred to her to ask why he had come for *her*.

He led her as rapidly as possible to the secluded area where the two Crow waited. She looked about, then turned questioning eyes to him.

"Where is he?"

The words were hardly out of her mouth when a hand covered it and other less than gentle hands bound her quickly. She saw the two Crows and knew what was happening. She glared her hatred at Fox for his betrayal.

"Be careful," Fox said to the two silent Indians. "Take her to the place we prepared and leave her. Come back here, and I will bring the other one."

Lone Star resisted, and one of the Crow struck her sharply, knocking her to her knees. Still anger and resistance sparkled in her eyes. The Crow laughed softly.

"We will see if you are so brave later, when we have more time."

There was no doubt in Lone Star's mind as to what they had planned for her. Her chin tipped up and pride glimmered in her dark eyes. She was the daughter of White Eagle, and she would not shame his name before these men who, she felt, knew no pride.

They dragged her away, and Fox made his way back to the village. He waited and watched closely until he saw Rayne leave his tepee and walk across the open area to White Eagle's lodge. When he went inside, Fox rose and moved toward his. He would try the same ruse with Falling Water. If it did not work, he would take her by force.

He stood before her tepee and gazed about him to make sure no one was watching. He had to catch her off guard. Without calling out, he stepped inside. Falling Water spun about in surprise.

"Fox!"

He acted upset and worried.

"Falling Water, you must come quickly. It is Rayne. He's been hurt."

She started to move toward him at once, then she stopped and looked at him. Some sixth sense cried an alarm within her. Yet she still half believed what he said.

"Where is he? What happened?"

"He's near the clearing behind your tepee," Fox said quickly. "There is much blood. You must hurry!"

When Rayne had left, he had told her he was going to speak to White Eagle and then to her father. She knew at once that Fox was lying. But Fox was quick, both to realize she was aware and to move. He dealt her a sharp blow that made her sag to her knees and then collapse into unconsciousness.

Swiftly he lifted her and slung her over one shoulder. Then he took the knife from his waist and went to the back of the tepee, slitting it neatly and stepping outside.

There were only a few feet between him and the sanctuary of the forest. He moved on silent feet, keeping her tepee between him and any who might see.

Once in the safety of the trees, he made his way to the others. Now they had to move past the guards again.

With quick and silent hand signals, the Crow made it clear they would never make it with the two women. The guards must die. Fox nodded in silence. Three lives meant nothing to him, nor did the people who trusted him. He had what he wanted.

They approached the area of the first guard. Fox bound and gagged Falling Water and laid her upon the ground. She had not yet regained consciousness. He motioned to the two Crow to wait. He slipped his blade from its sheath and slowly and silently made his way toward the unsuspecting guard. His back to the village and to his attacker, the guard was unprepared to defend himself. Within minutes he lay dead on the ground. Fox dragged his body to a place of some concealment, knowing that at least it would take a while before he was found.

He returned to see Falling Water slowly regaining her senses. She looked about her and realized whom she was with and why. She made no struggle, for she knew her attempts would be futile. She was bound well and could not move or make a sound. Using her bound hands, she forced herself into a sitting position. Fox walked to her side and knelt beside her. He reached a surprisingly gentle hand to brush dirt from her face, and the hand lingered to caress her hair. In anger, she jerked her head away from him and stared at him with the disbelief of what he was doing clear in her eyes.

"Do not be frightened. No one will hurt you."

Her eyes grew heated, showing him less fear and more fury. He laughed softly.

"It will do no good to be angry. You will learn. You belong to me now. You are Fox's woman, not the white man's. Soon you will forget him."

Falling Water shook her head furiously.

"Oh, yes," he said softly. "You will never see him again. Soon you will see it is wiser to be with me. These others"—he motioned toward the Crow—"will not be so kind to your friend."

Falling Water's eyes flew to Lone Star, who sat motionless. It was clear they both knew the fate the two grinning warriors had in store for Lone Star. Her eyes spoke another thing to Falling Water. She would die well. She would die knowing they could not reach her father or her tribe through her defeat.

Fox left Falling Water's side while he gestured to the Crow. Then he returned and lifted Falling Water to her feet. Lone Star was dragged to hers, and they began to move silently toward the next guard. Fox carried Falling Water over his shoulder, knowing she would run at the first opportunity if he unbound her ankles.

The other two roughly dragged Lone Star between them.

Again the guard was struck from behind without mercy. Now, only one man stood between them and the wilderness. It was Fox who stilled the breath of the last. They made their way to the horses. Lone Star was put up before one of the Crow and Fox took Falling Water and set her before him.

A few gestures passed between him and the other two captors. Falling Water and Lone Star could only gaze at each other with mute looks in attempts to convey the courage to face what might be coming.

After a few minutes, Fox drew his horse away from the others. Falling Water closed her eyes as she heard the hoofbeats of the others' horses slowly fading away.

Fox nudged his horse slowly forward. He held her against him, almost gently, but she knew what violence dwelt beneath the surface.

She set her mind on keeping calm and searching for a way to escape. She realized that Fox would be watching her closely, and she knew that he, like all Indians, could travel without leaving signs, could vanish into the wilderness, perhaps never to be seen again. Her only hope was to escape him and try to create some signal that would lead Rayne to her. She did not doubt for one minute that Rayne would follow as soon as he found her gone.

They moved slowly, and Falling Water was aware that Fox was being extremely careful. He did not speak to her.

Her hands and feet bound, she could not move. Her body was exhausted, and cramping pains tightened her muscles. Thirst made her throat dry and perspiration dampened her skin, but she refused to let the sound of her misery escape her lips. She also knew that he could not afford to stop now. They were too near the village yet. He had to put as many miles between him and his pursuers as he could.

The sun descended, and, as it touched the horizon, the sky grew blood red. Falling Water felt as if her body was burning. She was exhausted and her whole being cried out for water. Still they traveled on.

Fox used streams of water to hide his tracks. He found stony areas as often as he could to further camouflage his trail. Still they traveled on . . . and on . . . and on.

She slept from sheer exhaustion, her head resting against his chest. Fox drew his horse to a stop and remained motionless for a few minutes. He allowed the pleasure of simply holding her to wash through him. He tipped her head back and looked down into her sleeping face. Gently, he touched her cheek and drew his fingers down her throat, letting them slowly move over her slim curves. At that moment he wanted her more than anything he had ever wanted before. He smiled to himself. It would not be like this. He drew her close to him and nudged his horse forward again.

Lone Star too was feeling the discomfort of their rapid travel. They stopped for only moments, and, when she had to relieve herself, they still refused to let her out of their sight. They wanted to shame her.

The Crow and the Cheyenne had shared no love for a long, long time. The two warriors who held her now had had contact with White Eagle before, and White Eagle had proven stronger. Now they planned to revenge themselves on someone White Eagle held very dear—his daughter.

Lone Star knew that when they finally chose to stop, she would have to face that hatred and vengeance. She closed her eyes, praying silently to the gods for courage. The man who held her laughed and jerked her closer to him.

"Why do you not beg?" he demanded. "Maybe we would choose to let you go free. If you beg and be pleasant, we might think about it."

"I do not beg animals for mercy. I am Lone Star, daughter of White Eagle. I do not beg. And I do not play whore for filth like you."

They both threw back their heads and laughed.

"You will beg," the second one said. "You will beg and you will do whatever we choose. You will lie beneath us as often as we choose, and when we are finished with you, we will send you back to your father so that he will know."

Lone Star refused to answer. She knew well that she did not have the strength to withstand whatever they planned. She prayed now only to die quickly and cheat them of the pleasure they wanted. She prayed, but she knew they would keep her alive and make her suffer as long as they possibly could.

They rode on into the dusk, rode until it was no longer dusk but night. And still they rode.

Lone Star was in a state of utter exhaustion. Her bound hands and feet had held her so long that her limbs burned like fire. She would not ask for water, for she knew they would refuse it, and she would not give them that satisfaction. It was impossible for her to see the grudging respect in one captor's eyes.

Out of sheer exhaustion she felt herself slipping into darkness. It enveloped her, and she was oblivious to all but the constant movement and the pain.

It was dawn when she felt herself lifted down and placed on her feet. She immediately collapsed, her legs no longer able to support her.

They left her in a heap and moved about to rest their limbs and their horses. She knew it would be for a very short time.

One of them walked to Lone Star's side. He knelt down and took his knife from his sheath. She prepared herself for whatever he might do and was amazed when he cut the bonds that held her legs. Her eyes questioned him.

"Stand and move," he growled. "I want you to be well when it is time. I want you to know what is happening to you. You will curse your father when we are finished with you. I will find it a great pleasure to be the first to mount you. You said you will not beg," he added softly, "but you will. I promise you, you will."

He waited for her to stand, but she was unable. He reached down and jerked her to her feet and pushed her ahead of him, forcing her to move.

Circulation returned to her limbs. She was given a few drops of water, enough to keep her alive. Then she was again drawn up before the same warrior whose hard hands had not been averse to fondling her roughly.

She refused to make a sound when he chuckled close to

440

her ear as his hand slipped under her tunic to grip her flesh.

"Tonight," he muttered. "Tonight you will lie beneath me. I will make you cry in pleasure. I shall enjoy you very much."

She knew the words were meant to weaken her courage, and she refused to let him know just how close to success he came.

She had always dreamed that Little Eagle would be the man to whom she would give herself. She would never be able to imagine that the man who held her was Little Eagle. She knew that such brutality would not have been Little Eagle's way. She wished only that she could have belonged to him once before this terrible thing happened. They rode on toward the end of the day and toward the fate they had in store for her.

Falling Water awoke to the rocking motion of the horse. She tried to move, but her bound hands and arms were numb, as were her legs. She looked up at Fox, who seemed completely unperturbed by the forced travel. He felt her awaken and looked down at her.

"Soon we will stop for a while, and you will rest and eat."

She remained silent, knowing any argument would be useless. She had to be alert and watch for any slip on his part that might mean her freedom.

It was well into the day when they drew to a halt in what, to Falling Water's surprise, seemed like a previously prepared camp. She knew now that Fox had been planning her abduction for a long time. Rayne's warning to stay away from Fox came rushing back to her.

She knew now how right Rayne's words and instincts had been.

Fox dismounted and lifted her down beside him. He bent and cut the bonds that held her feet. She did not have the strength even to try to run, and her hands were still bound before her.

"Listen to me, Falling Water," Fox said firmly. "I am more of an expert here than you. I have lived off this land all my life. Even if you try to run, I will catch you. You cannot get far."

"Rayne will follow you," she whispered raggedly, her voice dry and hoarse from lack of water.

"No, he will not follow me. He is a white man. No white man will ever be able to track Fox across this land."

"You do not know him, Fox. He will follow. He will find you and kill you."

"No," he said. He reached out and took hold of her shoulders. He drew her resisting body close to his. "But if he does happen to find me, I will kill him."

"Fox, let me go."

"I cannot. You will go with me."

"Where?"

"Across those hills." He pointed to a spot off in the distance. "To a place no one can find."

"Why, Fox, why? Why are you doing this?"

"I will ask you why," he said angrily. "Why did you smile at the white one? Why did you make him your husband and take him to your bed? Did you not know that one day, when he became tired of you, he would have left you? What would you have done then? I have spared you that. One day you will be grateful. You will stay with me, Falling Water. From now on, you belong to me."

"Belong!" she said in fury. "I have not chosen you.

442

Who has the right to give me to anyone? I do not belong to you! I belong to my husband. You do not know him. Rayne would never leave me; he would never leave the people he has come to love. You lie to yourself when you think he will not follow. He will pour your blood into the ground."

"You were given to me because I asked for your life. Soon your village will be no more. Soon all those you love will be dead. The white leader at the fort is coming. He will destroy every life in the valley, every life but yours, because I asked for you. You see, you should be grateful that I did not leave you there to die."

"How do you know this?"

Fox went on to explain all that Martin Preston and John Chevington had planned. "The valley will be theirs, and White Eagle and his people will be no more. They will all die, except you."

"It would have been better if you had let me die with them," she whispered as the agony of his words engulfed her. "I would rather die with Rayne than live a moment after he dies. White Eagle is no fool. The white leader struck him once. White Eagle remembers too well. He will never surrender the valley."

"He does not realize what will happen."

"What?"

"Chevington will tell White Eagle he has you and his daughter. When Summer Rain signs the papers that will give the valley to him by the white man's law, then the white leader will strike. White Eagle will not be able to defend his valley. Soon," he added softly, "your white husband will be no more. Then you will live with me."

He drew her closer. She forced her bound hands up between them and looked defiantly into his eyes.

"If I cannot get away from you, if all you say comes to be, then I will find a way to kill myself. I belong to Rayne, and I choose to be with him always, even if it is in death."

Her defiance and pride pleased him. He wanted her so, but he would bend and mold that pride to suit him.

He gripped her bound hands and, with little effort, he drew them above his head and over his shoulders. She could not get away. His arms circled her waist and drew her close against him. He let his hands caress her slim curves and watched the fire leap into her eyes.

Slowly, with an amused smile, he continued to play his hands over her slim hips, gripping her buttocks and drawing her close to him. She could feel the pressure of his desire, and for the first time fear touched her eyes. Fox saw it clearly and smiled. He bent to take her lips with his, but she turned her head away. Grasping her hair, he drew her head back until she cried out. Then he kissed her firmly and with a fierce possessiveness that made her tremble.

She closed her eyes and thought of Rayne and the sweetness of their love.

Chapter 32

Rayne called out his presence and White Eagle invited him inside his tepee. He enjoyed speaking with White Eagle, and now, because he had become a member of the tribe, its future meant even more to him.

Once inside, he found Sun Knife already there. Rebecca sat toward the back of the tepee, leaning against a backrest. Her hands were busy mending some article of White Eagle's clothing, but she looked up and smiled at Rayne.

As were all others in the tribe, Rayne was still in awe of her rare golden beauty. Her skin was tanned now, and her startling light eyes dominated her face. He could easily understand how she had held the heart of the huge chief of the Cheyenne for so many years.

The conversation between the three men involved a discussion of the successful move and the strategic locations in which White Eagle had placed his guards. From those topics they went on to the next hunt and the Grand Council that would be held very soon.

"White Eagle," Rayne began, "I would like to go with

you and be part of the council. I would really like to be able to send Senator Miles the message that the tribes do not gather for war, but only for protection. Now I can give him some names, and he can attempt to put a stop to some of the pressure being placed on your people."

"I would be pleased to have you come."

"White Eagle . . ." Rayne hesitated, "if I could put a stop to such things . . ."

White Eagle smiled. "Neither you nor anyone else could ever stop what the gods wish for us. You have entered our life circle and we welcome you. We know your heart as we know the others. We know what is beyond your help. Our lives flow as the Great Spirit wishes."

"That you have chosen to stay with us is enough to allow us to know your heart, Rayne," Sun Knife added. "You said you would send a message. Have you decided not to go back to Washington?"

"Yes. When Grant and Martha go home, I will send a message to Senator Miles with them. I would prefer to stay."

"I will hate to see Grant and Martha go," Sun Knife said. "But they must leave before the snow falls, or they will be forced to stay the winter."

"I'm sure," Rayne remarked with a grin, "Night Sky will hate to see them go also."

"I have not seen my son for two moons. Has he gone to hunt?" White Eagle questioned.

"I don't know," both Rayne and Sun Knife said simultaneously. They had not seen Night Sky. None of them realized that Savannah had not been seen either. Only Grant and Martha knew, and no one had thought to ask them.

The conversation lingered on general talk of the welfare of the village, and not only its protection but Lauren's as well.

Nearby, in Grant's tepee, the conversation touched upon one of the same subjects.

"Grant, she's been gone for a whole day!" Martha exclaimed nervously.

"Martha, don't worry. She will come back unharmed."

"Are you sure, Grant?"

"He would be so shamed in this village that he would probably not be able to live here in peace again, not to mention the shame he would bring on White Eagle. I think he would die before doing that. She is safe, and she will be home shortly."

"I hope you are right."

"I know I am. Maybe Savannah will discover she's made a mistake about him. When I compare him to Paul Gregory, I certainly find Night Sky to be the better man. But she must make her own decision, and, if she wants to go back with us, we will say nothing more about it. I just want her to be happy, and I think she has to be more open in order to find that happiness."

"Will we be leaving soon, Grant?"

"I suppose we will have to go before the heavy snows. It will be too difficult to travel after that."

Martha watched Grant, a half smile on her face. "You're going to hate leaving here, aren't you?"

"I suppose," he admitted. "Cade and I have been friends a long time. Besides, I kind of like it here. It's so . . ."

"Free," Martha offered.

"Yes, I guess you might say that."

"Grant, why don't we plan on coming back in the spring?"

"Would you consider that, my dear?"

"If Savannah finds she wants to come back, and you do"—she laughed—"I think it would be a wise idea."

"We will consider it. I will talk to Savannah when they come back."

"Grant . . ."

"Now, Martha, don't worry. She's fine. I'd stake my life on it."

Martha sighed and Grant put his arm about her reassuringly.

It was well past the supper hour. Most of the village seemed deserted as Rayne left White Eagle's tepee and started back to his own. He was less than halfway there when he saw Running Wolf walking toward him. They stopped to speak.

"Rayne, have you seen Lone Star? She was to come for the pony I have been taming for her."

"No, come to think of it, it has been some time since I've seen her. Let's go to my tepee. Maybe Falling Water knows where she is."

They walked together to Rayne's tepee and went inside. Rayne was surprised to find it empty but did not yet notice the slit in the back of the dwelling.

"She cannot be far. I've told her not to go to the river alone, so she must still be in the village. Sit down, Running Wolf. Let's talk until she gets back."

They sat together and spoke of many things, but Rayne was plagued by the uncomfortable feeling that something was wrong. He moved to stand up, and his eyes caught the slit in the back of the tepee. His heart froze. Someone had entered his home, someone who must have been an unwelcome guest. Alarm surged through him, and he rose to his feet abruptly.

"Rayne?"

"Damnit!" Rayne shouted angrily. He drew Running Wolf's attention to the slit in the tepee hide.

It took only moments for the shock to enter their minds. They left the tepee hurriedly and began a rapid search, hoping against hope that both Lone Star and Falling Water were together somewhere. Their efforts were futile. In less than an hour, they were certain that both women were gone from the village.

The alarm was spread, and the men gathered together in the center of the village, each restraining himself with great effort while White Eagle spoke.

"It is necessary for us to find their tracks as quickly as possible. We will spread out from the village in all directions, for we do not know which way they have gone or how many were responsible. We will come back here as quickly as possible."

Rayne could feel his heart beating like a throbbing drum. Falling Water, he thought in anguish. Who had taken her? And where?

Slowly and meticulously, they covered the area around the village, each man carefully searching the ground. Gradually Rayne's worry turned into a deep, burning fury. His hands itched to kill the man who had touched Falling Water, who had tried to take her from him.

A voice called from behind Rayne, and he spun his horse about, hoping that one of the warriors had found

449

some sign, some track to follow. He rode back toward the voice. It was one of the younger warriors of the village.

"Come back to the village, Rayne," he said. "White Eagle would speak with you."

"Has he found something?"

"I think so, but he must tell you."

They rode together to the center of the village, where the others were beginning to reassemble. Rayne dismounted swiftly and walked to White Eagle, who had two young children standing wide eyed and frightened beside him.

"White Eagle?" Rayne questioned.

"Have patience, Rayne. You must listen to these children."

Rayne knelt before the two. It was obvious they were very frightened. He spoke gently, smiling at them and trying to soothe their fears.

"You have something to tell me about the ones who have been taken?"

"Yes," they said together.

"Will you tell me what you saw?"

The children were brother and sister, about eight or nine years of age. The girl was trying to hide behind her brother, who was doing his best to appear very manly and brave.

"We were near the river playing," he began. "We hid when we saw the Crow."

"Crow! How did they get so close to the village?" Running Wolf asked.

"They were with Fox."

"Fox," Rayne said softly. "What did they do?"

"They came into the village."

"Did you see them after that?"

"Just Fox. He was carrying something, and he was running."

"Did you see what he was carrying?"

"Not exactly. It looked big. Like a body. But I don't know."

Rayne sighed and stood up. For a moment he and White Eagle exchanged glances.

"It's obvious Fox led the Crow in. They have taken the women and gone," Rayne said with mounting frustration.

"We will not be able to find their tracks until daylight," Running Wolf said.

"White Eagle, there is more to this than we know," Rayne said. "If Fox wanted to do this, he could have done it long ago. There's something deadly in his timing that we do not see."

White Eagle turned to three braves who stood near. "Go," he ordered. "Ride out through the valley. Find the scouts and see why they allowed these men to pass them." They nodded and were quickly gone. White Eagle turned back to Rayne.

"We must wait for the sun. We can make no mistakes about the tracks. There will be no time for mistakes."

"You are right. There must be no mistakes. I intend to find Fox. And when I do, I intend to repay him."

White Eagle could only nod his head. He remembered too well the time the whites had taken Rebecca from him. He recalled the pain and fear he had felt then. And he recognized that same pain within him now as he thought of his captured daughter. He could understand completely what Rayne was feeling.

Rayne turned away and walked back to what was now a very cold and empty tepee. It was only a few short hours until dawn, but they would be the longest, hardest, and most lonely hours he had ever spent.

In his own tepee, word was brought to White Eagle of the deaths of his three scouts. It was another debt he added to the score he would settle.

He was thinking of this when a voice called out to him. It was Little Eagle, son of Sun Knife. He told him to enter.

"You would speak to me?" White Eagle questioned.

"Yes, my chief."

"Then speak."

"I was near the stream just before dark and noticed many strange tracks. I did not think of them then, but I realize now they must be the ones we search for. I know you do not intend to search until dawn, but I would ask a favor."

"What favor?"

"I would leave now and try to follow. If I am successful, I will send smoke. If I am not, I shall return by morning and ride with you."

White Eagle thought for a few moments, then he nodded his head. A quick, hesitant smile of gratitude formed on Little Eagle's lips, then he was gone. White Eagle sat quietly, wondering why he had not stopped him. It was only logical that they would need daylight to follow tracks. But he also knew he would have followed without tracks if it had been Rebecca. He was a chief and he had to lead with logic, yet he drew comfort from Little Eagle's eagerness to search for his daughter and Falling Water.

*   *   *

Little Eagle made his way to the stream. There he found the spot for which he searched. Sun Knife had trained him well. It was an almost imperceptible trail, yet laboriously he began to follow it. He knew the Crow well, and he feared for the lives of both women.

He could not ride, so he led his horse. He knelt often to search for the almost invisible trail. Hour followed hour. Then he came to a spot that he had to study very carefully. He knelt for a long time and read the story that had taken place there. One man had left two and had gone in another direction. He knew he had to decide which trail to follow.

He chose the path of the two, praying silently that he was right.

Rayne could not stand what would be hours of waiting. He left his tepee and began a slow search of his own. The sky was still black with a faint touch of grey at the horizon when Rayne found the first signs. He went back to where the herd was kept, took his horse, and saddled it. He made a pack of dried meat and left.

He also followed the trail until it divided. He knew White Eagle and the others would not be far behind him. He made his choice. He took the path of the single set of prints.

The warriors gathered in the center of the village again. White Eagle called the names of those who would go with him and those who would remain behind to protect the village. As the chief, he could not leave his people defenseless.

Grant and Thomas had both asked to ride with him. White Eagle had given his approval quickly and then announced that the selected warriors should prepare to ride immediately.

A loud shout from a scout on a nearby hill alerted everyone that there were riders approaching the village.

Everyone was completely shocked and in a vulnerable position when the cavalry troop rode over the hill and entered the village. At its head rode Martin Preston and John Chevington.

White Eagle knew his people were in no position to fight. Since they rode in without any threat of violence, he stayed any belligerent reaction on the part of his anxious warriors. They all had lived through an unprovoked attack by the same man. They would never trust him again.

The troop halted and a smug, smiling Chevington looked again into the eyes of White Eagle. Their gazes spanned the years and brought back old hatreds.

"Why do you come here again, white one? Have you not caused enough death?"

"I have come only to speak with you, White Eagle," Chevington said. "I have something I know you will be very interested in . . . as will Running Wolf."

White Eagle stiffened and grew alert. He realized that this visit had to do with the two women of his tribe who were now missing.

"Come," White Eagle said coldly. "We will talk."

Martin and Chevington dismounted and walked with White Eagle to his tepee. White Eagle had motioned for Sun Knife, Running Wolf, and Mack to follow.

Inside his tepee, White Eagle turned to Chevington. "What do you wish to speak to me about?"

"I would like to speak also to Lauren Brent . . . or Summer Rain, as you call her."

Running Wolf grew grim but said nothing. His eyes remained on his chief.

"Why?" White Eagle inquired coldly.

"What I have to say means a lot to her as well."

White Eagle turned to look at Running Wolf, who nodded slightly and silently left. He made his way to his tepee, where he knew Lauren would be. She had been crying; this he could tell by her eyes. Now she gazed at him, silently questioning.

"Come with me," Running Wolf said gently. "The white chief would speak with you also."

Lauren closed her eyes for a moment. She knew that this must mean Chevington knew where their child was. She rose and went to Running Wolf.

"Running Wolf," she whispered, "what . . . what will he do with her?"

He drew her into his arms and held her. He wanted to say so much, but there were no answers he could give to a woman who wanted only to see her child again. And, because he didn't know if she would, he left the question unanswered.

"Come," he said gently, and together they walked to White Eagle's tepee.

Running Wolf could feel Lauren's tension as they entered. When her eyes met Martin's, old memories returned—her hatred and his desire.

Martin remembered her as beautiful, but she had become even more so over the years. He could feel the embers of his passion leap to life with a new flame and with the knowledge that soon, very soon, she would be his.

"Now," White Eagle said firmly, "say what you wish to say. My patience grows thin."

"Keep your patience in control, White Eagle," Chevington said. "You have a great deal to lose."

"Say what you have to say, Chevington," Sun Knife said.

"Since the death of your father, Miss Brent, it seems you have come into possession of a piece of land that interests us very much."

"Did you have my father killed?" Lauren demanded.

"Miss Brent, I was at Fort Ramsey when your father met his death."

"Liar," Lauren said. Chevington's face grew cold.

"Don't speak to me so, or I may leave without stating my purpose. Believe me, you will regret it if I do!"

Lauren turned her face away from both men, as if she could not stand to look at either of them any longer.

"Tell us what you want," Sun Knife said.

"I want this valley. I want this tribe to remove itself from here within four days. I have brought the papers for Lauren to sign. Once you have turned the valley over to me, you will all go. I have three times this many men camped some miles from here. They will see to it you leave peacefully."

"Do you think we will run because you howl like a wolf?" White Eagle asked. "We will not. We will fight you. Do you wish to pay the price too?"

"Oh, I have forgotten one little thing," Chevington added. "We have two people from your village. Falling Water and Lone Star, I believe, are their names. I'm sure you wouldn't want to see any harm come to them."

It took every ounce of grim determination that White Eagle and the others possessed to keep them from

456

striking out at Chevington's smiling face.

"You have my daughter?" White Eagle asked coldly.

"And mine?" added Running Wolf.

"Yes, I do."

"What kind of man are you?" Lauren cried.

"I am a man who gets what he wants, no matter how many years it may take."

"What have you done with them?" Running Wolf asked.

"I'm not foolish enough to answer that. They are in a safe place. None of you will be permitted to leave this valley. My men will see to that. In four days, I will return. If Lauren signs the papers, you will be free to go, and, after you leave the valley, the two women will be returned. If you refuse to sign"—he shrugged—"they will both suffer for it."

The four men were filled with rage, and Lauren's face was white.

"I must reiterate one point. *No one* will leave this valley before the papers are signed."

White Eagle and Running Wolf still did not know that Rayne had already gone. They only knew that Little Eagle had left many hours before. Now their silent prayers followed him.

Chevington turned to leave, then he smiled at Sun Knife.

"I told you many years ago you might die with these savages. You chose the wrong path, Doctor. I am returning to my troops. If we see one rider leave this valley, there will be no more choices. The two we hold will die."

"You are a corrupt and evil man, Chevington," Sun Knife said coldly. "I proved once before that you were a coward. This time, no matter what, I will kill you."

"I am afraid, my brother, you will have to share that honor," said Running Wolf. He turned to Chevington. "If my daughter suffers at your hands, you will die very, very slowly."

"If anything happens to your daughter, it will be your fault. Convince your wife to sign the papers I bring, and further problems will be gone," Chevington replied coldly.

"Chevington," White Eagle said, "you walked my land once, a long time ago. I warned you then and was foolish enough to let you live. I will never do so again. If any harm comes to these women, you will regret the way you stepped upon my land again. This time you will never leave it."

White Eagle's eyes were cold and hard. He was a huge, fierce man whose fury could be felt like a roll of thunder filling the tepee.

His eyes held Chevington's for a long time, and Chevington's smile faded temporarily. Then it returned, for he knew that he had the upper hand and that White Eagle's threats could never be carried out.

Chevington understood the depth of the love these people felt for their children, and he knew that White Eagle would do whatever he had to do to keep his daughter safe. Chevington silently vowed that after he had the papers signed, he would make sure this man and all who followed him could never speak to him so again — would, in fact, never speak to anyone of what had happened here.

Word might reach Washington, but the distance and the lack of interest in what happened to bloodthirsty savages would bring it to nothing.

"You have four days," he said to White Eagle.

He left the tepee and Martin followed. The others stood in silence for several minutes.

"Running Wolf, take your woman to your lodge," White Eagle said gently. Lauren could not protest. She was too frightened to speak. Running Wolf took hold of her arm and drew her toward the door.

When they had left, Sun Knife looked at White Eagle.

"What will you do now, Brother? You do not really think they will keep their word, do you?"

"That man does not know the meaning of the word truth. He plans much more."

"What are your plans?"

"I don't know yet. One thing is good. Little Eagle left the village long ago."

"He is tracking the ones who stole Falling Water and Lone Star?"

"Yes."

"Good. He is an excellent tracker."

"First, I will speak to Rayne. Then we will decide what we must do."

"I will explain to Snow Blossom," Sun Knife said. "Then I will gather the men together again. We have four days to think of something."

"Yes," agreed White Eagle softly. "We have four days."

Chapter 33

"Rebecca," White Eagle questioned, "where is Night Sky?"

"I do not know, White Eagle. Maybe he has gone to hunt. You know he is like the wind. He is also much like his father. He likes to be free to wander."

"Yes, but he is needed now."

"He will return soon." She watched the worry lines on his face. "White Eagle, what are we going to do, leave the valley?"

"No, we will not," he said firmly. "Soon we will gather to talk. Word has been brought to me that Rayne also left before dawn to track. With Little Eagle and Rayne searching, maybe we will have them back before the four days. If so . . ."

"And if not?" she whispered. He came to her side and rested a hand on her shoulder.

"We will find a way, Rebecca," he said gently. "Because the wolf howls outside your tepee, it does not mean he will be able to make a meal of you."

She laughed softly. "I have never been afraid, from the

first day I met you. I refuse to be afraid now. Together we will find a way out of this."

"Yes." He smiled. "Together we will. I just wish Night Sky were here now. He is quick and silent and could slip out to track as well."

"He will be home soon. He always is."

White Eagle lay awake the balance of the night. His hopes were with Little Eagle and Rayne. If they could find Lone Star and Falling Water, there would be no question of his facing Chevington. He knew the white leader still did not know how to fight the Indian. He would surprise Chevington in ways the white leader had never known. If Rayne and Little Eagle could find his daughter . . .

Lone Star was more frightened than she had ever been before, but she tried to keep her fear under control. There had been another hard day of travel before the two Crow had felt safe enough to stop. Stopping was the thing that frightened her the most, for when they did, she knew their full attention would be turned to her.

The sun was setting when they came to a halt. They dismounted and dragged her from the horse, throwing her roughly to the ground.

They built a fire for the first time and sat beside it, laughing and eating. She was hungry and thirsty, but it would have given them too much satisfaction if she had asked for food or water.

She tried to move her legs, but they were so numb that she nearly cried out with the pain. Her movement drew attention, the one thing she didn't want. She closed her eyes for a moment when one rose and walked toward her.

He knelt beside her, a smile on his face. He unsheathed his knife and cut the bonds that held her hands and feet.

He stood, dragging her up with him. He had to half drag and half support her. He forced her nearer the fire where the other Crow warrior waited with a leering smile on his face.

The first warrior almost threw her to the ground beside the other. They laughed and spoke in low, guttural tones. Lone Star was grateful she did not understand what they said.

Suddenly the first warrior gripped her arms from behind as he knelt behind her. He held her while the second moved closer.

She glared up at him. They meant to kill her, but she knew it would be a long time between this moment and her death. She prayed she could bear what they had in mind for her.

The first struck her sharply several times, bringing unwanted tears to her eyes. Then he grasped her tunic and began to rip it from her. She struggled, but the arms holding her were too strong. She felt the night air touch her skin and then felt the rough hands of the man before her. Grimly she fought, twisting and turning, trying to keep him from touching her. They seemed to be enjoying her battle very much.

The first man slipped a knife from the sheath at his waist. He put the tip of the blade against her cheek. She quivered like a stricken doe though she knew in her heart that she would rather have the quickness of the blade than the shame they meant for her. They also knew this and had no intention of allowing her to die quickly.

The tip of the blade now moved to the flesh of her arm. It nicked the skin as the Crow drew a thin line down her arm, and blood soon began to seep from the shallow wound. She refused to cry out. He moved to the other arm and did the same. Very slowly he touched the knife to the skin of her hip. They meant to torment her for a long time, she realized again.

She spat at him and called him coward and everything else she could think of. Her body writhed in her fury and her fear. It did little or no good, for they acted as if she were giving them pleasure.

It was only when the first man began to loosen his clothes that she felt real terror strike. Now she began to fight in earnest. She felt the hands behind her grip more tightly and twist her arms. She groaned with the pain. She wanted to force her mind away from this shame and the only way she could find sanctuary was in thinking of Little Eagle.

Little Eagle followed the trail with eyes that missed nothing. He had done so for hours upon hours. He did not eat but only reached for his water sac occasionally to quench his thirst.

It was again nearing night, and the trail had become very difficult to follow. He crested a hill and drew his horse to a halt. His gaze roamed the darkness before him. Then his heart leapt. In the distance he could see the faint red glow of a fire. He smiled grimly. They must have felt safe enough to stop, he thought to himself. It would prove a fatal mistake. He moved his horse down the hill and into the surrounding trees.

He dismounted, took his bow and quiver of arrows, and checked the knife in the sheath at his waist. He would have to go the rest of the way on foot.

He moved with complete silence. Closer and closer he came. Finally there was only some brush and a few trees between him and the glowing fire. He moved close enough to see what was happening. Hot anger coursed through him as he witnessed the scene unfolding before him.

He knelt behind some brush. For a moment his stunned gaze remained fixed on the girl who was kneeling by the fire. Her body glowed in its flame and took him completely by surprise. He had always thought of Lone Star as a little sister, never giving her much thought at all. But now he saw that she was a very beautiful woman.

He heard her voice as she called them names, and it brought a smile to his lips. She was very brave as well. He saw the blood on her body but knew she was not yet hurt badly. She was fighting too hard for that.

She spat and fought until the one before her grew impatient. There was no doubt what he intended now. He struck her again, this time hard enough to send her senses spinning. The man who held her felt her sag in his arms. The first man hit her again. She tasted blood and blackness swirled before her. She cried out Little Eagle's name as they forced her to the ground. The first man now knelt over her. She could hear his laughter and knew she could no longer fight him. He bent closer, and, through the red mist before her eyes, she could see his animallike grin of lust. Then she heard the soft thud and saw the grin turn to a grimace. The weight of his body fell across her legs. She was as shocked as the second Crow, who leapt to his feet and tried to reach the weapons he had laid aside. It was too late. The second arrow quivered in his chest, followed closely by a third. He was dead when he struck the ground.

Little Eagle rose from the darkness and moved toward the fire. To Lone Star, he seemed to appear out of a mist. Gentle hands lifted her, and she felt the warmth of a blanket against her skin. She began to tremble as if the fear had just struck her.

"You are not hurt?" Little Eagle questioned.

"N—N—No. I am all right."

He drew her closer to the firelight and examined her face closely. He drew her arms from beneath the blanket, and, using the sac of water that lay near, he washed the blood away, then examined her wounds.

"They do not look too bad. I will take you back, and Sun Knife can care for them."

Lone Star had suddenly reached a limit. She began to shake, and tears she had refused to shed before now touched her cheeks. Little Eagle was alarmed.

"Lone Star, did they hurt you anywhere else?"

"No," she choked out. He realized then why she was acting this way. She needed comfort. She needed the knowledge that someone strong was near. He put his arms about her and held her close to him. Rocking her gently in his arms, he shared the warmth of his body with her. She clung to him, and Little Eagle received another shock. Despite the situation, she felt quite good in his arms. He promised himself that, when she was better, he would look into the matter more deeply.

"Come," he said gently. "We must get back to the village. Your father is worried. . . . Lone Star, what has happened to Falling Water?"

She began to speak, finding some relief in talking. His face was stiff with his anger, and he tried to control it only because she was so near the breaking point.

He cautioned her to remain close to the fire until he

465

went to retrieve his horse. She clung to him for a moment as if afraid he might suddenly disappear and the horrors return.

"Don't be frightened, Lone Star. I will return in a moment."

He left her side and disappeared silently into the night. Lone Star hugged the blanket about her. Now that the fear had abated somewhat, a whole new feeling took its place. She felt ashamed that Little Eagle had seen her so. She felt completely and entirely miserable.

It was not long before he returned, leading his horse behind him. He loosened the other two horses, one for her to ride and one to take with them.

Her clothes were badly torn, and he realized how difficult it would be for her to retain the blanket and ride as well. He made his decision immediately and informed her she would ride before him. There was no argument from her. Being close to him even for the ride back to the village would provide her with a cherished memory.

He threw dirt upon the fire, mounted, and reached down to lift her before him. When he had her comfortably seated, he tucked the blanket securely about her and urged his horse forward.

Lone Star rested her head against his chest and closed her eyes, enjoying his strength and the solid, secure beat of his heart.

The moon was bright and the path easy to travel. Little Eagle moved slowly, at first with his mind on the trail, but gradually he became aware of the slim form held close to his. His wayward body reacted in a way that startled him. He looked down at her at the same moment she was regarding him with the depth of her feelings clear in her eyes. Their gazes held, and both were shaken, he with a sudden knowledge, and she with the fear that again she had shamed herself.

Tears of self-pity filled her eyes, and she dipped her head to escape the sudden awareness of her she saw in his eyes. Her heart thudded wildly as he drew his horse to a halt. Gentle yet firm fingers tipped her head up to search her face. It was a profound moment of absolute silence.

"Lone Star," he said gently. "Truly you are well?"

"Yes, I am not hurt."

He chuckled softly. "Your face is dirty."

He was surprised that she seemed upset by his teasing words. He lifted his hand to brush the dirt and still-damp streaks from her face. It lingered to caress skin that felt incredibly soft beneath his touch.

He had seen awareness in the eyes of many women, but Lone Star's reaction was quite different.

"It is also very beautiful," he added.

She could not speak. No words would come. Instead, she gazed in wide-eyed wonder as he slowly bent his head and touched her lips very gently with his.

As he felt her lips quivering beneath his, he had to restrain an almost overpowering urge to deepen the kiss. He lifted his head to again look into her eyes. This is not the time to think the thoughts I am thinking, he cautioned himself. Because he knew how much she had been hurt and frightened, he resolved to keep his feelings within, for now. But after he returned her to her parents—when she was well and had her strength back— then he would see if what he felt now was still true. He pulled the blanket tighter about her, drew her close to him, and rode on.

*　　　*　　　*

For Rayne the tracking was not easy. Many times he cursed himself for missing the faint trail. Fox was an expert, and only the fact that he had Falling Water with him kept Rayne driving on.

He lost the trail over and over and continually had to backtrack to find it again. He wished he had taken Night Sky or one of the other warriors with him, for they were much better at this than he.

Now he sat upon his horse in the center of a shallow stream, trying to decide if Fox had ridden up or down it or had simply crossed to the other side. He moved forward slowly, but there was no trace of a horse and rider leaving the stream on the opposite bank. He knew he would have to go either upstream or down. He made a quick decision, for he had no time to agonize over it. He chose to move upstream, toward the hills. Very slowly, examining the ground thoroughly, he worked his way onward. He knew that if he made a mistake, it might prove to be a fatal one.

He found it suddenly, a very faint track, but it gave him new hope. Fox had left the stream here. He moved on slowly, searching the ground for any signs.

The night was cool, yet Rayne could feel the perspiration on his skin. His body was taut and filled with a bottled up fury that needed only the sight of Fox to create an explosion. He wondered if Fox had any idea he was being followed.

Rayne knew Fox's expertise, and he began to wonder if the man's conceit and confidence in his abilities had made him careless enough to leave behind the very few tracks Rayne now followed.

He was trying his best to keep his mind on tracking and not on Falling Water. When he thought of her, the rage he felt threatened to overpower him. He could not afford to be careless now. Slowly but determinedly he moved on.

Falling Water sat before Fox on the horse in silence. Several times Fox had tried to talk to her, but she refused. She thought of the brutal kisses he had forced upon her and dreaded what was to come. He had not stopped for any length of time since he had taken her from the village. The short stops were only made so that they could relieve themselves, drink, and rest the horses.

She was tired, so tired that she could barely keep her eyes open. She was surprised when the horse came to an abrupt halt. They were by another small stream. Fox lifted her down from the horse and stood her close to him. He motioned to the water.

"Drink," he said. "It will be a long time before we reach water again."

She moved to the bank of the stream and knelt. Cupping her hands, she scooped up the cool water and drank gratefully. The water poured into her parched body like a river of ice. It stabbed at her insides and her stomach cramped in pain. Her head ached terribly from lack of food.

Night was rapidly approaching, and the sky was aswirl with dusky gray and blue-black clouds. She gazed at them with renewed fear. If it should rain, any small trail they had carelessly left would be washed away.

Desperately she longed for Rayne and wondered if, at this moment, he was seeking the trail they followed.

She was torn with worry. She had watched Fox and realized he was a man who could blend with the country,

469

live from it, and, if given enough time, disappear into its depths.

She lay back on the stones. The earth beneath her was growing cool as night began to fall. She had closed her eyes, and now she opened them to see Fox standing over her.

Fox had watched her drink, saw the beads of perspiration on her brow, and knew that the cold water hitting her empty stomach had made her temporarily ill.

Despite this, he admired her slim beauty. By now Chevington and Martin had gone to the village. He doubted very much that they were being followed, but, even if they were, he was confident he had enough of a lead. He was a man proud of his skills, and he did not think anyone could find him now.

Tonight they would make camp, he decided. Tonight she would sleep in his arms, the first night of many nights to come.

He would make camp near this stream. He would see to it that she ate, for she had not had food since he had taken her. Then they would bathe together in the cool water and share the warmth of his blankets. His heart leapt at the thought, and he walked to where she lay and stood over her, looking down on her beauty, beauty he meant to possess. He smiled as her eyes opened, and she looked up at him.

She struggled to her feet, feeling her weakness, trying not to show it. Her head was reeling, and she put out her hand to steady herself. It was grasped by Fox, and she jerked her hand away. He seemed to enjoy her defiance, and she realized it was because he knew it was only a matter of time until he forced her to do what he chose.

He made a small fire and put the blankets near it. Then

470

he withdrew some food from the pouch he carried. Her hunger caused moisture to form in her mouth, and she swallowed heavily.

"You will eat, Falling Water, if I have to force the food down your throat. I do not want you dead."

"Let me go, Fox."

"Out here?" He laughed. "How far do you think you will get?"

"I will wait. I know Rayne is coming."

"You deceive yourself, Falling Water. I am better at this than he. If he tried to follow, he has found it impossible by now."

"Then I will die here," she whispered.

Fox walked to her side. Before she could move, he caught her to him, pinning her arms at her sides. His strength was far more than she could fight. She stood immobile while her eyes warred with his.

"No, Falling Water," he said softly. "You will not die here. I shall keep us both alive. I want you very much alive."

One arm held her while he tangled his hands in her hair to hold her still. Gently he began to kiss first her cheeks, her forehead, her eyes; then his hunger increased as his mouth searched and found hers.

She moaned softly and resisted with what strength she had, but he ravaged her mouth, proving that she had no hope of escaping whatever he planned.

And what he originally had planned was lost in the heat of his desire. He could not, would not, wait to possess her. The sooner she understood to whom she now belonged, he rationalized, the easier it would be for both of them.

"I have watched you for so long," he said, his voice

471

ragged with passion, "with that white one! He is not like us, Falling Water. He is white. He comes only to take. He could not make you happy. You will see. You will be mine, and we will go beyond those hills and live together. I will make you happy, Falling Water," he insisted, his voice dying to a whisper as he began to kiss her fervently. His kisses grew heated and wild with passion. Slowly he began forcing her to the ground.

"No," she gasped. He silenced her with a grinding kiss that bruised her mouth and stopped any more words of resistance.

He forced her down to the blankets, and the weight of his body pinned her there.

It took little effort for him to pin her arms over her head, where he held them immobile with one hand. The other hand slipped his knife from its sheath. At first she thought he meant to kill her. In moments she realized his true intention. He slid the blade beneath the ties of her tunic and sliced upward, splitting it open. Then he tossed the knife aside and pushed the garment open so his rough hands could seek the softness of her flesh.

"You belong to me. Always you will belong to me," he groaned. He caressed the softness of her flesh, then his mouth began a hungry exploration that ended as he caught one nipple and sucked fiercely, causing a burst of pain that made her gasp.

She wanted to cry out, wanted to beg him to let her go, but she knew he was beyong caring or hearing what she said. There was no escape. She was determined that he would have to take what he wanted—she would not surrender.

Her stomach churned, and a cold feeling filled her. A shudder she could not control caused her to shake violently. Fox deluded himself by assuming that she was beginning to feel what he was. He eagerly continued his rough exploration of her body. Falling Water gritted her teeth and closed her eyes against the sight and feel of him. She forced her mind to dwell on Rayne and his gentleness, trying to hold his beloved image before her in the face of what soon would come.

Suddenly, Fox ceased to move. Falling Water looked up in surprise. He was tense and seemed to be sensing the air. Then he reached for the knife he had discarded. Jerking Falling Water up to her knees beside him, he snaked his arm around her neck. She gasped as he nearly choked the air from her. The knife was cold against the skin of her throat. It seemed he had suddenly gone insane, and she tried to keep her mind calm in order to be able to take advantage of the situation that might arise. What happened next was completely unexpected.

"Come, where I can see you!" Fox called out.

There was no sound from the surrounding area.

"Come out, or I will kill her here and now!" Fox called again. To demonstrate his point, he rose to his feet carefully and pulled Falling Water up with him. He tangled his hand in her hair and drew her head back, placing the knife against her throat.

Still there was no sound, no movement. Falling Water could see no sign of anyone. Fox's eyes scanned the area. He was not fooled by the silence. He knew someone was there, and he also felt it could only be Rayne. He wondered if he had many others with him.

He drew Falling Water against him and let his hands roughly caress her skin. The tunic hung from her shoulders, and he casually drew it down until it hung just around her hips. He tightened his grip on her hair and

473

forced her face up, kissing her as if he had all the time in the world. The knife point nicked her skin slightly, compelling her to remain still. This produced the result Fox had expected. A voice came from the shadows of the trees.

"Let her go, Fox. We can settle this between us."

It was Rayne's voice, and Falling Water felt it reach within her.

"Come out. Unless you want her dead, come out."

Rayne stepped from the trees, a rifle in his hand.

"You will see her blood on this ground if you do not lay that rifle down," Fox said with a smirk.

"Let her go, Fox," Rayne said. He was now only twenty feet away. His eyes held Falling Water's as he tried to give her courage. She smiled at him.

"Put down the gun," Fox demanded. Rayne laid the gun on the ground and moved a little closer.

"I'm going to kill you, Fox," Rayne said coldly.

"No. The one who dies here will be you. Take the knife you wear and throw it down."

Slowly Rayne took the knife and tossed it beside him. He was silent, but his eyes burned into Fox, who refused to show the effect it had on him. It was as if Rayne could wish him dead.

"Turn around," he commanded.

"Is that how you fight, Fox, from the back?"

"I do not fight you, white one," Fox spat. "I take what I want, and I kill what gets in my way as I would kill the snake if it crossed my path."

Rayne had edged a little closer. Falling Water watched his face and knew he intended to do battle. She had to give him the best possible chance.

The knife at her throat had lowered slightly, and the

hand that held her was not as firm. He was ignoring her while he watched what he considered a more serious threat.

She smiled at Rayne, then suddenly let her entire weight drop. It all seemed to happen in seconds. Fox's face registered surprise, his eyes shifted to Falling Water, and Rayne leapt forward. They went down in a tangled heap.

Still it was an armed man against an unarmed opponent. They rolled over and over.

Suddenly they were both on their feet. Fox held the knife before him, a grin of triumph on his face.

Slowly he edged forward, and Rayne backed away, his eyes holding Fox. Fox struck out and Rayne dodged. Quickly he struck again. This time the knife caught Rayne's arm, and a touch of blood brightened his shirt.

It seemed a losing battle for Rayne, who was trying to move toward his own knife. Fox sensed this and smiled as he kept himself between Rayne and the weapon.

Falling Water knew it would only be a matter of time until Fox struck a fatal blow. Slowly, she began to move to where Rayne's knife lay. She lifted it in her hand. Over Fox's shoulder, Rayne saw her. He was afraid Falling Water would try to get close enough to use it. He knew Fox was much too quick for her and that she wouldn't stand a chance against him.

He backed away, leading Fox further from her, telling her to be careful and that what she planned to do was foolish. He did not take into account her courage and her fear that he would die. She followed, and Rayne could do nothing more than keep Fox's attention on himself.

He smiled at Fox and tried to keep just enough space between them that Fox could not reach him. Yet several times he misjudged the distance and felt the touch of Fox's blade.

He challenged Fox, calling him a coward and any other insulting term he could conjure. He spoke of Fox's mixed blood as if it were a disgrace.

"You have gotten the rottenness of both sides, Fox," he said with a grin. "You are nothing. No one knows what you are, even you."

Fox's anger made him careless for the first time. He let all his senses dwell on Rayne. It was a fatal mistake, for he had discounted Falling Water, who closed in behind him.

She struck. As she did, he moved slightly, and she caught him high on the shoulder. Letting loose an angry roar, he spun about. At that moment Rayne leapt, and the two tumbled forward.

Rayne rose and tried to drag Fox up. He was limp. The force of Rayne's body had driven him down on his own knife.

Chapter 34

Rayne took a trembling Falling Water in his arms. They held each other as relief flowed through them. They had both feared they might never hold each other again.

Rayne moved her a little away from him for a moment and studied her face.

"Are you all right, love? Really all right?"

"I am fine now that you are here. Oh, Rayne, he has given Lone Star to the two Crow who came with him. They will . . . they will kill her."

"Falling Water, I have no way to find them unless I start from the village. We have to go back right away. Maybe," he said, trying to sound hopeful, "we will be able to find them before . . ."

"Before they kill her," she finished grimly.

"We must hurry."

Rayne moved away from her, and her attention was drawn to the fact that he had been wounded and was losing a great deal of blood. Despite his protests, she made him sit until she had examined the wound, washed it carefully, and bound it with a ragged piece of her torn tunic. The rest of the tunic she gathered about her, but it now provided very little cover.

Rayne lifted a blanket. With his knife, he cut a slit in the center, then drew it over her head.

"Now we must leave. I want to get you home, where you'll be safe."

He had no idea how untrue his words were, and that there was no longer any safety in the village of White Eagle.

They mounted and started for home, unaware that, from two different locations, others were riding for the same destination.

Little Eagle held a very silent Lone Star before him. He would not speak of the new feelings within him until she was reunited with her family and over the shock of what had happened to her.

Lone Star was more than content to travel slowly and draw out their journey for she had no way of knowing what Little Eagle was feeling. Neither had any inkling that the four-day period in Chevington's ultimatum was coming to an end and that the village would be placed in great danger unless White Eagle learned they were alive and well.

Night Sky and Savannah rode along at an easy pace also; quite content that the journey was long. They had talked and had gradually discovered many levels on which they could communicate.

She had been utterly amazed that he had talked and

478

done nothing more. He had shared his food and water and, when night came and she felt her fear creep nearer, he had led her to the tepee and gently pushed her inside . . . alone.

At first she had been surprised. Then the realization came to her that, despite what she had previously thought, he did have a sense of honor and did not mean to molest her.

The next day he had awakened her early. They had shared a day that had increased Savannah's wonder at both the magnificent land on which she stood and the strange and very exciting man with whom she enjoyed its beauty.

He seemed so much a part of the world in which he lived. Somewhere deep within, she began to wonder if she were woman enough to be part of it also.

He saw the change in her. He wanted her to be a part of him, wanted to hold her and tell her how he felt. But he would not reach for her now. He had given his word, and that meant more to him than anything else.

He watched the sun glisten in her hair as she rode, heard her laugh and talk freely with him, and knew the fear had gone.

She enjoyed the pony he had given her. For the first time in her life she rode astride, and the freedom of it thrilled her. She became aware that she was learning many new things from Night Sky. She secretly wondered what new things would be in store if she decided to stay.

As Night Sky watched her awaken to the beauty about her, he sensed a new awareness of him in her attitude. It was enough for now. They would return to the village, then he would ask her to stay among his people for a while.

Together they made their way back toward the village, which could no longer offer them a secure future.

Rayne expected to see the first guards of the village and was surprised when no one appeared. It was through the narrow end of the valley that they rode, and Rayne could not know that the village lay between him and a troop of soldiers that was now threatening its existence.

Something about the situation bothered him, but he did not know what. A sixth sense told him to be cautious.

He dismounted and motioned for Falling Water to do the same. She came to his side.

"Rayne? What is it?"

"I don't know," he said grimly. "I guess I'm getting spooked. I've just got a feeling something's not right. Tether the horses. We'll wait here until the sun goes down. Then I'll move in and see if everything's all right."

She had been through too much not to believe in his instincts. She made sure the horses would not wander, then returned to his side. He slipped his arm about her and held her close.

"I'm sure it's just my jumpy nerves," he said, trying to laugh, though the sound seemed somewhat strained. "We'll stay here. You need to rest anyway. It will be dark soon. Then, when I'm sure it's safe, we'll go on."

Rayne gathered some wood. He knew it would be dangerous to build a fire, for someone might be watching, but he felt Falling Water needed its warmth. He made it as small as possible and silently prayed his instincts were wrong.

He sat by the fire and pulled Falling Water close to him. She was drowsy and becoming relaxed when, suddenly, Fox's words sprang into her mind. She sat up abruptly.

"What's the matter?" Rayne asked in surprise.

"I just remembered. Fox . . . he said . . ."

"All right, calm down." He drew her closer and kissed her gently. "Now tell me what he said."

Quickly she related the story of what Chevington and Martin had planned for the village.

"They must be near, much nearer than the fort if they plan on doing what Fox said," she finished.

"Yes, they must be. We must be very careful how we approach the village. It was a good thing that we stayed here. I will scout carefully as soon as the sun goes down."

"You must be cautious, Rayne."

"I know," he said. "I know Chevington and Martin, maybe a little better than anyone else out here. I'm sure Senator Miles is going to be quite interested in this."

"If you are able to tell him. He wants to kill everyone."

"Yes, but he doesn't know we know it. Don't worry, Falling Water. We'll think of some way to stop him."

He drew her close to him, and his lips lightly touched hers. Then the snap of a twig not far from them brought them both to immediate alertness. From the shadows of the trees two figures slowly approached. Rayne stood up, lifting the rifle from his side to point it in their direction. Then their identities became apparent. It was Little Eagle and Lone Star.

Falling Water ran to Lone Star's side and clasped her in her arms, grateful to see her alive.

Rayne brought them near the fire, and Little Eagle listened carefully while Rayne explained the situation.

Two others saw the pale glow of the fire and rode in its direction. It was a very surprised group of four who watched Night Sky and Savannah ride into their camp.

Again the situation was explained, this time to Night Sky, who was at first thoroughly enraged, then also ashamed. He felt he had deserted his parents and his people when he had ridden away without a word. It battered his pride to have been gone when the strength of his protection had been needed.

They waited impatiently for night to fall. Night Sky insisted that he be the one to creep stealthily toward the village. Under the protection of darkness he made his way from one shadow to another, blending easily.

Outside his father's tepee, he called out in a soft whisper. He knew that from the time of the first attack on his village White Eagle had always slept lightly. In seconds he appeared.

He never questioned Night Sky about where he had been, but in swift words he told his son of the situation in the village.

"They hold your sister and Falling Water," he said grimly.

"No, Father, you are wrong," he declared and explained where the others waited.

White Eagle was overcome with relief.

"Tell them to come in. I'm sure they can do so without the useless white scouts seeing them. The white chief comes tomorrow to see Summer Rain, to make her sign upon the paper that gives him the valley. We will have more than one surprise for him."

Night Sky nodded and was about to leave. Then he turned back to his father, who knew what he was feeling.

"My father?"

"Yes."

"I am deeply sorry that I was not here when you

needed me. I will tell you why I was gone and hope you understand."

White Eagle smiled. "My son does not need to explain to me where his heart lies. I have seen it for a long time. She is a very beautiful woman."

"I have the eyes of my father in my choice of women," Night Sky said with a grin. "She is as gentle and beautiful as my mother."

"You have asked her to remain with you?"

"No, Father, I have not. It is too soon. She does not know my heart yet. I have asked her to stay for a while and listen with an open mind to all that occurs about her. She has agreed to that much. For now, that is enough."

White Eagle nodded his agreement. In a few moments Night Sky was gone as silently as the air that whispered about a satisfied and very pleased White Eagle.

With the help of Night Sky and Little Eagle, the rest were silently returned to the village. Savannah, Lone Star, and Falling Water were given food and water and told to rest. None of them could, for they knew that plans were being made in White Eagle's tepee that would determine their futures.

White Eagle bent closer to the men who sat about his fire.

"They will come here in the morning, expecting Summer Rain to be ready to make her sign on the paper. We will let them come," he said with a smile tempered by dark memories and deep anger. "But this time we will be ready to handle them. They will get what they have asked for, but in a much different way from what they plan. This time they will take back the story that White Eagle and his people will hold this valley forever."

The plans were made, and, on silent feet, they were carried out. Then a stillness touched the village. It waited for the touch of the sun that would herald the arrival of the white intruders.

The sun was just rimming the horizon when Chevington stepped out of his tent. He smiled as he pulled on his gloves and gazed at the group of mounted men awaiting his order to ride.

Martin strode toward him. Both men were secure in the knowledge that their plans had finally come to fruition. They would own the land they had sought for so long. They would have their revenge on the people who had thwarted their plans for years.

Both John and Martin were elated as they walked to their horses. Half of the men had been sent back to the fort, and only forty men would ride with Chevington. His arrogant pride had rejected the notion that more troops might be necessary.

Jess joined them, and they smiled at him, knowing that two of the mounted men had been ordered to make sure Jess was a casualty when the village was destroyed.

Chevington mounted and Martin and Jess followed. A shouted order, and the group was on its way.

"Ah, Martin," Chevington said, "it is a beautiful day."

"I agree," Martin replied. "This day will bring us all we have sought for a very long time." He did not understand then the irony of his words.

They entered a village that seemed subdued and silent.

White Eagle stood before his tepee. He had dressed well for the occasion in fringed white buckskin, elaborately beaded and outstanding in its grandeur. On his head, he wore a full-feathered headdress that told of his bravery. He stood cold eyed, his arms folded across his chest, and watched the troop of men ride down the center of his village.

Beside him stood Rebecca. She was dressed in tawny buckskin, her golden hair held by a beaded headband as it flowed down her back like a golden river.

Chevington gazed at her and remembered vividly the last confrontation they had had. She had almost been his then. She would belong to him now. He would see the mighty Chief White Eagle die in the dirt like a beast in the wilderness. He smiled at the thought. But first he had to get Lauren Brent to sign the paper Martin had in his pocket.

He drew his horse to a stop in front of White Eagle. Without a word, he and Martin dismounted. They took the few steps that brought them face to face with a silent White Eagle. Chevington's gloating arrogance was quite obvious, as was Martin's smug smile.

"Well, White Eagle—" Chevington inquired, "where is Lauren Brent?"

"She is within my tepee."

"Bring her out. Let's get this signing over with. I want to see you moving out of this valley immediately. My men are here to see that you move with as much speed as possible."

Before White Eagle could answer, Lauren appeared behind Rebecca.

"Ah, Miss Brent," Chevington said. "We have brought the papers for you to sign. Do so quickly. I want to see this village on the move."

"And if I still refuse to sign?" Lauren asked softly.

"Now I thought we had already discussed the consequences of a refusal," Chevington replied.

"Lauren," Martin said gently, and her eyes turned to him. It was easy for her to read the lust and satisfaction in his eyes. "You do not want your friends to pay the price for your obstinacy, do you?"

"No, I would not like that. Why do you not free them and leave here, Martin?"

"I cannot do that."

"No, he cannot do that," Chevington reiterated. "I want this valley. I have what you want, and you have what I want. Why do we not just strike an agreement. Make a bargain. I will give you the lives of your friends in return for this land. Is this land worth their lives to you?"

White Eagle's eyes were cold with his fury. This man would have been responsible for his daughter's death if Little Eagle had not rescued her. He would have casually taken the lives of Lone Star and Falling Water, without the slightest concern for the ways they might have suffered.

"Do you keep your bargains, white one?" White Eagle questioned.

"Yes, I do," Chevington replied.

"Then I will make a bargain with you. I will give you a chance to leave my valley now, while you still have your lives."

Chevington laughed. "You forget who has the power here."

"You will not go?"

"Not until those papers are signed."

"And then you will return our women to us?"

"Yes, I will."

"When do the Crow return women they have stolen? When will Fox return the one you told him to take? You do not speak the truth, white one. You lie. Always you lie."

Chevington jerked to alertness. How did they know about the Crow and Fox, he wondered, unless . . . He gazed at White Eagle, who smiled and pointed to the tepee closest to them. Chevington and Martin watched in utter amazement as Lone Star and Falling Water stepped out into the sunlight.

They were stunned, momentarily unable to move. Then their eyes turned back to White Eagle, whose gaze had hardened. They found no mercy there.

Behind Rebecca and Lauren, Rayne and Mack appeared. And if that were not enough, Martin was further shocked by the appearance of Thomas.

"Thomas! I thought . . ."

"That I had run away to hide like a little boy, Father. No, I didn't. I tried to right some of the terrible wrongs you have done. I am ashamed of my name and of you. I will spend some time here trying to erase some of the damage you have wrought."

"I," Rayne said, "am sending a message to Senator Miles, who has been suspicious of you for a long, long time. I'm afraid you won't find your greeting in Washington very warm. In fact, I think you are finished, Chevington."

Martin's face grew grey, and without a word he turned and mounted his horse.

Chevington's eyes burned with the hatred of a fanatic. He glared at White Eagle as if he would destroy him through desire alone. Then his gaze swept from White Eagle to Rayne and Mack. His fury was almost beyond control. He raged with the lust to see these men dead, to kill everyone within his sight.

He turned slowly and mounted. Then he moved away. Rayne and White Eagle watched him go, knowing that his hatred was too overpowering for him to contain it so easily.

At the edge of the village, Chevington spun his horse about, and his men followed suit.

"I told you, White Eagle," Rayne said softly.

"I am glad you had us prepare for this," White Eagle replied. He raised his hand, and, from the borders of his village, armed warriors rose from their concealment.

Now Chevington knew he was completely beaten. It was more than his delicate mental state could withstand. The men under his command, led by Sgt. Randolph Parker, could not believe he would order them to attack. But Parker recognized the insanity in Chevington's eyes, and he made his decision at once, just as Chevington spun about to face him.

"Attack!" he commanded. "Kill them all—every man, woman, and child!"

"Colonel Chevington," Parker broke in. "We don't stand a snowball's chance in hell. They outnumber us two to one, and they are ready. We have to get out of here, if we want to stay in one piece."

"I said attack!" Chevington shouted. "Are you deliberately disobeying my command? I'll have you court-martialed!"

"Maybe," Parker agreed. "But I'm not gettin' these men killed. Besides, after what I just heard, I don't think you really want a court trial to come out of this. They didn't start this trouble, Colonel, and I think we're lucky to be getting out of it with our skins in one piece and our hair still on our heads."

"Damn you! Are you a coward?"

"No, sir, I'm not. But I'm not a fool, either. We ride in there, and not one of us will come out alive."

Chevington could see he had again been beaten. His rage now completely overrode his logic, and nothing reached his mind but the obsessive desire to kill White Eagle, his golden-haired wife, and the two men who had destroyed all his plans. In his present condition, he was unable to consider the extreme tension under which White Eagle's armed warriors had been placed.

With a loud cry, Chevington drew his saber and charged toward what he thought was an unarmed, unprotected White Eagle.

Long before he reached the chief, ten or more arrows thudded into his body. He fell from his horse, dead before he hit the ground.

The warriors' nerves had frayed beyond control. Pandemonium ensued. Unheard cries were too late. Before White Eagle could get them under control, his braves had sent their arrows winging. Jess tumbled from his horse without a sound. Martin followed, his eyes still gazing in disbelief as his life came to an end. White Eagle regained control of his warriors, and he turned to face Sergeant Parker.

"Go now," he said. "Take your dead and thank your gods you are not among them. You know that what has happened here today was not our choosing. Think carefully before you or any other whites enter our valley again."

"I now know all that happened," the sergeant replied.

"I'll make sure my story satisfies the commander. I'll also do everything in my power to keep everyone out of this valley. White Eagle, I'm sorry I was part of this. I hope you plan to end it here."

White Eagle smiled. "It is ended. Leave in peace, and keep your word. I will keep mine."

Sergeant Parker nodded. He ordered his men to retrieve the bodies. In less than half an hour, they were moving away from the village.

The entire tribe seemed to breathe a sigh of relief. The threat was gone. Now they could return to the peace and harmony they had known before the coming of Chevington and Martin.

The tepees glowed that night, and the sounds of celebration echoed in the crisp air. The beating drums heralded a new time. For some it would be a time for beginning, a time to cherish peace . . . a time for lovers.

Epilogue

Rayne lay on the grass-covered bank of the river and watched Falling Water emerge from the water. He folded his hands behind his head and admired her graceful beauty.

She came to him and knelt beside him. Smiling up at her, he reached up to touch her soft skin, feeling the drops of water that still lingered.

"I can still remember the first time I saw you. Just like this. Fresh from the water and so beautiful I could not believe it."

She bent to touch her lips to his.

"It is time for us to return to the village. Today Night Sky and Savannah are to marry. We do not want to miss the celebration," she said with a soft smile.

He grasped her wrist as she tried to move away. "The wedding will not take place for a while yet, and I plan on our doing a little celebrating of our own."

She laughed as he drew her into his arms, but she did not pull away. She would have been content to remain there for any length of time he desired. She always found her peace, security, and pleasure in the arms of this man.

He caressed her lightly and tasted her moist, warm lips.

"Our son will be crying for his mother," she whispered.

"You know he will be well cared for." Rayne chuckled. "Your father does not let him out of his sight. It is our son's father who needs a little attention."

She put her arms about his neck and lowered her willing mouth for his kiss. Always he could stir this flaming need within her with just his touch.

"Rayne?"

"Hmmm?"

"Do you ever think of going back to the place you knew, to the life and the people you loved before?"

"No, Falling Water. I don't ever think about it. I sent the message the senator wanted. I wrote my parents and my brother and told them I'm happy here. Leaving you is a thought that never enters my mind. Why?" He grinned. "Are you tired of me and trying to rid yourself of my presence? Do you have some other buck in mind?"

"You know I think of no one but you."

"That is a good thing to hear."

"Oh?"

"I'd hate to have to hang some brave's hair on my lodge pole, but I'd do it before I'd let you get away." He touched her lips with his. "I love you, woman," he whispered, "and I'd rather give up my life than the moments we share."

"And I love you," she murmured as his lips claimed hers in a kiss so consuming that it forced everything from her mind but the love and strength of the man in her arms—the man she loved and would love until she breathed her last breath.

Once again, as they would through a long and happy life, they shared the magic that had united them in the past and inspired the promise of their joining each time they touched.

Author's Note

I have enjoyed the letters and comments of my readers. I hope to keep my books a pleasure to read. You may write to me at

Box 45
Edinburg, PA 16116

CAPTIVATING ROMANCE FROM ZEBRA

MIDNIGHT DESIRE   (1573, $3.50)
by Linda Benjamin
Looking into the handsome gunslinger's blazing blue eyes, innocent Kate felt dizzy. His husky voice, so warm and inviting, sent a river of fire cascading through her flesh. But she knew she'd never willingly give her heart to the arrogant rogue!

PASSION'S GAMBLE   (1477, $3.50)
by Linda Benjamin
Jade-eyed Jessica was too shocked to protest when the riverboat cardsharp offered *her* as the stakes in a poker game. Then she met the smouldering glance of his opponent as he stared at her satiny cheeks and the tantalizing fullness of her bodice—and she found herself hoping he would hold the winning hand!

FORBIDDEN FIRES   (1295, $3.50)
by Bobbi Smith
When Ellyn Douglas rescued the handsome Union officer from the raging river, she had no choice but to surrender to the sensuous stranger as he pulled her against his hard muscular body. Forgetting they were enemies in a senseless war, they were destined to share a life of unbridled ecstasy and glorious love!

WANTON SPLENDOR   (1461, $3.50)
by Bobbi Smith
Kathleen had every intention of keeping her distance from Christopher Fletcher. But in the midst of a devastating hurricane, she crept into his arms. As she felt the heat of his lean body pressed against hers, she wondered breathlessly what it would be like to kiss those cynical lips—to turn that cool arrogance to fiery passion!

Available wherever paperbacks are sold, or order direct from the Publisher. Send cover price plus 50¢ per copy for mailing and handling to Zebra Books, Dept. 1669, 475 Park Avenue South, New York, N.Y. 10016. DO NOT SEND CASH.